ALIEN AGENDAS

Smith left Hunter alone with Kelsey.

"How the hell do you do it, Commander?"

"Do what, Admiral?"

"Time after time you go up against these guys and don't end up in prison."

"Talent, I suppose. Or pure dumb luck."

"What were you doing ashore, Commander?"

"I had to go to the library, sir. Overdue book."

Kelsey looked pained. "Commander, can you be serious for five minutes?"

"No, really, sir. I had some research I needed to do. I do not trust the computer network here at Dreamland, okay? So I went to the Clark County Library to use their machines."

"What were you looking for?"

"Stuff I don't want Mr. Smith or his cronies to know. Sir."

ALIEN AGENDAS

SOLAR WARDEN, BOOK THREE

IAN DOUGLAS

HARPER Voyager
An Imprint of HarperCollins*Publishers*

HarperCollins books may be purchased for educational, business, or sales promotional use. For information, please email the Special Markets Department at SPsales@harpercollins.com.

Harper Voyager and design are trademarks of HarperCollins Publishers LLC.

FIRST EDITION

Library of Congress Cataloging-in-Publication Data has been applied for.

ISBN 978-0-06-329946-7

23 24 25 26 27 LBC 5 4 3 2 1

For those everywhere who prefer thought to irrational nonsense, truth to wild conspiracies, and honesty to the self-serving agendas of fear-mongering propagandists

And to Brea, who is MY truth and beauty both

ALIEN AGENDAS

PROLOGUE

Conspiracy Theory in America is about the transformation of America's civic culture from the Founders' hard-nosed realism about elite political intrigue to today's blanket condemnation of conspiracy beliefs as ludicrous by definition. This cultural reversal did not occur spontaneously; it was planned and orchestrated by the government itself.

LANCE DEHAVEN-SMITH,
CONSPIRACY THEORY IN AMERICA, 2014

May 1951

GÖTTERDÄMMERUNG . . .

Flashes lit the distant clouds on the dark horizon like lightning, and the sound of thunder rolled in unending cacophony. Berlin was now under bombardment by the Soviet army, their tanks already at the outskirts of the city.

The Twilight of the Gods.

The end of everything. . . .

Herr Oberst *Viktor Albrecht watched the light show for a moment, the somber notes of Wagner's opera of that name running through his mind. That the word* Götterdämmerung *was, in fact, a mistranslation, the Old Norse* Ragnarok, *the fate of the gods, misconstrued as* ragnarokker, *the twilight of the gods, was a minor historical footnote that changed nothing. Albrecht was aware of the linguistic error . . . but, like most modern Germans, was willing to see "twilight" and "fate" as very much the same.*

Either way, the thousand-year Reich was falling into darkness. But there was hope. . . .

Generalleutnant der Waffen-SS *Hans Otto Fegelein stood at Albrecht's side.* "You are clear on what you must do, Herr Oberst?"

"Ja wohl, Herr Generalleutnant," *Albrecht replied with stiff formality. It was a bald-faced lie, of course . . . but one did* not *tell the commanding general of the* Waffen-SS *that his orders were vague to the point of complete incoherence.*

"The future," Fegelein said, almost as though he'd read what Albrecht was thinking, "is a dark and uncertain place. But our allies assure us that social and economic conditions in the future, both in Europe and in the United States, offer us a chance to rebuild."

"It . . . it seems like madness, Herr Generalleutnant." *He gestured with the locked briefcase he carried.* "If half of what is in here is true, with such magical new technologies, why couldn't we . . ." *He trailed off, uncertain of what to say.*

"Why couldn't we what, Herr Oberst?"

"I don't know, Mein Herr. *Go back in time and kill Lenin while he was on that train heading to Russia to redirect his revolution? Communism becomes irrelevant, nonexistent, and we face a weak and divided Russia today. Or . . . or do we go back and see to it that the English never colonize North America in the first place. The place is divided by the empires of France and Spain, and never becomes a serious threat. . . ."*

"And how do you know these things have not already been accomplished?"

Albrecht swept his arm to encompass the distant bombard-ment of Berlin. "I would say this argues rather forcefully against it, Mein Herr. The Soviets are here. And it appears the Americans will be here soon as well."

"Our . . . allies have explained to us that changing history causes that history to branch, to follow all possible paths. To make a difference in this reality, we must make a change farther down this path. We will change the future for our Reich."

"Our allies. The damned Lizards."

"The Eidechse have been most supportive. And they will be there in the future to help."

"My impression is that they have abandoned us."

"Not at all. They continue to fight for the Reich behind the scenes, as it were."

Albrecht looked out at the horizon, engulfed in the strobing flashes of shellfire. How much longer did they have?

"The Wunderwaffe promised by the Lizards came too slow, too late, too . . . too insignificant in the larger effort," he said. "Jet aircraft are all well and good . . . but if they had given us those superbomb weapons they promised . . . or one of their time ships . . ." He shrugged. "They made no difference to the cause."

The general took a moment to strike a match, lighting a ciga-rette. He did not offer one to Albrecht. "This sounds disturbingly like defeatism, Herr Oberst," the SS leader said with calm assur-ance. "If you would rather stay here, we can find other officers, loyal officers, to further our cause in the future!"

"Nein, Mein Herr." He hesitated. How much could he say? "But I do fear Berlin is lost. We have nothing here to face the Soviets *except for children and old men. If I can make a difference in the future, I will."*

"Good. You will find others who have gone forward as well."

"Kammler?"

"SS Obergruppenführer Hans Kammler," Fegelein said slowly, "will leave for the future in a few weeks, on board Die Glocke. *As I understand it, he will be traveling just twenty years into the future . . . but he or someone from his organization should be there to prepare the way for you, and for others."*

"The Bell" was one of the secret wonder weapons, one under Kammler's direct supervision, a German-made time ship under Eidechse *control. Evidently, the Lizards didn't entirely trust humans yet with transtemporal technology.*

"You have had your immunizations?"

Albrecht rubbed a shoulder still painful from the injections. He'd been told that there were diseases in the future to which he was traveling to which he lacked immunity. "Ja, Mein Herr."

"Excellent. I envy you, actually. An opportunity to further the Reich into the most remote reaches of futurity. And to escape this . . . hell."

"And you, Herr General?"

Fegelein scowled. "I return this evening to the Führerbunker. It is der Führer's birthday today."

The Führer, Albrecht knew, had retired to his underground stronghold in the heart of Berlin in mid-January, and had not emerged since. General Fegelein had been with him for much of that time.

"You don't sound . . . enthusiastic."

A casual shrug. "I will not be coerced into a suicide pact. I have other plans. But I envy you your chance to continue serving the Fatherland."

"You said General Kammler was going twenty years into the future. What about me? I didn't see that mentioned in my orders."

"Ah. You will be going considerably further. As I said, the social and economic atmosphere will be perfect for your arrival. You will find willing supporters, and social chaos that you and the others can exploit. I am told that you will find ground even more fertile than that which the Führer used to establish himself twelve years ago. We are counting on you."

"And . . . how far am I to go?"

"Seventy-five years."

The figure was like a punch to the gut.

CHAPTER ONE

Alas, our technology has marched ahead of our spiritual and social evolution, making us, frankly, a dangerous people.

STEVEN M. GREER, MD,
UFOLOGIST, FOUNDER OF CSETI

4 October 1967

"WHAT THE HELL is that?"

Captain Pierre Carbonneau's attention had been snagged by something unusual in the distance, off the port side of his aircraft. At 7:15 p.m., Air Canada Flight 305 was en route from Halifax to Toronto. At the moment, they were at an altitude of twelve thousand feet above the city of Sherbrooke in southeastern Quebec, as the last trace glow of evening light faded from the sky. Carbonneau's copilot, Bob Ralphington, leaned forward in his seat so he could see past the pilot.

"Yeah . . . that's weird," he said. "Is that all one thing? Or something big getting chased by little ones?"

From the cockpit, the object appeared to be an enormous black rectangle, brilliantly lit, flying on a parallel course to them several miles away. Trailing behind the main object were four smaller objects, at this distance visible only as bright stars.

Carbonneau reached for his microphone. They were in Sher-

brooke's air control space. They should be seeing this on radar. "Sherbrooke traffic control, Sherbrooke traffic control, Canada Air 305."

"Go ahead, 305. Sherbrooke tower, over."

"Ahh . . . I have traffic off my nine o'clock, estimate range five miles. Please advise, over."

There was a long pause. "Three-oh-five, Sherbrooke. Nearest traffic to you is twelve miles at your one o'clock, Ottawa 97 on approach to Valcour. We have nothing at your nine o'clock. Over."

" 'Curiouser and curiouser,' said Alice," Ralphington quoted.

"Okay, Sherbrooke. Thank you. Three-oh-five. Out."

They watched the light show for several more minutes as they slowly drew ahead of the objects. "Wish I had some binoculars," Carbonneau said.

"Shit . . . I've never seen one before."

"Seen what?"

"A real, live flying saucer. A UFO."

"There's no such thing."

"Okay, Captain. What the hell is it?"

"Damned if I know."

A brilliant pulse of light flared around the black rectangle, bright white swiftly fading to blue. The cloud seemed to hang behind the object as the four orbs passed through it. Carbonneau checked the clock on the control panel. It was 7:19 p.m.

Two minutes later, a second silent flash illuminated the southern sky, leaving another blue cloud hanging behind the craft. At this point, the four orange orbs closed in on the rectangle, and Carbonneau had the distinct impression that he was seeing small craft following a much larger one.

Were they helping the larger craft after it had suffered some sort of accident?

Or were they attacking a larger enemy?

Carbonneau had no idea . . . but he was beginning to think he needed to revise his self-assured belief that UFO stories were nonsense.

In a few more minutes, as they approached Saint-Jeans, the group changed direction, swiftly moving toward the east until they fell astern and they lost sight of it.

Of course all hell broke loose when they reported the incident in Toronto.

The Present Day

HIS TAIL was back.

Lieutenant Commander Mark Hunter, head of the supersecret 1-JSST and an active-duty Navy SEAL, paused at a newsstand on the concourse of the Gold Coast Janet terminal. Headlines glared at him from the racks: anti-migrant riots in Germany . . . a random beheading of a social worker by a Muslim jihadist in Paris . . . Brexit-triggered economic chaos in London . . . yet another resurgence of COVID19 in Brazil and in India . . . another police shooting in Michigan . . .

The world, Hunter decided with a sharp grimace, was one royally fucked-up place. . . .

Hunter was in an obscure corner of the Janet terminal, located in Las Vegas's McCarran International Airport. Just getting into this terminal required a clearance of top secret or above, and there were armed MPs and G4S camo dudes everywhere, as well as surveillance cams at every junction, all making certain the terminal's security remained sacrosanct. In civilian clothing, he'd had to jump through all kinds of hoops to get a pass from his base—the notorious Area 51 just seventy miles north of Las Vegas.

He knew he should have expected it . . . but the Men in Black had been shadowing him ever since he'd landed here that morning.

Hunter picked up a copy of *USA Today* and paid the COVID-masked newsstand attendant. What kind of security clearance, he wondered, did a guy need to get a job like that *here*—pretty high, he guessed. Hunter had already passed through two security checkpoints, and there was another just ahead, leading to his gate. Leaning with his back against the wall, Hunter pretended to study the paper. In fact, he was using the maneuver to mask what he was doing . . . taking a long, hard look out of the corner of his eye at the people in the concourse behind him.

Perhaps a quarter of the people were wearing masks. As Hunter understood it, the SARS-CoV-2 pandemic had largely abated, and life across the planet was very slowly returning to whatever it was that passed for normal nowadays, especially now that several new vaccines were available. However, many people continued to wear masks and maintain their distance from people they didn't know. The COVID virus was a nasty and persistent adversary, and it kept popping up again in places thought safe from its deadly wrath. Hunter was just glad he'd been off-world through the worst of it . . . and that he and his people had been vaccinated while they were still up at Lunar Operations Command. By all accounts, back on Earth during the year 2020 had been a small slice of hell. . . .

Ah! There he was. Your stereotypical Mark 1 Mod 0 Man in Black. Wearing a dark suit, with tie and dark glasses, the guy stood out like a lit flare in a dark basement. He even wore a black mask across his face. Curiously, and atypically, the MiB wasn't wearing a fedora; possibly that was his concession to blending in. Most of the people on the concourse were casually dressed or in military uniform. Hunter had been pretty sure this clown was following him . . . and now he was sure.

What the hell was this guy playing at?

It occurred to him that the MiB *wanted* to be noticed by his quarry if the goal was simple intimidation rather than covert surveillance. Hunter had had run-ins with these people before, and he was getting sick of it.

Hunter wanted to have a little chat with this guy, who appeared to be alone. He scanned the rest of the crowd; a backup might well not have the suit and glasses, if suit and glasses was what they wanted him to see.

Folding the paper, he strolled farther up the concourse toward the next security checkpoint, presenting his orders, his pass, his carry-on bag, and his ID to one face-masked camo dude, and submitting to a temperature check and a meticulous wanding by another. These were private security guards, members of a company once called Wackenhut, now known by the blander and more anonymous G4S Secure Solutions. They were the security firm used on the perimeter out at Dreamland—the popular name for Area 51. They were tough, no-nonsense men wearing camouflage fatigues, holstered pistols and Motorolas, and permanent scowls when they weren't masked. Hunter considered asking these two to detain the MiB behind him . . . but the MiB would have ID, and might even be working here with their knowledge and consent. No, he would need to handle this himself.

Past the security checkpoint was a passenger lounge—rows of seats sectioned off for appropriate social distancing beneath a large picture window overlooking the tarmac. Beyond, the Luxor Hotel and Casino towered thirty stories above the city just on the other side of the Strip, an enormous Egyptian pyramid just five and a half meters shorter than the original Great Pyramid of Giza, with black, mirror-polished sides. Out front, on the Strip, were a life-size Sphinx and an obelisk displaying the name Luxor in a cartouche.

The Gold Coast, the private Janet terminal located on one corner of McCarran International, was quite close to the Luxor, which had always amused Hunter. According to popular belief, aliens had built the Pyramids . . . and here one had unaccountably popped up right next to the gateway to Area 51.

"Coincidence?" Hunter muttered to himself in a conspiratorial tone. "I think not!"

But he was looking for something other than pop culture . . . something closer at hand. There were only a few passengers waiting in the lounge for their flight, all absorbed in their books, newspapers, or telephones. He lingered at the entrance to the lounge until he saw the MiB pass through the checkpoint and hurry toward him.

Good. . . .

To his left, a short hallway led off from the lounge and ended in a locked door. Dropping his bag and using a pair of short and tough plastic strips pulled from his luggage's outside pocket, it took him all of three seconds to pick the lock. As he'd expected, it was a janitor's storeroom. The legend "JANITOR" on the door had been his first clue. A yank on a pull chain turned on the light, revealing mops, buckets, and bottles of cleaning solvents.

Pocketing the picks, he returned to the short hallway's entrance, counting down silently as he moved. The MiB would reach him in another three . . . two . . . one. . . .

Movement emerged from behind the corner to his right. Hunter snapped out his arm and used the target's own momentum to swing him off-balance, forward and around the corner.

Navy SEALs are proficient in a number of hand-to-hand combat techniques, but one of the most viciously effective is Krav Maga, a form used by Israeli commandos and special forces. Its central tenet is "maximum damage, minimum time." Stressing the practical over the flashy, Hunter's instructors had emphasized that a hand-to-hand encounter should take no more than three to four seconds; any longer than that and the attack had failed.

As the surprised MiB spun around the corner and into the short hallway, Hunter met him with a knife-hand jab to the throat and an elbow to the side of his head; the man sagged, gasping, and Hunter pulled him around and shoved him into the closet.

No one in the lounge reacted. The attack had been so quick and silent that no one had looked up from their phones.

Dropping his bag nearby, Hunter stooped and checked the man's pulse. He hadn't intended to kill the guy, but . . . good. Alive but unconscious. So far, so good.

The man's glasses had been knocked ajar by the blow to his head. Hunter removed them, and caught the gleam of microelectronics reflecting the room's light. Tucking those into his shirt pocket, Hunter then removed the man's mask.

Shit. His tail was . . . not right. Not quite human. The skin was so pale that Hunter thought the MiB was an albino at first, and a close inspection showed a trace of . . . were those *scales*? No hair . . . no beard growth. Hunter peeled back a closed eyelid and got a real shock: from the deep socket a black-and-gold, slit-pupiled eye stared up at him. Hunter had seen eyes like that before—on alligators, on venomous snakes . . . on domestic cats . . .

. . . and on Saurians.

No wonder the guy wore dark glasses.

He was *not* a Saurian, however—one of the Malok engaged, as Hunter understood it, in an eons-long war against the highly evolved humans of Earth's remote future. Those critters walked on digitigrade legs—the knees reversed from the human plantigrade articulation, like a bird—and they were distinctly scaled, with snouts filled with teeth more like a shark's than a man's. This guy looked human in his joint articulation and the overall design of his body . . . but with hints and traces of more reptilian characteristics.

There were several hanks of clothesline on a shelf at the back of the storeroom. Perfect.

"Let's have a closer look, shall we?" Hunter said to his unconscious prisoner. "Maybe a quick alien autopsy . . . ?"

Ten minutes later, the Man in Black no longer wore his suit. Hunter had peeled him completely naked and tied him hand and foot, hanging him head-down from a hook high on the wall. A rag from a nearby shelf stuffed in his mouth would keep him quiet when he came around. "Huh," Hunter said, mildly curious. "I thought lizards had two penises. Read that somewhere . . ."

But there was one significant difference in an anatomy normally hidden by clothing.

The man had no navel.

Hunter gave this some thought. No navel meant no placenta or mother's womb . . . and that suggested an artificial birth. The Saurians, Hunter knew, possessed sophisticated medical technologies, technologies advanced to the point of being able to keep human abductees alive for years inside transparent cylinders filled with a greenish perfluorocarbon solution and drugs to keep them asleep. Maybe they raised their babies that way, too.

Or had this guy been hatched from an egg? No. Somehow, he looked just a bit too human for that.

He decided that he was going to need to have a long chat with Dr. McClure, the senior xeno-wonk back at Area 51.

Hunter continued going through the MiB's clothing. He could see more thread-fine wiring woven in through the man's shirt, his shoes, and even in his underwear. Man, the tech people on base were going to *love* this! Hell, the guy was a walking RadioShack. He realized that he would have to hurry, though. The wiring was part of a complex communications array at the very least, which meant someone was almost certainly tracking him.

Commander Hunter had had run-ins with the so-called Men in Black before. He knew he was under almost constant surveillance when he was on Earth and away from the above-top-secret compound at Groom Lake, and he was willing to accept that people in charge of the Solar Warden program wanted to make sure he didn't talk to unauthorized personnel about secret Earth space programs, about secret alliances with both aliens and humans from the far future, or about Saurians working within human governments with secret agendas of their own.

But he also strongly suspected the MiBs had been responsible

for abducting a young woman with whom Hunter was romantically involved—Geri Galanis. They hadn't actually admitted to
having taken her . . . but they kept turning up as Hunter searched
for her. He thought they'd snatched her as a precaution, something
to hold over him to ensure his obedience.

And he didn't like that. What they seemed to have missed was
the fact that Navy SEALs are *very* good at keeping their mouths
shut. Until just now, Hunter had assumed, like most people
within Solar Warden, that the Men in Black were simply members
of one or another of America's intelligence services—the CIA,
perhaps . . . or Navy Intelligence.

But there was a lot of hardware here that Hunter couldn't even
begin to identify. What was it all for? A careful search revealed
nothing like a battery. How was this gear powered?

Microphone on his shirt collar, probably a military-grade
comm system. Sidearm—a small Glock 27 .40 mm pistol in a
concealed shoulder holster. Oddly, the prisoner was carrying no
ammunition, no spare magazines.

And there was something about the Glock. As a Navy SEAL,
Hunter was intimately familiar with a large number of weapons,
and he'd used Glocks plenty of times on the range. This one was
too light, and somehow didn't feel right in the hand. *Awkward.*

Too many questions. He'd not originally planned on stealing
the MiB's clothes and gear . . . but he needed the xeno and high-
tech whiz kids back on the ship to take a close look at all of this,
probably with an electron microscope.

The prisoner groaned. With blood flowing into his head in
his upside-down position, he was regaining consciousness more
quickly than Hunter had expected.

"Welcome back," he told the man. "Sorry for the discomfort. I'm sure your people will be along soon to cut you down."

The prisoner's reply was a gag-muffled roar—pure rage and defiance. He struggled against the clotheslines.

"Don't hurt yourself, mister," Hunter told him. "I'm a sailor. That means I'm *very* good with knots."

The prisoner simmered down, but he was seething, puffing hard and glaring up at Hunter as the SEAL began going through the man's wallet. Those golden eyes were . . . disturbing.

Hunter ignored the prisoner for a moment, focusing instead on the contents of his wallet. No money at all . . . and almost nothing in the way of what intelligence services referred to as "pocket litter," the bits and scraps and detritus of everyday life that people intended to accumulate in their pockets or billfolds. No credit or debit cards. Huh . . . How did this guy get along in modern society?

There were a number of ID cards, though, and Hunter found these fascinating. No fewer than seven driver's licenses from different states, with seven different bland, "John Smith" kinds of names. The list of US government agencies represented was impressive: CIA, of course . . . but also US Navy, US Air Force, FBI, NSA, CDC, and NRO. There was also a separate ID holder, the kind that could be flipped open to show a card or a badge, and this one was for one "Dennis Young" of the US Marshals Service. The silver star identified him as a US deputy marshal.

"Well, Marshal," Hunter said at last. "I see you get around. Maybe you can tell me what happened to a friend of mine . . . Geri Galanis? I *know* you people have her. . . ."

That provoked another muffled bellow and another round of

struggling, and Hunter decided that it would be too risky to pull the gag out of his mouth.

"Now don't go getting all red in the face. If you're going to be like that, I'll have to leave you here. Like I said . . . I'm sure your friends will be along soon." Those disturbing eyes . . . and now Hunter could feel the delicate brush of another mind within his own.

Shit . . .

Both Grays and Saurians could read human minds, at least to some extent, and could even influence a person's actions.

This guy's mental touch was extremely weak, but the SEAL was not going to take any chances. Hunter grabbed the prisoner's hips and spun him around, so he was facing into the corner. Without eye contact, the intrusion seemed to fade.

"You tell your buddies that I want Geri released, safe and un-harmed," he said. Stooping, he emptied his spare clothing from his carry-on bag—a couple of dirty civilian shirts, underwear and socks, and a pair of slacks—and stuffed the bag tight-full of the MiB's clothing, wallet, and weapon. He was taking a horrendous risk, he knew. There were enough electronics woven into the guy's clothes that it was a forgone conclusion that someone was tracking him. Worse, Hunter now was inside the Janet airport's innermost security zone . . . but there might be additional hidden devices at the gate that would pick up . . . say . . . a Glock pistol hidden in the bag.

He actually considered ditching the pistol in a waste can, but . . . no. He would brazen it out. Despite what popular culture claimed, a Glock pistol was *not* a "plastic gun" indetectable to a security scan; the frame was indeed a plastic polymer, but there were plenty of small metal parts detectible on a magnetic or X-ray scan.

But the missing ammo bothered him, and he wanted a closer look. Besides, he didn't want some janitor finding the shit-canned gun and possibly hurting himself, or someone else.

In any case, the microelectronics in the clothing were probably at least as much of a danger to him as the Glock. His carry-on had been checked several times, though, and he doubted that the airport would hold up boarding at the gate for *another* scan. He would take the risk.

How, he wondered, had the MiB gotten through the security checkpoints? Simply by flashing an ID? Or was there more to it than that?

"You hang tight, pal," he told the prisoner, then delivered a stinging slap to the man's backside. "And you tell your bosses that I want Geri delivered alive and safe!"

He let himself out of the closet, locking the door behind him. His discarded clothing went into a trash can at the entrance to the passenger lounge. He found a seat, sat down, and waited for his flight to be called.

This afternoon, he knew, was going to get him into trouble . . . *big* trouble, the sort of trouble that might have him up on charges for assault, attacking a government agent, treason, malfeasance, chewing gum without a license, and anything else that they could throw at him and make stick. He might be lucky to get a transfer to Adak, Alaska; Rear Admiral Benjamin Kelsey had once threatened him with prison and even hinted at the possibility of his being killed if he didn't toe the line. They took this stuff *seriously* in Solar Warden.

But no matter how deep the secrecy, abducting an American citizen and holding her prisoner for . . . what? Over a year now? Two? That was about as illegal and just plain *wrong* as it was possible to be. Hunter's oath of service had sworn to uphold the Constitution of the United States from all enemies, foreign and domestic . . . and that meant upholding the rule of law.

He would deliver this bag-load of goodies to the ship's technical staff, and accept the official ass-chewing when it came.

He waited five minutes, occasionally glancing toward the locked janitor's closet . . . but no one appeared to be interested in that door. No one paid any attention to anyone else in the waiting room; the culture of working at a highly classified base tended to isolate people. They didn't chat, didn't even acknowledge anyone else around them.

Hunter did catch sight of one man he knew in the group— Master Chief Arnold Minkowski, like Hunter a US Navy SEAL, and now a member of the 1st Joint Space Strike Team, or 1-JSST. The "Just One" was an ad hoc unit, currently at company strength with sixty-five men, way too small to be called a battalion, but divided into four smaller companies of fifteen to eighteen people each. The personnel had been drawn from elite units throughout the US armed forces—SEALs, Green Beanies, Rangers, Delta Force, even CIA direct action teams.

Minkowski looked up and met Hunter's gaze, but gave only a slight nod of recognition. Good. Hunter didn't want to attract attention to himself or to his people, just now.

He spotted three other Just-Oners scattered among the waiting passengers.

Master Sergeant Bruce Layton, the senior NCO and acting

CO of Charlie Company; Marine Sergeant Miguilito Herrera, his linebacker frame squeezed into his narrow seat; and EN1 Thomas Taylor, another SEAL from the old unit.

Hunter felt cold. If the camo dudes or MiBs showed up and took him away, four of his people were liable to come to his rescue and that would not end well.

Thankfully, the gate attendant called their flight—Janet 6— and he stood up and filed out of the building into the blast furnace of Las Vegas's heat, trotted down the stairs, and stepped out onto the tarmac with about twenty other passengers.

The Janet flight was a modern-looking Boeing 737-200, painted white with a red stripe along the line of windows and no tail numbers or other markings. Janets were notorious within the general UFO community. Based out of this private terminal on the northwest corner of McCarran International, they shuttled workers from their homes in and around Las Vegas to various highly classified destinations, including the more secret portions of Edwards Air Force Base, the Tonopah Test Range . . . and the infamous Area 51.

Camo dudes with H&K submachine guns watched the line as it filed across the concrete and up the boarding stairs into the 737, but no one called out or yanked him out of line. It was cooler inside as Hunter stowed his bag and took a seat. He couldn't see outside; the windows were blacked out. He sat there for an agony of minutes, wondering if someone would hold the flight at the gate, and send someone out to remove him from the plane.

But at last the passenger jet backed away from the terminal and began taxiing toward the runway. Five minutes later, acceleration shoved him back into his seat, and the aircraft howled as it lifted into the clear blue of the desert sky. Only then did Hunter allow himself to breathe . . . though he was fully aware that there likely would be a reception committee waiting for him at Groom Lake.

But he would deal with that when the time came.

"DID YOU pick up any impression at all of *time*?" Dr. Bennett asked.

"Not really, Doctor." Julia Ashley sat at a desk, several scrawled, almost childlike drawings in front of her. "I was in the past, I'm sure. The airliner didn't feel modern . . . like it might have had propellers instead of jet engines."

"That's not evidence," Bennett said. "We still have turboprops in service today."

"I know. So . . . maybe fifty years? Sixty?"

Bennett made a note on his tablet. "Close enough. And . . . what was your impression as to how these lights were interacting?"

"It felt like the small ones were attacking the big one. I . . . I think they shot it down. . . ."

Julia Ashley let her pen drop, marveling at how slowly it reached the desktop in one-sixth of a G. She'd been working in the small, close compartment deep within the warren of lava tubes beneath the far side of the Moon. She'd come ashore off the USSS *Hillenkoetter* days before, leaving the huge spacecraft carrier parked inside the cavern converted into a subsurface hangar. That low gravity was a constant reminder that she was a long way from home. Despite that, she was exhausted, as she always was at the end of a particularly grueling RV session. She'd made the sketches in front of her while remote-viewing target coordinates given to her by her new handler, Dr. James Bennett.

Remote viewing, the ability to see what was happening in another place and even in another time through the power of the mind alone, had been practiced by the government since the 1970s as part of the Stargate Project. Officially, the program had been shut down. Unofficially, it had continued under other names; how could it be otherwise, when program directors reported successful hit rates of *over 90 percent*?

But Julia had something special. During the last deep-space deployment of the USSS *Hillenkoetter*, she'd encountered a kind of hive mind on the alien asteroid-ship Oumuamua, and that touch had . . . *changed* her. Rather than the usual protocols where she would get snippets and snatches of impressions without attached meaning, she now could send her mind more or less anywhere and any *when*. That first time when she'd found herself seemingly on the streets of LA during the Battle of Los Angeles in 1942 had profoundly shocked her, shocked her enough that she still hadn't admitted to her handlers the depth and clarity of her new mental vision.

"Okay," Bennett said. He pushed one of her drawings toward her. "Tell me about this one."

On the paper was a crudely sketched rectangle, shaded in black, but with a white band around the perimeter.

"You remember the monolith in *2001*?" she asked.

"Yes."

"It looked like that . . . but the edges were lit up really bright."

"How big was it?"

"I'm not sure. Huge."

Bennett seemed to be digesting this. Ashley knew he still wasn't sure about her reporting. When you did a controlled RV, the viewer wasn't supposed to interpret or analyze, and a great deal of training went into the mental gymnastics required to keep the mind from leaping ahead and putting meaning on what was being viewed. The drawing was a way to record shapes or impressions without examining them or guessing at what they meant.

Ashley had seen considerably more than *this*, however. She was still shaking inside at the memory. For a moment, *just* for a moment, she'd glimpsed the occupants of that craft.

"And these?"

"I think they were small ships," Ashley admitted. "Nothing more than orbs . . . orange lights. They were trailing behind, at least until the end."

"And they attacked the big one?"

"I'm not sure, sir. I'm not supposed to analyze."

"You can analyze now, Julia. Tell me what you felt! It's important!"

"It might have been an attack. I didn't see beams or missiles or anything like that, but the rectangle seemed to be trying to get clear, and then there were two really bright explosions, a couple of minutes apart. I think part of the rectangle kind of broke away, like pieces were falling off. Then it changed course and looked like it was trying to get away."

"And the orbs followed it?"

She nodded. "Yes, sir."

"Anything else? Anything at all?"

She hesitated. "No, sir."

Bennett sighed, leaning back in his chair. "Okay, Julia. Good session. I need to go over this with the others, see what the rest of the teams came up with. You can stand down until we call you in again. We're going to want to follow this up with another session . . . maybe in a couple of hours or so."

She sagged a bit inside, releasing a pent-up breath. "Thank you, Doctor."

By not telling Bennett *everything* she'd seen, she was breaking an oath she'd sworn when she'd signed on as a government contract worker, one bound by military discipline and rules. The problem was . . . how much could she tell Bennett? Would he think she was unstable, like Eric?

Eric Lassiter had been a fellow RVer on the recent *Hillenkoetter* deployment, a gifted, nineteen-year-old RV savant, but his brush with the Oumuamuan Mind had left him incoherently babbling, unable to relate at all to anyone around him. She shuddered. Why the encounter had done that to him but left her with the ability to pick up such vivid impressions, she didn't know.

What she *did* know was that she'd seen the crew of the rectangle.

And she feared if she described them to her handlers, she would end up on a locked ward, too.

And that thought terrified her more than her brief glimpse of those . . . *things.* . . .

CHAPTER TWO

Decades ago, visitors from other planets warned us about the direction we were heading and offered to help. Instead, some of us interpreted their visits as a threat, and decided to shoot first and ask questions after. It is ironic that the US should be fighting monstrously expensive wars, allegedly to bring democracy to those countries, when it itself can no longer claim to be a democracy when trillions, and I mean thousands of billions of dollars, have been spent on black projects [about] which both congress and the commander in chief have been kept deliberately in the dark.

PAUL HELLYER,
FORMER CANADIAN MINISTER OF NATIONAL DEFENSE

4 October 1967

JULIA ASHLEY STOOD on a line of rocks at the edge of a broad bay opening into the ocean, the surface of the water dark and wind-swept, the foot-high surf curling in to splash just below her feet. She could hear wind and wave, but not feel them.

She was, in fact, present only in her mind.

She still knew nothing about where she was, or when. She knew she was supposed to report on what she saw, however, and what she was watching at the moment was a very large, rectangular craft of some sort descending toward the waters of the bay. She was pretty sure it was the same craft she'd seen earlier from the vantage point of Air Canada 305. The craft appeared to have experienced some difficulties, and was settling toward the water with a curious rocking motion, almost like the falling of a leaf. She could hear a high-pitched, descending whine that sounded like a falling bomb, though the object wasn't moving fast enough to be screaming through the air. Five people, three men and two women, were getting out of their car on the highway behind her, pointing and talking among themselves.

Ashley knew they couldn't see her. After all, she wasn't really there.

Swiftly, with that part of her mind still back on board the Hillenkoetter, *she began sketching her impressions on the sheet of paper in front of her.*

Present Day

HUNTER GLANCED around the aircraft cabin. The other passengers continued to occupy their own, private worlds, perhaps a quarter of them anonymous behind their COVID masks. Minkowski was reading an in-flight magazine in the window seat on the opposite side of the aisle four rows back. There was no one next to him. Hunter stood and walked aft, as though headed for the restroom, but swung around and sat down next to the master chief. "We've got to stop meeting like this, Mink," he said, sotto voce. "The aliens are getting suspicious."

Minkowski looked up, startled, then glanced around. "Hey, Skipper . . ."

"I need your help."

"Absolutely, sir. What's going down?"

Hunter continued to whisper. "In the overhead luggage bin above my seat, there's a carry-on bag. Black nylon, Velcro flaps. When we deplane, I want you to get it and take it with you."

"And why can't you carry your own damned bag?" Minkowski was senior NCO of the JSST's Alfa Platoon, and had been in Hunter's SEAL company before that. The two had an old and easy relationship that trumped the protocol of rank.

"Don't ask questions, Master Chief," Hunter replied. "And don't open the bag. I want you to take it straight to Becky Mc-Clure when we touch down. If you can't find her, then find Elanna, but tell her I want Dr. McClure to see what's inside and then pass it on to her xenotech people."

"Looking for what?"

"I want a rundown on the technology. There's comm stuff in there, and probably a tracking device. I want to know what else. I want them to pay particular attention to the Glock."

Minkowski's eyes opened wide, and he looked around again. To his credit, he didn't comment on Hunter having smuggled a weapon onto the plane.

"Will do, sir. And why can't you deliver the bag yourself?"

"The less you know, the better, Mink. There's a good chance that I'm going to be picked up by the camo dudes when we land. I do *not* want them intercepting that bag."

"Shit. What can *we* do?"

"Nothing. I don't want the rest of you involved any more than you are already. Just get that bag to Dr. McClure."

"Aye, aye, sir."

"Good luck."

"You, too, sir."

Hunter stood and walked the rest of the way aft, washed his hands, then returned to his own seat. Minkowski was watching him with an expression of mingled concern and curiosity, as were Layton, Herrera, and Taylor from their various seats. They knew *something* was going down . . . but Hunter didn't want any of them to be sucked too far into this. One ruined career this morning, he thought with an inner glower, would be quite enough.

Fifteen minutes later, the Janet flight began its descent into Groom Lake.

Hunter wondered if there would be an official reception committee waiting for him when he deplaned.

IN HER *mind, Julia Ashley floated above the surface of the bay, scant meters from the object that had crashed. The thing didn't look like any spaceship Ashley had ever seen or imagined—a jet-black rectangle over a hundred meters long and less than half that wide, its perimeter ringed by a single, continuous panel blazing with a dazzlingly pure white light. It was large enough that it appeared unaffected by the waves. But Ashley could tell it was settling slowly, with one corner already completely submerged, and waves breaking over the rest of it as the swells rolled in from the ocean.*

She'd been ordered to look inside. Penetrating the hull in front of her was a simple matter of will and the logic of dreams; she would imagine herself moving through to the interior, and she would be there.

But she was struggling to force her mind to move. She'd had a glimpse of those . . . things, and they were worse, worse by far, then the swarm of abyssal group-mind mites she'd glimpsed in-

side Oumuamua. She knew they couldn't hurt her physically . . . but some entities she'd encountered while in this altered state had been able to see her, and to touch her mind.

With a deep shudder, she once again remembered poor Eric, remembered his shrieks and the tumbling babble a psych tech had called "word salad." I don't want to end like that!

Still shaking inside, however, she forced herself to move toward the sinking vessel.

Though sleek and smooth-skinned on the outside, with a surface like polished black obsidian, the alien ship's interior was organic and complex, like a cavern with rippled flowstone walls and surfaces. She saw nothing like instrument panels or controls, nothing but large, rounded masses like water-eroded boulders on decks, protruding from bulkheads, and even hanging from the overhead. Unseen light sources cast bewildering shadows everywhere, sparkling off wet surfaces like diamonds. The light seemed dim to her mind's eye, and with a distinct reddish cast to it.

She heard a noise behind her, and turned. . . .

The being was terrifying . . . large and bulky, vaguely tube-shaped, but with a heavily rugose, corrugated hide glistening with beads of moisture. A dozen squat legs held it up, while seven beady black eyes with no apparent symmetry to their placement watched her from the front of the body, all but lost in those thick wrinkles.

Steadying herself with a deep breath, Ashley studied the being, rapidly sketching what she saw on her tablet back on board the Hillenkoetter. As she worked, she became aware of . . . a name? An occupation? An identifying telepathic symbol? Sometimes, she knew, information could flow spontaneously across a

*particularly close telepathic link. The being in front of her, she
knew, was Dorava . . . though whether that was its name or its
title was unknown.*

*Somehow, knowing the thing had a name helped her get past
her initial surge of panic. The appearance in and of itself, she realized, was not really terrifying. Strange, yes, but not frightening.
It took her a few moments to realize that the terror she was feeling
trembling inside her . . .*

. . . was coming from the creature.

It was aware of her.

*It was trying to speak to her. She stilled her mind . . .
listening . . .*

"Help us!"

Present Day

"COME WITH us, please, sir."

They'd waited to pick him up as he stepped off the bus that had
taken them from the Janet flight to the personnel barracks—two
armed camo dudes and a grim-looking but very polite MiB. Hunter
exchanged a quick and meaningful glance with Minkowski, then
followed them out of the queue to a waiting black Cadillac.

An hour later he was seated at a small, bare table in an office
somewhere around ten floors down, a part of the secret underground city that was the hidden realm of Area 51. Standing across
from him were two of the ubiquitous Men in Black, plus Rear
Admiral Benjamin Kelsey, the former Navy SEAL and JSOC officer who'd recruited Hunter into Solar Warden in the first place.

"What the hell happened, Hunter?" Kelsey said without pre-amble. He sounded more like a father disappointed in his way-ward son than angry.

"I haven't heard any charges as yet, sir," Hunter replied.

"Do not play sea lawyer with me, Commander," Kelsey snapped. "You *will* lose."

"Yes, sir."

"You assaulted a special agent of an American intelligence ser-vice. You stole his weapon and his clothing and left him tied up in a storage closet. Why?"

Hunter considered dragging the game out, but knew it was pointless. They'd obviously found the Man No Longer in Black and would have heard his side of the story.

Hunter glared at the two suits standing behind Kelsey, dark and silent specters. Neither wore sunglasses, thank God, and both had human-looking eyes. That, at least, was *something*.

"These . . . people have been following me everywhere I go, sir. I'm sick and tired of it."

"Commander . . . Solar Warden may be *the* most important and most secret program in the history of our country. The program takes a significant risk each and every time you or one of your men goes on liberty, every time they make a phone call home. There is a significant danger that anyone could leak something. Of *course* they're going to keep tabs on anyone who sets foot out-side of a secure facility."

Hunter noted Kelsey's use of the word *they're*, not *we're*. That was significant, he thought.

"I have no whistleblowers in my unit, sir. *I* am not a whistle-blower."

"Not deliberately, perhaps, no. But a careless word in the wrong ear—"

"With respect, Admiral, don't give me that shit!"

"Commander—"

But Hunter could not hold back. His only chance here, he believed, was to go on the offensive, all-out locked and loaded.

"Sir! I have reason to believe that these people—the organization behind them—kidnapped a dear friend of mine two years ago. I can only assume that they have her as a kind of hold on me, to make sure I behave! That violates so many laws, violates the Constitution I am sworn to uphold, violates common *decency* to the point where I don't even know where to begin! These people are abducting American citizens, and they may be working for a foreign power with hostile intent. It's *wrong*, and I want them to release Geri Galanis and all the rest, and I want them to do it *now*! If they don't, they damned well *will* have a whistleblower on their hands, and they're not going to know what hit them!"

"I suggest, Commander, that you watch your tongue. You are on extremely thin ice right now." Kelsey's voice was level and controlled, warning Hunter that if he became too much of a nuisance, he *could* easily be eliminated. Not by Kelsey, but there were plenty of stories of Men in Black threatening to take uncooperative witnesses out into the desert where they would never be found.

"Are you aware, Admiral, that the . . . person I accosted at the Gold Coast was not completely human?"

"You know perfectly well that we have treaties with several alien groups. Some are not from this planet. Some are human, but not from this time. The Talis, for instance . . . as human as you or me, but from roughly ten thousand years in our future. The Grays . . . also human, but from a species of humanity evolved across over a million years."

"That clown I took down at the airport was not Talis, Admiral. And he wasn't a Gray. He was part Saurian. I think he was Malok."

Malok was a Talis term applied to the reptilian Saurians, a species also from Earth . . . but from a civilization of highly evolved dinosaurs who'd somehow escaped the global cataclysm of sixty-five million years ago. The Talis also applied the word to those of the myriad Gray cultures and groups who'd already been co-opted by the Saurians and were working against Humankind's best interests. There was a far-flung interstellar war being played out not only across the Galaxy, but across time as well.

"I thought you didn't believe in alien hybrids, Commander?" Hunter had had this conversation with Kelsey before.

"I'm not sure what I believe at this point, Admiral. But the guy who was following me . . . he wasn't like any other human out there; this guy had *scales*. He also didn't have hair anywhere on his body. His eyes behind his sunglasses looked like Saurian eyes . . . slit pupils, reptilian. And no belly button! If he's human, someone's tampered with his genetics big time."

"Commander," one of the MiBs said. Hunter was pretty sure it was the one who'd once stereotypically introduced himself as "Smith." "Do you have *any* idea how vast and complex spacetime truly is on a galactic scale? How enormous and diverse the human species has become in a million years-plus? Or how advanced technology has become in all that great gulf of time? From *that* vantage point, natural evolution and humans both have been manipulating the human genome for a very long time indeed. You should see the weird variety of shapes, sizes, and the overall plasticity of the human genome in all of that time."

Hunter was surprised. Smith generally wasn't so flowery in his speech, which tended to consist of rather blunt threats and attempts at intimidation. Maybe this wasn't *that* Smith at all. "I know that aliens—real, *nonhuman* aliens—are generally *so* alien it's tough to identify them as intelligent beings." He glanced at Kelsey. "That's why I don't believe in alien hybrids, sir. We're more closely related to . . . to *cockroaches* than we are to anything out there."

"True," Smith said. "But all life on Earth shares the same DNA base pairs, the same biochemistry, the same genetic dynamics. A sufficiently advanced genetic technology has no problem at all taking certain genes from, let's say, reptiles and inserting them into the genome of a human. Jack is one of our colleagues from over four thousand years in our future."

"'Jack'?"

"The agent you attacked, Commander. His name—part of it—is Gja'aak." The alien name slipped smoothly from Smith's mouth. "For obvious reasons we call him 'Jack.'"

"Enough of this," the second MiB said. "Ask him about Jack's stuff."

Hunter pulled his best "who, me?" look. "I don't know what you mean."

"Commander," Kelsey said, exasperated, "you were caught on camera." He held up his smartphone and pressed a button. The screen showed an overhead view of Hunter emerging from the janitorial closet, with a carry-on bag and an armful of clothing. The clothing went into a litter can by a wall. Hunter's image strode off with the luggage.

"We recovered what you placed in the trash can," Smith told him. "Civilian clothing, obviously yours. What became of the bag, Commander?"

"I ditched it. I thought you might be able to track it."

"The only place you could have hidden it was on board the airliner. We watched you leave the aircraft after it landed, and you did not have the bag. We searched the plane. It was not there."

Hunter was relieved that they'd not had surveillance cameras on the Janet flight.

"Then I really don't know what to tell you."

"You'd better talk, asshole," MiB Number Two said, "or we'll bury you so deep that whale shit is gonna look like shooting stars to you!"

Hunter looked at Smith. "Where'd you pick up this character?" he asked. "The Mafia? Or maybe he was a DI in Marine boot camp?" That whale-shit comment, a variant of it rather, was an old one from Navy OCS as well as both Marine and Navy recruit training. His use of it was hilarious, and the guy's melodrama only made it worse.

"Wait outside, Johnson," Smith said. "I think we can reason with Commander Hunter."

Johnson? *Johnson?* Who did these clowns think they were kidding?

The second MiB glowered at Hunter, but left the room. For his part, Hunter had no doubt whatsoever that the room was being monitored, and that "Johnson" would continue to watch the conversation from outside.

"Commander, the only reason you are not already inside a very small prison cell at the Colorado Supermax is because you have been so successful in creating the JSST, putting it together from such disparate military units. Your contribution to Solar Warden's success has been noted . . . and appreciated." Smith stared intently at Hunter.

"Glad I could help. Where's Geri?"

Smith hesitated. "I'll tell you the truth, Commander. I don't know. However . . . if I promise to make inquiries on your behalf— on *her* behalf—will you return Gja'aak's property? It is important to my supervisors that my organization not be compromised by . . . unsanctioned leaks."

"If you people don't have her, who does?"

"I can't tell you that."

"Can't? Or won't?"

"Both, Commander."

"Meaning your organization works for the Saurians and you won't admit it."

That got Smith's attention. He actually looked startled. "That's nonsense."

"Really?" Hunter felt as though he'd just scored a small advantage in this game of cat-and-mouse. He decided to push for all he was worth. "I know *exactly* where she is . . . inside one of seven undersea domes on top of Sycamore Knoll, four hundred feet down just off Point Duma, on the Malibu coast. They're keeping her in some sort of biological containment inside a damned acrylic tube, along with a great many other human prisoners in other tubes."

"And just how do you know all of this, Commander?"

"A friend told me."

He decided to keep Julia Ashley's name out of this. He'd met the talented remote viewer on board the *Hillenkoetter* during their last mission. Impressed by her ability to peer inside the alien Oumuamuan ship, he'd asked her help in finding Geri.

And she'd come through.

How she'd done it, he wasn't entirely sure. And he didn't want to get her into trouble by saying too much.

But if he could shake Smith hard enough to enlist his help, Hunter would do it. He looked at Kelsey. "Sir, MJ-12 is playing both sides of the game here." He was guessing, now, but he was fairly sure he was on the right track. "I think Majestic is fragmented into factions, with some of them supporting Solar Warden, but others controlled by the damned Lizards. The Lizards have been abducting our citizens for decades, now, God knows why. I think our leaders—I think Eisenhower himself—signed a treaty with the Saurians that let them kidnap our citizens in exchange for technological help, and that's about as wrong, as plain, downright *evil* as it gets!"

Kelsey looked at Smith. "How much of this is true?"

"It's . . . it's conspiracy-theory crazy talk! Tinfoil hat stuff!"

"Really?" Hunter said. "We know MJ-12 exists, that it was established by Truman in 1947 . . . along with the CIA. We know MJ-12 was the guiding hand in suppressing UFO sightings and speculation for the next seventy years. We know they're behind the creation of Solar Warden, the building of a secret space fleet using technology acquired from aliens . . . and from time-travelers from the far future. I don't think we have to connect too many more dots to see the picture, Mr. Smith."

Smith regarded them both for a long moment. "This . . . material is so highly classified we could *all* be killed just for thinking about it."

Hunter wasn't sure if Smith was speaking metaphorically, or with dead seriousness.

He wasn't sure he wanted to know which.

"Sir," Hunter said. "Anything I know now is covered by my security oaths, plural. I am a US Navy SEAL. I *know* how to keep official secrets, okay? But kidnapping Americans and holding them against their will is wrong by any standard. If the Saurians have penetrated our government this deeply, if they have secret bases from which they operate against American interests . . . don't you think we ought to *do* something about it?"

"What we have to do," Smith said, "is figure out what to do with you."

"Really? And maybe you'll never see Jack-off's gear again until it turns up on the evening news. Or maybe an insightful documentary—*Majestic-12: The Inside Story.*"

"Is that a threat, Commander?"

"No, sir. It's a promise."

Smith sighed and suddenly looked much older. "Commander Hunter, you might make promises but I cannot. Ms. Galanis's . . . situation is completely outside of my control. I know of the facility you mentioned, but I don't know if she is there or not. Besides, even if I promised to have her released in exchange for the contents of that luggage . . . would you believe me?"

Hunter leaned back in his chair. "I guess not. You people don't exactly inspire trust."

"What if I agree to try to find out something about her—find out whether she is indeed held prisoner, as you say—would you agree to return the contents of your luggage and not to talk to the media?"

"As I said, I know how to keep secrets."

It felt like a Mexican standoff. By now, Hunter believed that Smith truly didn't know if he could find out anything about Geri or not. He also was beginning to believe the agent's sincerity. Surely, if Smith was going to blow smoke up Hunter's ass he would promise him anything to elicit his cooperation, whether he planned to keep that promise or not.

The situation was far from ideal, but it was probably the best Hunter could hope for.

"So . . . will you return the material?"

"It will take me a while to get it. But yes."

"I suppose that we will have to trust you, Commander."

"As I'm trusting you not to throw me in jail."

"Indeed. While you're at it, believe me when I say, we *will* be keeping a cell at the Colorado Supermax ready for you. If you get out of line, you will never see daylight again."

The return of Smith the bad cop was jarring after Hunter had begun thinking of him as Smith the *good* cop.

Smith left Hunter alone with Kelsey.

"How the hell do you do it, Commander?"

"Do what, Admiral?"

"Time after time you go up against these guys and don't end up in prison."

"Talent, I suppose. Or pure dumb luck."

"What were you doing ashore, Commander?"

"I had to go to the library, sir. Overdue book."

Kelsey looked pained. "Commander, can you be serious for five minutes?"

"No, really, sir. I had some research I needed to do. I do not trust the computer network here at Dreamland, okay? So I went to the Clark County Library to use their machines."

"What were you looking for?"

"Stuff I don't want Mr. Smith or his cronies to know. Sir." Among other things, though, he'd wanted to verify the geographical information Julia had given him about Geri, and which he'd just used in his all-out assault on Smith—Point Duma, Malibu, Sycamore Knoll. You could actually *see* the underwater feature on Google Earth.

"Uh-huh." He didn't sound like he believed Hunter. "Did you find what you needed?"

"Yes, sir."

"And that's where the Men in Black found you?"

"Someone was waiting for me the moment I touched down at McCarran, Admiral. He followed me all the way into East Flamingo Road. I didn't see him inside, but he was waiting for me when I hit the street again and tailed me back to McCarran." Hunter shrugged. "I was getting pissed at being followed, so I decided to have a chat with him."

"That must have been quite a chat."

"Yes, sir."

"They consider you to be a loose cannon, Commander. You do know that, right? And they have a long history of dealing with loose cannons, starting with James Forrestal."

Hunter nodded. James Vincent Forrestal had been the nation's first secretary of defense and, according to some conspiracy theories, a member of the first MJ-12 group formed by Truman in 1947. Rumor and speculation from the tinfoil-hat crowd suggested that he'd insisted the American public be told about what had been found at Roswell and of subsequent treaties with aliens. If any of that was true, Forrestal certainly *had* been a loose cannon, threatening to break ranks with the ultrasecret organization. Officially, he'd committed suicide by jumping out of a sixteenth-floor window at the Bethesda National Naval Medical Center where he'd been committed for severe depression.

There were rumors, however, that he'd been suicided.

And Hunter was going to have to be damned careful if he didn't want to end up the same way.

"So . . . is that it?" Hunter asked. "Am I free to go?"

"You are confined to the base, Commander. You are also relieved of duty until this thing gets straightened out."

"Aye, aye, sir."

"These people will want to interview you again. But they also *really* want that clothing back, so this is your chance to retrieve it. Where is it, by the way?"

"Where is what, sir?"

"Damn it, Hunter! You know what I mean! If you have that agent's shit, you *will* return it! We know you left it on the plane. We know it's not there now. Who has it?"

"I would rather not say, sir." Hunter looked about the room. "Like they say, the walls have ears." And probably eyes as well.

"We know that four of your men from the JSST were on that Janet flight—Layton, Taylor, Minkowski, and Herrera. It's pretty easy to imagine that you arranged for one of them to take the carry-on off the plane. I would imagine that they'll be picked up soon for questioning. If you care about your men, you'll come clean. If you don't, you're going to have company in Supermax."

"I doubt that, sir. They don't allow prisoners to fraternize there."

Supermax was the one federal supermax prison currently open in the United States, though there were numerous lesser state-level facilities with the title as well. The United States Penitentiary ADX Florence, in Florence, Colorado, was *the* place reserved for terrorists like the Shoe Bomber, the Unabomber, and the Boston Marathon Bomber, as well as drug lords like El Chapo, and other characters so vicious the authorities couldn't risk putting them in less secure facilities. There, prisoners were in solitary confinement twenty-three hours a day for the first three years . . . *not* a pleasant lifestyle.

"Bring that stuff to me, Hunter. Believe it or not, I'm on your side . . . and I think Smith might be as well. But if you pull anything, anything at all, we will not be able to save you. We won't be able to save your men. And that would be a serious loss to the program."

"Yes, sir. I'll take care of it, sir."

Hunter had been willing to gamble with his own life and career, but the lives of his men were something else. SEALs shared a camaraderie utterly beyond any civilian's understanding, and in the JSST that loyalty extended to men and women from other units as well. They'd been to Zeta Reticuli and back together; they'd been to Aldebaran and back together. They would *not* let one another down, no matter the personal cost.

Hunter wondered if Doc McClure had seen that stuff yet, and if they'd had a chance to examine it closely.

CHAPTER THREE

Commanders and subordinates are obligated to follow lawful orders. Commanders deviate from orders only when they are unlawful, risk the lives of soldiers, or when orders no longer fit the situation. Subordinates inform their superiors as soon as possible when they have deviated from orders. Adhering to applicable laws and regulations when exercising disciplined initiative builds credibility and legitimacy. Straying beyond legal boundaries undermines trust and jeopardizes tactical, operational, and strategic success; this must be avoided.

ADRP 6-0; MISSION COMMAND,
DEPARTMENT OF THE ARMY, MAY 2012, SECTION 2-19,
CONSPIRACY THEORY IN AMERICA, 2014

4 October 1967

"WHAT WAS IT? What did you see?"

"I saw nothing, Pilot Kedawa. Nothing visible. But there was a . . . mind."

"A mind? What kind of a mind?"

"I'm not certain. It tasted like nothing with which we are familiar. It may have been one of the inhabitants of this world."

"Nonsense. The inhabitants of this planet are primitives. Their cogitative index has been determined to be zero-one-point-three . . . sentient, but only marginally aware."

Dorava turned their ponderous bulk to face the ship's pilot,

regarding them with all seven eyes. "Then perhaps, Pilot, our
determinations are in error."

Present Day

"WHERE DID he get this?"

Dr. Becky McClure held the Glock pistol at arm's length between thumb and forefinger, as if worried that it might go off by
itself. They were in McClure's xenobiology lab deep within the
subterranean fastness of S4, just south of Area 51.

"He didn't say, ma'am," Minkowski told her. He'd just given
her Hunter's carry-on, and they'd emptied it of clothing and the
weapon. "He just told me to bring it to you or Elanna, and to examine all of this stuff carefully."

"And what happened to him, Master Chief?" Elanna asked.

"He . . . he got picked up by the camo dudes," Minkowski replied. He tried not to stare at Elanna's eyes. A Talis, a human
from ten thousand years in the future, 425812 Elanna had an unexpected effect on present-day males that Minkowski found disturbing and uncomfortable. Her unusually large eyes were deep
and luminous, with a way of looking all the way down into your
soul. Evolution and far-future genetic engineering together had
fine-tuned certain aspects of her sexuality. Scuttlebutt had it that
her pheromones were more potent, too. Mere twenty-first-century
males could find the effect overpowering.

Of course, Minkowski had also heard that Elanna had lived in
Nazi Germany for years, taking on the identity of a psychic and
leader of the Vril Society named Maria Orsic. Although the Solar

Warden brass seemed to have accepted her, he wasn't certain she could be trusted, not with baggage like that.

"He was arrested?" McClure asked. She set the Glock carefully on the table. "Why?"

"I don't know, ma'am. I don't know for sure that he was arrested. They just pulled him out of line and put him in a black limo, and that was the last I saw of him." Minkowski paused. "Thing is . . . he told me beforehand that he might get picked up. He didn't tell me why. He just told me that the less I knew, the better . . . and that he didn't want the camo dudes getting that bag."

"This is beginning to sound like some weird sort of conspiracy," McClure said. "Cloak-and-dagger stuff."

"All of Solar Warden is one enormous conspiracy," Elanna pointed out.

Curious, Minkowski pointed at the Glock. "May I?"

"By all means."

He picked up the weapon, immediately aware that it was too light to be a semiautomatic pistol, even one with a polymer frame. There appeared to be a nine-round magazine in the short grip . . . but pressing the release lever did not drop it into his hand. He tried to jack the slide back and couldn't. The weapon appeared to be a perfect replica of the Glock 27 but a nonworking one, a dummy. What the hell was this . . . ?

Meanwhile, McClure was going through the clothing. "I'm going to need a large-stage microscope," she said. "I can see circuitry woven all through the fabric, but I don't know what it does."

Elanna pointed to the collar. "Voice pickup, for communications," she said. She pointed at the sleeves. "Those are probably ion-flow collectors that turn body heat into electrical power. I recognize the technology. That's how the system is run."

"No batteries."

"No batteries. Not as you would think of the term."

"And this?"

Elanna peered at the wiring in the back of the suit coat. "At a guess . . . some sort of tracking device."

"Are they getting our location now?"

"No one is wearing the coat," Elanna said. "No power."

"Thank God." McClure dropped the jacket. "Looks like Commander Hunter got everything, even the guy's underwear. I don't see anything technological in there, though. What's this?" She held up the trousers.

Elanna looked puzzled. "Interesting. If I didn't know better . . ."

"What?"

"I was going to say a phase-shifting device. But the power requirements would be larger than this collector could provide."

"Phase-shifting?"

"It's . . . technical, and extremely advanced. The Malok use this technology, but we don't. It generates a field that can bend local space."

"For camouflage? A cloaking device?"

"Among other things."

"Careful with that, Master Chief," McClure said, interrupting the conversation. Minkowski was still examining the pistol, puzzled.

"It's okay, Doc," he told her. "The thing is a dummy, like a movie prop." He held the weapon up, aiming at a large wall chart showing the periodic table of the elements. "See?"

He squeezed the trigger . . . and a bright flash engulfed the wall chart, accompanied by a piercing crack and the sharp smell of ozone. McClure jumped; even the usually unflappable Elanna spun to see and looked startled.

The chart now had a huge burn-through stretching from magnesium to argon, and the concrete block wall behind it had a deep crater in it, with charred rubble on the floor beneath. "My God," McClure said. "What did you *do*?"

"I'm sorry! I . . . I thought it was a fucking prop!"

"Obviously," Elanna said, "it is not. Let me see that."

Minkowski handed her the weapon. He gave McClure a sheepish look. "Doc . . . I really am sorry!"

"I'm just glad you didn't point it at one of us!"

"*That* wouldn't happen. You never point a weapon at anyone unless you're planning on taking them out, even if you think it isn't loaded. Or not a real weapon."

"This is Malok technology," Elanna said. "Saurian. As is the phase-shift technology."

"You're sure?" McClure asked.

"Yes. No safety. And their hand weapons are considerably less . . . *elegant* than ours." Carefully, she placed the weapon back on the desk.

Someone banged on the office door. "What the hell happened?" Dr. Kresge, from the office next door, peeked into the room, an assistant crowding in behind. "You ladies alright?"

"We're fine, Kres," McClure told him, positioning herself so the newcomers couldn't open the door farther and see the crater in the wall. "A little lab experiment, louder than we expected."

"It sounded like a gunshot!"

"And we're not allowed to carry weapons in this facility. I know. Everything is fine."

Kresge looked unconvinced, but McClure shut the door on him.

"Why didn't you show him?" Minkowski asked.

"Mark, I mean *Commander Hunter*, obviously didn't want to share his find," she said, "and he didn't want anyone to know he was sending it to us. I think we keep it under wraps for now, until we can talk with him."

"I agree," Elanna said.

"Assuming," Minkowski said, "he hasn't been thrown into prison for stealing this stuff."

He picked up the weapon again and examined it, thoughtful.

"I'M SORRY, Commander," the camo dude said. He handed back Hunter's ID. "Your Crypto 20 has been revoked."

"So how am I supposed to get in there, mister?" Hunter demanded. He was standing at the first security checkpoint inside S4, the highly classified facility south of the main base at Groom Lake. The place, buried inside a mountain, was where most of the research into UFOs and Solar Warden's near-magical technologies actually took place. "I'm supposed to see someone here."

"Sorry, sir. Your ID is only showing USAP clearance. You shouldn't even have been able to board the tube."

He tapped the security badge he wore. "This didn't go off." The color-coded badges would trigger an alarm if he wandered into the wrong-colored area.

"But you need TS Crypto 12 to be here. *Above* top secret."

"Now listen here . . ."

"No, Commander. *You* listen. Your card reads as level USAP, which does not allow access to this facility. In fact, at that level you're not even supposed to *know* about it! So the staff sergeant here is going to escort you back to the tube boarding station, and you're going to have a quick ride back to Dreamland. You can check in with main security there, and maybe they will straighten things out."

Hunter pointed at the landline phone on the guard's desk. "Can I make a call?"

"No, you may not." The watchdog almost smirked. "Now get the hell out of here, or I'll have Staff Sergeant Hanson escort you all the way back to Area 51." He jerked a thumb at a prominent notice posted on the wall next to him—a long list of security regulations ending with the ominous phrase "USE OF DEADLY FORCE AUTHORIZED." "I suggest that you comply."

Hunter pocketed the ID, seething. He knew the MiBs back at Kelsey's office wanted him to find that carry-on bag. Minkowski would have brought it here, to the xenotech labs several floors below this one, where both Dr. McClure and Elanna worked. He'd been given special clearance to board the underground maglev tube shuttle that connected S4 with Area 51 proper . . . but these clowns obviously hadn't gotten the word.

In the clandestine and often twisted world of US military security, there technically were just six levels of clearance: restricted, confidential, secret, and top secret, plus two special classifications—special compartmented information and unacknowledged special access program, or USAP. That last one was a kind of placeholder for personnel still being cleared for higher levels. The Top Secret Crypto levels went up to at *least* twenty-eight; the President himself was only cleared to TS Crypto 17.

Supposedly, there were even higher levels beyond Crypto 28, far up and away in the murky realms of Majic-12.

Hanson snapped to attention. "If you will come with me, sir?"

He glared at the camo dude. "I *will* be back."

"Not without something better than USAP clearance, you won't."

Hanson escorted him into the tube car boarding chamber. The tunnel between here and the main facility was kept in vacuum, allowing for much faster accelerations than a mere subway, but that meant the boarding chamber had to maintain a vacuum seal to allow both boarding and exiting the car.

They had to wait for the car's arrival.

"You're military, Staff Sergeant. Marine?"

"Negative, sir." But Hanson volunteered nothing. He was probably Delta or one of the other Army special forces. Hunter had little use for the G4S Security Solutions employees who handled most security functions on and around this base, even though most of them were ex-military themselves. So far as Hunter was concerned, they were civilian mercenaries, one step removed from hired thugs.

"Would you be able to get a message to someone here in S4?"

"No, sir. I would not."

So much for that idea. Security's job was to act as a sort of buffer, keeping unauthorized personnel out of secure areas, and that extended to personal messages as well.

The tube car pulled up, visible through the thick windows of the boarding platform, and they waited while the docking coupler connected with the vehicle's door and hissed into a firm seal. The door opened, and Hunter was swiftly on his way back to Area 51.

Hunter decided he would have to see about recruiting Hanson to the 1-JSST. Just-One took volunteers from a number of elite special forces across the US military community, and Hunter, as its operational commander, was always on the lookout for fresh meat.

Hanson appeared to be sharp and on the ball . . . *and* he would already have the necessary security clearances.

Hunter actually was not all that disappointed by security's refusal to let him into S4. He would return to Security and try to get them to update the file on him in the base computer. The delay, meanwhile, would give McClure a bit more time to study the contents of his luggage.

And if he couldn't get the computer reports changed . . . well . . . it wouldn't be the first time the government's left hand didn't know what the right was doing.

"THE THING about that is," Minkowski said, gesturing toward the faux-Glock, "it's way, way better than the laser sidearms they issue to us. If *this* kind of technology is available, why the hell don't we have it?"

McClure and Elanna, as well as Joshua Norton and Simone Carter, were in the S4 xenotechnology lab, all members of the USSS *Hillenkoetter*'s science department. Dr. Simone Carter was head of biological sciences, while Dr. Norton was in charge of xenotechnology. They'd all shuttled down from the *Big-H*, now tucked away in her subselenian hangar bay on the lunar Farside, in order to study new technologies acquired during the recent mission to Aldebaran.

But Hunter had just provided them with a treasure trove.

"It's happened before," Elanna said. "How's your history?"

"So-so . . ."

"You know the Battle of the Little Bighorn?"

"No, ma'am."

"Most people nowadays call it Custer's Last Stand. The native peoples called it the Battle of the Greasy Grass. Five companies of the US Seventh Cavalry were completely wiped out by ten times their number of Lakota and Cheyenne natives."

"Okay . . ." He wondered where Elanna was going with this. *Damn*, those blue eyes were disturbing. . . .

"The Seventh Cavalry was armed with Springfield trapdoor rifles—single-shot breechloaders, standard-issue for the day. At least ten percent of the natives carried the very latest in repeating rifles—Winchesters and Henrys, especially. Something like two hundred of the Native Americans were actually far better armed than their opponents."

McClure looked at her with surprise. "How the hell do you know all of that, Elanna?"

"Yeah," Norton added. "You ain't from around here. . . ."

"But you have to admit I *do* get around."

Minkowski blinked. He'd heard rumors that the Talis were somehow force-fed volumes upon volumes of history, sociology, and politics before they traveled back into their past, turned into walking encyclopedias. If that were true, it still begged the crucial question of *why*? He didn't see how working in the twenty-first century demanded an intimate knowledge of nineteenth-century breechloading rifles.

But her information did raise the next question.

"Okay. Why?" he asked. "If the US government had access to

better weapons, why did they deploy their cavalry with obsolete equipment . . . ?"

"Because military procurement was an ass," Carter said. "Still is, so far as I'm concerned."

"Back in the day," Elanna continued, "government procurers didn't want to foster wastefulness, right? If you had a weapon that fires five or seven times between reloadings, you *obviously* are going to waste ammo . . . and they couldn't have *that*, now, could they?"

"And you think something like that is why they issued us those crappy Type I Sunbeams?"

"That must be it," Carter said. "I can't speak for government purchasing agents in the eighteen hundreds, but I know there's concern nowadays about power packs and expendables. The guys in charge also want weapons that us poor, dumb humans can repair in the field." She indicated the Glock. "High technology requires sophisticated support and maintenance."

"This thing isn't actually a laser like the Type I," Norton said. "It must have a *very* potent energy cell inside the grip. It probably releases a bolt of directed electricity, several thousand volts' worth, instead of coherent light."

"I was wondering about that," Minkowski said. "It made a hell of a loud crack when it went off. Lasers don't usually do that."

"You heard the thunderclap associated with a bolt of lightning, yes."

"Well . . . shit. We're expected to fight with those, those *toys*— junk that doesn't have nearly the same impact downrange. Just four shots, and they need to be reloaded! How does that even compare to this thing?"

"We haven't tested that yet," Norton replied.

"Saurian power cells *are* extremely high-density," Elanna said. "They're good for forty or fifty shots before they need their cells swapped out."

"Damn it, it's not right!"

"You'll have to take that up with the people in charge of the program, Master Chief," McClure said. "Assuming they'll listen to you, of course. Like they say, beggars can't be choosers."

"The JSST are *not*—"

He was interrupted by a squeal from a speaker on one wall. "Attention, attention," an authoritarian voice declared. "Master Chief Arnold Minkowski, please report to S4 Security. Master Chief Arnold Minkowski, report to S4 Security, immediately."

"What did you do now, Master Chief?" McClure asked with a sharply raised eyebrow.

"I just said it isn't right! Were they listening? Okay . . . I'd better go see what they want."

But he was pretty sure he knew the answer to that.

HUNTER WALKED into a large aircraft hangar back at the main Groom Lake facility. It wasn't the first time he'd been stuck on a red-tape merry-go-round, but he was swiftly becoming fed up. The JSST was lined up in ranks doing morning calisthenics—T-shirts, shorts, and military-issue running shoes. Lieutenant Billingsly, the unit's XO, was leading them in jumping jacks, the *stomp-stomp-stomp* of forty men and women jumping in unison echoing through the enormous, empty structure.

The JSST's personnel roster currently stood at 120, but two-thirds were still on board *Hillenkoetter*, out on the far side of the Moon. Passes to take a shuttle back to Earth, *especially* passes to visit Earth and go off-base, were damned hard to come by. Hunter was beginning to wish he'd elected to stay on board. His attempts to find Geri so far had been nothing but trouble.

Billingsly saw Hunter standing off to one side and signaled for Sergeant Aliya Moss to break ranks and come forward to take over the calisthenics. At least, Hunter thought, the men will have something nicer to look at than Billingsly's long face. The unit's executive officer joined Hunter. "What's up, boss?"

"Need you to do me a favor, Lieutenant."

"Yes, sir."

"Let's go over there."

He led Billingsly to a private corner. "You scheduled to go twelve-plus anytime this morning?"

"Going twelve-plus" meant entering any passageway or office in the complex restricted to TS Crypto 12 or higher . . . the most secret sanctum sanctorum within a facility already so secret.

"Negative, Commander." Hunter heard the question behind the statement.

"I'd like to borrow your ID for about an hour."

Billingsly's eyebrows shot up on his forehead. "So . . . you're looking at . . . what? Ten years and ten thousand dollars?" That was the basic penalty for violating their various secrecy oaths.

"This is not an order, Jim," Hunter replied. He explained what had happened when he'd tried to get into S4. "I need to see Doc McClure and Elanna. I do *not* want to call them, because all calls in this place are monitored." Personal cell phones were prohibited here, of course, and every landline call was recorded. "I could ask you to deliver a message . . . but that means getting you involved. Deeply involved. I don't want to do that."

"And you don't want to tell me what this is all about. . . ."

"Let's just say that I'm already in it up to my neck, okay? If I go under I don't want to drag you with me."

Billingsly considered this.

"If you'd rather go in my place," Hunter added, "I have no problem telling you everything. But . . . take it from me, you'd really be better off not knowing."

"No problem, Skipper." He pulled out his ID card. "You need the badge, too?"

"No," Hunter replied, removing his card and handing it to him in exchange. "Those still work. But I need this to get past the computer scan at the checkpoints."

"Well . . . if I end up in the brig, come see me once in a while, okay?"

"It won't come to that. If anyone challenges you on it, tell them I gave you a very specific order. I'll back you on that. That might get you a security review, but I'm the one they'll be coming after."

At least, that was Hunter's hope. What they were doing was so far above and beyond the strict rules of military security that The System might well decide to eliminate them both. But Hunter also felt a binding connection with both McClure and Elanna, along with any of the other scientists who might have been roped into this thing.

"Thanks, Lieutenant." He slipped the card into his wallet. "I'll look you up in a bit to return it."

"Sure . . . if you're not in the brig." But he grinned as he said it.

Hunter knew his team possessed a camaraderie worthy of the Navy SEALs.

THE BEING known as Charaach despised humans, detested them with a cold-blooded fury belying the fact that the circulatory fluid flowing through her veins was hot. Her particular faction of the Ve'hrech'na, a phrase shortened to Vach, the People, saw little point in keeping the creatures alive. Some wanted to maintain a breeding population as a food source, but Charaach disliked both the taste and smell. They were swarming vermin, overrunning the world of the Vach, fouling their nests, polluting everything they touched, threatening to render the entire planet uninhabitable by either Vach or human. How the Kagag faction of her people could even consider working *with* the ugly, semi-sentient mammals was completely beyond her.

She knew that humans called her species Saurian or Reptilian. In turn, she called them *Ghech*, which denoted a foul-smelling lump of excrement. Charaach—with the "ch" pronounced like the guttural "ch" in *Bach*, a human composer—was not a personal name as humans understood it. It meant something like "Truthful Lies," and was a description of her place in the Few's order.

Truthful Lies missed her home . . . her *real* home lost now in the distant past. She and her fellows called themselves Ve'hrech'na— roughly "We Surviving Few."

At times, though, she wondered if survival was worth it.

She floated at the center of the Place of Viewing, surrounded by virtual displays showing feeds from a dozen different surface locales. A riot was underway in the Ghech hive called Berlin . . . large numbers of the mammals launching themselves at one another with rocks and clubs and water cannons. Over the past years, the Vach had been encouraging such behavior, amplifying the natural Ghech tendencies toward xenophobia and paranoia. Larger and larger numbers of homeless migrants from the south had been crowding into Berlin and its sister hives, seeking work, seeking government subsidies for healthcare and the needs of basic living, until the local social infrastructure tottered on the brink of destruction.

The recent pandemic, though not created by the Vach, had certainly been used by them to foment crisis upon crisis. Charaach worked in the Vach propaganda bureau, disseminating what the humans would have called "fake news," quite literally "truthful lies": that the new vaccines were tainted, that they would only be given to the wealthy, or that the entire pandemic was a hoax, created by rich humans who wanted to gain supreme control over the entire, faction-riddled planet. Individual Ghech believed whatever paranoid fantasies spoke to them best, echoed what they heard endlessly, bringing the planet closer and closer to collapse.

Charaach would have been just as happy to have released a *real* killer plague, a genengineered disease with 100 percent lethality that would eliminate the filthy, swarming mammals entirely. She'd been overruled by the Ve'hrech'na Council, however. The Kagag, along with the allied Grushek and Nivgheer factions of the Few, insisted that humans would have a place in the new world once the Vach assumed full, outward control of the planet. Even the Rareek wanted the humans kept around as food animals and for entertainment. But that made things very difficult for the planners who were trying to engineer a takeover.

There were barely two hundred thousand of the Ve'hrech'na

in this epoch, two hundred thousand against well over seven billion of the loathsome Ghech. Were the Vach to emerge from their hiding places across this world and elsewhere in this star system, they would find themselves outnumbered by tens of thousands to one. Worse, the locals had an unpleasant propensity for deploying primitive nuclear weapons. No one on the Council had any illusions about the Ghech attacking with primitive atomics should the Vach threaten them overtly.

No matter how well they were armed, the Vach would be annihilated or, at the very best, they would annihilate those teeming billions and find themselves in possession of a ruined world.

So the Council long ago had decreed that the Vach would conquer this world by stealth; by pitting the Ghech against one another; by inspiring wars, massacres, bloody uprisings and divisive religions, and ideologies that would end with the collapse of what passed here for civilization.

And that was a large part of Charaach's hatred for these creatures. *Vachaad was the home of the Vach!* Rightfully, it belonged to *them*, to the *Vach* . . . not to upstart mammals that should have gone into extinction sixty-five million years ago.

Charaach watched the humans battling one another in the streets of Berlin. It would be so easy, so *very* easy, to annihilate that city . . . and then to extend the annihilation to the rest of the planet.

The Council, at times, could be so idiotically conservative . . . so self-limiting . . . so *wrong.* . . .

CHAPTER FOUR

Most Americans will be shocked to learn that the conspiracy-theory label was popularized as a pejorative term by the Central Intelligence Agency (CIA) in a propaganda program initiated in 1967. This program was directed at criticisms of the Warren Commission's report. The propaganda campaign called on media corporations and journalists to criticize "conspiracy theorists" and raise questions about their motives and judgments.

LANCE DEHAVEN-SMITH,
CONSPIRACY THEORY IN AMERICA, 2014

20 March 2020 to the Present

THE TIME SHIP *broke through from the abyss and into a somewhat saner continuum, one with a mere four dimensions.* Oberst *Viktor Albrecht had left* Götterdämmerung *far behind . . . seventy-five years behind if the Lizard piloting the craft had gotten its sums right. The time ship descended above a sprawling, alien metropolis.*

"That . . . that is Berlin?" he asked, amazed.

The being at the controls ignored him. The Eidechse—*the Deutsch word meant "Lizards"—were hard to comprehend. Some interacted with humans openly and even enthusiastically. Others were sullen and uncommunicative.*

Albrecht wondered if this one had read his thoughts, had picked up what he thought of them.

He stared into the console display, transfixed. When the time ship first had dropped into normal space, Earth had been spread out below him, an enormous blue globe masked by swirls and streaks of cloud. He'd recognized the continental outlines of Europe, however, and could tell they were descending over Germany. The city passing below must be Berlin; he thought . . . he thought it might resemble the Berlin he knew. That, surely, was the Spree River running through the center of the metropolis . . . and if that river it joined with was the Havel, that *district must be Spandau, on the northwest side. They were drifting south over the city's center, descending steadily. A sprawling airport lay ahead . . . surely not* Tempelhof*! The airport he remembered would have been swallowed by this gargantuan sprawl of concrete.*

Abruptly, the scene blurred, and Albrecht felt an inner twist of acceleration. Daylight vanished, replaced by a vast and shimmering galaxy of light—the lights of the city illuminating the night. "What was that?" he demanded. "What just happened?"

A field fluctuation, caused by your radar. *The words formed themselves in his mind, emotionless.* We were in danger of being seen.

"And this is Berlin? In the future?"

It is Berlin . . . more than seventy years after the city you knew. The facility below is new—Berlin Brandenburg Airport.

"It looks like I'm going to have some catching up to do," he said, more to himself than to the small, alien pilot. Like all of the Eidechse, *the pilot was disturbingly humanoid . . . but scaled,*

bluish on the back, pale in front. The eyes were large, golden, and with pupils slitted like a cat's.

The eyes bothered him the most. When the being looked at him, he could imagine himself being read, studied as if he were a small and peculiarly revolting insect.

It matters not whether you catch up or not, *the voice in his head replied.* Your sole purpose here is to bring down the local authority.

The city, ablaze with light, seemed magical in its scope and bustle and luminous output . . . so far removed from the rubble of Götterdämmerung.

His job—his purpose, *as the creature had called it—seemed impossible in its scale and scope.*

The Present

"WHERE'S MINKOWSKI now?" Hunter asked Elanna.

He'd found her along with Doctors McClure, Norton, and Carter in S4 X-Tech. He'd had no problem this time getting through security but was worried his ruse would be discovered. He needed to talk to these people and then get back before Billingsly got into trouble for the ID card swap.

"He got called up to Security," Norton told him. "It sounded important."

I'll just bet it did, Hunter thought.

He didn't like Norton. The guy was a civilian with strong anti-military feelings who'd been put in charge of a VBSS boarding team sent into the asteroid called Oumuamua during *Hillenkoet-*

ter's last mission. He'd fired his hand laser at an alien being that might, *might* have been trying to communicate . . . though how to exchange greetings with those living, semisolid mountains forming out of swarms of tiny black creatures was somewhat of a problem.

The VBSS party had been lucky to get out alive. One of the team scientists, Roger Kellerman, had not been so lucky, cut in half by a superhigh pressure stream of water.

Since that episode, Norton had been more . . . restrained, no longer assuming the worst about military personnel, no longer the arrogant know-it-all whose blunders had nearly wiped out the boarding party. However, Hunter still didn't trust him and kept an emotional distance.

"He did bring us your little present," Elanna told him. "I assume this was from a Malok agent?"

"A genuine Man in Black," Hunter told her. "An *alien* Man in Black. It looked like there was some high tech in there, and there's something different about the Glock."

"I'll say," Simone Carter told him. "Minkowski put a crater in the wall . . . nearly gave us a window to the lab next door."

Hunter raised his eyebrows. "More powerful than a Sunbeam?"

"More powerful than a *Starbeam*," Norton said, referring to the larger, more massive laser rifles issued to the JSST.

"Well, I wanted you science-types to have a look," Hunter told them, "but I'm going to need to take it all back. Kelsey's on my case about playing nice with the Majic people . . . and I have a couple more MiBs breathing down my neck."

"Too bad," Norton said. "I'd love to study this stuff for the next year or so."

"Any idea what any of it does? Or how?"

"Don't ask me," McClure said, grinning. "My specialty is xenobiology, not alien toys."

"Well, I figured you'd get the stuff to the right people," Hunter told her. He looked at Elanna. "How about it? Are these your toys? Or are they Malok?"

"Malok," the Talis told him. "Definitely. The weapon is typical of Saurian hand weapons—powerful, somewhat clumsy, rugged. This person you took these items from . . . you said he was alien?"

"I assumed he was Malok, actually," Hunter said. "But he was a lot more human than the Saurians I've seen. Very light scaling. Human enough to pass for one in a bad light. But a reptile's eyes. Very large, like he was used to lower light levels than us. I never believed in all of that alien-hybrid crap . . . but now I'm wondering."

"Malok genetic technology is quite good," Elanna told him. "Good enough that they *can* tinker with the human genome, splicing in DNA segments from other organisms, including themselves. You are correct that hybrids between truly alien organisms and humans is not possible."

"That's right," McClure said. "The respective DNA sequences are too different, assuming the alien life-form even uses deoxyribonucleic acid in the first place."

"But the Saurians, as you call them . . . they have DNA," Elanna said. "They are, in fact, life-forms that evolved on Earth millions of years ago, as you know."

"Dinosaurs," Hunter said. "I'm still not sure I buy *that*."

"Well, they are life-forms as closely related to the original dinosaurs as birds are now. They developed a highly technical civilization on Earth some sixty-six million years ago. Eventually they developed star travel, which, of course, requires time travel to get around the Einstein limit."

"The speed of light?" Hunter asked.

Elanna nodded. "Then their civilization was destroyed—an asteroid impact that wiped out seventy-five percent of all species on the planet. Some survived for a time in subterranean cities—many Saurian hive-cities were located underground to begin with. A large number remained on other worlds, or in space. Several hundred thousand of these brought their ships back to the Sol system, rescued some of their struggling fellows, and decided to shift their civilization into the remote future."

"But they found *us* in their future," Carter said. "That must have been a shock."

"We believe they established a number of colonies through the eons," Elanna told them. "They established their primary base of operations in the early Pleistocene, very roughly two million years ago."

"Interesting," Hunter said. "That date."

Elanna looked uncomfortable. "We're not supposed to discuss that, Mark."

"You're reading my mind?"

"I don't need to. I see the question in your eyes."

Hunter knew everyone in the room wondered the same question: Had the Saurians been involved with human evolution? Two million years ago, the closest thing on the planet to humans had been a three- to four-foot upright ape called *Homo habilis*. A few hundred thousand years later, *H. habilis* was making the evolutionary transition to *Homo erectus*, a giant step on the long road to modern, intelligent humans. *Homo sapiens*, an archaic form of him, wouldn't appear in the fossil record until around 300,000 years before the present.

So had intelligent, time-traveling dinosaurs done their genetic tinkering with a species of ape they found roaming the African savannahs, and ultimately created modern man? Hunter had noticed that the Talis, who would probably know, seemed unwilling to discuss that question. However, Hunter had not pushed. He suspected that the Talis were afraid of rocking the boat for modern human civilization by suggesting that it hadn't been God in the Garden of Eden that brought forth people, but scaly, toothy humanoids with crocodile eyes.

Fiat hominidae . . .

Hell, the ancient astronaut theorists on the History Channel would just eat that stuff up.

Hunter didn't really care one way or another. He wasn't religious to begin with and had always had an abiding respect for Darwinian natural selection. But if ancient aliens—or intelligent dinosaurs—had created Humankind, the overriding question had to be . . . *why*?

"Those questions," Elanna said, "are best left alone."

Damn it, she was doing it again: reading his mind. He shrugged. "Whatever. My concern right now is for the suits in the dark glasses, human and reptile both. I need to get this stuff back to Kelsey . . . or end up in prison."

"Would they *do* that?" McClure sounded incredulous.

"I've pissed them off pretty badly. Some of them want to lock me up and throw away the key. Or eliminate me entirely."

"This is more like some wild conspiracy theory every moment," Carter said. "Pure, unadulterated paranoia."

"Hey," Hunter said, "like they say . . . just because you're paranoid, it doesn't mean they're *not* out to get you."

"Give us twenty minutes, Mark," McClure told him. She gathered up the clothing. "I'll get high-def macros of the visible wiring. We'll make do with that."

"What about the gun?" Norton asked.

"You're a xenotech. Go ahead and take it apart. Just be sure you put it back together inside of twenty minutes."

"And try not to blow us all up while you're doing it," McClure put in.

McClure, Carter, and Norton gathered up the MiB's accoutrements and vanished into the back recesses of the lab. Hunter was left alone with Elanna.

"The Saurians," she said gently, "wish to destabilize human civilization. They will do anything to accomplish that, including leading us into bloody and fruitless wars. They use religion to set us against one another. They seed human cultures with . . . *stories*. Conspiracy theories. Tales that would be laughable in most circumstances, but which take on a certain plausibility in times of stress, heightened paranoia, and fear."

"Like this COVID19 thing?" Hunter asked.

"Exactly. *COVID was created by the Chinese as a bioweapon. COVID is a hoax perpetrated by governments to assume greater control over their populations. COVID is no worse than the flu. COVID vaccines don't work. COVID vaccines inject people with microchips.* Every one of these stories has been circulating since the pandemic began. None can be proven. All are to some degree destabilizing."

"I don't think I see the point."

"*Don't trust the government.* That one has been around since the Vietnam conflict. *We never went to the Moon.* That gets us to question our own past, our own worthiness . . . and to question the government's truthfulness in dealing with the American public. *The US government engineered 9/11 to create a reason to invade Iraq.* An insidious one, that, again making us question our government."

Hunter noticed that Elanna was including herself, using the words *us* and *our.*

"It's been my experience that the government *does* lie," he told her. "It *does* cover things up. It *does* overdo secrecy. It *does* rip off the taxpayers seven ways from Sunday."

"Of course. Every government does. Every government is made up of people, and people are ignorant, fallible, greedy, afraid, and at times malicious. But . . . the Moon landings were faked at Area 51? *Really?*"

"I've always hated that one," Hunter admitted. "Cherry-picking idiots pretending they're in on the greatest secret ever."

"Ten percent of the American population believes it," Elanna said. "*Eighteen* percent of Americans in their twenties."

"Good God. Sometimes I mourn for my species. . . ."

"You should take heart from the fact that human ignorance has had so much help."

"And you're suggesting the Saurians planted that rumor? In God's name how?"

"By abducting a disillusioned and deeply depressed former technical writer who'd once worked for Rocketdyne and programming him with the necessary lies and misinterpretations. He went on to write the first of the Moon-hoax conspiracy books in the mid-1970s."

"Yeah, but . . . *how*? You can't just reach into a guy's brain with a screwdriver and make adjustments."

Elanna smiled. "It's not quite that easy. You're aware that the Saurians have large numbers of humans in stasis. Submerged in vats of hyperoxygenated liquid either comatose or in a twilight sleep."

Hunter shuddered. All of those naked people, suspended in their own, personal aquaria . . .

He'd been having nightmares about that lately.

"Yes . . ."

"The Malok have a keen understanding of the human nervous system, of brain function. Are you aware of how easy it is to generate false memories?"

"I've heard that."

"Or how a person with a particular emotional investment in an idea will cling to that fantasy regardless of attempts to sway them with logic, reason, or facts?"

Hunter nodded.

"They understand this and use it. They are telepathic, as you are aware, and can reach inside a person's mind to implant new ideas. They link those ideas to certain emotional responses that make them feel solid, obvious, even proven and absolute."

"That explains . . . a lot." Until now, Hunter had simply assumed people were idiots. But something else occurred to him. "Wait . . . are you saying that eighteen percent of Americans in their twenties have all been abducted by aliens? That's ridiculous!"

"I'm not saying that at all. But they could abduct a few, program them, and give them the subliminal urge to convert others."

"So how many have they abducted?" He knew that Eisenhower had agreed to a treaty with aliens that allowed them to abduct and release a few citizens a year in exchange for technology.

"We don't know. Some surveys suggest one person in twenty-five worldwide. For the United States, that would be over thirteen million. That seems unlikely."

"Yeah," Hunter agreed. "Where do they stash them . . . in the attic? Under the bed?"

But he was remembering those rows upon rows of transparent cylinders, like props in some incredibly hokey sci-fi thriller.

"A better question to ask might be how many people go missing each year? Police statistics claim the number is in excess of six hundred thousand."

"Six hundred thousand missing people a *year*?"

"The vast majority are people escaping abusive relationships, people seeking to start a new life, or runaway children. Some are kidnap victims, often by parents in custody battles. But a few . . ."

"So the Malok would have a steady supply of victims to turn into conspiracy theorists."

Still . . . so many cylinders, each with its solitary, sleeping prisoner.

"They would," Elanna agreed.

"I was wondering what the hell they did with all of those abductees. I saw hundreds of them at Zeta Retic, and then at Aldebaran. Surely visiting aliens would have learned all they needed about human reproduction decades ago. Or stolen all of the genetic material they needed from a handful of people. Why so many locked up and held captive?" He felt a growing excitement, as though he were finally being allowed to see a reason behind this madness. "It almost makes sense. . . ."

He stopped himself and gave Elanna a sharp look. "So why are you telling me all of this? You Talis have been pretty tight with your behind-the-scenes info with us."

"Not all of us are in agreement as to the best course of action in working with twenty-first-century humans," she told him.

"Afraid of scaring us to death?"

"Not at all. Humans are remarkably resilient. It's true that some do still fear causing a catastrophic social collapse of human civilization. Your economies, religions, even your willingness to pursue your own agendas regarding science, redressing social wrongs, improving the human condition . . . It would be a grievous wrong if your culture simply sat back, folded your hands, and said 'Let the aliens do it.' Such a dependency on older, more advanced cultures could cripple you, might even lead to your extinction as a species."

"Which would eliminate *you*," Hunter observed, "since we're your ancestors."

"Exactly. You people, your civilization, are assets to be cherished and protected, but not held back."

"Like *Star Trek*'s noninterference directive. I'll buy that. I'm not sure how I feel about being anyone's *asset*, though."

"I mean no offense, Mark. But humans of this era have become chess pieces in an unimaginably vast and far-reaching contest. The Malok would enslave you, and in so doing eliminate those humans in your future—us, and the free Grays. You are vital to their interests, and that's the reason they're at war with us . . .

though they appear to be divided among themselves over what to do about you. As for us, your destruction or enslavement would be an existential threat to us. Of course, we will try to help you . . . *if* we can do so without affecting your development."

Time travel was one hell of a bucket of worms. How *did* you help a past civilization without stunting its growth, making them become dependent on you? As he understood it—and that wasn't very well—there were no such things as time-travel paradoxes, no *grandfather* paradoxes. Go back in time and kill your own grandfather, and you didn't wink out, and therefore fail to go back and kill the guy . . . an endless loop of causal mayhem. No, quantum physics, as currently understood, said that by killing your grandfather, you would immediately find yourself in an entirely new universe, a new branch of reality in which you did not exist. The universe you'd come from, though, would still exist . . . as one of an infinity of parallel realities.

You just could never go home, could never return to your original reality again.

The Talis appeared to have a tightly shaped and guarded reality, and they'd been working for God alone knew how long to protect it. Something else nagged at Hunter. So long as Elanna was being chatty . . .

"What about the Grays?" he asked.

"What about them?"

"They're from even farther in the future than you are. What . . . a million years?"

"A little more than that."

"So far, most of the Grays I've seen have been working for the Saurians. Is that a reality you're trying to change?"

"That is a difficult question to answer, Mark. Remember, there is no single Gray civilization. A million years from now, there are hundreds of thousands of offshoots of humanity, some so alien you would have difficulty recognizing them as anything related to you. Do you understand?"

"I suppose so." He didn't, not really, but he wanted to.

"Some branches have been . . . overtaken by the Saurians. Like the Saurians, they are Malok, a part of that culture. Others are free. Remember, the original abduction events were attempts by some Gray cultures to break a genetic bottleneck in your far future, to correct certain problems the Grays themselves created along the way by manipulating their own genome."

"Those must've been catch-and-release."

"If you like."

"And the Saurians, with their long-term catch-and-keep programs?"

"The Malok, both Saurians and the Grays under their control, are determined to take back the Earth." Elanna stared into Hunter's eyes for a long moment, as though she were trying to make up her mind. Finally, she lifted her arm and touched Hunter's forehead.

The thrill of her touch was sharp, tingling, and distinctly sexual in its intensity. For just a moment, he could see an unfolding scene: a montage of historical scenes. He could see workers building the Egyptian pyramids . . . shaven-headed Sumerians working in open-pit mines . . . a temple filled with humans on their knees before an enthroned Reptilian . . . and always, always, hanging in the skies overhead, the dark and sinister shapes of gigantic ships. . . .

Hunter heard Elanna's voice in his head. *For the Saurians, that means returning human civilization to what they were created for in the first place . . . docile slaves serving their needs.*

The shock of that vision forced Hunter back a step. She'd said it! She'd finally said it!

"So the Saurians really did genetically engineer us," he said. "Why didn't you tell us?"

"Because doing so would advance the Malok agenda," she told him aloud.

"What? How?"

"How do you think many of your fellows would react to this . . . this revelation?"

He thought about it. "I don't think they would believe it. Some would, I suppose. . . ."

"And you would have thousands of programmed disseminators of Malok conspiracies. Conspiracy theories upon conspiracy theories . . . all united only by the mistrust of any authority, and the conviction that those who are not with us are against us."

"You're saying there would be a war between the two camps?"

"An unimaginable war, Mark, a *horrific* war, one pitting believers against nonbelievers; old religions against new religions *and* against one another; the poor seeking to better their lot against the rich seeking to keep them in their place; haves against have-nots; democratic nations against totalitarian states; liberals against conservatives . . . Who could win such a conflict?"

"The Malok," Hunter said, reluctant, but seeing the truth. "The Saurians."

"The Malok, standing amid the smoking ruin of a once proud and promising civilization, ruling over the handful of filthy, ignorant, broken survivors by sheer right of force."

Even though Elanna was no longer touching him, Hunter could see a city blasted into utter desolation, with skyscrapers broken and burned and thrusting up through mounds of rubble, a Saurian in gleaming combat armor standing on a fallen statue over cowed and naked worshippers crouching in the street, over *animals*. . . .

"My God." Hunter had to take a few deep breaths as the vision faded. "I guess I understand why you people held that stuff back," he told her.

"It is difficult to know how best to move forward," she said. "As you already know, the Saurians subverted the German people, enabling the Nazis to take over, helped the Nazis with advanced technology. I and some of my fellows attempted to influence that tragedy, to stop them. We failed."

"The Nazis were stopped," Hunter told her. "I'd say you succeeded."

"The Nazis, the Italian Fascisti, and Imperial Japan all were destroyed, yes . . . but human civilization as a whole remained strong," she said. "Despite widespread destruction across the planet, the Americas and most other places remained untouched.

"For the next forty-five years, East and West were poised to annihilate one another. We came very close, agonizingly close, to losing the entire game in your so-called Cold War. Somehow, we managed to block a number of Malok attempts to initiate a nuclear war. Somehow you survived . . . and we guided you in the creation of a true space navy, one that will help you stand up for yourselves against the Saurian threat.

"Remember, it is absolutely imperative for the Malok to utterly crush modern human civilization, to bring it to its knees."

"Why? Wouldn't they want to incorporate what we have into their infrastructure?"

"Your people," Elanna reminded him, "number in the billions. The Malok number a tiny fraction of that. They *know* they cannot win a straight-up, out-and-out war with Humankind. So they will do what they can to get you to kill one another; to reduce your industrial output to nothing; to wreck your economic, scientific, and academic foundations; to leave the survivors broken, dispirited, and starving . . . to the point where surrendering to slavery is the only option."

"I guess I understand." He sighed. "Maybe I understand too much. So why *did* you tell me? I know you people are usually real careful about telling us too much."

Again, she reached for his face. This time, though, there were no nightmare visions. Elanna gently stroked his cheek, touched his ear, smoothed his hair, and Hunter felt himself, just for a moment, teetering on the brink of allurement.

"Because I know we can trust you, Mark. We trust you not to share this with others in a way that would undermine your people's confidence in themselves. We trust you not to carelessly reveal information that would advance the Malok agenda.

"And we trust you to be one of our . . . assets, a very *important* asset, to make certain that the Malok vision is never realized."

Hunter didn't know why she'd chosen him . . . but in that moment he knew he would have died for her. It wasn't sexual desire, it wasn't simple respect, it wasn't anything he could put a name to.

The closest he could come to naming what he felt in that moment was pure awe. . . .

CHAPTER FIVE

Chemtrails: Since the early 1980s, the government has been covertly putting various chemicals into the atmosphere, dispersing them by means of commercial jet exhausts, dubbed "chemtrails." These chemicals may be intended to increase planet Earth's albedo in order to secretly combat global warming, or, alternatively and more likely, they may be used to control the minds of the population below.

POPULAR CONSPIRACY THEORY,
1980S ONWARD

The Present

VIKTOR ALBRECHT STEPPED from the time ship and out onto the grass. It was dark, but the lights of Berlin painted a pale orange glow across the northern sky. They'd set down in a clearing in the forest, and he could hear the keek and peep of insects in the undergrowth.

Someone was supposed to meet him.

The Zeitschiff *glowed behind him, its energy fields slowly dissipating. The craft looked nothing like* Die Glocke, *the bell-shaped time ship laboriously reconstructed by German technicians from a recovered crash in Bavaria back before the war. This* Zeitschiff *was more modern, more alien, a gleaming metallic disk ten meters across, a craft given to the Reich by the* Eidechse *for research purposes. The Lizards, evidently, didn't trust this more modern technology in human hands; even* Die Glocke, *he knew, would have an alien pilot when it made its maiden flight into the future.*

Bitter, Albrecht wondered if Eidechse *help for the Reich's war efforts had been worth anything at all. They'd provided some technical advances, certainly . . . and the promise of many, many more—antipodal bombers, a single bomb that could obliterate an entire city.*

And the time ships, of course. But other than depositing him here in this dark forest near an impossible city, he hadn't seen much concrete aid from the mysterious aliens.

Step away from the ship, *a voice said, speaking in his mind.*

"Eh? What?"

We have appeared on the enemy's radar, *the voice continued.* Step away from the ship while we move ourselves out of phase.

Albrecht stepped back, moving a few meters across the clearing. The light from the time ship dimmed, brightened, pulsed . . . and then the entire disk-shaped ship faded, becoming first translucent, then transparent, the black tangle of vegetation beyond clearly visible through its hull. The illusion wasn't perfect, but, still, how did they do *that?*

Invisibility!

What the Reich could have done with that one trick. . . .

A screeching thunder sounded from behind, then boomed directly overhead. Startled, Albrecht looked up in time to glimpse two aircraft flying over the forest at very nearly treetop height.

Albrecht had seen German jet-fighter aircraft, which had first become operational the previous summer, in 1944, but these looked nothing like the Me 262. They were delta-winged, and possessed tiny canards forward, beneath canopies set almost as far forward as it was possible to go. Instead of the twin engine pods slung beneath the wings, these were powered by single engines in their tails. Orange flame stabbed from behind both aircraft. They looked sleeker, heavier, more powerful than the Me 262 . . . or any other aircraft Albrecht knew of native to the Earth. He caught a glimpse of a black cross outlined in white on the side—a Teutonic Knights' iron cross rather than the Balkenkreuz *usually emblazoned on Nazi aircraft.*

And then they were gone, vanished in thunder beyond the trees.

"Was zum Teufel waren das!?" he exclaimed. But there was no answer in his mind, and when he looked down from the sky, the time ship was gone. Thinking it might have made itself completely invisible, he stumbled forward, hand outstretched, searching . . . but the craft truly was gone.

"Typhoon," someone said behind him. Albrecht spun, and saw a lean, bent, almost wizened man wearing strangely cut civilian clothing. He looked ancient; he must be . . . what? In his nineties? There was something about his eyes . . . as if they weren't quite focused on Albrecht, but on something else, something indescribably more distant.

"I beg your pardon?"

"Eurofighter Typhoons," the man said. "Hunting for the Zeitschiff. *They'll never find it, of course. . . ." He broke into harsh, cackling laughter.*

"Who are you?"

The man stopped laughing, and appeared to think about this for a moment, as though he wasn't quite sure of the answer. At last, though, he drew himself up straighter. "Kammler," he said.

"SS Obergruppenführer *Hans . . . Hans Kammler.* SS Obergruppenführer und General der Waffen-SS *Hans Kammler.*"

Shock rocked Albrecht. He snapped to attention. "Herr *General!*".

"Ja . . . ja . . . *But that was a very, very long time ago. . . .*"

"I'M GLAD to hear you trust me," Hunter said, shaking his head. "But I don't see what that has to do with telling me all this stuff. I'd think that it all was strictly need-to-know."

"But it *is* need-to-know, Mark. You need to know it."

"Why?"

"We want the JSST to carry out a mission for us. A very special, highly secret mission. One of which even your MJ-12 will be unaware."

"What? I thought Majic-12 was running this whole Solar Warden thing."

"We have had reason to suspect for some time that MJ-12 is not operating in Humankind's best interests. Saurian operatives may be using telepathic influence to shape their decisions."

That shook Hunter. They couldn't trust their own command structure?

Don't trust the government. . . .

As he thought about it, however, he realized that the idea made sense in a nightmarish way. MJ-12, the above-top-secret coterie of defense, scientific, and intelligence executives who had first conceived of reverse-engineering crashed alien spacecraft to create a space navy, would have been a key target of enemy operatives from the outset. It would have taken the Malok years to penetrate the tangled layers of security, but eventually they'd find a way in.

"What chance is there, then?"

"That is, as yet, unknown, Mark."

I thought you people were supposed to know the future, Hunter thought. That, of course, was unfair. As time-travelers changed events in their past, they created new continua and picking your way through all the interlocking decision trees was not as simple as might be suggested by a history text. Elanna's people were in the business of preventing the Saurians from wiping them out of existence by changing Hunter's present. Hunter and the JSST, while they wanted to help the Talis, were primarily there to stop the Saurians and their allies from destroying or enslaving the human species.

The intricacies of intertemporal warfare could give you one hell of a headache.

"So what's the mission, Elanna?"

"Later."

At that moment, McClure, Carter, and Norton emerged from the far corner of the lab. "Are we interrupting you two?" Norton asked. His smirk suggested he thought Hunter and Elanna had been engaged in other activities than discussing the Saurian threat.

Hunter ignored the jibe. "What did you learn? Anything?"

"We got a lot of images," McClure told him, "including electron microscopy scans. We also ran some of these under an XRF gun to read the chemistry."

"'XRF'?"

"X-ray fluorescence," Carter told him. "It uses X-rays to cause the elements within a sample to fluoresce. The process tells us what it's made of."

Hunter had heard of that. "So what did you find out?"

"Not as much as we'd like to," McClure told him. "Lots of microelectronic circuitry . . . quite possibly nanotech."

Norton nodded. "Gold, silver, niobium, tantalum, and some weird-ass alloys that I'd love to pick apart. Quite possibly super-conducting."

"Communications, tracking . . . and there's some stuff we can't begin to identify," Carter added.

"Elanna thinks it's for camouflage, maybe bending light around the wearer," McClure put in.

"That is certainly a part of it," Elanna added. "It might also phase-shift the wearer enough to allow limited dimensional trans-lation."

Hunter decided he was going to need to continue his conversa-tion with Elanna.

"Are you sure we can't hang on to this stuff a little longer?" Carter asked him.

"Very sure, Doctor. At least two careers depend on getting these back to Admiral Kelsey." He started packing the stolen articles of clothing and the weapon into the carry-on bag. "Dr. Carter . . . do you still have a pneumatic mail tube running between S4 and Dreamland?"

"It's not pneumatic," Carter said. "It's electromagnetic."

"Okay, okay. EM. Can you zap all of this stuff to Kelsey for me?"

Frequently, researchers at S4 needed to send samples back and forth between there and Groom Lake, and EM delivery was faster and more secure than hauling it around by hand. The system su-perficially resembled the transfer tubes used by banks, but it used

EM linear induction identical to the base's maglev passenger tube cars, not compressed air. The tubes were less than a meter wide.

Minkowski had managed to smuggle the clothing and fake Glock into S4, obviously, but with the base now under a security alert he didn't want to try smuggling it out.

"Glad to, Commander," Carter told him.

"Thanks. I'll catch you guys later."

"Where are you off to, Mark?" McClure asked him.

"Security. To bail out Minkowski, of course. If he's in trouble, it's my fault."

"TUCK IN tight, chickies," Lieutenant Commander Hank Boland called over the Starhawks' tactical frequency. "Let's show 'em how the *Navy* does it."

Lieutenant David Duvall, "Double-D," adjusted the trim on his F/S-49 Stingray space fighter with a microscopic nudge to the stick. Outside of atmosphere, of course, a fighter's attitude didn't count for shit. He could be hurtling along his flight path *backward* and it wouldn't mean a thing, but the skipper wanted them looking sharp, so he carefully aligned his ship with the other three, flying in tight formation toward the rusty, cold, desert world ahead.

From just under a million kilometers out, the planet showed a small but distinct red-orange disk, the southern polar cap just visible to the naked eye.

Mars. Duvall had always wanted to go there ever since he'd been a kid. That had seemed less than likely in the early aughts, so he'd joined the Navy instead and become a fighter pilot, always with the slim possibility in mind that he might manage to leapfrog from there to the astronaut corps.

And somehow, against all expectations, it had worked . . . though not quite in the fashion he'd expected. He'd never made it to astronaut training, but he'd been asked to volunteer for Solar Warden.

That had been after his encounter with a real, live UFO, back when he'd been flying off the USS *Nimitz* in the Pacific off San Diego. He'd jumped at the chance, of course. What fighter jock wouldn't? As a member of SFA-05, the Starhawks, he flew higher and he flew faster than he'd ever dreamed was possible. He'd been all the way out to the star Aldebaran, a distance of sixty-five light-years, which beat the 43,000-foot operational ceiling of an F/A-18 Super Hornet all hollow.

Hell, even a quick training jaunt to Mars was nothing by comparison.

"Hawk Three copies, Skipper," Duvall said. "Tight formation."

He glanced out his Stingray's cockpit at Tamara Lasky's Stingray, Hawk Four, just a hundred meters to starboard. She was flying as his wing this time. Like its namesake, the Stingray fighter was long and flat save for the dorsal swell along the spine that included the cockpit. Diamond-shaped in plan view, it was forty feet long from nose to tail, and painted a matte black that drank light and made the fighter difficult to see, even at this range. Lieutenant Commander Boland and his wing, Lieutenant Frank "Hobbie" Hobson, were port, high, and a bit ahead of them, range now half a kilometer, the pair invisible in the encircling night.

"How about it, Tammy?" he called to Lasky over the private channel. "You ever been to the Red Planet?"

"Once, Double-D," she replied. "My first solo in a '49. Dreary place."

"You landed?"

"Oh no. Just a flyover. Looped around the night side and straight back to the Moon. But from the sky the surface looked like the Wyoming Badlands. Colorful rocks, impressive canyons, some sand dunes, that was about it."

"You didn't land at the base, then?"

"Base? That's news to me."

She must not have been cleared for that choice bit of scuttlebutt. He gave a mental shrug. She would be hearing the skipper's clearance request in a moment, so there was no reason not to fill her in. Solar Warden's obsession with secrecy could be bewildering at times.

"There are supposed to be, I don't know, four or five of them at different places. I touched down at Ares Prime a couple of years ago. Several hundred people and a lot of aliens."

"Aliens?" Lasky asked. "Or time-travelers?"

"Grays, lots of them . . . and a few Nordics."

"So time-traveling humans, then."

"I still think of them as alien. They don't *think* like we do, y'know?"

"Temporalist."

"Beg pardon?"

"You're prejudiced against people from a different time period than you."

"I'm prejudiced against know-it-alls who try to tell me what to do."

"And you joined the *Navy* . . . ?"

Duvall chuckled. "Belay that, Tammy. Hey, it seemed like a good idea at the time."

"Okay, listen up, Starhawks," Boland's voice cut in over the tac channel. "Time to check in with Ares Station."

"Tell 'em Double-D and Tammy say 'hi.'"

"Ares Station, Ares Station," Boland called. "This is Starhawk Flight Sierra on approach vector one, requesting clearance for a loop-and-scoot, over."

There was no reply. After a moment, Boland tried again.

"Ares Station, Ares Station, Starhawk Sierra. Do you copy, over?"

Duvall strained to hear a response but heard only the empty EM static of Sol and Jupiter and empty space.

Flight Sierra was a routine training run. Hobson and Lasky were both raw newbies, only recently arrived on board the *Hillenkoetter* as replacements for the Starhawks. The entire squadron had been all but wiped out at Aldebaran, and Solar Warden Command had been scrambling to make up the losses. Boland and Duvall were the old hands now, the only 'Hawk survivors, but pilots always were looking for the chance to put in hours and stay in practice between missions. The four of them had left *Hillenkoetter* in her Farside subselenian cavern on the Moon just two hours before, topping out at 37,500 kilometers per second en route. As they approached Mars, they'd slowed steadily to what amounted to a crawl for interplanetary gravcraft—roughly one thousand kilometers per second. Their flight plan called for them to reduce speed a great deal more—down to about two and a half kps—to allow the planet to sling them around its mass in the "loop" part of their flight.

At a thousand kps, it would take another thirteen minutes to reach the planet.

"Ares Station, Ares Station, Starhawk Sierra. Do you copy, over?"

Ten minutes.

"What do you think the problem is?" Lasky asked over the private channel.

"Damfino," Duvall replied. "I suppose their comm suite could be down. Dust storms play hob with the electronics."

"That must be it . . ."

"Ares Station, Ares Station, Starhawk Sierra. Please respond, over."

Eight minutes.

Boland, Duvall thought, must be feeling like he was trapped in a box. Radioing back to the Moon base for instructions wasn't in the cards right now, because at their current alignments, Earth and Mars were fifteen light minutes apart. By the time a call reached the *Hillenkoetter*, and an answer had returned, thirty minutes would have passed, and Starhawk Sierra would already be around the far turn and headed back to the barn—fighter slang for their home base.

Mars was already quite a bit larger now, as wide as a full Moon seen from Earth. Two tiny stars were caught now in ID reticules on Duvall's heads-up display, identified by his computer as Deimos and Phobos, the planet's two tiny moons.

He was worried now. He'd always wondered . . . what, really, had happened to *Phobos 2*?

The Russian probe had been launched in 1988 and had functioned nominally until it was in orbit around the planet, returning thirty-seven high-resolution photos of the tiny moon Phobos.

Then suddenly it had stopped working. The final three frames of imagery showed . . . something, a shadow . . . a lenticular shape . . . *something* closing with the spacecraft.

Duvall had always assumed the probe had simply died; Russian Mars probes, back in those days, had possessed an uncanny habit of doing that. But now, knowing that the spacecraft of other civilizations operated almost as a matter of routine throughout the Solar System, he began to wonder what it was that had silenced *Phobos 2* . . . and whether the same thing had happened to the human outposts on Mars.

"*Starhawk Sierra, Starhawk Sierra, Ares Station on emergency channel one-niner . . .*"

The voice was weak and static-blasted.

"Ares Station, this is Starhawk Sierra. Go ahead! Over."

"*Wave off, Starhawk, wave off! Snakes inside the perimeter . . . repeat, snakes inside the perimeter. Do not attempt—*"

And the transmission went dead.

Duvall's computer marked a spot on the Martian disk ahead with a brilliant ruby pinpoint, a red star growing brighter . . . brighter . . . then fading. The data feed next to it said only that there'd been a release of energy at that spot . . . a small matter of some 5×10^{13} joules. That was a fraction less than the fifteen-kiloton weapon that had leveled Hiroshima.

Someone had just nuked the Martian surface.

"Snakes?" Lasky asked. "What did he mean by snakes?"

Obviously, she wasn't all the way up to speed on the world of Solar Warden.

"Saurians," Boland replied. "Sounds like the Lizards came in and took over."

"What do we do, Skipper?" Hobson asked. "Was he telling us to back off?"

"We're committed to the pass, Hobbie," Boland replied, his voice grim. "Stick to the flight plan."

"I've got bandits, Skipper," Duvall announced. He couldn't see them optically, of course, but he could see three blips on his forward radar, small ships coming up from the planet's surface.

Coming up *fast*.

"Copy Hawk Three. I see them."

"And me without my one-twenties," Duvall said.

Stingrays were designed to carry standard AIM-120 AMRAAMs as warloads, the same air-to-air missiles currently mounted on Super Hornets and other blue-water Navy aircraft. However, this had been a routine training flight, and enemy contact had not been expected. AMRAAMs were expensive—$400,000 a pop—and Lunar Operations Command had limited numbers of them available for the Solar Warden navy. Stingrays also mounted XM93 hellpods with integral 800-kilowatt lasers but these had also been removed for this flight. Some idiot thought the rookies might accidentally discharge their weapons—a bad idea while they were still on board the *Big-H*.

Duvall was wishing he could swap seats with that guy right now. He'd show him a fucking accidental discharge or two. . . .

"Shit," Hobson called. "Are we gonna hit?"

"Way too much empty space for that," Boland told him.

A forty-meter Stingray was an insignificant speck in the vastness of the Void. Still, if the bogies *tried* a close intercept . . .

For this training flight, none of the twin-seat Stingrays was carrying a back-seater, a RIO, or radar intercept officer. Duvall suddenly feared that they would soon be missing their help in tracking targets.

"Okay . . . here's what we do," Boland went on. "On my mark, we boost, boost *hard* until we get behind them. Then we decelerate to ten kps for our flyby. That'll still be slow enough to let Mars bend our trajectories, and we can correct them to get back on course for Earth on the other side. We'll shoot a planet-grazer pass, and let the fireball mask us. Once we're clear and lined up, we run like hell, full boost, and yell our heads off for help. Maybe we can get the *Big-H* out of her barn long enough to give us a hand, or get an assist from the *Inman* or the *McCone*. Everybody on the same page?"

"Hawk Four copies."

"Yessir!" Hobson sounded scared.

"We're with you, Skipper," Duvall added, rounding off the recital. "Just give the word."

He wondered, though, if this maneuver could possibly work. Everything, *everything* depended now on the enemy ships' technological provenance, their "TP."

No time to think about that. He concentrated on inputting simple commands into his computer. The chances of a head-on collision might be remote, but the Stingray's computer should be able to make last-instant corrections, if need be, to avoid a deliberate impact.

"Okay . . . stand by. Accelerate on my mark in three . . . two . . . one . . . *hit it!*"

Stingrays used one of the new Aerojet Rocketdyne antigravity propulsion systems, which meant the pilot was essentially weightless even under extreme acceleration. The only evidence of that acceleration was the rapid growth of the Martian disk ahead, and the sudden appearance of the three hostile spacecraft coming at them from dead ahead.

He didn't have time to react. His Stingray was closing with the hostiles at speeds in excess of 1,000 kps, and he had only the very briefest glimpse of something flat and lenticular and *big* directly in his path.

White light flared to his right, impossibly brilliant, brighter than the sun. . . .

Once the flash passed, he found himself still accelerating toward Mars, with the three bogies somewhere behind him.

Where the hell had that light come from? It had been brief, as brief as the passage with the hostiles. A chill ran down his spine as he looked at his screen and saw the radar data.

Tammy Lasky's Stingray must have collided with one of the bogies.

Fragments of the alien ship would have continued traveling out and away from the planet, carrying their original momentum once they were no longer in the grip of an inertia-canceling field. Tammy's fighter, the debris from the collision, would have continued on her original course toward the planet, moving at a thousand kilometers per second. "Hawk One, Hawk Three!" he called. "Hawk Four . . . Hawk Four is destroyed!"

"I saw it, Double-D. God in heaven . . ."

On his radar screen, one alien ship had fragmented—the one that had collided with Tammy. Another, hanging back, appeared to be in trouble . . . and Duvall thought from its position that it might have caught some high-velocity fragments of Tammy's fighter, sprayed into its path like the pellets of a shotgun blast.

Good! Serves the bastards right!

He was numb. Though Tammy had joined the squadron only two weeks before, the two of them had found time to enjoy some close camaraderie. They'd spent three delightful nights together—two of them in all-night bull sessions discussing Solar Warden and the alien threat to Earth, and one enjoying some spectacular low-G gymnastics in bed. He couldn't say he'd loved her . . . but she'd been a good friend and a fun companion.

And now she was gone. . . .

Ahead, a mass of tiny, bright pinpoints of light scattered across the face of Mars. It took Duvall a moment to recognize what he was seeing . . . fragments from Tammy's fighter vaporizing in the thin Martian atmosphere.

Behind them, the one surviving hostile was decelerating now, as the three remaining Stingrays continued to boost. They hit the atmosphere with a shock that felt like a solid wall, with ionized atmosphere blazing around them, turning them into three bright, shooting stars streaking across the dark Martian sky. Duvall gritted his teeth as the vibration rattled him to the bones, threatening to rip his Stingray into burning fragments in a sudden blaze of atmospheric friction. The air pressure was a tiny fraction of Earth's, at this altitude very nearly a hard vacuum, but hitting it that fast was like hitting the ocean . . . or a brick wall.

Then they whipped past the planet, cutting their acceleration and slowing sharply as they did so. Duvall had a brief glimpse of the surface sixty kilometers below, blurred by speed . . . then whipped away as they passed the terminator and circled over the planet's night side.

Punching clear of the atmosphere they began accelerating

once more, as Duvall scanned the sky around them for any sign of the remaining alien spacecraft. Had it followed them around the planet? Pulled back to see what the Stingrays were going to do? Or stopped instantly and taken up a new position in front of them?

Technological provenance . . .

Jokes about toilet paper aside, TP was a vital consideration in Solar Warden's efforts against both hostile aliens and reptilian time-travelers. Visitors from off-world came from an enormous variety of civilizations, both in the future and, in the case of the Saurians, from a high-tech Earth in the remote past. As writer Arthur C. Clarke had famously said, *any sufficiently advanced technology is indistinguishable from magic.* Just *how* magical was a function of the culture's provenance in time and the age of its culture. The Talis were from about ten thousand years in Earth's future, which was bad enough. The Grays were from over a million years ahead, and there was a bewildering variety of subspecies from countless different times and cultures and origins. The Saurians were technically from the past . . . but they were in conflict with the Talis far into the future, and possessed a technological civilization that might well span hundreds of millions of years.

Those ships, presumably, had been Saurian. They might be fairly close to current human technology—no more than a few hundred years more advanced. Or they could be pure, Clarke-ian magic.

Duvall saw no sign of the alien.

"Mayday, mayday, this is Starhawk Flight calling Luna Operations Command." Boland's voice over the radio was calm and measured, but possessed an unmistakable sense of urgency. "We are on a direct vector, Mars to Earth, with hostiles in pursuit."

Boland went on to give rapid-fire details of what had just happened . . . the distress call from Mars warning them off, the appearance of three probable Saurian warships, the destruction of Hawk Four. They were still well over twelve light minutes from Earth, so the conversation was strictly one-sided. It would take long minutes for Boland's words to crawl all the way to LOC, and longer still for any response.

The question, of course, was whether there would be any help coming at all. The political situation, the balance between present-day humans and the Saurians, was highly debatable. Technically, the Lizards were currently at war with the Talis, but it was a highly limited form of warfare given that it was a war across time as well as space. There'd been a number of skirmishes recently in which Solar Warden ships had taken part—at Zeta Reticuli and at Aldebaran—but nothing as blatant as a full-blown, lasers-blazing Saurian attack on Earth. Scuttlebutt held that the Talis didn't want to risk all-out war since defeat might well result in the extinction of *Homo sapiens*. Why the Saurians were holding back was less clear, but since they claimed that Earth by right belonged to them, perhaps they simply didn't want to damage the merchandise.

Time wars became *very* tangled very quickly.

It appeared, however, that the Saurians had just pulled back the restraints. By attacking human bases on Mars, they'd upped the ante big time.

And it was possible that present-day humans had just been dragged into all-out war.

A war of competing magics that Humankind could not possibly win.

CHAPTER SIX

Pandemic Hoax: COVID19 is a hoax perpetrated by the government in order to freely assume more sweeping powers and to control a cowed population. The wearing of masks is useless, but employed as a symbol of submission, somewhat akin to the Star of David worn by Jews in Nazi Germany. COVID19 vaccines are covert means of injecting citizens with microelectronic devices for the purposes of tracking, for mind control, or, alternatively, for genocide.

POPULAR CONSPIRACY THEORY,
2020 AND ONWARD

VIKTOR ALBRECHT FOLLOWED *Kammler into the southern outskirts of Berlin and down a set of stone steps to a sunken door. Kammler gave an obviously coded knock, the door opened, and they were admitted into the near-darkness of an underground pub, a smoke-filled rathskeller crowded with dirty-looking youths watching their entrance with suspicious eyes. Many, Albrecht saw, wore masks over their lower faces, but not all . . . and the masks looked more like surgeon's masks than any attempt at anonymity.*

"Why all the masks?" he whispered to Kammler.

"Ah . . . you wouldn't know. A global pandemic. Millions dead . . . nearly a hundred million infected. We think it was the Talis."

Albrecht didn't know who or what the Talis might be but decided to hold his questions. This place, this crowd, felt dangerous . . . and he was very much on his guard.

Kammler led him into the back of the rathskeller, where five men and one woman were seated at a round table, beer steins in front of them. A kind of impromptu stage rose off to one side, occupied at the moment by a nude blonde writhing to a raucous, pulsing noise that Albrecht presumed was music. It was nothing like anything he'd ever heard before, something more akin, he thought, to the sound of tortured cats.

Nearby, a two-meter poster hung on a brick wall, the art showing a throng of young Aryan-looking people standing with their hands raised in a mass Nazi salute and proclaiming the eventual victory of the AfD.

Albrecht had no idea what AfD might stand for.

One of the seated men looked him over, a cigarette dangling from his unmasked lips. He badly needed a shave, and probably a shower as well. "Wer ist das?" *he growled. Who is this?*

"Our courier from the Reich," Kammler replied, speaking German. He dropped into an empty seat. "Herr Oberst Viktor *Albrecht. He's only just arrived."*

"Well, then, sieg heil, *Herr Oberst," the woman said. She looked and sounded bored.* "Willkommen in der Zukunft."

Welcome to the future.

"So where the devil are our promised legions?" another man demanded. He jerked a thumb over his shoulder at the poster.

The woman nodded. "The Sternenmann *has been promising us help since forever!"*

"Herr Albrecht is here to deliver important documents to

the Sternenmann," *Kammler said. "And to discuss with him the schedule."*

Damn it, that . . . atrocity these people label as music was so loud it was difficult to hear them.

"I think," he said slowly, "it would be best if you filled me in on the situation. I'm not entirely sure of what temporal zone I'm in, and I'll need you to catch me up."

The first man nodded. "Ja. Germany has changed somewhat since your day, Grandfather."

And he began to talk as the naked blonde twisted and writhed onstage to the pounding beat of the noise.

"YOU, SIR, look like hell."

Hunter took a sip of his coffee, then leaned back in his chair. He and Minkowski were in a subterranean mess hall in the depths of S4. "It's been a long day, Mink."

"Yeah, well . . . those goons in Security just wanted to know if I'd been in cahoots with you. I didn't admit anything. No harm, no foul."

They'd still lucked out, Hunter thought. When he'd walked into the security office, he'd been nabbed by a quartet of Air Police who'd told him they were going to throw him and Minkowski into solitary. A call to Admiral Kelsey, however, at Hunter's urging, had established that the missing package had been returned and Minkowski and Hunter were to be released.

Even then, judging by the goons' expressions, it had been a near thing.

But the near-escape was not responsible for Hunter's bedraggled state. He was digesting the overload of information Elanna had dumped on him shortly before, information he knew he could share with no one, not even his own men. The Saurians—responsible for the creation of Humankind . . . ?

If he didn't believe in God now, he certainly still remembered when he had—as a kid, raised by devout Baptist parents. It all had seemed so simple, then, the way they'd laid it out in Sunday school. God, the Father, the loving, benevolent and all-powerful Creator . . .

To have all of that declared to be myth by someone who ought to know . . .

He felt as though the stakes in this game had just been raised clear out of sight. He would have folded if he could.

But he knew he had to ride it out.

He couldn't tell Minkowski . . . or anyone else in the unit, not without breaking a vow to Elanna, not without betraying her trust.

Mark Hunter had never felt so alone.

"Attention, attention," a loudspeaker in the ceiling announced. "All JSST personnel report to Hangar One for immediate embarkation."

Now what?

"No rest for the wicked," Minkowski said, rising from the table.

"Mink, you appear to be gifted with a true mastery of understatement."

"CAPTAIN IN the bridge!"

Captain Frederick Groton strode down the steps and across the deck toward his console inside the bridge pit, careful of how he moved. With the Moon's gravity, one-sixth that of Earth, it was possible to step too hard and take a most undignified slow-motion tumble. "As you were," he snapped. "What's the tacsit, Bill?"

Commander William Haines swung himself out of the command chair, standing to one side as the captain took his seat. Around them, thirty members of the bridge crew sat at their consoles, readying the huge carrier for space.

"One of our training missions ran into trouble, Captain," Haines replied. "Starhawk Sierra, four Stingray fighters, on a quick jaunt out to Mars and back."

"Trouble? What kind of trouble?"

"We got a mayday from them about ten minutes ago, sir. They report unknown alien spacecraft jumping them as they approached the planet, about eight hundred K out." He hesitated. "It . . . sounds like Saurians, Captain. They got an emergency radio call warning them off, saying 'snakes' were in the base. Then whoever was transmitting got nuked. Sir."

"Nuked? They're sure?"

Haines shrugged. "No information on that, sir. Sounds like an enormous discharge of energy. Might have been a tactical nuke. Might have been something else."

Groton knew the Saurians had plenty of powerful and deadly weapons in their arsenal. Their bases on Mars had been small scientific and research outposts, lightly armed, if at all. Damn it, they wouldn't *need* to throw nukes around. . . .

But, then, this *was* the Saurians they were talking about. *Bastards.*

"LOC has ordered us to go out there and see if we can rescue our fighters. One was destroyed on approach to the planet, but three more are on their way back now, possibly with snakes in pursuit."

"Then we don't have much time. Make preparations to get underway, Mr. Haines."

"The orders are already given, Captain. We need five minutes to clear away the gantry and hoses."

For those guys fleeing Saurian spacecraft, five minutes would be an eternity. But launching a spacecraft carrier of *Hillenkoetter*'s size and complexity was an involved and demanding process. With massive gantry scaffolding surrounding parts of the ship, and dozens of hoses piping in fresh water and high-pressure liquid air to fill her expendables tanks, it would take time.

Time that neither they nor those fighter jocks could spare.

"Incoming call, Captain," the communications officer reported. "Admiral Winchester."

"Open the channel. This is Groton, Admiral."

"What the hell is going on, Captain? I've got a report here of some of our fighters under attack."

"Don't know the details yet, Admiral. We're going to check it out."

"I'll be right over—"

"Negative, sir," Groton replied. Winchester's office was at least fifteen minutes away inside the vast lava-tube cavern housing Farside. "They're breaking down the gantry now. No time."

"You don't have a full crew, man."

"We have a full watch, sir. We'll be fine."

"Gravity at ninety-eight percent," the engineering officer called from a console forward. "All normal."

"Inertial dampers on," Groton ordered.

"Inertial dampers on, aye, sir."

"Inertial mass to fifteen percent."

"Inertial mass at one-five, aye, sir."

"I'll have them launch the *Inman* as well," Winchester said. "I'll transfer my flag to her."

The *Bobby Ray Inman* was a cruiser also berthed within the cavernous docking bay of Lunar Operations Command.

"Very well, Admiral," Groton said. "But we won't hang around waiting. It is my intent to rendezvous with our fighters as soon as we clear the cavern." *If those fighters are still alive.*

"We have power, Captain."

"Very well. Energy feed to five percent."

"Energy at five percent, aye."

Groton could feel the rising hum of power coming up through the deck. *Hillenkoetter* was coming alive.

He'd glossed over the ship's readiness for space with Winchester, and he was uneasy about *Hillenkoetter*'s readiness—*especially* if she was going to go into combat. She had weapons, both beams and missiles, but what she didn't have was her complement of seventy-two Stingray fighters in her hangar deck. All of her fighters had been off-loaded into the LOC hangars for a thorough maintenance inspection and servicing, with replacements being prepped to come on board and bring *Hillenkoetter*'s fighter complement up to a full seventy-two craft.

He would be glad of *Inman*'s support out there . . . just in case.

"Give us lift, Mr. Larimer," Groton said. "Five meters above the gantry."

The gantry structure had folded down against the deck beneath *Hillenkoetter.*

"Positive lift, up to five meters, Captain, aye, aye."

Groton looked toward the large flat-screen mounted in front of his command chair, saw the black, volcanic rock of the lava-tube wall sliding slowly down. The tunnel, the way out, hung gaping before them.

"Ahead slow, helm. Take us out."

"Aye, aye, Captain," the woman at the helm console said. "Ahead slow."

Slowly, the tunnel mouth grew, a yawning opening hundreds of feet across. He could just make out the faint shimmer of the magnetokinetic induction screen across the entrance. The helm officer eased the giant ship through the impalpable barrier, transitioning from atmosphere to vacuum.

"External atmosphere now at two times ten to the fifth particles per cubic centimeter," a bridge officer reported.

"Outside atmospheric pressure at three times ten to the minus fifteen bar," said another.

Hard vacuum, or near enough.

"Base, *Hillenkoetter*," Groton said. "Ready to open the roof doors."

"Copy that, *Hillenkoetter*. Opening roof doors."

"Overhead doors are open, Captain. Alignment within acceptable parameters."

"Positive lift, Mr. Larimer," Groton ordered. "Slow exit, five mps."

"Positive lift, aye, aye, sir. Emerging at five meters per second."

The ship, a slightly flattened cigar some twelve hundred feet long, rose above the lunar surface, emerging into the harsh, white glare of sunlight. Similar in length to an oceangoing aircraft carrier and massing perhaps half as much, she was the first of several spacecraft carriers, capable of bending both time and space to circumvent the implacable tyranny of Einstein.

"Lieutenant Keel." Lieutenant Janice Keel was the ship's senior avigation officer.

"Yes, sir?"

"Plot a course to intercept Starhawk Sierra on a straight-line Mars-to-Earth vector."

"Plotted and laid in, Captain."

"Weps? We'll go to General Quarters now, if you please."

"Aye, aye, sir," responded Commander William James, *Hillenkoetter*'s tactical officer.

A moment later, an alarm Klaxon sounded, followed by James's voice. "Now General Quarters, General Quarters! All hands man your battle stations!"

"Helm, ahead one-half."

"Ahead one-half, aye, aye."

And the *Hillenkoetter* began to accelerate, the twin spheres of Moon and Earth dwindling rapidly until they were lost in the starry vastness astern.

"YOUR TEAM is going to Mars," Kelsey said.

"What in God's name for? Sir."

"To fight Lizards. More than that I can't tell you."

Hunter's eyebrows rose. "This might be taking the secrecy thing a bit too far, Admiral."

"I can't tell you because I don't know." He went on to describe the events of the past half hour and confirmed that the USSS *Hillenkoetter* was on her way to rescue three surviving pilots.

"We don't know the current situation on the Martian surface,"

Kelsey continued. "One of the Sierra One pilots did report an energy discharge, possibly a small nuke, that apparently silenced the people on Mars they were talking with."

"Ouch." If the damned Saurians were tossing nukes around, the quasi-war between them and the Talis, and, by extension, with modern-day humanity, had just become very, *very* hot.

"The JSST will deploy in four TR-3W transports," Kelsey told him. "Your objective is Ares Prime. You will secure the base, ascertain the situation globally, and report back." He hesitated, as though considering how much to tell Hunter. "You and your team will stay there for a time."

"Oh? If we take out the bad guys . . . why hang around?"

"To tell you the truth, I want you out of Groom Lake . . . off Earth . . . off the Moon for a while, until things calm down around here. You made waves with that little joyride you took to Las Vegas and back . . . big waves . . . tsunami size. It'll be easier smoothing things over if you're not here and visible."

Hunter sighed. "I understand, sir."

"I take it you had some scientists examining the stuff you stole. By way of Minkowski, I'm assuming?"

There was no point in denying it. "Yes, sir. But he was following my orders."

"Mm. Who'd he give it to?"

Hunter decided he could employ some subtle misdirection. "I'm not sure, sir. I wasn't there."

"The Talis girl. And Dr. Carter. Science department. They would have been the obvious choices."

Hunter didn't comment.

"We'll find out, Commander. Or *they* will." He glanced up at the overhead as he said that last part, indicating unnamed personnel farther up the command tree.

"I don't see what the point is, Admiral. The horse is out of the barn, right? We know that at least some of these Men in Black dudes are alien hybrids of some sort. And that calls into question the whole MJ-12 organization. It's been penetrated by the enemy."

"Technically, the personnel of the MJ-12 Intelligence Service are not our enemies, Hunter. Neither are the Reptilians."

"Even after blowing up some of our people on Mars? Destroying one of our fighters? Killing one of our pilots?"

"After *you* started a gunfight with them at Zeta Retic *and* at Aldebaran. They might easily see this action as . . . justified."

"This proves what I've been saying all along, that some of these agents were kidnapping American citizens. They're the *bad* guys, damn it!"

"*Some* of them are bad guys, agreed. We can't have them dropping nukes on our personnel on Mars or anywhere else, and I expect the JSST to address that. But it is imperative that these . . . skirmishes be limited to just that, skirmishes. The JSST is *not* to go in all guns blazing. This is a reconnaissance in force, and if the situation can be resolved peacefully, you *will* do so. The JSST will be there as a show of force. Your ROEs will be to fire only if fired upon. Understand?"

"Yes, sir."

"MJ-1 does not want this to turn into a general war . . . a war that humanity can't possibly win."

"And what if MJ-1 is one of *them*?"

"Just follow your damned orders, Hunter. I'll try to sort things out here, but you need to stay out of the limelight for a while."

"Yes, sir."

MJ-12—sometimes called Majestic Twelve, though it often used other designations—was the organization that ran Solar Warden and Earth's secret space armada. At the top were twelve people, referred to only by the numbers one through twelve. Suppose the bad guys had penetrated this inner circle? They would be in a position to completely nullify Solar Warden's usefulness as a planetary defense force.

And right now, Solar Warden was the only thing standing between Humankind and an all-out takeover of Earth by time-traveling dinosaurs.

It sounded so ridiculous that Hunter wanted to laugh, if it wasn't so damned deadly serious. By all reports, the Saurians had infiltrated governments, corporations, and banking institutions all over the planet. They were, effectively, already in control.

What more, Hunter wondered, did they want?

He was almost afraid that someone might tell him.

The intercom on Kelsey's desk squawked. "Admiral . . . one of the Talis representatives is here to see you. She says it's important."

"Not now, Claire," Kelsey replied. "Closed meeting."

But the admiral's door slammed open a moment later, and 425812 Elanna strode into the office. "Ms. Elanna," Kelsey said, looking up. "Not—"

"You damned well *will* see me, Admiral. I'm the closest thing on this base right now to a Talis ambassador, which makes me this planet's one hope for success in a very nasty conflict. And *this* man," she gestured at Hunter, "has done you and your cause a tremendous service by confirming Malok involvement in your own intelligence operations."

"Did you assume I was disciplining him, Ms. Elanna?"

"I believe the colloquial term is 'reaming him a new one,' yes."

Kelsey smiled. "Maybe a small one. However, the point of this meeting is to send him off-world for a period, to get him away from your 'Malok involvement.'"

"Off-world where?"

"Mars. The Saurians may be engaged in hostilities against our interests there."

"Likely," she said, nodding. "They've been bent out of shape over your bases there and on the Moon since the bases were created. They didn't like it when your Apollo program landed men on the Moon and warned you off, remember?"

"I wasn't there personally," Kelsey said. "But I know the story, of course."

"Care to come with us, Elanna?" Hunter asked, keeping his tone light. "We're going to need a science team. And I need to ask you some questions."

"That actually might be a good idea," Kelsey said. "If . . . certain elements decide that you've been helping *this* unsavory character . . ."

"I wouldn't miss it," she said.

"I'd also like to bring along that remote viewer from the last mission. Ms. Ashley?"

"I think she's still at LOC. Either there or on the *Hillenkoetter*."

"None of us have been to Mars, Admiral. I don't like going in cold. Julia Ashley could let us know what to expect. A psychic scout."

"I'll give the order. One of the Trebs can make a quick stop at Lunar Farside if she's there. Otherwise, she can transfer when you meet up with the *Hillenkoetter*. If she's willing to play along."

Julia Ashley was a civilian, and under military discipline but not actually a part of it. But Hunter hoped she would be willing to come to Mars. He had some questions for *her* as well, questions which he felt were better *not* shared with Kelsey.

"So," Elanna said, looking at Hunter, "old unsavory here isn't in trouble?"

"Oh, he's in trouble, miss. But we're not going to shoot him at sunrise. We just need him out of the way."

"Good. Because, Admiral, you *need* this guy. I'll line up a team heavy in the biology and planetology sciences, okay?"

"Biology?" Kelsey asked.

"Of course. If we're dealing with Malok life-forms—both Gray and Saurian—we may need people to examine their bodies."

"'Bodies'?" Hunter put in. "Elanna, I've been ordered to resolve this thing peacefully if I can. A 'show of force,' I believe the admiral told me."

"Oh . . . there *will* be bodies," Elanna said with a shrug that did delightful things inside her jumpsuit. "With the Malok? Count on it."

And Hunter was very much afraid she was right.

"HE'S BACK," Hobson called over the tactical channel. "And he's brought friends."

Duvall checked his radar. The newbie was right: three bogies were on their six, evidently coming from Mars. They might be friendlies . . . but given the reception they'd already had approaching the red planet, he doubted it.

"They might all be fresh replacements," Boland said. "That one chasing us was pretty badly dinged up."

Duvall studied his screen. The bogies were a hundred thousand kilometers astern but closing fast. According to his combat computer, they would intercept in fifty seconds.

"Skipper . . . these clowns are getting on my nerves," Duvall said. "We need to do something to scrape them off our tails."

By *we*, of course, he really meant *I*.

"Okay, Double-D. What? I'm open to suggestions."

"Permission to break formation."

He didn't wait for the requested permission, and he didn't hang around to argue. Duvall flipped his F/S-94 end-for-end so that the Stingray was now traveling backward, and the three snakes were in a cluster directly ahead.

And closing.

Fast.

He accelerated, which, given his new attitude, meant he was slowing sharply. Hobson and Boland vanished astern, still boosting for Earth, but the three hostiles seemed to leap forward with an aggressive surge.

It was an illusion, of course, caused by his sudden decrease in velocity. He continued to slow, pushing his spacecraft as hard as he dared, gently working his control stick back and forth to put himself in the perfect position.

At a range of less than a thousand kilometers, the hostiles came to a halt relative to local space. Duvall was accelerating now, whittling away the remaining kilometers in a blur of speed.

These guys, Duvall reasoned, probably didn't know the fighters were unarmed. At least, he sincerely hoped that was the case.

They also didn't know humans well enough to guess whether Tammy had hit one of them by accident . . .

. . . or if it had been deliberate, a kamikaze run made in desperation.

The targets ahead seemed to hesitate. They were pulling back now, but Duvall was still closing fast. Three hundred kilometers . . .

Two hundred . . .

The three hostiles broke left, right, and high on his screen. Duvall picked one, the closest hostile moving toward his starboard side, and lunged starboard as well.

What was going through their Reptilian brains right now? *He's trying to ram us, like that last one! He's going to engage with his beam weapons! It's a bluff!*

At the last possible instant, he cut his forward power and decelerated. He had no intention of deliberately ramming one of those Lizard saucers, but *they* didn't know that. And his ploy appeared to have worked; the three were scattering widely now and jinking to make themselves difficult targets.

Duvall's gravitic drive allowed him to move freely, but it wasn't as good as the enemy's maneuverability. Where he could mask about 80 percent of his Higgs-field inertia, the hostiles appeared to be able to eliminate it completely, allowing them to stop on a dime or make an instantaneous right-angle turn at high speed long observed in UFOs over Earth. They *must* know he couldn't deliberately ram them. Tammy's collision, after all, had been either bad luck or a momentarily inattentive Lizard . . . or both.

The three halted, at varying distances, now waiting.

Then abruptly they all vanished, as though suddenly wiped from the sky.

CHAPTER SEVEN

5G Genocide: The fifth-generation cellular network technology, or 5G, is a kind of Trojan horse designed to reduce the global population through widespread genocide. It is no coincidence that the advent of 5G coverage took place the same year as the appearance of the COVID19 pandemic. The network was first thought to cause cancer but may in fact weaken the human immune system making it susceptible to the coronavirus. Alternatively, 5G radiation causes mutations within the body that *create* the virus in the first place.

POPULAR CONSPIRACY THEORY,
2019 AND ONWARD

IN BERLIN, HANS Kammler *led Albrecht through the smoke-heavy pit of the rathskeller and up a flight of steps to a large office, one with doors flanked by a pair of blond, blue-eyed Aryans armed with automatic weapons. Inside, a dozen men stood around a large map spread out on a table . . .*

. . . and one other he'd not been expecting to see.

This, he thought, must be the Sternenmann.

The Starman.

He'd seen them before—most recently at Himmler's occult fortress at Wewelsburg—one of the Eidechse. *It stood over two meters tall and had distinctly scaled jewel-green skin. The head was large, with a pronounced snout and crocodilian teeth. The most mesmerizing part, though, were the eyes—large, golden, and slit-pupiled.*

You are our courier from the past. *The words formed them-selves in Albrecht's mind. These things were telepathic, at least to some extent. Albrecht suppressed a shudder of revulsion. It was impossible to read these things' expressions, but he suspected that it could pick up his fear and disgust.*

Albrecht felt an echo of its emotions. The thing was . . . amused.

The war in the Germany you knew is lost, *the thing said in his mind.* The fight continues here and now.

"You abandoned us," Albrecht said. "You failed to deliver the help, the weapons you promised, and the Reich was overwhelmed by its enemies."

The humans in the room stiffened, some angry, some shocked, all afraid. "You should not say such things, Herr Oberst," one shouted at him. "The Sternenmänner *are our friends!"*

Gently, *the* Eidechse *said in their minds.* Remember what and where Herr Albrecht is coming from. He deserves your under-standing.

Was the Lizard trying to win him over? Why?

He felt something moving inside his head . . . a crawling, slith-ering something as cold as ice, as implacable as Guderian's pan-zers. He started and found he was paralyzed as the . . . the thing moved deeper into his brain. Though, the paralysis passed . . . as did his anger.

He felt . . . loyalty. A sharp devotion to duty . . . honor . . . the Führer *. . . the Fatherland . . .*

Albrecht snapped to attention, clicking his heels . . . though his civilian shoes didn't carry the same authority. "Mein Herr," he said. "I am here to serve the Reich."

"Sehr gut," *the* Eidechse *said, speaking out loud with a deep-throated gargle sharp with sibilants, a chilling sound.* "Herr General Kammler . . . tell our visitor about Projekt Rückkehr."

Operation Return? What within the vast and mighty ramparts of Valhalla was that?

"COWARDS!" DUVALL screamed.

There was no rationality to the taunt. He'd been so focused on delaying the Saurian ships by any means possible and had been all but certain he would be killed in the attempt . . . the palpable sense of liberation and relief when they turned tail and ran shook him to his core, leaving him gasping for breath and more than a little drunk with the emotional release.

"Run! Run! Damned fucking cowards! Run away!"

A shadow fell across his Stingray, breaking the wild-eyed harangue. *What the hell . . . ?*

He flipped his Stingray around, and found himself looking up at the *Hillenkoetter*, a looming shape now close enough to block out the sun.

"Hawk Sierra Three, *Hillenkoetter* CIC. Stand down and prepare to come aboard."

"Are you okay, Double-D?" Boland's voice added. "We heard a lot of screaming."

"I'm . . . okay," he replied. He took a deep breath, figuratively shook himself, and let himself sink into the embrace of his seat. "Yeah, I'm okay. . . ."

"Sierra Three, CIC. Do you require assistance? We have a tug standing by."

"No. No . . . I can bring it in." He paused. He'd been so intent on the Saurians he hadn't even noticed the approach of the *Big-H* on radar.

Situational awareness, he thought ruefully. *What's that?*

Still shaking, he guided his Stingray down the hull of the spacecraft carrier, following beacons to the long, flat slit of the docking bay access. Like the airlock tunnels back at Lunar Operations Command, the bay was walled off by magnetokinetic induction screens. Technically, they went down for a fraction of a second as a ship passed through them, closing again before the bay could be subjected to explosive decompression. In effect, as he flew across the threshold, those screens pressed close around his fuselage, allowing him to pass through within his own maginduct bubble. He didn't know how it worked—it was alien technology after all. He just hoped the fail-safes kept the thing working, because the ship would be in a world of hurt if those screens ever went down.

His fighter touched down gently on the flight deck and was immediately surrounded by the green-shirted maintenance crew. *Hillenkoetter*'s flight deck personnel wore the same color-coded liveries as on aircraft carriers back home—red for the "mag rats," the ordnance crews; yellow for deck handlers and directors; blue for handlers. The only color missing was purple. Space fighters used zero-point energy and didn't require fueling from the "grapes." During both launch and landing evolutions, the flight deck was a ballet of colorful garb and choreographed motion, mingled with the dozens of electric forklifts shifting ordnance and equipment.

Chief Gonzalez, a plane director in a brown vest, climbed a ladder to help Duvall exit his craft. The cockpit cracked with a hiss, then opened up, and Duvall unstrapped and climbed out into the crowd. "Where the hell did you guys come from?"

"Ten minutes ago, we were on the Moon, sir," Gonzalez told him. "I've never seen such a goddamned scramble in my life!"

"Well, I'm damned glad to see you boys."

Nearby, he saw two other Stingrays surrounded by maintenance personnel and handlers—Boland and Hobson. *We made it!*

Then memory, suppressed by battle lust, rose fresh and raw. *All except for Tammy . . .*

"SO WHAT do you know about reptiles, Becky?"

Hunter was in the passenger compartment of one of the huge TR-3B shuttles based at Groom Lake. Dr. Becky McClure sat on his left; Elanna was on the other side of her

"As in reptiles in general?" she asked him, eyebrows arching. "Or the Saurians specifically?"

"Maybe a little of both. I've heard a lot of wild things about the Saurians, but it's all pretty speculative, and sometimes it's tough to tease out fact from speculation . . . or from outright conspiracy, fringe-group nonsense."

She dimpled. "Like them being from the constellation of Draco?"

"Yeah. Or worse, from a *planet* called Draco. Reptilian aliens from a constellation named 'the Dragon' is just a bit too contrived, don't you think? That's not even good pulp fiction."

Around them, other people were filing on board, stowing carry-ons and finding seats. TR-3Bs, affectionately known as "Trebs," had passenger compartments laid out similar to those of big commercial jets, with seating for around 250 people. Hunter knew that a lot of personnel from the *Hillenkoetter* had been on Earth and were being scrambled back aboard the ship.

"I like the one about the Queen of England being a Reptilian in disguise," McClure said.

"Not to mention both Clintons and both Presidents Bush," Hunter added, laughing. "Plus anyone with a net worth of more than a billion dollars. You're supposed to be able to tell by looking at their eyes."

"According to that line of reasoning," Elanna put in, "the Malok have already taken over the planet, and we all serve secret masters."

"Is that what the Malok want?" McClure asked. "To make us all slaves?"

"I wouldn't put it past them," Hunter said with feeling. "They were operating a huge slave camp at Aldebaran. I understand our people are still shuttling those people back to LOC and trying to deprogram them. That was . . . man. Horrible doesn't begin to describe it."

"Most of them were Nazis," Elanna pointed out.

"So? It was still horrible. And I seem to recall that most of them weren't the original generation of Nazis, right? They were the *kids* of Nazis, born and raised on the Paradies colony. You can't condemn them for the crimes of their fathers."

"The Malok simply see humans as resources. As slave labor and food. Even as entertainment. And we are occupying the world they *know* to be their home, sixty-some million years later. If they can get what they need operating behind the scenes, with humans none the wiser, they will remain in the shadows. They are too few in number to challenge *Homo sapiens* directly."

"Okay," Hunter said. "How do they stay in the shadows? Are they really shape-shifters, the way the conspiracy nuts claim?"

"Not really," Elanna told him. "Some can use a form of hypnotism, but that depends on how suggestive an observing human is. There's no magical ray or mind power that will make a crowd of people all see them as human. And they certainly can't change their shape physically."

"You said the clothing from that MiB I took down had something in it . . . What did you say? A phase-thing, something like that?"

"Phase-shifting device," Elanna said. "This instrument can bend space around the wearer and make him difficult to see. It can't make him invisible, though it's effective in a darkened room, or literally in the shadows. It's mostly used for moving from one place to another."

"God. You're saying teleportation?"

"They can phase-shift through multiple dimensions, yes. Your own people are working on that now, Mark."

"Huh. 'Beam me up, Scotty.'"

"It's more like stepping from one room into another. The adjoining rooms just happen to be far apart."

"You said that takes a lot of power."

"A *lot* of power, yes. That agent you apprehended probably just used his to better blend into the shadows while he was following you."

Hunter thought about Men in Black invisibly lurking in the shadows of his room at night, and shuddered. That kind of technology couldn't be allowed out and into the world, not without serious safeguards.

But how the hell did you stop something like that?

Hunter was thoughtful for a moment. The TR-3B gently lifted from the floor of the huge hangar and drifted through the open door. It was just past sunset outside, the desert sky still an intense blue at the horizon, but deepening to almost black directly overhead. The stars were coming out.

"Becky . . ." he began after a moment. "I wonder . . ."

"What, Mark?"

"It's kind of embarrassing."

"I don't embarrass easily."

"No, but maybe I do. Look . . . I read once that lizards have . . . uh . . . two penises."

"Order Squamata. Yes."

"Squamata?"

"The order of reptiles that includes snakes, lizards, and Amphisbaenia . . . that's a kind of legless lizard, called a worm lizard. They have organs called hemipenes, which are tucked away inside their bodies and evert for reproductive encounters. Some of them are quite complicated, with spines or hooks to aid with the coupling process."

Hunter winced. "Ouch. Okay. But when I captured that MiB at the airport, I stripped off all of his clothing, right? And he had a penis that, well, it looked almost completely human."

"'Almost'?"

"He had a very light pattern of scales all over. To tell the truth, I wasn't looking that closely. I just wanted to make sure he wasn't wearing any microelectronics—you know, tracking devices, or a radio."

"Those *were* there, but inside his clothing. But only Squamates have the hemipenes. Archosaurs and turtles have single penises, like humans."

"'Archosaurs'? Like dinosaurs?"

"The order that includes crocodiles, birds, and avian dinosaurs."

"Okay. I was beginning to think I'd missed something."

McClure laughed. "No, it sounds like you saw everything you needed to see."

Silently, the Treb lifted from the Groom Lake runway. On a monitor affixed to the seat in front of him, Hunter could see the horizon falling away, could see the sky deepening and the stars coming out in uncountable numbers.

They were on their way.

"But what I still don't get is this whole alien-hybrid thing. The conspiracy theorists have been claiming for years that aliens are mating with humans to . . . I don't know . . . make us more like them, or something. This guy at the airport had *scales*. And, my God, his eyes . . ."

"Aliens having sex with humans?" Elanna said. "Not possible. You'd have better luck mating a human with a tree shrew; at least they're related."

Hunter nodded. "I had this lecture earlier from an MiB. With good enough genetic technology, you can play mix and match with the human genome."

"Exactly." Elanna smiled. "It's just *much* more fun doing it the old-fashioned way."

"I think what Mark is asking," McClure said, "is why? Having guys running around looking human except for weird eyes seems counterproductive."

"Right," Hunter said. "The cost in sunglasses alone would be ridiculous."

"Remember that the Saurian agenda has at least two objectives. They are trying to control the modern human population for reasons of their own, yes. But they are also fighting us, in your future. By changing the human genome here in the twenty-first century, they send more and more drastic changes rippling down through the millennia. They are attempting to create new varieties of humans in the far future."

"The Grays," Hunter realized. "Dozens, maybe hundreds of different species, and they all look remarkably like the Saurians. Does that mean the Saurians have won? Or I mean, *will* win? Wait, hold on." Hunter looked as if he was struggling to figure out a *very* complex puzzle. ". . . Damn it. *You* know what I mean. . . ."

"English grammar and time travel are incompatible," McClure said.

"They at least don't get along well together." Hunter fixed Elanna with a hard stare. "And what you're carefully not saying is that the Saurians have been doing this throughout human history, right? We twenty-first-century humans have already been modified in the Saurian image."

Elanna didn't reply, and Hunter pushed ahead. "I'm thinking that if they hadn't popped up, oh, say, two million years ago and started tinkering with the genome of *Homo erectus*, then today we'd look more like Sasquatch."

"Your speculations are more accurate than you realize," Elanna said after a moment. "But please . . . keep your conclusions to yourself. This information could have serious implications, serious repercussions for the entire human species."

"What . . . today? Or the species in *your* time?"

"Yes."

"Okay, stupid question."

The Moon appeared on the seat monitors, in half-phase. Hunter could see it visibly growing moment to moment.

"Looks like we're stopping at the LOC first," he said. Good. Julia would be boarding this Treb, and he might have a chance to talk with her.

Hunter still had little understanding as to why the opposition had kidnapped Geri and been holding her, presumably, for over a year now. At least, he *hoped* they were holding her . . . that she was still alive, though in the past months he'd found himself more and more reconciled to the possibility that she was dead. So far as he knew, the only possible motive for the kidnapping was the enemy's desire to keep him under control, a means of ensuring his cooperation and his submission. *Do what we say, or your girlfriend will be dead. . . .*

Yet, he'd been over it repeatedly, and that reasoning still didn't make sense. Thousands of people—scientists and military personnel both—were part of Solar Warden, and so far as Hunter knew none of them had been subjected to that kind of coercion. Those thousands went back and forth between space and Earth on a more or less regular basis. Military personnel went on liberty. Scientists took vacations, or even had weekends off. The Saurians apparently were holding many thousands of people as prisoners in those nightmarish tanks of theirs, but he'd never heard that any of the men and women in the JSST were related to them in any way.

So why Geri?

The moon filled his monitor screen now, vast and radiant with an intense white light. The closer they got to the surface, however, the more that light faded, until the landscape was the "dirty beach sand" described by Bill Anders during Apollo 8. Craters large and small drifted across the screen in tangled profusion. The Treb was dropping lower and lower as it lined up for an approach with Lunar Operations Command, hidden away in its subselenian cavern on the Moon's far side.

He hoped that Julia Ashley would have the answers he needed.

JAMES BENNETT knocked, then stuck his head in the door. "Ms. Ashley? They're here."

Damn . . .

"Coming."

Julia Ashley grabbed her bag and followed, somehow managing to keep her grumbles to herself. Bennett had told her less than an hour ago that a TR-3B was on its way from Earth, that Commander Hunter had specifically requested her, and that once she was on board they would be going to Mars.

Mars! Great gods of the Galaxy, why *Mars*? She was feeling stressed, *really* stressed, pulled between the demands of her various duties. Bennett had her working on that alien crash. She'd been trying to get time off for a visit home, but the people who ran LOC were always wary when it came to granting leave for Lunar personnel, both military and the small community of civilians stationed at the base. Some of that had to do with COVID, of course. Using draconian screening methods, they'd managed to keep COVID19 off the Moon—so far, at least—but things had been tight even before the pandemic had exploded across the human world, and they remained tight now that vaccines were available and the pandemic was receding. She was pretty sure most of their reluctance arose from fears that someone was going to turn whistleblower.

Either that, or they were avoiding the mountain of paperwork attending each request for time off.

They checked out a public electric cart, one just slightly more robust than a golf cart, from a charging station in front of the place where she'd been staying, and the quiet little machine whisked them down silent streets toward the docking facilities.

And what, she wondered as they cruised past the massive block-house containing LOC headquarters, would be so terrible about someone spilling the cosmic beans? The powers above had been keeping all of this so secret that even the President didn't know. It was mind-numbing—it wasn't just alien contact, but *treaties* with both extraterrestrial species and humans from the future; secret human colonies on both the Moon and Mars; an entire top-secret government program established to defend Humankind from extrasolar threats and to explore beyond the cramped and narrow confines of Sol, complete with space-going battleships and aircraft carriers.

Besides that, all of the wild conspiracy theories that had been swirling through human consciousness for these past few years paled into absurdity, fading away when compared to the reality of Solar Warden.

Could all of these ludicrous conspiracy theories—tales of COVID being a hoax, QAnon nonsense of satanic cults and child trafficking—been planted to create a distraction from the *real* conspiracy? Ashley wondered if she could use her RV skills to find out . . . then decided that she simply couldn't face that particular rabbit hole. For months now, she had been engaged in mental contacts with increasingly strange and alien minds, some—the Saurians—implacably hostile and apparently telepathically aware of her. When she managed to sleep at all, she descended into nightmares, and lately she'd been obsessing over the beings in that crashed ship who'd asked her for help.

She was exhausted and on edge, worried about her father back on Earth, and feeling frustrated and depressed.

She knew she was showing the symptoms of burnout, and she didn't know what she could do about it.

"Question?" she said after a long moment.

"Shoot."

"That crash I saw. My last assignment. Can you tell me anything about it?"

Bennett was silent for a long time, and Ashley began to think he was ignoring her. Finally he responded, "What about it? What do you want to know?" His words were guarded, his expression unreadable.

"I had the impression it was in the past."

"It was. We think you were dialed in on the Shag Harbour incident in 1967."

"Shag Harbour?"

"Nova Scotia. A 'shag' is a kind of cormorant, a bird that lives there."

"Did we get them out?"

"What do you mean?"

"They asked me for help. With time travel, we could go back and maybe rescue them."

He sighed. "And how would I explain that to our Talis friends? You know they don't like us doing stuff like that."

There seemed to be nothing more she could say about it.

They slipped through a final tunnel entrance and entered the high-vaulted lava-tube chamber of the landing bay.

A number of Solar Warden ships were parked there—a heavy cruiser, a couple of light escorts, other vessels she couldn't identify. The TR-3B was resting on its landing legs on the deck just ahead, steaming as water in the air touched the black hull still hot from the unfiltered sunlight in space and turned to vapor. A sentry in the Treb's shadow checked their IDs, and they walked up the ramp and into the waiting craft.

Moments later, Ashley was on her way to Mars.

"THE BALANCE of the JSST will be on board in thirty minutes, Captain," Navy Commander Philip Wheaton said. He was *Hillenkoetter*'s senior intelligence officer, normally reporting to the ship's operations officer, or "ops," Commander Donald Kelly. He and Kelly had been summoned to the carrier's Combat Information Center by the skipper, Captain Fred Groton. They were gathered now in the ship's large, low CIC along with several staff officers, studying a Mercator projection of the planet Mars displayed on a screen that took up much of the forward bulkhead.

"About damned time," Groton replied. "What was the holdup?"

"They had to pick up special personnel at Farside."

"What special personnel?"

"The psychic and her new handler."

"*That's* all we need . . . the damned crystal-gazers!"

Wheaton held his peace. Groton didn't care for the idea of remote viewing, largely because a handler had almost gotten a landing party killed during the last mission inside the alien asteroid-starship Oumuamua. Wheaton, however, had noted how one viewer had provided valuable combat intelligence for the JSST at Aldebaran.

"Remote viewing will give us some battlefield intel, Captain, and intel is our biggest need right now. At this point we have no idea whatsoever what's going on inside Ares Prime."

He looked up at the map. Ares Prime lay close to the intersection of the Martian equator with the planet's prime meridian, in a region called Meridiani Planum. The base had been built back in the late '80s, shortly after the creation of Solar Warden, and was one of five secret military and scientific installations on the planet. All had been built with Talisian help, and staffed by a number of the enigmatic Grays, as well as by modern Earth humans. Wheaton wondered if some of those Grays had been Malok; the Talis acknowledged them as humans working for the Saurians for whatever reason. Someone had taken down those bases. None, now, were responding to radio requests for information.

"I suppose so," Groton conceded after a moment's thought. "How should we proceed?"

"We need Hunter in on the planning, sir. It'll be his boots on the ground, after all. But a quick guess, we provide air cover with our fighters and with *Hillenkoetter*'s heavy weaponry from space while the JSST goes in on their Trebs. They kick in the door . . . and then we play by ear."

"Have there been any reports of the big-ass thing that killed *Phobos 2*?"

"Our only reports of hostile ships were the ones our fighters encountered. Those were Malok *Zegrest*-class—standard thirty-meter disks armed with laser and directed energy beam weapons. The *Big-H* should be able to handle small stuff like them, no problem. But we shouldn't rule out the possibility of running into something bigger."

"I don't intend to rule out *anything*. We still don't know what the black hats have been doing out here . . . maybe for the past few million years."

Wheaton nodded. Mars had always been a mysterious world, the place where early twentieth-century astronomers had glimpsed the threads of *canali* and filled uncounted volumes of pulp fiction with tales of dying civilizations on an arid, desert planet. When the canals had proven to be illusory, Mars instead became a dead body like Earth's Moon; the Mariner probes in the early '60s had revealed rugged craters and no sign of the lost cities of Barsoom.

But later spacecraft had turned up . . . anomalies. Seasonal outgassings of methane best explained by alien biology beneath the Martian surface. Strange landforms that tugged at human perceptions, suggesting pyramids and enormous stone faces, as well as other fragments of what might have been a vanished civilization. Suddenly, Mars had become an early target for Solar Warden's classified research. Nothing had been published as yet, but there were rumors that native biology had been discovered and that certain mysterious rock forms and mesas were in fact the detritus of a civilization vanished long ago.

"We should learn more when we get there," Wheaton said.

"*If* we get there," Groton said, scowling. "I'm concerned about that *Phobos*-killer. Captain Macmillan?"

"Yes, sir." Andrew Macmillan was *Hillenkoetter*'s CAG, the commander aerospace group in charge of the spacecraft carrier's six fighter squadrons and various auxiliary craft.

"What do we have outside the ship now?"

"Two squadrons on CAP, Captain. The Firedrakes and the Sunhammers, just arrived from LOC."

Groton nodded. "Okay . . . I suggest you get two more squadrons spaceborne, stationed between us and Mars. If there's a threat out here, it'll come from that direction."

"Very well, Captain," Macmillan replied. "The Star Raiders and the Blood Demons are on ready-five. I can give the order to launch immediately."

"Which leaves us with . . . what? The Lancers and the Starhawks?"

"Yes, sir. But both of them are almost all newbies . . . replacements after Aldebaran. I'll hold them in reserve."

The table of organization and equipment, TOE, for *Hillenkoetter*'s fighter squadrons had been an abysmal mess after Aldebaran. For a while, Macmillan had cobbled together a replacement group from survivors of the regular squadrons, called the "Dino Killers." That name had been deemed . . . undignified by the admiral back at LOC, and the original squadron name had been brought back online. But the Starhawks and the Lancers, and to a lesser degree the Thunderbolts and the Firedrakes, were flying with over 50 percent replacements. The 'Hawks had been the worst off, with a casualty count of over 80 percent, staggering losses for any combat unit. Replacements from Earth had brought the squadrons back to full strength, but most of those pilots hadn't had the chance yet to fly combat missions with the others. They would be very much unknown quantities until they had some experience working together.

"Okay," Groton said. "But put them in if you have to. They need combat experience? Sounds like this is where they'll find it."

"Yes, sir."

Macmillan did not sound happy, but the ship's CAG turned away to give the necessary orders. Wheaton knew the *Hillenkoetter*'s CAG cared deeply for the men and women under his command and didn't like tossing newbies into the fire.

But the nature of combat was such that officers like Macmillan often didn't have a choice.

Given the nature of this enemy—devious, militant, and technologically advanced far beyond Humankind—*none* of them did.

CHAPTER EIGHT

Ripped Blue Jeans: Though a popular fashion trend off and on since the 1970s, the current fad of ripped denim jeans, as reported by Islamist newspaper *Yeni Akit*, is in fact a secret mode of communication between foreign agents and local traitors who intend to destroy Turkey. The patterns of tears in the fabric are actually deliberately created in code to transmit secret intelligence among spies, a conspiracy fabricated by either US or Israeli intelligence services to undermine the Ankara government, Islamic influences within that government, or both.

CONSPIRACY THEORY,
2021 AND AFTER

"WE'VE BEEN CALLING it 'memenbau,'*" Kammler told him. "Memetic engineering. Using memes—ideas or beliefs or fads that carry cultural ideas or symbols from person to person, spreading them throughout an entire population. We have been literally remaking human culture."*

"But to what end?" Albrecht asked. Under the watchful eyes and mind of the alien, Kammler had been explaining the Eidechse *program on Earth, a scheme that had been playing out for centuries and that was now nearing a climax.*

"Division," Kammler explained. "Divide and conquer, yes? Using wildly divergent and antithetical ideas. Using memes created for the purpose and invested with strong emotional con-

tent, we set nation against nation, race against race, community against community, individual against individual until Earth's entire population is at the point of tearing itself to pieces."

"Giving your movement an opportunity for attack."

"With luck, the humans will beg us to march in and restore order."

Albrecht blinked. Kammler had said the word humans *as though . . .*

He chose to ignore the slip. Kammler might well consider himself different from the humans of this future age.

"And who will do the marching, Herr *General? Those young thugs I saw out there in the main room?"*

"Of course not. They are useful idiots, tools for inciting riots and protests, waving signs in front of television cameras, and shouting down the voices of calm and reason. They are too undisciplined for serious work."

"Then who—"

"Men like the two of us, for a start, brought from Greater Germany to serve the cause. And the descendants of German soldiers taken to other worlds during the war, carefully trained, carefully indoctrinated. There are tens of thousands of them now, waiting for the commencement of Projekt Rückkehr.*"*

"The Return . . . ?"

"The return of the thousand-year Reich. The return of strong men willing to take control of a shattered and divided world. The return of Übermensch *who will finally irradicate the subhumans who drag us down from our rightful place in the cosmos. The return of* order.*"*

Albrecht didn't like the expression behind those wildly staring eyes . . . and then Kammler shrieked and clawed at his face, dropping to his knees. "Herr General! What is it?"

As Kammler writhed on the floor in apparent agony, Albrecht looked up for an explanation from the Eidechse. He was jolted to see that the creature had vanished.

Albrecht had not seen it leave.

"PERMISSION TO come aboard."

"Granted. Welcome aboard, sir." Lieutenant Commander Jeremy Winslow was one of *Hillenkoetter*'s engineering officers, currently standing watch on the ship's vast, open flight deck.

"Captain Groton?"

"He's in CIC, sir," Winslow told Hunter. "And he—"

"Wants to see me as soon as I come on board. Yes, I know."

"You've been hanging out with those damned Talis for too long, Commander," Winslow said, grinning. "You're becoming psychic."

"No, it just seems like every time I step on board this ship, the skipper wants to see me. You'll take care of my people?"

"Of course, Commander. They're to muster in the oh-two rec lounge, compartment 2715."

"Just so I can find them later," Hunter said. "I'd hate to lose an entire combat company."

Except the 1-JSST wasn't a full company now, and he wouldn't exactly call it combat-ready. On paper, 1-JSST rated 120 people, a full company of four platoons. Eighty of those, thank God, had been on board the *Big-H* when the hurry-up-and-boost order had come down to Groom Lake. Half of those on liberty, though, had been elsewhere when the order had been received—visiting wives or girlfriends for the most part, or on various necessary personal errands, like Hunter. Only twenty had been available to board the shuttle with Hunter, which left him twenty short.

Worse, they'd suffered casualties at Aldebaran, casualties that had been replaced, but who hadn't had the time to integrate fully with the unit. They were raw newbies, and Hunter's platoon commanders were going to have their hands full looking out for them.

Hunter still had no idea as yet what precisely the JSST was being ordered to do. Kelsey had given him the bare bones about the training flight and told him that this would be a reconnaissance in force, but no more than that. Their objective was the largest human base on the planet, Ares Prime . . . but details as to how they were to get inside and what they were to do there were annoyingly lacking.

Presumably, Groton would have some more details up in CIC, and then it would be his job to brief his people.

"Commander! Commander Hunter!"

Master Chief Vic Torres was *Hillenkoetter*'s supply chief, and he was carrying a clipboard. *What now?* Hunter wondered. "How's it going, Master Chief?"

"Good, sir. I need a signature."

"What . . . again? I just gave you one of those last week."

"And now I need another one, sir." He handed the clipboard to Hunter . . . ten or twelve pages of printed documents.

"What is it?"

"Your requisition for .45, 9-mil, and 5.56-mil ammo was approved. We have eight crates of the stuff; just came on board at LOC."

"Excellent." Hunter pulled the pen from its holder on the board and scanned through the pages, looking for boxes to initial or sign.

"Thanks, Commander. There's more . . ."

"What?"

Torres grinned. "Looks like the tech wonks came through for you at last. We've got your uprated PEWs."

"PEW" stood for "personal energy weaponry," and such weapons had been a sore point with Hunter and the soldiers under his command ever since they'd signed on for Solar Warden. The laser pistols and rifles first issued to the JSST had worked okay, but their battery life was sharply limited. A Type 1 laser pistol carried enough juice in its grip housing for *four* shots, which was pathetic in a stand-up firefight. And the bulky RAND/Starbeam 3000 laser rifle, linked by a power cable to a PLSS backpack, was no better. The power output was adjustable, and depending on the setting, you could get between four or five "fifty shots." The fifty-shot setting *might* let you light a campfire on a cold night, assuming the local atmosphere had oxygen, but it did nothing if the target was armored.

As a result, many JSST personnel now carried weapons they'd brought aboard themselves, slug-throwers like .45 Colts and CQBRs—the Navy's Close Quarters Battle Receiver, which transformed the standard-issue M16 rifle into a compact and deadly weapon ideal for combat in confined spaces, like shipboard. Getting those weapons to the Moon was a challenge that often involved a bottle of good whiskey as a thank-you to a willing supply officer Earthside. Hunter knew Master Chief Minkowski had broken down his beloved M4 shotgun and mailed the packages to himself over the course of several weeks.

Somehow, an arsenal of slug-throwers didn't carry quite the same mystique of Buck Rogers ray guns, but they had one important advantage: they *worked*.

Hunter had been complaining about the inadequacies of the personal energy weapons issued to the JSST ever since he'd signed aboard with Solar Warden, but to little effect. Scuttlebutt had it that the Nordics—like Elanna—didn't want the really advanced stuff in the hands of twenty-first-century knuckle-draggers, while ultraconservative naval commanders didn't want them shooting holes in their ships.

But maybe, just maybe, someone had finally been paying attention. "Uprated PEWs?" Hunter repeated, genuinely surprised. "For real?"

"Yessir."

"How uprated?"

"Don't know, sir. I just haul 'em off the transports, check 'em off the req forms, and hand 'em out. Sign . . . *here*, sir."

Hunter scribbled the requested signature and handed the board back to Torres. As he took back the form, Torres added, "We also have sentrybots. XKS-4 GIWS units."

Hunter had to think a moment, then nodded. "I think I saw a report Earthside. . . ."

"Right. Perimeter defense. Those are going on board the transports."

The receipt of decent weapons, while a pleasant surprise, was not unalloyed good news. The new ones would have their own

idiosyncrasies, their own limitations, and, perhaps most impor-
tantly from a unit commander's perspective, their own learning
curves. You couldn't just hand these things out to the men without
the appropriate training.

"Going our way, Commander?"

It was Elanna, stepping off the Treb's ramp, and Julia Ashley
was with her. The rather grim-faced civilian behind Julia must be
Bennett, her new handler.

"I am if you're on your way to see the captain," he told them.

"Lead on, mighty Torbad," Elanna said. "We follow you will-
ingly through the balefires of Hell."

"'Torbad'?"

Elanna laughed. "Sorry. Famous line from *E'kagre e Torobat.*
You would say, ah . . . *Torbad the Conqueror* is close enough. I
guess it was written a little after your time."

"How much after our time?" Ashley wanted to know.

"Oh, a couple of thousand years or so. It's a POV opera . . . an
ancient classic in my century."

"And what, pray tell, is a POV opera?" Hunter asked, puzzled.

"Point of view. The interface inserts you as a cast member—
your choice." She dimpled. "Most males and maletrans choose
Torbad, of course. He gets to have lots of POV sex between arias."

"What if you're like me and can't sing?"

"Doesn't matter. The interface takes care of the details. All you
have to do is *experience.*"

As they climbed into an in-ship tube transport and accelerated,
Hunter realized they really knew far too little about their Talis
allies. They were definitely humans, but with a technology and
social structure sundered from his own by ten thousand years.

Hell, he could better understand the heart and mind of someone from ancient Sumer than of a sex goddess called 425812 Elanna.

They were waiting for them as they walked into the dimly lit Combat Information Center—dimly lit to better showcase the dozens of computer screens and the large, bulkhead map of Mars. Shipboard Marines in full combat armor snapped to attention on either side of the door as they entered. Not part of the JSST, the ship's Marines belonged to the master-at-arms, serving as a ship's security force. Hunter wondered if he should talk to someone about getting some of them on loan to beef up the JSST for the op on Mars.

Groton was in conversation with his executive officer, Commander William Haines, and the *Hillenkoetter*'s CAG, intelligence officer, and operations officer. Commander Philip Wheaton looked up as Hunter and his small entourage approached and beamed. "And here's the man of the hour now!"

"Ah, good," Groton said. "Welcome aboard, Commander. Ms. Ashley. Elanna . . . and you are?"

"Jim Bennett," the civilian replied. He nodded at Ashley. "I'm with her."

"Thank you, sir," Hunter said, replying to Groton's welcome. "I gather we have a planet to capture."

"With a single company?" Wheaton said with a chuckle. "I very much doubt *that*, Commander."

"Hey, when you march through balefire anything is possible," Hunter said, laughing.

"Not when you're outnumbered a hundred to one," Groton said. He looked at Haines. "Number One? Take over here. We'll be aft in CIC Brief."

"I have command, aye, aye, Captain."

"If anything, *anything* changes—if you even get a peep out of the opposition—call me."

"Aye, aye, sir."

"This way, people."

Groton turned and led the small group back through the maze of CIC consoles and workstations toward the rear. Phil Wheaton joined them.

As they walked, Hunter remembered his earlier conversation with Elanna, about how the Saurians used sneak tactics, staying in the shadows while influencing the humans who made the decisions behind the scenes.

Would it be possible for humans to employ similar tactics? That didn't seem likely, not when Humankind remained in ignorance of every detail of Saurian existence. *If we don't understand the Talisians*, he thought, *this is worse. We don't know a damned thing about their culture, about their beliefs, about their leaders or where they're based, nothing.*

Kelsey had called this Mars op a reconnaissance in force. That would be an excellent place to start.

Leaving CIC through a pressure-tight door guarded by two more Marines, they entered a small, brightly lit compartment with slanted bulkheads and what appeared to be a solid mahogany table, lined with office chairs like a conference room. Another large-screen monitor was built into the forward bulkhead.

"So . . . have you been to Ares Prime, Commander?" Groton asked him without preamble.

"No, sir."

"You're not missing a great deal. Have a look. . . ."

He clicked a hand controller, and the bulkhead screen illuminated with a photograph taken from the air. Hunter could see what looked like a dozen cylindrical Quonset huts snugged up together side by side, centered among a scattering of domes, low buildings, and communications masts and dishes. A very large hut made of blue-green glass squatted in the foreground—it looked like a greenhouse. The whole facility had a modular look to it, with pieces hauled from Earth and assembled like LEGO bricks.

A rectangular pad or platform in the distance held three TR-3S black triangles, the smaller cousins of the 3W and the enormous 3B shuttles. A single 3B Treb rested on the pad as well; nearby were stacks of large cylinders, presumably holding expendables brought out from Earth, primarily water and air. Piles of metallic boxes nearby might store food or equipment. Hunter could see ground tractors among the supply stacks.

One structure, a huge silvery doughnut, was larger than the rest. Set near the center of the complex, it connected with the Quonset huts by means of a narrow tube lying flat on the ground. Everything was coated by a thin layer of ocher dust, giving it a dirty, used feel. The planet itself appeared as flat as the prairies of the American Midwest, dull ocher and butternut in color beneath a red-tinted sky.

"The big thing at the center is Mars Center Headquarters," Groton told him. "MCHQ. Think 'Pentagon,' but with fewer corners. It's our operational headquarters on the planet."

"*Was*," Wheaton clarified. "We've not been able to raise them for hours. You're going to need to go down there and let us know what happened."

"I'm gathering the Saurians launched an attack on a training flight from there?"

"From Mars, certainly," Groton replied. "The entire planet is now out of communications. We have to assume that hostile forces have moved in and taken over."

"Admiral Kelsey did say 'reconnaissance in force,'" Hunter said. "How old is this photo?"

Wheaton indicated a tiny date and time stamp in the lower corner of the image. "Three weeks. Why?"

"I was noticing that all of the spacecraft down there seem to be ours."

"There's a fair-sized population of Grays at the base," Groton told him. "One hundred twelve, at last count. They come and go in small ships—mostly either Talis Arnold-class scouts, or time ships from various future Gray cultures, *Tovad*- or *Salec*-class, usually. None of them happened to be at the port when this shot was taken."

"Nothing bigger?"

Groton gave a tight, worried grin. "Like the Phobos-killer? No. Not that we've seen, anyway. Nothing obviously Saurian."

"It would be best to assume they have something larger than the *Zegrest*-class vessels your fighters encountered," Elanna told them. "The *Zegrests* are not time-capable. They would require a carrier ship to bring them to this system from elsewhere, else *when*."

"I agree," Groton said. "And for that reason, this vessel will remain on high alert. Having a large fighter assault on us would be bad enough. Going up against a carrier as big as or bigger than we are would be infinitely worse."

"Can we bring in cruisers, or other support vessels?" Hunter asked.

"LOC is working on that," Wheaton told them. "The cruisers *Inman* and *McCone* are supposed to be flight-ready, but they're still working at recalling their personnel. It might take a while."

"Ms. Ashley," Groton said, looking at the young psychic. "Might you be able to scan Mars and its environs and pick up on any large space vessels? Maybe look for underground bases or hangars?"

"That's not how remote viewing works, Captain," Bennett replied. "She would need a specific target, with appropriate coordinates."

"I take it you're Ms. Ashley's, ah, handler?"

"I am. I've been with Project Stargate almost since the beginning."

"Stargate," Hunter knew, was an insider's term for the highly classified government remote-viewing program.

"Ms. Ashley," Groton continued, ignoring the man, "you've done some amazing work for us, for this ship, in the past. Coordinates didn't appear to be a big issue for you."

"The coordinates are important," she said, "as a means of validation."

"But you have . . . seen things without them?"

She hesitated, glancing at Bennett. "Yes, sir."

Groton jabbed a thumb at the photo of Ares Prime on the screen. "Do you think you could peer inside that base, tell us what's waiting for us in there?"

"Yes, sir." But she didn't sound entirely convinced.

"I can help," Elanna said. "I can work with Julia to help her pinpoint specific areas inside the base."

"You've been there? To Ares Prime?"

"No. But I can sense Saurian minds and tell where they are clustered. That should do for a start."

"Good."

"*If* you can trust her reports," Bennett said, "without validation." He looked at the psychic. "No offense, Julia. You know that's how it works."

"Dr. Bennett," Ashley said, "you've had me working on that UFO sighting for a week, now. You've been trusting everything I've reported . . . from inside an airliner cockpit, from the side of a harbor, and even inside an alien craft. How am I supposed to validate all of that, when it just comes to me out of the air?"

"You saw inside the alien ship?" Bennett was surprised.

"Yes," Ashley said reluctantly.

"You didn't report that!"

She looked at him squarely, drawing herself up straight. "Would you have believed me if I had? Sir."

"What UFO?" Hunter asked, intrigued.

"We're still piecing it together," Bennett admitted, "but we think she's been cueing in on the Shag Harbour affair back in 1967. Apparently, Ms. Ashley hasn't been entirely forthcoming with her information, and that just points to what I've been saying. The consequences of mistaken reporting, of guessing, aren't nearly as important as this!"

"I know what I saw," Ashley said, stubborn. "What I *heard*. Those creatures wanted my help!"

Hunter followed this exchange with interest. Julia Ashley, he knew from experience, could return absolutely astonishing psychic information from alien locals and even from back in time, with very little to go on for the attempt. "Captain," he said, watching Ashley, "I have *personally* validated things Ms. Ashley has reported. She really does see what she says she sees. I trust her one hundred percent."

"I see. Commander Wheaton? How do you feel about it?"

Wheaton frowned. "Well, sir . . . I guess I'm old-school when it comes to intelligence. I'm not sure I believe in . . . magic."

"I've seen Ms. Ashley in action," Groton said. "I don't like . . . *magic*, but if Commander Hunter is willing to risk his deployment based on information she provides, so am I."

"But—" Bennett started to say.

"*So am I*, Doctor," Groton said, with an unspoken *and that settles it* at the end. He looked at Ashley. "You'll tell us everything you pick up down there?"

"If I can," she told him. "If I'm sure of what I'm seeing. Yes."

"All the intel in the world," Hunter observed, "or on Mars, I guess, doesn't help us with getting inside that base. Looks to me like incoming ships touched down on a landing pad outside. So just how are we supposed to get inside that base in the first place? I'm assuming we don't want to shoot the place full of holes."

"No. Lunar Operations Command has given us very specific orders. They want to preserve the base's airtight integrity if at all possible."

"You're just full of cheery news, Captain," Hunter said. "What are we supposed to do? Knock on the front door?"

"You're a Navy SEAL," Groton said with a grin. "What is it you guys say? 'Improvise, adapt . . .'"

"And overcome. That's the jarheads, sir. The Marines. But I take your meaning. Are there external defensive weapons on that base? Missile batteries, lasers, that sort of thing?"

"There *weren't*," Groton said. "Not as of yesterday."

"If the Saurians have their own ships down there now," Elanna pointed out, "they have such weapons. Even Arnold-class scouts have laser weaponry."

Hunter smiled. "'Arnold-class'?'"

"A man named Kenneth Arnold saw a flight of them in 1947," Elanna told him, "over the Cascade Mountains. The newspapers quoted him as saying they were 'skipping like saucers across the water,' and the name 'flying saucers' stuck. Even though those particular scout craft are crescent-shaped, not saucers."

"I know," Hunter said. "I was briefed. I just find the name incongruous when the other Saurian ships have Talisian names."

"It seemed appropriate."

"Well, in the absence of blowing a hole in the side of that big metal doughnut," he said, "I think what we're left with is putting a small team on the ground at some distance, have them sneak in close, and study the place. If we find a way in, we call down the rest of the team."

"'We'?" Elanna said, her eyebrows arching.

"We. I'm not going to risk my people down there without my being with them." He was thinking of his last op as a Navy SEAL several years ago . . . dug in on the slopes of a mountain watching a North Korean nuclear test facility.

It seemed an age—a part of an entirely different lifetime—in the past.

"Sounds good," Groton said. "Captain Macmillan will be the

one to tell off the landing craft, of course. Anything else you'll need down there?"

"A couple of Predators for the first leg of the march," Hunter said thoughtfully. "Some time to brief my people on the new weaponry that just came on board . . . and about damn time, too!"

"Not *too* much, though," Groton said. "I don't like just sitting out here between planets . . . especially when those bastards know we're here."

"An hour or two will do it."

"I think we can manage that. A corporate rep from RAND came on board with them. He'll be able to brief your troops."

"I'll set it up," Hunter said. "And while they're playing with new toys, I can be sitting down with Julia and Elanna for a long-distance look-see at that base."

"Very well," Groton said. He stood. "We'll find suitable quarters where the RV team can set up. Phil? Back to work."

"Aye, aye, sir."

And they filed out of the room and back into the CIC.

But all Hunter could think about was that base seen from the sky.

It looked like it was going to be a *very* hard nut to crack.

CHAPTER NINE

Moon Landing Hoax: The United States never went to the Moon. The landings were faked in a secret sound stage at Area 51 in Nevada and filmed by director Stanley Kubrick, who'd recently completed his epic *2001: A Space Odyssey*. Kubrick, unhappy with the deception, deliberately incorporated mistakes in the filming, including the oscillations of the flag as the astronauts set it up and the fact that there were no stars visible in the sky, in order to reveal the truth. The hoax was perpetrated to win national prestige in the space race with Russia, and to fulfill the martyred Kennedy's admonition to "go to the Moon within this decade."

POPULAR CONSPIRACY THEORY,
1976 AND ONWARD

"WHAT DO YOU want from me!?"

"A precise timetable for the Return."

"All . . . all of that was in the briefcase I gave you."

The man behind the desk stared at Albrecht, stared through Albrecht, as if trying to decide whether he was telling the truth or not. Albrecht had the feeling that if the man thought he was lying, the consequences would be . . . unpleasant.

What had happened to Hans Kammler? Two men had come in moments before and dragged him out, still screaming. Albrecht studied the man, who had replaced the Eidechse *behind the desk—tall, thin to the point of cadaverousness, with long, aristocratic features. He had identified himself as "Max" when he'd* simply taken control of the conversation. Three other men in the room who appeared to be guards seemed excessively deferential.

"That was all they gave me . . . all they told me! I swear!"

"What was in the briefcase were assurances from our people in 1945 that a German colony had been established on a planet in the star system of Aldebaran, and that we would be able to draw upon that colony now, in the twenty-first century, for sufficient manpower to create the new Reich."

Albrecht's eyes widened. The rumors were true!

"What our people in 1945 fail to realize is that the colony they speak of—Paradies—has been attacked by a fleet of American warships and is no longer under our control."

"I . . . I know nothing of any of this." Was the man behind the desk a general? He was certainly a military officer. Albrecht decided to play it safe and added the words "Mein Herr."

"Ja . . . I imagine the situation was . . . grim where you came from. Grim and confused."

Albrecht shrugged. "Berlin was in flames, the Soviets on the outskirts of the city. Everything was falling apart." He didn't add that the Eidechse had failed to help the Reich as they'd promised. He found his newfound sense of loyalty to the Reptilians was . . . fading.

"And now we're giving you the chance to set things right."

"I don't understand," Albrecht said. "They gave me the briefcase with information for you. What else do you want of me . . . expect of me?"

"Herr Albrecht . . . do you truly believe that our organization would use an Oberst as a messenger boy?" The word translated as "colonel."

"*I did wonder about that, yes. . . .*"

"*Trust me when I tell you,* Herr Oberst *Albrecht, that you have been chosen to fulfill a far, far more important destiny.*"

"*What destiny?*"

"*We are creating a new Reich here,* Herr *Albrecht. And you have been chosen to be the Reich's new* Führer."

The shock was like a stinging slap across the face. This man couldn't be serious!

Albrecht began to laugh.

ASHLEY'S MIND reached out . . . reached down . . . reached until she became aware of . . . *impressions*. Red and ocher sand . . . a low, dust-scoured bluff of red-brown rock . . . dust . . . lots of dust . . . swirling in weak winds and piling itself into dunes stretching to the horizon under a pale red sky . . .

And the base, sprawling and cluttered and glittering in thin sunlight against drifting sand.

As always when she was remote viewing, she was aware of a sense of duality, of lying on a chaise in an office on board the *Hillenkoetter*, pencil in hand as she sketched her impressions out on a pad of white paper, but also of floating gently down through the thin Martian atmosphere, toward the base of Ares Prime spread out below her.

She could see the doughnut, the central governing core of the entire base stretching for a hundred yards or more across the sand. She'd seen images of the structure back in the CIC briefing area, so this wasn't a controlled viewing in the RV rulebook by any means. She'd known what the place actually looked like going in. But the landing pad off to the side . . . *that* was different. . . .

"There are ships on the ground," she said aloud. "I see . . . five . . . no, six saucer-shaped craft."

"Can you describe them, Julia? How big are they?"

Bennett's voice seemed to be coming from far away. When she was in a session, it was all too easy to lose completely that doubled sense of identity, the feeling of an existence back in the room where her physical body remained, of her handler guiding the session.

"They're . . . they're not very large," she replied to Bennett's question. "It's tough to judge scale without a known reference."

"The doughnut is a hundred and fifty meters across," Bennett told her. "Try using that for comparison."

"Okay, the largest is . . . I'm not sure. Maybe forty . . . fifty yards across?"

"I can see them," Elanna's voice put in. She was somehow riding Ashley's mind, seeing through her psychic eyes, guiding her down toward the base. "Definitely *Zegrest*-class. About thirty meters. And definitely Malok."

"The smaller ones are maybe half that . . . or a little bigger." Her hand, unseen, was sketching and writing rapidly, laying out impressions of central domes, of landing gear, and even of tiny, silver-suited humanoid figures moving in the round shadows the saucers cast on the tarmac.

"I believe the smaller ones must be *Zdal*-class," Elanna put in. "Malok scouts, probably eight to ten meters across."

"Are they armed?" That was Hunter's voice. Ashley hadn't realized he was in the semi-darkened room as well.

"Lasers and particle beam weapons on the *Zegrest* vessels," Elanna told him. "Light lasers on the scouts."

"Let's have a look inside, Julia," Bennett told her.

Descending, she slipped down through the walls of the gleaming doughnut. The interior place was a mess. . . .

The corridor in which she found herself was filled with smoke, and there were scorch marks on the walls. An overhead light fitfully flickered on and off.

"I . . . I see bodies," she told them. She'd stopped sketching her impressions and concentrated on holding her emotions in check as she described what she saw. "Humans . . . and lots of Grays as well. They look like they were just shot down in the corridor. No uniforms. No weapons. I think they're all civilians."

"I'm sensing living minds," Elanna's voice said, and Ashley felt a nudge in *that* direction. "Through here. . . ."

Her point of view drifted through a wall, and she emerged within a large and circular room, bigger than *Hillenkoetter*'s CIC, an empty space within which a large, metal frame had been set up, incongruously out of place. Aliens—*Saurians*, she corrected herself—filled the room, and they were armed with devices strapped to their bodies that Ashley recognized as weapons. Their attention appeared to be focused on that erect framework. One held something the size of a laptop computer and was making adjustments to a touch screen where the keyboard should have been. Two others wore circlets on their scaled heads that had the look of technological devices of some kind.

"What is this framework for?" Bennett's voice asked, coming from very far away, now. "Can you tell?"

"No. It's . . . big. Maybe nine, ten feet across at the bottom? And a good fifteen feet high. Not a rectangle. The sides kind of converge toward the top . . . narrowing down from ten feet to about half that. There's . . . something inside it. Movement. Darkness. I can't tell. . . ."

For just a moment, Ashley caught a clear glimpse of the frame's interior. It was like looking through an oddly shaped and placed door, and she thought it might be some kind of monitor. She saw more Saurians moving in the shadows beyond the frame, but, weirdly, the image was cocked out of alignment with the room in which she stood, as though the other side of the strange door was canted seventy or eighty degrees off the horizontal.

And then they sensed her.

It had happened to Ashley before. Various alien species, apparently with psychic powers, were able to see her spectral, out-of-body form, and Saurians had noticed her on more than one foray into their worlds. She became aware of dozens of golden, vertically slit eyes turning toward her, of dagger teeth bared in question or sharp anger, of blunt and scaly muzzles, of hostile minds hammering at her own thoughts as they sensed her unwanted intrusion. She was aware of a black shadowy figure that resembled a net, unfolding toward her, closing on her, and she jerked backward at its icy touch.

She screamed.

HUNTER SPRANG forward as Ashley fell off her chaise. Elanna got there first, embracing her, cradling her, helping her off the floor. Her pencil and sketchbook had flown across the room.

"What happened?" Hunter demanded. "Is she alright?"

Ashley's eyes opened, and for just a moment Hunter glimpsed

depths of horror there he'd never seen in anyone before, not even in combat.

"She's okay, Commander," Elanna told him. "One of the hazards of remote-view spying on a sensitive species."

"So what did she see?"

"I'm not sure what she saw, Commander, but I know *they* saw her . . . saw us. Julia? Are you with us?"

Ashley struggled to sit up, then looked around, breathing hard as though she'd just awakened from a nightmare. "I'm . . . okay, Elanna. Thanks."

"What did you see, Julia?" Bennett asked her. He sounded less worried than he did curious. Hunter wondered if this sort of thing was routine for the remote-viewing intelligence community.

"Eyes . . ." she said, and Hunter recognized that expression— the thousand-yard stare of combat personnel too long in the line of fire. "Eyes. And . . . I think it was a door."

"Door?" Bennett asked, frowning.

"A gate. That trapezoidal frame is a gate to . . . to someplace else. . . ."

An hour later, Hunter sat with Bennett, Elanna, Wheaton, and Captain Groton around the CIC briefing room table. Julia had been packed off to *Hillenkoetter*'s sick bay, though she'd insisted she was fine. Hunter, though, had told her he wanted the docs to check her out.

He didn't like that stare.

"So what are we up against?" Groton asked Elanna. "You saw what she saw?"

"Some of it," the Talisian told them. "It's not good."

"Tell us," Wheaton said.

"I think that she entered a room inside Ares Prime that held a Saurian Dimensional Gateway."

"A what?"

"A kind of gate that uses hyperdimensional folds past normal space."

"You mind putting that in English?" Hunter said.

"You've read *Flatland*, Commander?"

"No."

"I have," Bennett said. "In high school. Written by 'A Square'?"

"Yes. The author was actually a schoolteacher named Edwin Abbott, all the way back in 1884, long before Mr. Einstein came along. Flatland was a fictional world of only two dimensions, okay? The inhabitants are two-D shapes, squares and polygons, that know of only two dimensions and cannot even conceive of a third."

"I think I did read that," Hunter said. "A long time ago, in high school, maybe. The two-D shapes were rather upset when a three-D being, a sphere, entered their world. You're saying the Saurians come from the fourth dimension?"

"No . . . but they can fold gateways through higher dimensions. Like Mr. Abbott's sphere-being, they can enter a locked room without bothering with doors. Their gateways can let them step from one location to another without going through the space in between. A useful technology. . . ."

"How far?" Groton demanded. "What kind of range are we talking about here?"

"Not interstellar," Elanna confirmed. "That would require

power at levels beyond even their abilities. But from a ship in orbit to the surface, certainly. Even from one planetary surface to another within the same system."

"Sounds like black magic to me," Wheaton said. He winked at Elanna.

"In a way, remote viewers accomplish the same thing with their minds," Bennett pointed out. "The viewer is *here* . . . but she can look into a locked room on the other side of the planet."

"Exactly," Elanna agreed. "In fact, the best Solar Warden xenotech people are already studying the technology."

Hunter looked at her in surprise. He was all too aware that the Talis didn't like giving technology to twenty-first-century humans that was *too* far advanced, for fear of destroying their civilization. "And your people *allowed* that?"

"No," she told him. She sounded unhappy about it. "Your government acquired it from a crashed Saurian time ship."

"Roswell?" Hunter asked.

"No. Before that. Your people have been scavenging Saurian wrecks for a long time."

"Where, then?"

She paused as though considering what she could tell them. "You call the event the 'Battle of Los Angeles.' Early in World War II, a time ship was seen in the skies over the city during the middle of the night and came under fire. A single large aerial vessel, which authorities claimed officially was a balloon, was undamaged by hours of concentrated antiaircraft fire. A smaller vessel, a *Yoruzta*-class ship launched from the first, was damaged and crashed in the waters southwest of Los Angeles, near the island of Catalina. A secret Navy recovery force managed to retrieve the ship almost intact and transport it to a secure facility at Emerald Bay on the north coast of the island."

"Just in time for World War II?" Hunter wondered: If the United States had had teleportation technology in 1941, why hadn't they used it in that conflict? The Normandy landings would have been infinitely easier if the invading forces could just . . . *appear*, deep in enemy territory. Or instead of losing hundreds of B-17s in bombing runs over Dusseldorf or Ploiesti, just teleport a few thousand tons of explosives directly into the enemy's industrial plants or into the Führerbunker, for that matter.

"Your people didn't have the technical or theoretical background to develop such devices," Elanna told him. "Not then. And it was fortunate that the Malok didn't simply give the technology to the Nazis. The recovered Dimensional Gate equipment remained in storage for two decades, first at Wright-Patterson, then at Groom Lake, until various reverse-engineering programs began to catch up with the technology. According to my sources, a crude prototype has only recently been developed by Section Six."

Section Six was the rumored research and development bureau within Solar Warden, overseen directly by MJ-12. Almost nothing was known about it, and many claimed it was the Space Force equivalent of an urban legend. But Hunter reasoned that *someone* in the deep, dark background was working at developing recovered alien gadgetry and merging it into existing human technology. How else could you explain antigravity and interstellar travel in the early twenty-first century . . . or the existence of a secret Solar Warden fleet?

"You know . . . this little op to take back Mars," Hunter said, "would have been made a whole lot easier if we'd had access to that."

"I said 'crude prototype,'" Elanna replied. "I doubt that you would want to trust the lives of yourself and your men to such an untested device."

Hunter didn't reply. He was wondering, though, how much of the story was concern for human lives, and how much was reluctance on the part of the Talis to release such powerful technology to primitives.

"So . . . what's the setup?" Wheaton asked. "Do you need two gates, one at the sending end and one at the receiving end?"

"Most Malok devices can be used with a single gate, the transmitter. However, accuracy is better if two gates are linked. You don't want to emerge inside a wall at the target."

"I can see how that would be inconvenient," Groton put in.

"To say the least. Not to mention catastrophically explosive as two solid bodies attempt to interphase with one another. One of the biggest issues with the technology is the problem created by conflicting motions and velocities."

Bennett nodded understanding. "You mean things on one side of the gateway are moving in one direction, while on the other side—"

"Exactly," Elanna told them. "Even if the two sites, transmitting and receiving, are both located on the surface of the same planet, two points at two different latitudes will be traveling at different speeds, do you see? And if those two points happen to be on different planets, the velocity differences are enormous. Having two gates makes linking the two sites so much simpler."

"The question remains," Groton said, "what the Saurians are

doing with that gate. Are they using it to bring their soldiers to Mars from someplace else . . . from a transport ship, maybe? Or . . ." He let the question trail off.

"Or are they getting ready to use it to send troops to Earth," Hunter said, completing the thought. "We know from the intel we gained at Aldebaran that they were planning on using their own, homegrown Nazi army to impose a new Reich on Earth."

"A plan," Wheaton pointed out, "that we managed to kick over."

"Right. So now maybe they're going to rely on their own people." He grinned. "Humans are *so* unreliable."

"I doubt that, Commander," Elanna said. "As we've discussed, Saurian numbers remain extremely small compared with the population of Earth. They would much rather use expendable proxies. And Aldebaran wasn't unique. They *do* have other worlds with captive human populations."

"What worlds?" Hunter demanded. "Give us something to work with here."

She shook her head. "I have no hard data. Sending you off to find such worlds on nothing but hearsay and rumor would be worse than useless."

"In other words," Hunter said, "we have to police our own backyard."

"That's part of it," Elanna agreed. "Your culture must grow of its own accord, and not have everything handed to it."

"Even when your own survival is at stake?" If Earth was openly taken over by the Saurians, the Talis might well be destroyed.

She didn't reply to that, and Hunter always wondered how much twenty-first-century humans could really trust the Talis. He'd often heard that the Talis were humans from "ten thousand years in the future," or thereabouts. He'd also heard other figures—eleven thousand, or even twelve thousand. He'd heard Elanna claim that her home base was in the 101st century . . . which would mean only eight thousand years into the future from the twenty-first.

So which was it? *When* was she from? And why was she so deliberately vague about it?

And if Elanna couldn't be trusted to reveal such basic information about her own culture, what else might she be, to say the least, less than forthcoming about?

He became uncomfortably aware that Elanna was staring at him, staring *through* him, as though she were reading his mind.

Damn it, he thought. *You have to admit that it's damned suspicious! Why won't you level with us?*

And then he heard her voice answering in his mind. *You know why, Commander. The less you know about us, the less the Malok can learn. And the less risk of violence done to this timeline. Or to ours.*

He sighed. He'd been on this merry-go-round with her before.

"I think," Groton said, almost as if he was hearing those thoughts himself, "we're going to need to trust our Talisian offspring. You have to admit that they have a clearer idea of what's going on than we do."

"Yes," Hunter agreed. "Because they deliberately keep us in the dark."

The harsh bleat of an alarm startled them all. "What the hell . . . ?" Bennett said, looking around wildly.

"Captain to CIC," Haines's voice called over the intercom. "Captain to CIC . . ."

Groton touched a control on the desk. "Groton. What is it, Bill?"

"Sir! Intruders! Intruders in Secondary Engineering!"

"How the hell did they get on board?"

"Sir . . . they just *appeared*! Out of nowhere!"

"Shit," Groton said. "Okay. On my way." He looked at Hunter. "You're with me."

"Now we know," Hunter said, rising, "what they were planning on using that gateway for."

LIEUTENANT COMMANDER Jeremy Winslow jumped back as a dazzling flash of light illuminated the secondary engineering deck and a water condenser exploded in molten fragments and a white cloud of steam. "Stay back, sir!" a battle-armored Marine yelled through his helmet speakers. "Stay under cover!"

"Screw *that*!" Winslow snapped back. "Let me have your side-arm!"

The Marine was cradling a bulky Starbeam laser rifle in his gauntleted hands, but a Sunbeam laser pistol was holstered at his thigh. The Marine hesitated, then snatched the pistol from its holster and tossed it to him. "The safety—" he started to say.

Winslow snapped the safety to off, then pressed the small, red charge button. "I know how to use it, Sergeant!"

When the compact little weapon showed a full ready charge, Winslow leaned around the corner of the primary coil housing, aiming the pistol in a two-handed Weaver grip. Back on Earth, before he'd volunteered for Solar Warden, he'd been a serious contender with the Navy's pistol team, and had collected several Distinguished Pistol Shot badges. This thing felt more like a toy than a match-grade M1911A1, but he figured it had a right end and a wrong end, and all he had to do was point and shoot.

Twenty yards down the passageway, a Saurian stepped out of thin air.

It was one of the big ones. Saurians, Winslow knew, came in a variety of shapes and sizes, from a little smaller than a man to hulks like this one, eight feet tall and built like a pro-football lineman. Winslow aimed, not for the center of mass as he'd been taught, but for the thing's crocodile-grinning face. It was wearing some sort of armor, like Kevlar, but the head was unprotected. He squeezed the trigger . . .

. . . too late! The Saurian warrior had seen him emerge from cover and ducked aside into the shadows. Even the big ones could be blindingly fast.

Damn!

But more Saurians were appearing every moment, materializing out of the air and moving forward, as if to make way for more at their backs. Winslow shifted aim, and caught one in the side of its head, burning through scales and flesh as the thing keened an unearthly shriek. Beside him, the Marine fired his laser rifle, and the pulse of coherent light nearly took a Saurian's head off at the shoulders.

Winslow shot another one . . .

. . . and another . . .

. . . and suddenly his weapon cheeped in his hands, warning that the battery had been drained.

Something exploded inside Winslow's head, a searing pain that left him blind and dizzy and paralyzed. He hit the deck, and he could hear the thud of approaching boots through ringing ears.

Someone grabbed the collar of his uniform, and he felt himself being dragged backward. He hit the low partition at the airtight hatch—that peculiarity of Naval ship design popularly known as a "knee-knocker" because you had to pick up your feet to step over it as you moved down the passageway. His unseen rescuer dragged him over, and he heard someone slam the hatch home and dog it.

"You're gonna be okay, sir," a helmet speaker said close by. "Corpsman!"

The paralysis was already wearing off with pins-and-needles sensations sweeping across his limbs. His sight was returning, too. He could make out hulking shadows hovering above him, cradling him, moving with him through the passageway.

"Where you hit, sir?" a new voice said in his ear. He thought it must be the corpsman . . . the Navy equivalent of combat medics serving with the Marines.

"I don't . . . I don't know. I think I was just stunned for a minute. . . ."

"Some minor burns on the side of your face," the corpsman told him, turning his head. "You're lucky, sir. I think fifty thousand volts or so just zapped past your head and missed you by a hair!"

Sounds of gunfire crashed from the other side of the airtight door.

"Let's get back in there, people," one of the Marines said. The armor helmet turned to face Winslow. "You stay out here, sir. We can handle this."

Winslow was more than happy to agree. The Marines were part of the *Hillenkoetter*'s complement—not part of the JSST.

Winslow watched them undog the hatch, open it, and when the movement didn't draw fire, slip back into Secondary Engineering. *God help them*, he thought.

Winslow stood up, still feeling quite weak and a bit wobbly in the knees, and made his way to an intercom panel on a nearby bulkhead. "Engineering," he called. "This is Winslow."

"Engineering. Ramsey. Go ahead."

Commander Thomas Ramsey was the ship's CHENG, or chief engineering officer. He sounded rushed.

"Sir! Intruders are inside Secondary Engineering! Dozens of them! The Marines are in there trying to push them back."

"They're up here in Primary, too, Jerry. Just stay put and—"

The deck under Winslow's feet lurched hard, and it seemed as though the entire ship rang like an enormous gong.

"Commander!" he yelled . . . and then a second explosion blasted the ship. The overhead lights flickered and went out . . . and so did *Hillenkoetter*'s artificial gravity.

"Oh, *Christ*!"

If both primary and secondary power had been shut down . . .

Warning! Warning! a woman's voice intoned, the mechanical drone of a recording. *Major hull breach. Atmospheric pressure dropping. Warning!*

. . . then the USSS *Hillenkoetter* was in very serious trouble indeed.

CHAPTER TEN

US Concentration Camps: The Federal Emergency Management Agency (FEMA) has been secretly building concentration camps on US soil in preparation for the imposition of martial law and genocide. Executive orders are already on the books giving the government the right to detain, arrest, and incarcerate individuals without due process.

CONSPIRACY THEORY,
UNITED STATES, 1980S

"YOU CAN'T BE serious!"

"On the contrary, Herr Oberst, *I am completely serious. You were chosen by Heinrich Himmler himself to become the new* Führer.*"*

"Won't the old one have something to say about that?"

"I doubt it. He committed suicide a few days after you left."

"The Reichsführer-SS? *He would never betray the* Führer!*"*

"He did. He'd made his plans, told Hitler that he would never leave his side . . . and then fled the holocaust of Berlin. He tried to open negotiations with the Americans and the British through a Swedish consulate, telling them that Hitler would soon be dead, and that he was the provisional leader of Germany. He was denounced by his own people, captured, and finally killed himself while being interrogated."

"Why are you telling me all of this?"

"*Because you should know. So that you can take command here.*"

"*What I* know, Mein Herr, *is that we all were betrayed by the* Eidechse. *They promised us weapons, they promised us victory . . . and they allowed us to go down in fire and blood!*"

"*And all of that,* Herr Oberst, *was precisely according to plan. . . .*"

LIEUTENANT ROGER Caidin, flying CAP with SFA-07, was less than a kilometer from the *Hillenkoetter*'s starboard side when the ship went on full alert.

"What the hell is going on, Dodge?" his rear-seater asked, using Caidin's handle. "Sounds like they're up against it!"

"I wouldn't be a bit—"

And then the magnetic shielding covering the flight deck entrance failed, multiple sets of backups failed, and the ship's atmosphere exploded into space.

Explosive decompression created a short-lived hurricane wind rapidly dissipating into vacuum. It caught Caidin's Stingray and flipped him into an uncontrolled roll, coupled with a savage yaw to port.

"Hang on, Pops!" he yelled at his RIO, whose handle came from him being the oldest student in his flight school class—all of thirty-one.

"Hanging!" Pops, Lieutenant Jeff Greer, yelled back. There wasn't anything else the radar intercept officer *could* do . . . except, perhaps, pray. Stars and the ponderous cliffside of the *Hillenkoetter* swung past the cockpit, and Caidin felt the heavy drag of centrifugal force.

Caidin nudged his controls enough to stabilize the craft, stopping both the roll and the yaw. By the time he had his ship back under control, they were drifting through a debris field of equipment, papers, and detritus sucked out of the *Big-H* and flung into space. An ordnance forklift, a Hellfire missile still strapped in its grabs, sailed past the cockpit.

And corpses. He saw two, a man and a woman, air-wing maintenance personnel to judge by their green vests, tumbling through space nearby, arms and legs flailing, mouths wide open in silent screams. God . . . they were *still alive* . . . though they wouldn't be for long.

And there was not a damned thing Caidin could do to help them.

"God, Lieutenant!" Greer said from the rear seat. "What happened?"

"The pressure screens blew," he replied, voice tight. "Obviously."

The magnetokinetic induction screens across the broad opening leading in to *Hillenkoetter*'s flight deck had failed. Damn it, that wasn't supposed to happen! When he'd first reported aboard the *Big-H* he'd learned there were multiple fail-safes, guaranteeing that even if the ship's power went down there were backup generators in place to take up the load. Without those screens, however, *Hillenkoetter* was wide open to space, her atmosphere spilling explosively into hard vacuum. Automatic pressure doors throughout the ship should close when a pressure drop was detected, but that wouldn't help the personnel working on the exposed flight deck.

Another body pirouetted past his fighter, a brown shirt this time, eyes wide open and blood frozen across the face. He tried desperately to think of a way to help, but there was nothing, *nothing* he could do. He was sealed inside his fighter, and even if he could open the pressure-locked canopy in vacuum, there was no room inside the cockpit for a passenger.

"Isn't there anything we can *do*?" Greer said. He was close to sobbing.

"If you think of anything," he replied, voice hard, "let me know."

And in any case, by now the people blasted into space would be dead.

A plastic box struck his port side, spilling a cascade of electronic cards and parts in a glittering swarm. Carefully, he swung his Stingray around and approached the stricken spacecraft carrier.

"What's on radar, Pops? I didn't see any bandits!"

"Zilch, Dodge! Sky's clear!"

"Damn it, there must be *something*. . . ."

"Negatory, Lieutenant."

If no one was attacking from outside, it must have been something internal. But what kind of onboard accident or systems failure would take out two separate engineering decks and several armored generator stations all at the same moment?

"Prifly, Prifly, this is CAP Oh-seven, Prifly, CAP Oh-seven. Do you copy?"

He got static in return.

"Prifly, CAP Oh-Seven, Prifly, CAP Oh-Seven. Do you copy?"

"They're off the air, Lieutenant," Lieutenant Commander Jason White replied. White was SFA-07's CO, affectionately known as "Whitey" in spite of his dark skin. "Shit. What's going on in there?"

"Don't know, sir. They must be under attack, but the sky's empty!"

"Might have been an accident," another Stingray pilot put in. "Someone hit the wrong button with all of that alien high tech."

"Unlikely, Boomer," White replied. "Okay, people, listen up. We will redeploy along vector one-eight-seven. Eyes sharp for bogeys. They might try to sneak ships in while our pants are down."

"Copy, Skipper," Caidin said.

"Skipper, if we don't have a place to land," the other Drake pilot called out, "we are *screwed!*"

"Stow it, Boomer. If necessary, LOC can deploy another carrier or one of the cruisers to pick us up. Stay cool. Okay . . . everyone checked in and lined up? Alright . . . execute!"

Caidin engaged his Stingray's drive, carefully easing out of the debris cloud, then falling into formation with the rest of the squadron.

Like Boomer, though, and probably every other pilot and RIO with the Firedrakes, he wondered if they would have a barn to which they could return.

HUNTER HAD just returned to the CIC with *Hillenkoetter*'s captain when the ship went dark, with the overhead lighting and every monitor screen and control panel in the compartment down. It wasn't *completely* dark, thank both God and the engineering teams behind Solar Warden. The emergency glow strips—operating on their own independent batteries—put out a faint, green gleam, not enough to illuminate, but people were able to orient themselves.

Hunter felt his ears pop, and that meant shipboard pressure was dropping. Before long, the airtight doors would automatically seal. He knew there were override codes . . . but it was safer if they weren't opening internal doors and hatches during an explosive depressurization emergency.

Technicians and CIC crew had managed to pull themselves down into their seats, and were now looking to the *Hillenkoetter*'s captain for guidance.

"The induction screens must have blown," Groton said. "All of the power generators went down at once."

"Unless they put a whopping big hole in our hull," Haines said.

"The bastards hit the engineering spaces," Groton replied. "They're buried too deep inside the ship's core for that. They probably deliberately targeted the power generators."

"Sir," Hunter said. "Sounds like a precisely coordinated attack. And they knew *exactly* where to hit us."

Groton nodded. "From the inside. Any external attack that got both primary and secondary engineering would have taken out our entire ship!"

"Can you fix it if we secure the engineering decks?" Hunter asked.

"Depends on how badly they wrecked it. We need a combat team in there, stat."

"I can divide my people into two strike teams and clear them out, sir." He rubbed the back of his head, thinking. "But getting down there's going to be tricky. . . ."

"The tube cars still ought to be working," Haines told him. "They run on batteries. And the tube magnets are powered by a separate generator forward."

"Well *that's* convenient." Hunter felt immense relief; he knew they needed every bit of luck.

"The workers needed a way to get around inside this beast when they were building her, right?"

"Your people will need weapons and armor," Groton said.

"I thought we'd head for the armory, then deploy from there."

"Sounds good." Groton thought for a moment. "Staff Sergeant!"

One of the Marine sentries floating by CIC's main door came to attention—an odd-looking maneuver in zero gravity. "Sir!"

"Take one of your men and escort Mr. Hunter down to where he's going."

"Aye, aye, sir!"

"Good. Bill?"

"Sir!" the XO said.

"Get me some personal comms. Emergency locker."

Haines carefully moved away and fumbled with something in the darkness. "Got 'em."

Returning, Haines handed what looked like two small cell phones to Hunter.

"Those will let your teams stay in contact with one another," Groton told him. "They might even reach us here. Press one to talk between these two units . . . and push two to talk to me. Or try to. The signal might not make it through so many decks and bulkheads."

"If not I'll send a runner to let you know when we're clear."

"Yes, do that," Groton told him. "Though if we don't have gravity restored by then, he'll have to be a swimmer."

"Once we get our SAS on, we should be able to talk with you."

"One more thing, Commander," Haines said. He took one of the comms back and entered a five-digit number, then repeated it for the second unit. "If you run into sealed airtights along the way, press this button. It'll transmit the code and open the door. Do it again to reseal. *Please* don't forget to reseal."

"Don't leave the doors hanging open behind me. Got it."

"Commander Ramsey."

"Sir!" a man floating beside a console a few yards away said, turning.

"Get together two engineering teams. If . . . when Commander Hunter is successful, I want your people in there patching things up."

"Yes, *sir!*"

"Good luck, Mark," Groton told him. "With luck, maybe the bastards will have cleared out by the time you get down there."

"Yeah . . . but I won't count on it, sir. They might have decided to invite a few of their friends."

Carefully, using handrails set into the bulkheads, Hunter made his way out of the claustrophobic darkness of CIC and into the even darker and more claustrophobic passageway outside, with two armed and armored Marines in tow. A green-yellow glow strip guided him to the nearest tube car station. The lights on the helmets of the two Marines helped illuminate the corridor, though their movements sent shadows flicking wildly across the bulkheads.

Tube cars were a convenience back at S4 and Groom Lake. Here they were a necessity. The USSS *Hillenkoetter* was a dark and tangled maze of passageways and compartments in which even an old hand could easily get lost, a problem infinitely worse in zero gravity, with no up or down, and no way of telling if what had been a right turn now, with your body in a different orientation, was a left. Inside the waiting tube car, the three of them strapped down, and Hunter touched the destination panel. A light blinked on, telling him the transport was powered up. "Oh-two deck," he said aloud. "Compartment 2715."

He felt the gentle shove of acceleration as the transport car began moving.

On board ship, the "oh-two" referred to the second deck above the main deck that, on a spacecraft carrier like *Hillenkoetter*, was the level that included the midship flight deck. Decks below the main deck were identified as "first deck," "second deck," and so on. CIC was on the main deck forward, buried at the ship's core. The armory was . . . where? He typed out a request and pulled up a ship's schematic. There actually were several places on board where weapons and suits were stored; the nearest would be on the first deck, aft of the fighter service bay . . . so just three levels down from where the JSST was waiting.

Getting to the JSST would not be a problem. Transporting the JSST down to engineering in near-total blackness and zero G was going to be the fun part.

Moments later, the tube car pulled to a halt at another station. Hunter checked the map once more to get his bearings, then set out for compartment 2715, located down a long, straight corridor, followed by a right turn. He had to maintain his orientation, though, because if he got his up and down confused, his left would become a right. Following the glowing lines, however, and with help from his Marine escort, he found the door.

As expected, it was sealed now against the dropping pressure.

He transmitted the code on his communicator and the door opened with a hiss of escaping air. Damn . . . they had to get the landing bay screens up and running again fast, or before very long every bit of air was going to leak out into surrounding space. In fact, each time someone opened one of those doors, the pressure dropped a bit more, and there might well be enough damage within the engineering decks to have compromised the internal airtight security.

If any of the pressure doors leading into the vacuum had failed, there would be another hurricane.

He used his comm to transmit the access code, and the door opened with a sharp hiss. Inside, in the darkness and with no up or down, sixty-some men and women floundered in a disorganized tangle. It was noisy with everyone talking at once.

Hunter pressed into the room, but came up almost at once against a drifting commando.

"Get your butt out of my face, please," Hunter growled.

"Sorry, sir!" EN1 Taylor replied, recognizing his voice, and Hunter felt the body floating in front of him gently rotate and move aside. He pushed himself forward. Somehow, Hunter had to get this motley crowd organized.

"*Attention on deck!*" Taylor bellowed. The people in the room couldn't come to attention, but the talking stopped.

"Okay, people, listen up!" Hunter yelled in his most authoritative bellow, straining his voice to be heard.

"Sir!" someone in the crowd called. "What's going on?"

"You heard the Skipper!" Minkowski's voice added. "*Shut the fuck up!*"

"Everybody . . . stay calm!" Hunter yelled. "Keep your wits about you! The Lizards have taken both engineering decks. We're going to go take them back!"

The noise in the compartment stilled as he spoke. The unit was well trained and responsive and there was no panic . . . but in the near-darkness, they were acting like sixty-five separate individuals, and he needed them to work as a team.

"Anyone in here have a weapon on them?"

There was a long silence. Hunter had expected nothing else. Shipboard regulations were strict about carrying weapons on board; an accidental discharge could be disastrous in a confined space.

"Okay," Hunter continued. "We need to get our asses down to the armory. That's on the third deck. I want you all to form up in a queue, single file, just like a conga line. I'll be in the lead. Minkowski, you bring up the rear."

"Aye, aye, sir!"

"Ready, people? Okay, let's go!" Hunter ordered, and the JSST moved into the passageway. It was clumsy going in microgravity. They'd not trained extensively in zero G since their ships usually manufactured gravity to order.

They made a strange and eerie sight, threading their way out of the Deck 02 Lounge in a long, twisting line, bouncing gently off walls, floors, and ceilings while grabbing belts or ankles ahead to keep together. The Marines helped guide them. "Careful when you stop, everyone," one of the Marines called, his voice rasping from the helmet speaker. "If you pile up on a bulkhead you've got a hell of a lot of mass following you in!"

Hunter hadn't considered that. The line of personnel would be acting like a single mass, the total mass of all sixty-five people. Once in motion, that mass stayed in motion. When Hunter reached the bulkhead at the first turn in the passageway, he had to brake his movement with his arms, then push out of the way before the next trooper in line piled into him.

There were numerous bruises along the way, but they managed to reach the tube car station in fairly short order. One of the tube cars had seats for twelve, though they could crowd more into the narrow compartment if people didn't mind getting friendly. A Marine helped pack sixteen into one car and sent them on their way, before calling a second car . . . and then a third, and finally a fourth. The final car, where Hunter squeezed into along with the last Marine, had nineteen people in it. It wasn't bad in zero gravity . . . but when the car accelerated, the compartment suddenly became *very* crowded. Hunter was in one of the seats with Army Staff Sergeant Lynn Pauly in his lap. With acceleration, she became very heavy indeed.

"Sorry, Commander. . . ." she said.

"No problem, Staff Sergeant," Hunter replied with a grin. "We'll talk about putting you on a diet later."

"Sir!"

At the end of the trip, they extricated themselves and pulled out of the car, floating down a broad passageway to reach the armory.

"Hey, Skipper!" That was TM1 Frank Nielson.

"What is it?"

"Sir . . . scuttlebutt says we got new weapons on board! Upgraded PEWs!"

Rumor, Hunter thought, was the only thing besides starships that traveled faster than light. "You heard right. But we take what we can get."

There were, in fact, several armories on board the *Hillen-*

koetter, and a good chance that even if the new personal energy weapons were in this one, they hadn't yet been broken out of their shipping cases. Torres had told him the weapons had only just come on board.

However, what they found in the armory racks, illuminated by the Marines' lights, were the old standbys—RAND/Starbeam rifles and Sunbeam Type 1 laser pistols. Hunter was actually relieved when they couldn't find the upgrades. There was a lot of exposed and fragile equipment on an engineering deck, and more powerful weapons in unpracticed hands could inflict even more damage than the ship had suffered already.

As the JSST personnel collected their weapons, they moved on to the racks holding their Mark VII Space Activity Suits, nicknamed Seven-SAS. The team helped one another suit up, wiggling into the metal pressure shells and sealing the Kevlar over that. Lights began winking on throughout the compartment, dazzling now after the near-darkness. Each suit included a PLSS backpack—a portable life-support system that included the batteries for the massive plug-in Starbeams. Many of them also picked up slug-throwers—.45 pistols and CQBR-fitted M16s; a few disdained the lasers for the old-fashioned weapons . . . not that Hunter blamed them.

Fully suited and armed, the team divided into pairs, each person carefully inspecting his or her partner to make sure all joints were sealed, latches closed, and straps tight. Ten of them carried spare battery packs for both weapon types in canvas pouches attached to their SASes, and would serve as ammo runners if it came to a firefight.

And now, Hunter thought, holstering his Type 1 on his thigh and snapping the catch, *for the hard part. . . .*

ELANNA AND Julia Ashley floated together in the close darkness of Julia's sleeping quarters. Fortunately, the rooms were just a short way down the passageway aft of CIC, and one of the Marine guards had been able to guide them there. Ashley was trying to focus on the large room within Ares Prime where she'd seen the crowd of Saurians, but was having difficulty. The odd sensation of weightlessness—a feeling like she was endlessly and helplessly falling—was distracting enough to break her focus and cut her off from remote viewing.

"Relax, Julia," Elanna told her. "Just let your thoughts drift."

"I'm trying. . . ."

"You're trying too hard. Just let the impressions come." Ashley could feel Elanna riding her thoughts, holding her, strengthening her. The feeling was odder than that of zero gravity, but not unpleasant. It felt warm, comfortable, even. And she was finding the darkness actually helped, a means of shutting out the room and letting her hone in on her thoughts.

But it was no use. She could not connect with her target.

She found her thoughts turning back to Shag Harbour, and the aliens she'd seen inside the crashed ship off Nova Scotia. What had they wanted of her? What did they expect her to *do*? Could she even do anything at all in a situation that had unfolded over fifty years ago? *Hillenkoetter*'s alien-derived technology could do some pretty wild things with time, but rescuing aliens trapped in a submerged spacecraft half a century in the past seemed ludicrous.

"You're thinking about the Zshaj," Elanna told her. It was not an accusation, but a simple statement of fact as the Talisian read her mind.

"I can't help it. They saw me. They were asking for help. . . ."

"The Zshaj are remarkably perceptive," Elanna said.

"Zshaj. Is that what they're called?"

"It's the Talisian name for them. They communicate through telepathy. No words, and no names."

"That's weird."

"Not weird, Julia. *Different*."

"I was wondering . . ."

"Yes?"

"Well . . . *Hillenkoetter* travels through time when it travels faster than light, right?"

"In a manner of speaking. Backward in time, forward in space."

"Could we go back to 1967 and help them?"

Elanna frowned. "That might not be a good idea."

"Why not?"

"The chances of a temporal branching are quite large. We change history, even by a small amount, and our own present, yours and mine, become closed to us. There are no such things as temporal paradoxes, remember. Instead, a new timeline branches off, one with a different future. And there is no way for us to jump from one reality to another."

"I'm not sure I understand."

"It is difficult to grasp, I know. The multiverse, remember, is a vast—some believe infinite—web of different realities, constantly unfolding and growing more complex as choices are made. In *this* reality, I flip a coin and get heads. In *that* reality, I get tails, because all possible outcomes *must* be expressed. In a majority of cases, with such small events, the new reality merges with the old immediately. In one reality, the Zshaj explorers perish in the seas off Nova Scotia. In another, we rescue them. Is there a difference between the two timelines? Maybe there isn't . . . and everything is fine. But if the two universes express differently . . ."

"The people who messed it up go home to a different reality. I get it." Ashley drew a long breath. "Okay . . . thanks. It helped talking about that. It's been gnawing at me."

"Are you ready to try visiting Mars again?"

Ashley drew a deep breath, then nodded. "I think so. Let's give it a try. . . ."

"EVERYBODY STAND ready," Hunter ordered.

"A little hard to *stand*, Commander," Minkowski said. "We don't know which bulkhead is the deck."

Hunter ignored him. "Mr. Winslow. Where's Winslow?"

Half of the JSST floated in the passageway outside another airtight door, this one under a big sign reading "Primary Engineering." The other half were forward with Lieutenant Billingsly, Hunter's XO, assaulting the other engineering space. With them were a half dozen engineers and engineering techs under the command of Lieutenant Commander Winslow, whom Hunter remembered from the flight deck. Winslow had been in the fighting here earlier, but escaped along with several shipboard Marines. The Marines would be going in with the strike team, but . . .

"You keep your people outside and out of the scrapping, Mr. Winslow," Hunter told him. "We'll need you inside when the place is secured. Understand?"

"Yes, Commander."

"You people with slug-throwers," he told his team members, "remember to brace, or the recoil will send you spinning. Everybody set?"

"Ooh-rah!"

"Let's go, Skipper!"

"Yeah! Let's smoke 'em!"

Hunter pulled out the handheld comm. "In three . . . two . . . one . . . *now*!" He pressed the button and the door slid open, a puff of air from inside rushing out past them. Minkowski was first through, holding his shotgun at the ready. A new kid named Bonnowitz followed with his Starbeam laser. These doors were only wide enough to admit one person at a time and those robust 7-SASes created a much tighter squeeze. Hunter heard the boom of Mink's shotgun, muffled and distant. Was the air so thin already that sound transmission was dulled? Or was it being muffled by his suit?

One of the ship Marines crowded ahead next, and Hunter followed close behind, gripping his pistol. He couldn't see any targets, but the place was a mess, with bits and fragments of machinery adrift everywhere. It didn't look good.

"US Space Force!" he yelled over his suit radio. When he heard no response, he called to the Marine. "What channel are your people on, Staff Sergeant?"

"One-one-seven, sir. But I'm not hearing anything. . . ."

Then a trio of gray, armored figures simply materialized out of the air five meters in front of them, energy weapons snapping bolts into the JSST troopers. Two of Hunter's men were killed instantly.

CHAPTER ELEVEN

Agenda 21: The presence of intact trees around burned homes after devastating wildfires proves beyond doubt that the US government has been using powerful and secret laser weapons from space to set those wildfires throughout the American West. They are doing this as part of an organized plan to force rural Americans to live in cities where they can be more easily watched, controlled, and disarmed.

There has been no suggestion yet as to what Agendas 1 through 20 might have been.

POPULAR CONSPIRACY THEORY,
2020 AND ONWARD

A MOB GATHERED that evening in the Pariser Platz, just in front of Berlin's historic Brandenburg Gate. It was dark; city authorities had refused to illuminate the plaza, but torchlight flared and danced, sending shadows across the massive pillars of the gate and the statue at the top of the goddess Victory in her chariot—the quadriga. This gathering, Albrecht was told, had been conceived as a rally for the AfD, the Alternative für Deutschland, *the far-right populist political party that currently controlled around twelve percent of the German parliament. For Albrecht, however, there were clear and startling connections with the Nazis' rally . . . the flaring torches, the shouting, chanting crowd, the upraised fists as men on the temporary stage raised in front of the Brandenburg itself screamed invectives decrying membership in the European Union, unrestricted foreign immigration, and Islam.*

Most of what was said was alien to Albrecht, and he struggled to understand. What was this European Union several speakers were railing against? Why had Germany joined such an organization in the first place?

One ideology alone he understood: instead of Jews, the enemies of all mankind were the Muslims. Evidently, unprecedented numbers of them had been migrating from the Middle East, had taken up residence in Germany, taken jobs, taken money from social programs, undermined the German social structure, raped German women, and set up their own isolationist enclaves in German cities where Islamic law superseded the laws of Germany.

One prominent speaker called for all Muslims to be expelled from Germany, or for them to suffer the consequences, and Albrecht was forcibly reminded of a similar speech he'd heard at Nuremburg in 1935. That had been the Rally of Freedom, the one in which the Nuremburg laws had been introduced, stripping the Jews of their rights to be citizens of the Reich.

This rally, his mysterious companion told him, was der Kundgeburg für die Rückkehr, *the Rally for the Return.*

"The Return?" he'd asked, astonished. "They know about the Return?"

"For them," Max told him, " 'the Return' is the return of Germany to greatness. Only a few know the plans formulated by our . . . friends."

Meaning, of course, the Eidechse. *But the spirit of the crowd was a searing, white-hot flame, uniting, empowering, sweeping all up together in a shared vision of greatness.*

Perhaps, he reasoned, there was something worth saving in this future Germany.

But why were the Eidechse *interested in populist German politics?*

And more to the point, could they ever be trusted?

AS HUNTER tried to get his bearings inside Engineering, Minkowski's M4 boomed again, the detonation startlingly louder inside the compartment despite the thin air. The JSST trooper had his feet braced against the bulkhead behind him, firing "up" at the oncoming shadows. One of the armored Saurians spun crazily backward into the dark, legs and arms flailing, as Minkowski's heavy slug caught the thing high in the chest.

It was pitch-black inside the compartment, save for the wildly dancing shadows cast by the powerful lights on the teams' suits. With thirty-some men throwing those shadows across bulkheads and deck, constantly moving, the entire engineering space appeared to be alive, writhing as if in agony. The effect, like moving strobes, was both disorienting and dizzying. Hunter felt his stomach twist in response, and fought the nausea back.

He thumbed on his laser pistol's battery, brought it up in a two-handed grip, and triggered a pulse of coherent light, aiming for a nearby Saurian's snouted face. Most of the Lizards he could see emerging from the darkness were wearing armor—lightweight stuff by the look of it. Yet, Hunter knew their technology gave them a serious advantage. None of those he could see had fully helmeted heads, however. Their faces were exposed, and even his little Sunbeam could cause serious damage to scaly but un-protected skin. His target vented a shrill, hissing screech, gloved hands over his burned face.

But others were firing into the JSST troops crowded in front of the door. Prescott and Andrews both had crumpled and were helplessly adrift now, with savage punctures burned through their suits. Casey was screaming, clutching frantically at the stump of her leg burned off at the knee, as droplets of blood expanded into the room, reflecting light like a glittering galaxy of brilliant red stars.

"Spread out!" Hunter yelled. "Everybody spread out!" The Lizards were trying to catch them in a three-dimensional cross-fire, englobing them with the door at their backs. Herrera nailed one with his Starbeam, missed a second, killed a third. There was enough dust floating in the air, making the beams faintly visible and only appearing as brief, hazy threads of light, flashing. Then, the brightness was gone in an instant. Against the throbbing, un-folding shadows, they added a weirdly surreal effect.

Beside him, Sergeant Liu took a bolt of high-energy plasma in his side, the hit burning into his PLSS. A cannister of high-pressure gas in the backpack unit ruptured, sending him tumbling backward and into another trooper.

The attackers' weapons looked like small, flat boxes strapped to the front torsos of their armor. The things were uncannily ac-curate; the hazy beams they fired seemed to deflect left or right, up or down as needed to target the humans, and Hunter decided the Saurians were controlling the things somehow without touch-ing them . . . quite likely with their thoughts. Nearby, Sergeant Allen's helmet exploded in a gory spray of blood and fragments, though the Saurian who'd fired was angled a good twenty degrees off-target. Hunter turned his laser pistol on that Saurian, scoring another head shot, another kill.

But the human strike team possessed one advantage, an advantage in numbers if not technology. As they spread out into the large room, more and more of the Saurian intruders were caught in crossfires; more were hit, several were killed. From what Hunter could make out in the shadowed dark, the intruders were of two separate species—Saurians and Grays. Some of the Grays, Hunter noticed, were armed, but most were not. Perhaps they were technicians or workers of some sort.

His pistol emitted a shrill tone, and a red light blinked, indicating that his battery was dead. He thumbed the release button and shook the dead battery free of the grip, slapping a fresh one home, taking aim, and firing again.

This time, he aimed at a Saurian's torso-mounted weapon . . . arguably a more vulnerable and easier-to-hit target than its eyes. At the touch of his laser, the shiny casing of the device deformed, melting under the intense heat, and the reptile screamed, slapping at the red-hot device.

"Go for their weapons!" Hunter yelled to his team. "Disarm them unless you're sure of a clean head shot!"

Slowly, steadily, shot by shot, the strike team was gaining the upper hand. The unarmed Grays all had vanished, while those with weapons were pulling back, swallowed by the cavernous black of the engineering space. More and more of the Reptilian intruders were dead or incapacitated. Many were breaking off and diving for the shadows.

Then three more Lizards materialized out of thin air . . . at ex-

actly the same place where the last three had entered the compartment. Hunter killed one with an assist from Herrera, as the other
two were taken down by concentrated fire from Layton, Bonnowitz, and Gomez. Combining the fire from several weapons was
definitely more effective than trying to pick them off one-to-one.

As Hunter took aim at another Saurian, one of the attackers
collided with him from the side, its gloved hands scrabbling at
the slick surface of Hunter's suit as if it were trying to claw his
opponent. It was one of the big Saurians, seven feet tall at least,
and it seemed to be attempting to overpower Hunter by sheer
brawn. For a brief second or two, he stared into the alien's golden
eyes, slit-pupiled and crocodilian, and twisted hard, breaking
the creature's hold, and pushed it back. Turning, he fired his laser
into the Saurian's face at point-blank range. When the first bolt
didn't kill it, he fired again, burning into its scaly, grinning face.
It thrashed in midair for a moment, then drifted into the shadows
among several generator units and went still. Its weapon, he saw,
had been burned to twisted junk. Disarming them, obviously, left
them almost as dangerous as if they were armed.

More were coming through from elsewhere, arriving three by
three. Something caught Hunter in the side and spun him around,
bits of molten armor splattering off his suit. He didn't return fire;
his pistol was so under-powered there was little point, and the rest
of the team was concentrating their fire now on the intruders in
a steady, flashing fusillade that burned into the crowd of Lizards
before they could disperse, leaving several floating in the middle
of the compartment, others writhing and wounded.

Hunter felt dizzy. His helmet instrumentation told him he
was losing suit pressure, and there was a serious danger now of

decompression sickness. He ignored the headache and dizziness and focused on directing the JSST's fire, aiming to burn down as many of the Lizards as possible.

After an anxious and furious several moments, the last of the attackers died . . . or stepped back through the gateway, in full retreat now.

That space where they'd materialized . . . that must be the targeted focus of the device at Ares Prime teleporting the Saurians onto the *Hillenkoetter*. The realization gave them a chance . . .

"Englobe that area!" Hunter ordered, pointing. "The place where the Lizards are materializing. Shoot them down as they step through! Be careful of scoring an own goal!"

And an instant later, three more heavily armored Saurians appeared as though walking in through a door. They staggered in place, suggesting that they'd been moving within a gravity field and then suddenly stepped into zero G, leaving them momentarily confused.

Good.

The concentrated fire from ten RAND/Starbeam 4000 rifles caught them all simultaneously in a fusillade of energy bolts. Hunter noticed these Lizards wore massive helmets that concealed their faces, helmets lacking even transparent visors. They would certainly be immune to the weak output of a laser pistol . . . but the concentrated crossfire from the heavier weapons burned into armor in dazzling, searing flares of white light and splatters of molten fragments. Before any of them could adjust to darkness and weightlessness, all three were dead.

But more were crowding through . . . and more . . . and *more*.

Those helmets, Hunter reasoned, meant that the Lizards back at Ares Prime were watching what was happening here, probably through their dimensional device. And *that* meant . . .

"Can anyone see anything there? Anything like a doorway?"

Lieutenant Joel Foster, an Army Ranger fairly new to the team, raised a gauntleted hand. "Sir! Over here!"

Hunter kicked off and swam across empty air to join Foster. Sure enough, from this one angle he could see . . . hell, what *was* that? A dim patch of light against the darkness only as big as a hand's breadth. Move a few feet in any direction, and the light vanished. Within the light, he could see movement . . . no detail, but he glimpsed shapes, grainy and indistinct as though on the screen of a low-res television set.

The patch of light abruptly expanded, forming a circular opening a couple of yards across. The images resolved themselves into close-packed ranks of armored Saurians. It was as though Hunter was staring into another room, one right over there . . .

. . . and a couple of million miles away.

"Hit 'em!" Hunter yelled. "*Hit 'em!*"

Again, the deadly crossfire of glowing threads of light snapped and stabbed, this time actually entering the room beyond with deadly effect. As Hunter had suspected, only fire from a relatively small area—where the light patch was visible—could reach through to the other side of this Dimensional Gateway.

But if the Saurians were getting images from *Hillenkoetter*'s engineering deck, it was because light was passing from one side of the gate to the other, from here to there.

And that meant that they would be able to see into Ares Prime from the *Big-H*. If light could pass through to Mars from *Hillenkoetter*'s engineering decks, well . . . lasers were nothing but tightly focused and coherent light.

With the suddenness of a slammed door, the opening snapped shut.

"Cease fire!" Hunter called. The portal might reopen at any moment. Would they reopen it here, at the same spot? Or would they come pouring in from someplace else? He didn't know how the Dimensional Gateway worked, if it was locked into its original coordinates or constantly changing. He would have to cover all of the bases.

He was panting hard, partially from exertion, partially from the thin air.

"Bonnowitz . . . Taylor . . . Dubois. You three watch this spot . . . right here. If you see that gate opening again, if Saurians start teleporting in, sing out, and hit the bastards with everything you have. Understand?"

"Yessir!" Taylor said.

"Lieutenant Foster. Pick out ten troopers and spread out. Watch for any sign that they're opening a gateway someplace else in here."

"Yes, sir."

"Mr. Winslow . . ."

"Right here, sir."

"Get your people in there and work your magic. The rest of my team will set up a perimeter around you, provide security. Understand?"

"Yes, sir. Watkins! Epstein! All the rest of you! With me!"

The engineering team had assembled outside. They came spilling into the compartment now, each carrying a case of equipment and tools. Winslow began giving orders, and Hunter's men gradually moved into position around them.

And the repairs on *Hillenkoetter*'s primary engineering spaces began.

"THEY SEEM confused. . . ."

Julia Ashley drifted above the chaise in her quarters, Elanna, unseen in the darkness, beside her.

"I think they've been attacked," Elanna said, thoughtful. "Unexpectedly attacked. Something's happened for which they were not prepared."

In Ashley's mind, the Saurians milled about, their attention focused on one unarmored Saurian seated within a horseshoe-shaped console. The being was working the touchscreen controls. The lights and display screens were meaningless to her.

"That's their Dimensional Gateway?"

"The controls for it, yes," Elanna told her. "It looks like there's a second unit on the other side of the room."

"I see it." The second frame was dark, the horseshoe console unoccupied.

"That first one. Can you . . . can you change your point of view over to the left? I'd like to see what's directly in front of that instrumentation."

"I'll try."

In Ashley's mind, the scene shifted, her point of view sliding around until it was directly behind the Saurian seated at the controls, looking over the creature's shoulder. She expected to see a kind of gateway or opening there, but she could see nothing but

the far wall. Several of the Saurians were kneeling, busily working on two reptilians, lying injured on the deck. She could make
little sense of what she was seeing.

She was getting used to having Elanna's mind riding with her
own, however. Together, the two had much greater control and
clarity . . . assuming Ashley could relax and just let the images
come.

Abruptly, then, the lights came on . . . followed an instant later
by the gravity. Ashley dropped a foot or two into her chaise, hitting with a jarring thump. Elanna, somehow, managed to land on
her feet.

"Looks like they got things working," Elanna said.

"I've lost the connection," Ashley told her. "Damn . . . that
jarred it right out of me!"

"Not surprising." Reaching out, she patted Ashley's arm. "Let's
call this one, Julia. You get some rest. You've been working hard!"

"I'm supposed to rest with those creepy critters jumping in
through another dimension? Yeah, right. . . ."

But she was tired—exhausted, even—and was going to relish
the downtime.

"LOOKS LIKE you finally paid the electric bill, Captain. That didn't
take long," Hunter told Groton. Leaving his strike teams on guard
in the two engineering spaces, he'd returned to CIC to confer with
the captain.

"Strictly a cobbled-together temporary fix, CHENG tells me,"
Groton replied. "He says Winslow's got one lone generator running in primary, with lights, communications, and gravity all

wired into that. We still have no induction screen or defensive fields, no weapons, and no drives. We're dead in space, and helpless except for our CAP."

"So the flight deck's still in vacuum?"

Groton nodded. "At least the slow leaks have mostly stopped. We're holding at nine, nine and a half psi throughout the rest of the ship."

"That's . . . what? The equivalent of twelve thousand feet back on Earth?"

"Something like that. Are your people adapting to altitude?"

"Some headaches," Hunter admitted. "Lots of fatigue . . . though that could be the aftereffects of combat. I was feeling pretty short of breath when my suit was breached. Most of my people are still sealed up in their suits."

"Keep them there. We don't know what else the Lizards are going to try. And altitude sickness is no joke."

"Can they help down in sick bay?"

"The medical department is pretty well swamped right now with barotrauma cases. We had a lot of people badly hurt adjacent to the flight deck when the pressure first dropped, before they were able to reach pressurized compartments. Everything from busted eardrums to full-on cases of the bends. And your people took some hits as well."

"Yes, sir." He'd already turned in his casualty report—five dead in primary engineering, and Billingsly's team in secondary had lost three. Most of the wounded had suffered minor cuts and burns, thanks to their armor. Hunter had dispatched three to sick bay for more serious injuries.

"How many lost on the flight deck?"

"Unknown. Perhaps as many as eighty. We're checking."

"Ouch." He was picturing the terror those people must have felt as the invisible wall holding in their air had suddenly switched off, and their atmosphere had abruptly exploded out into empty space. Considering their surface area, around twenty-six square feet, and weight, the wind blasting them into space had done so with the force of over a ton across their bodies.

They never stood a chance.

"We were damned lucky, Commander. It could have been much, *much* worse."

"I'll pass the word to stay suited up, sir," Hunter said. "But we're going to have to get out of our Seven-SASes at some point if we run out of spare O_2 tanks."

"I'm giving priority to bringing up the pressure inside living quarters and mess halls," Groton told him, "as well as the sick bays, the bridge, and CIC. I've got techs jury-rigging portable air-locks over the hatchways to those areas. That should alleviate the leakage problem."

"Yes, sir."

"In the category of *good* news, we've also made contact with the cruiser *Inman*," he continued. "Admiral Winchester is on board. They should be here very soon, and they'll be able to give us emergency support."

"Excellent. *Very* good news." Hunter hesitated, then pushed ahead. "What does this mean for the mission, Captain?"

"We're on hold," Groton told him. "I want to avoid combat un- til the ship is working again. The admiral might want to press on with the *Inman*, but that's for him to say. Right now, our biggest need is damage control . . . and security against further enemy incursions."

"I would suggest, sir, that we form flying squads based out of engineering. Engineering is probably still the principal Lizard target—one or the other or both—and we can leave the larger part of troops where they are now. That way, we can respond to other intrusions . . . but not leave the engineering spaces undefended. An attack elsewhere might be a diversion."

"Do it."

"Aye, aye, sir. Next. We need to have those new uprated weapons issued to my men. We had a hell of a lot of trouble on the engineering decks."

"That," Groton said, shaking his head, "won't be possible. Not yet."

"Fuck, why?" Hunter shouted. To have those weapons within reach . . .

"Look, I know how you feel, Mark," Groton told him. "I requested clearance to issue those weapons specifically from Admiral Winchester when the *Inman* joined us. He point-blank told me no."

"Why the hell not? We have better weapons. Let's use them!"

"Apparently they're still debating the issue back at LOC. Our Talisian friends are still nervous about their timelines. And the admiral doesn't want us shooting the crap out of the Mars base because we can't exercise appropriate fire control. Your people haven't been given the training."

"Hasn't the man heard of on-the-job training?"

"The word came down from MJ-12 itself. No uprated weapons yet."

"That," Hunter said with considerable feeling, "is bullshit."

"Maybe," Groton said. "But we're going to play this by the book. Strictly by the book. Understand me?"

"Sir," Hunter replied, neither confirming nor denying.

"And see to it that your people get some rest in shifts. You especially. You look *terrible*!"

"Yeah, but you should've seen the other guy."

THE SAURIAN saucer appeared out of nowhere, streaking in from Mars, coming in so quickly it registered on Caidin's vision as the briefest of blurs. He triggered his Stingray's lasers, and scored a clean miss.

"Bogey at one-seven-niner!" he warned. "Bastard slipped right past me!"

"Got him, Dodge," White replied . . . and the sky behind Caidin went silently white for an instant. "Scratch one bandit!"

The twelve aerospace fighters of SF-07, in charge of patrolling, were strung out along a perimeter line ten kilometers from the *Hillenkoetter* and some two million miles from Mars. At this distance the planet showed as an exceptionally brilliant red-orange star. Their patrol had been uneventful until just ten minutes before, when they picked up incoming spacecraft . . . not on radar, but with infrared sensors. The enemy ships obviously were trying to slip past the fighter screen to reach *Hillenkoetter* while she was disabled. The humans were at somewhat of a disadvantage because the Saurians were using screens that scattered radar returns, and even IR was scrambled by their drive fields. Attempts to lock on with radar-guided missiles had failed; they were limited to laser fire . . . and that was only when they managed to see their targets.

Even so, with Whitey's shot just now, the squadron had scored three kills so far. How many more were out there?

"Whoa," Greer said over the intercom. "Prifly just came back on the air!"

"Thank God. Maybe we can go home after all."

"Doesn't sound like they have the fight deck screens up and running, yet. But they have power."

"That's a start, Pops." So long as the induction screens were down, *Hillenkoetter* was particularly vulnerable to an attack. Caidin could picture one of those nimble little Lizard saucers slipping right inside the open flight deck and causing untold destruction.

They needed to . . .

There . . . a long string of lights off to the right, like bright stars, but moving quickly, sunlight gleaming off their silver hulls. It looked like they were trying to flank the Firedrakes' defensive formation in order to strike at the carrier.

"Sunhammers, Sunhammers, Firedrakes," White's voice called. SFA-09, the Sunhammers, were positioned closer to *Hillenkoetter*, and were in a better position to intercept the enemy formation. "You have inbound at three-one-five."

"Copy, Drakes," a voice replied. "Thanks for the heads-up. We're on 'em." A moment later, a dazzling sphere of brilliant white light strobed against the darkness, expanding, fading, and dissipating in a second or two.

"Nailed him!" a different voice called, exultant. "Scratch one Lizard!"

A second pulse of bright light. "Scratch two! They're not fighting back! What's with these guys?"

"They want the *Big-H*. We're small fry. Keep after 'em!"

"Close in, Hammers! Get in close! Make it count!"

"I'm hit! I'm hit!"

"Break off, Bates! Get clear!"

Three more strobing flares of brilliance illuminated the sky in rapid succession.

And then, suddenly, the string of saucers reversed direction, hurtling back toward Mars as though they'd been smacked away with a racquet.

"What the hell . . . ?"

"Radar contact, boss!" Greer called. "*Big* contact . . . coming up astern!"

Caidin turned in his seat, trying to see what was going on just as a huge shadow engulfed his Stingray. At first he thought it was the *Hillenkoetter*, under power and galloping in to the rescue.

Then he looked up and saw a flattened cylinder over five hundred feet long, less than half the length of the *Big-H* and massing as much as a wet-Navy Aegis-class cruiser . . . the *Bobby Ray Inman*. A squadron of Stingrays, like tiny, glittering toys compared to the giant ship, streaked past, between Caidin and the cruiser's keel.

Reinforcements had arrived at last.

CHAPTER TWELVE

The New World Order:
The Bilderberg Group is a shadowy world government/political/financial cabal of rich, powerful, and greedy men working behind the scenes to further sinister goals. . . .
or . . .
The Freemasons are a shadowy occult/political/financial cabal of rich, powerful, and greedy men working behind the scenes to further sinister goals. . . .
or . . .
The Illuminati are a shadowy occult/political/financial cabal of rich, powerful, and greedy men working behind the scenes to further sinister goals. . . .
or . . .
The Bohemian Club is a shadowy political/financial cabal of rich, powerful, and greedy men working behind the scenes to further sinister goals. . . .
or . . .
The British royals are a shadowy imperialist/political/financial cabal of rich, powerful, and greedy people working behind the scenes to further sinister goals. . . .
Take your pick.

POPULAR CONSPIRACY THEORIES,
EIGHTEENTH CENTURY AND ONWARD

THE RIOTING THAT followed the Rally for the Return had been terrifying, even for someone as hardened as Albrecht. He'd seen shop windows smashed before, seen places of worship burned, seen people chased through city streets by baying mobs, caught and stripped and beaten and left for dead in the gutters. He'd seen . . . and he'd approved. If the Jews were responsible for Germany's ills, as the Reich proclaimed, extermination was the only option . . . the final *option.*

Somehow, it felt wrong this time, and he wasn't certain why. It took him some time to figure it out.

In the Nazi Germany of the 1930s, Jews had been hunted down by mobs of ordinary citizens, yes, but it was the state, *the Reich that carried out the bulk of the persecution. Albrecht had been a part of that state, following orders and carrying out those orders because he'd been convinced that the state was acting in the national interest. It was obvious . . . wasn't it?*

At least that was how Viktor Albrecht had seen things at the time.

In this Germany of the 2000s it seemed like the state had nothing to do with it. Those mobs had hunted through a Muslim community with a personal hunger, a mindless, unreasoning hatred that seemed more animal than human.

No . . . that wasn't right. Animals don't hate. *They hunt for food or fight to defend their young or territory in ways that conform to their nature. This . . . this was something else, something insane, something wrong in its sheer bestial savagery. What was right for the state operating in the national interests wasn't necessarily right for citizens operating on their own.*

No . . . that couldn't be right. It made no sense. What was right?

Albrecht felt as though he'd been cut adrift, with no Reich, no orders from above to guide him, to tell him what was right.

Worse . . . if this persecution of Muslim civilians was wrong . . . did that mean the Final Solution of the '30s and '40s had been wrong as well? Had it been the state operating legally . . . or had it been men giving cold orders with the same blind hatred as these . . . these animals?

He saw a message crudely painted in red across the side of a building: Unruhen funktionieren.

Riots work. A stark and bitter statement when it was the state that offered security and stability.

And there were others. Muslime gehen nach Hause: *Muslims go home.*

Nein zu Eurabia; *that one required an explanation from Max. Eurabia, according to his guide, referred to the idea that Muslims from the Middle East were moving into the European Union in numbers that soon would overthrow the current governments and transform Europe into a collection of Islamic states.*

And still another sign, one with which Albrecht was quite familiar: Deutschland über alles.

Germany above all.

He was finding it difficult to identify with the emotions expressed in those graffiti. Even that last now seemed part of some other, distant world. After watching the German Reich burn, after watching the flames of Götterdämmerung, *he wondered if Germany above all was even a rational concept now.*

The sight of a student with a shaved scalp waving the torn and bloodied burqa ripped from a young Muslim woman over his head as he danced in the street would be with Albrecht for a long time to come.

HUNTER WAS just sitting down to a long-deferred dinner in the mess hall when Elanna found him. He'd given the necessary orders and divided command responsibility between himself and Billingsly, organized two groups of twelve troopers each who would serve as his flying squads, and seen to it that everyone had some downtime. He was exhausted—the accumulated aftereffects of lack of sleep and the stresses of combat.

At least he'd been able to get out of his 7-SAS armor. Ten hours after the fight in the engineering spaces, pressure was slowly being restored throughout the giant ship. The magnetokinetic induction screens had just been brought back online, and the flight deck was being repressurized. The word had come down from the bridge that it was now safe to move through the ship in shipboard fatigues. Personnel no longer had to wear space suits all the time.

And so Hunter was having something that might be tuna casserole, and as soon as it was done he was going to hit the rack.

"Hello, Mark," Elanna said. "Mind if I join you?"

Hunter stood, gesturing to an empty chair. "Please."

"You're a hard man to track down," she said, taking the seat. "I've been looking all over for you."

"That's because I'm usually the Hunter," he said, smiling as he sat again. "Not the hunted."

She laughed . . . a sound Hunter found utterly bewitching. "Do you use that line often?"

"Not so much." He looked at her, puzzled. "But I thought you telepathic types could track down anybody, no matter where they might be."

"That's not how it works, actually," she told him. "In a confined space like this ship, I'm aware of many, many minds . . .

a kind of cloud . . . or a glow. It's extremely hard to narrow my awareness down to a single individual. Besides . . . I try to be ethical about it."

"Meaning you don't want to snoop?"

"That's one way of putting it."

"Well . . . it's good to see you, whether you're a snoop or not. You were looking for me?"

She nodded. "I want to finish our last conversation."

"About what?"

"About trust."

He thought back a moment, then remembered the discussion with Elanna and the captain interrupted by the appearance of the Saurian intruders.

"Ah . . ."

"Mark . . . it is vitally important that you do trust us, even though we can't always answer all of your questions." Leaning forward, she reached across the table and placed her hand on his wrist. "I want to know what we can do . . . what *I* can do to ease your suspicions."

"And why is my trust so damned important?" Gently, he pulled his hand away. Her touch, light and warm, was . . . disturbingly sensual. It was distracting him.

She looked around. "I'd rather not discuss it here," she told him. "Come with me back to my quarters."

Hunter wasn't entirely sure that was a good idea, but he nodded. "Okay. *After* we finish dinner."

She was right. He *didn't* trust the Talis, and he was suspicious of their agenda, whatever that might be.

But it was important they be able to work together. The Talis, after all, were on the side of twenty-first-century humanity.

At least . . . he hoped they were.

"I SEE . . . it's a forest. I'm in a kind of forest. And beyond that, a plain. It's covered with . . . it's not grass. Not quite. All of the plants are . . . strange. Alien."

Ashley had returned to remote viewing, lying on the recliner in her darkened quarters with a sketchbook open on her lap. Dr. Bennett sat nearby, listening, asking questions, taking notes.

"An alien planet?" Bennett asked.

"I don't think so," she said. "I was definitely homing in on Earth. But it's . . . it's a very alien Earth."

"Sixty-six million years ago," Bennett said. "The end of the late Cretaceous. What's the climate like?"

"Warm. Pretty dry." She frowned. "I thought it would be wetter. This is *not* jungle. I thought it would be a rain forest."

"According to the paleontologists," Bennett told her, "the upper Cretaceous was a lot warmer than Earth today. No icecaps or glaciers anywhere, and seas covered eighty-five percent of the planet's surface."

"The future of global warming," she said.

"Could be. Do you see any animal life?"

"Birds. I *think* they're birds . . . They're pretty far off. Very brightly colored, though . . . red and blue . . ."

As Ashley studied the prehistoric landscape in her mind, she became aware of something else, something on the horizon beyond the plain, something that should not have been there. It looked like what might be a city . . . a scattering of enormous, dome-topped pillars, like mushrooms above the forest canopy where they gleamed in the sun, with dozens of low, white domes in the green shadows below. She wanted to move closer, to explore it . . . but at the same time she was afraid. The Saurians more than once had somehow sensed her mental presence, and she still wasn't sure what they might be able to do about it when they caught her.

She began sketching on the notepad, with rapid, sweeping movements of her hand.

At Bennett's suggestion, she was trying an experiment with remote viewing, using the mental fix she'd picked up from one of the Saurians earlier. It was as though she'd read its mind, read memories locked away in its brain, though she'd not been aware of it at the time. Possibly, as with regular remote viewing, she'd simply read a kind of coordinate set from the Saurian, a sort of mental roadmap she could use to navigate through RV space.

She was pretty sure the Saurian associated the scene she was seeing now with the concept of *home—earth from sixty-six million years ago* . . . a fact which had left both her and Bennett mildly astonished.

Obviously, the being wasn't sixty-six million years old. But that meant it must be a time traveler like the Talis and the Grays, an inhabitant of the upper Cretaceous who'd come forward all those millions of years to . . . what?

Ashley found herself adrift in sheer wonder at such depths of time.

Movement caught her mental eye to her left. She imagined herself turning, opened herself to new imagery, and gasped.

"What is it, Julia?" Bennett asked. "Describe what you see."

"A wall . . . a *living* wall! My God, it's *moving*!"

HE SAT on the edge of Elanna's bed. He'd not been sure of the . . . propriety of that, but the Talis woman had taken the only chair. He'd once read a briefing document by Doc McClure that had explained Elanna's intense sexual alure. According to McClure, either natural evolution across the relatively short span of ten thousand years or some genetic tinkering along the way had fine-tuned some of the biological traits that made humans sexually desirable, including the pheromones exuded by her body.

The worst of it was that she knew what she was doing to him right now, and he wondered if bringing him here to her quarters was a deliberate attempt at seduction. Her enormous eyes were . . . entrancing. . . .

He looked away abruptly, breaking eye contact. No, she wasn't using hypnosis on him, or any kind of mind control, but her close-ness was unsettling.

One entire wall of Elanna's quarters was given over to a view-screen, showing, at the moment, the depths of space, with Mars as a tiny, bright orange disk in the distance. A pair of Stingray fighters slowly drifted past in the panorama's foreground, close enough that Hunter could read the squadron markings painted on their hulls: SFA-09, the Sunhammers. The technology was casu-ally impressive; a tech-toy, perhaps brought back to the twenty-first century from Elanna's home time. As far as Hunter was aware, there was nothing like that in modern-day electronics.

Or was it a part of *Hillenkoetter*'s original design, something recently learned from the Talis and simply not yet on the store shelves? Sometimes it was hard to tell. Hunter didn't have anything like this in *his* quarters.

Elanna moved her head slightly in a body gesture that Hunter thought was her far-future equivalent of a shrug.

"The viewall is not scheduled to become available on Earth for another eight to ten years," Elanna told him. She was reading his mind again. "It's simply an extension of your current LCD television screens."

"For which you people provided the technology?"

"In part. Blitzer and Slottow invented the first plasma flat-screen TV in the 1960s, at the University of Illinois. Thirty years later, we helped the Sony and Sharp corporations refine the idea, and increase the size of the screen."

"Huh. I thought you always insisted that you couldn't contaminate the past—contaminate *us*—by explaining stuff from the future."

"We don't want to give you details of your future, no. That might lead to unacceptable repercussions; alternate realities that might threaten our own future."

"But it's okay to come back in time and outright give the Nazis superweapons?"

Her expression hardened. "It wasn't like that, Mark."

"Jet fighters? The Haunebu flying saucer?"

"That was the Malok," she told him. "The Reptilians and their slaves."

"And what about this ship we're riding in right now?"

Again, Elanna shrugged. "Your own scientists reverse-engineered much of it. And the Malok helped with what you had. We simply tried to *guide* you. . . ."

"Ah. I'm so sorry I misunderstood. But you can't tell us about the future?"

"Certain information is prohibited, yes," she told him. "And certain items are prohibited from intertemporal trade. Weapons, for instance."

"Wait a minute," Hunter said, trying to grasp this. "Are you seriously telling me that there's some sort of trade network . . . across *time*?"

"Of course. What did you expect?"

"I'm having a little trouble wrapping my head around that."

She seemed to study him for a moment. "I don't think you understand where—or when—I'm from."

"You got that right. You exist in a vacuum. I see you . . . but there's no substance to what I see. No history . . . no culture . . . no background. 'From the future' just doesn't cut it. Does that make sense?"

She nodded slowly. "I think so. We, all of us, are the products of our societies, our cultures. We don't quite seem real if those are hidden."

"And what I do know, I don't like. You . . . you *personally*, I mean, were helping the Nazis. Giving them weapons."

"As I've said before, that was a mistake. From ten thousand years away, the details of history can seem vanishingly small. They get lost in the murk of deep time." She smiled at him. "And believe me, we *do* make mistakes!"

"So how the hell are we supposed to trust you?"

She reached out her hands, touching the sides of his face. "Perhaps this will help. . . ."

An image flickered through his mind and he jerked back as if her touch burned. The image was gone before he could tell exactly what he'd seen, but he had the lingering impression of a vast, open hall, of a throng of people in bright colors, of shapes and structures and dazzling, colored lights that refused to submit to analysis.

"What the hell . . . ?"

"Memories," Elanna told him. "Just relax. Open your thoughts . . . let them drift. Let them simply *be*. . . ."

The image slowly reformed within his mind. The space he was looking at was part cathedral, part shopping mall, part EPCOT, and entirely strange and alien. Thousands of people were traveling through the structure, some on moving pathways, some walking, some floating or flying. Those pathways deserved a second look. They appeared to be liquid, but supported the people standing on them. Overhead was some sort of transparency, a cathedral ceiling so far above him he could see the clouds of an internal, local weather. Beyond the transparency were stars.

He couldn't tell if he was looking through an actual transparent window, one big enough to cover a football stadium, or a viewscreen like the one in Elanna's quarters.

He looked back at the crowd around him. Most were human, though in a bewildering variety of sizes, colors, and body shapes. There were lots of Grays and even a few Saurians. What were they doing here? And there were others; a bloated near-human with legs like tree trunks stood nearby, at least ten feet tall and colored a vibrant purple. Some nearby Grays scarcely came up to his knee.

And there were truly alien creatures—beings so strange Hunter couldn't begin to understand what he was seeing. A pillar of flesh in iridescent robes, twelve feet tall and moving on a writhing ball of tentacles. Its . . . head, if that was the proper term, looked like a cluster of grapes, each sphere the size of a cantaloupe. Sensory organs, like eyes? Or something Hunter would never be able to understand?

Clothing ran the spectrum from vividly elaborate to complete nudity. Human taboos and mores, clearly, had changed with time. Skintight garments like the silvery utilities Elanna wore were popular but ranged in color from gray or black or silver to dazzling neons; many had surfaces displaying animated imagery. Hunter studied one young woman who appeared to be covered head to foot in moving pictures. Then she turned enough so he could see her nipple, and he realized that those were *tattoos*, designs on her body somehow given life and motion across otherwise bare skin.

"An example," Elanna said in his ear, "of nanotechnology as art form."

The panorama of shapes, colors, textures, and light and alien people was bewildering and overwhelming. "I . . . I . . . What am I looking at?" Hunter asked in his mind.

"Kalenviat Limbis," Elanna told him. "I was born here."

"I thought you said you were from Earth?"

The view suddenly drew back, as though his mind's eye was suddenly propelled backward through crowd and walls and transparent overhead . . . and he found himself looking down at a world of blue and green and white encircled by rings as gorgeous and as perfect as those of Saturn. An alien world, he thought . . . and then he recognized the westward bulge of Africa, the near-kiss of Gibraltar with the northern coast of Morocco, the boot of Italy close by the triangle of Sicily.

Much, though, was changed. The Sahara was . . . green and cloud-flecked, with a pale-azure sea connected to the Mediterranean south of Tunis. Shorelines, while recognizable, were ragged and different from what he remembered, as though portions of the coast had flooded. He wondered . . . was the flooded Sahara a result of global climate change?

"The Saharan Sea was a terraforming project from the fifty-third century," Elanna told him, following his mental train of thought. "Geoengineering on a massive scale."

"Impressive," he said, with a steadiness he did not, *could* not feel. "Are you people sure you know what you're doing?"

"As I told you, we *do* make mistakes."

As his viewpoint continued to recede from the planet, he saw the black slash of a vast, curved shadow across the southern hemisphere.

"Ringshadow," she told him. "We use it to fine-tune Earth's insolation and gently control the climate."

"But there's still coastal flooding."

"You should have seen it before the terraforming efforts began in earnest."

Hunter found himself mesmerized by the sight of those glorious rings. As with Saturn, they reminded him of a close-up of an old-fashioned vinyl record, with each groove a separate ring, but so close together they appeared to be a solid surface, dazzlingly iridescent in the sunlight. As his point of view again drifted closer, he began to see the ring was composed of myriads of structures, many, perhaps most, interconnected by threads of light. There were dust motes that might have been the size of individual houses or skyscrapers, all interspersed by larger structures that must have been hundreds of miles across. Gaps in the rings were occupied by planetoids bristling with industrial-looking structures.

He fell forward through a particular key-shaped island within the cloud, and entered once more the teeming cathedral hall of color and light.

Kalenviat Limbis.

"Is Kalen . . . Kalenviat what you call the whole ring?"

"That is the name for just this one hab, a kind of city orbiting with some billions of others. It is one small part of Earthring."

Within the colorful crowd, a centaur—a woman's head, arms, and torso rising from the body of a horse—walked past.

"Many people choose to . . . express themselves through genetic enhancement."

A translucent orange dragon writhed sinuously through the air. Another genetic enhancement? Or some sort of holographic advertisement?

"A remote avatar," Elanna told him. "A virtual visitor."

"When . . . when *is* this?"

"In your calendar, this would be the year 11,995. Almost ten thousand years from your present."

"And you were born here?"

"In 10,801."

"I heard you say once you were twelve hundred years old. . . ."

"Close enough."

"But you said once your home base was in the hundred and first century. . . ."

"It is. Here. . . ."

The crowded cathedral vanished, replaced by a world, a *different* world, one with much of its northern hemisphere submerged within a single, broad sea, its skies filled with the white brush-strokes of cloud, its land areas green and red-brown.

Hunter recognized the world from speculative artwork he'd seen. It was Mars, but . . .

"Terraformed," Elanna said, completing the thought.

"And when did that happen?"

"Sometime in the thirtieth or thirty-first century," she told him. "There was a thousand-year delay because humans discovered native life beneath the Martian surface back in your time. There was a long debate . . . but eventually large preserves were set up and maintained to protect it. They remade Mars to be quite similar to the Earth of three billion years ago."

Hunter's viewpoint dropped down into the Martian vista. He saw a city below, and a tower agleam in the sun like burnished steel. Within the tower, the lights and strangeness were as confusing as they'd been in Earthring. It wasn't as crowded, and there were many uniforms in evidence. The architecture was different as well . . . but still beyond his understanding. Numerous structures the size of city blocks floated in the sky above their own shadows—a casually offhand display of massive antigravitic architecture.

In front of him a pair of people in pale blue and white uniforms materialized out of empty air, walking purposefully, engaged in conversation.

"This is Prime Center," Elanna told him. "The year is 10,062 . . . the hundred and first century. It is my . . . you would call it my military headquarters. It coordinates our operations against the Malok."

"So you're from the hundred twentieth century *and* the hundred and first. . . ."

"Try to understand, Mark. The numbers mean nothing. Humankind operates freely throughout a vast expanse of time, from millions of years in the past all the way through to over a million years in the future. The population of Earth numbers in the hundreds of billions. Throughout the civilized Galaxy, it numbers in the hundreds of *trillions*. We trade and interact with and learn from over forty thousand technic civilizations, which are a part of this tapestry of life and culture spanning millions of years of galactic history. Humankind itself has split into thousands of distinct species and subspecies, mostly through genetic engineering. The ones you know as the Grays comprise several hundred species extending far into the future. Earth in your time remains as a kind of preserve, protected from outside contamination."

"Except that the Saurians are muddying things up."

"As you say. . . ."

"But why are you keeping us *ignorant* of all this?"

"Consider," Elanna told him, "what might happen if a Neolithic inhabitant of Gobekli Tepi was snatched up out of his own time ten thousand years before yours and deposited on the streets of New York City. How much of what he was seeing would he understand?"

"He'd probably be run down by a cab," Hunter said. "Some of those drivers . . ."

"Human civilization has remade itself many, many times since your time. We don't have cabs in our era. But comprehension would be just as difficult for someone from the twenty-first century."

"Okay, so we're knuckle-dragging troglodytes. Rude, crude dudes. I get it. But we've also had ten thousand years of technological evolution beyond those ancient Neolithics. We wouldn't be *completely* lost."

"Indeed. Do you understand the detailed workings of a television set?"

Hunter opened his mouth to answer, reconsidered, then gave a mental shrug. "Of course I do. Magic."

He heard her laugh . . . and the panoply of lights and shapes in his mind faded away. Hunter again sat on Elanna's bed, as she drew back from him. "There may be hope for you yet, Mark!"

Elanna's jumpsuit, Hunter thought with embarrassed discomfort, was extremely fitted, hugging her beautiful curves perfectly. A single small, emerald-green pin or decoration the size of a pea glowed at her throat.

Very slowly, she reached up and touched the stone. Her jumpsuit seemed to blur, then turn grainy, as though it had somehow become a low-res image of itself.

And then it vanished, leaving her gloriously nude.

Hunter blinked, but couldn't look away. "What the hell . . . ?" Hunter didn't expect to see her completely bare, despite being in her bedroom and their close proximity. Suddenly, Hunter felt many emotions rushing through him.

"Another example of applied nanotechnics," she told him, her voice honey, and eyes wide. "Let's get to know one another better, okay?"

CHAPTER THIRTEEN

Superior Universal Alignment: A group founded by Valentina de Andrade in Altamira, Brazil, and including two doctors, a wealthy businessman, a police officer, and other prominent community members. According to de Andrade, the world is about to end, there is no God, Jesus was an alien spaceship pilot, and all male children born after 1981 are the embodiment of pure evil. If these children are castrated and killed, the aliens will accept that as payment and arrive to save those who believe and take them to heaven.

By 1993, nineteen children in the town, ages eight through thirteen, had disappeared; the bodies of five eventually were found dead—tortured, castrated, and murdered.

CULT CONSPIRACY BELIEF,
1980S TO 1990S

"*HUMANS, IT SEEMS,*" *Max said with a matter-of-fact lack of emotion,* "*will believe nearly anything. And no matter how unlikely their beliefs, they will defend them to the death.*"

They'd returned to the office above the Berlin rathskeller. Albrecht was struggling with conflicting thoughts and emotions. Earlier, when he'd first arrived and found himself in the presence of one of the alien Sternenmänner, *he'd felt his distrust of the creature evaporate as it touched his mind. While watching the massed crowds at the Rally for the Return, however, and later as the crowds had flowed through the Muslim quarter of Berlin looting and burning, beating and raping, his . . . questions had resurfaced. He felt deranged, torn between unswerving loyalty to the* Sternenmann *and burning distrust and—yes—fear. Were they allies from the stars, or a terrifying enemy, more vicious, more implacable, more deadly than the Soviets?*

A part of him raged against what he recognized as the ultimate violation, the invasion of his mind, the remolding of his mind by an outside intellect, one cold and dispassionate. Each time he wrestled with the thought, however, it slipped away like smoke, leaving behind only a burning loyalty to a kind of Übermensch *mentor.*

Viktor Albrecht felt like he was going insane.

Was that what had happened to Kammler?

JULIA FELT as though she were standing on an open plain beneath a hot sun in a deep cobalt sky. Fifty meters away, a pale gray monster plucked and nibbled at the tree canopy at the edge of the forest, a canopy easily fifteen meters above the ground. Its movements were ponderous but indescribably graceful.

"Describe what you're seeing, Julia," Bennett's voice said in her ear. "A living wall, you said?"

"It's a dinosaur," she replied. "I don't know what kind. Very long neck . . . long tail . . . small head . . ."

"A sauropod," Bennett said.

Ashley was rapidly sketching what she saw, drawing blind on her tablet. The thing was a true leviathan, perhaps one hundred feet long. Unlike any depiction of similar dinosaurs she'd ever seen, this one had a row of bony, triangular plates down its long neck and back, a strange-looking cross of an apatosaurus with a stegosaurus. The tail was held straight out from the creature's body, parallel to the ground; the neck, the long, *long* neck, stretched upward at perhaps a forty-five-degree angle.

"You're sure about those jagged things down the back?" Bennett asked. "That doesn't look like any species of dinosaur I've ever heard of . . . except maybe in cartoons."

Ashley was about to disagree, surely not all species of dinosaur had been discovered, when fresh movement ripped at the brush and small trees behind her and to her right. Swiveling her point of view, she looked in that direction, and gasped.

There were five of them . . . typical Saurians, and they were clearly focused on the giant close by. It was difficult to guess their size, but she assumed they were roughly as big as adult human males, or perhaps a little larger. They were dwarfed by the monster, though, none of them reaching as high as halfway up to its massive shoulder.

"What kind of equipment do they have?" Bennett asked her when she told him of these new arrivals.

"Nothing," she told him.

"What? No harnesses? No armor or weapons?"

"Just their scales," she said. "And . . . and those claws. . . ."

Gleaming iridescent in the hot sun, the pack of Reptilians rushed the giant, leaping with outspread forearms and legs, claws flashing. Though she usually didn't register sound in her RV sessions, she could hear a shriek, far off, a sound piercing and sharp above the thunderous rumble of the monster prey.

A hunt. It could be nothing else. The Saurians were hunting the sauropod, had stalked it, closed with it, and now were leaping high up onto its flanks. She saw a sudden gash opened in its side, hot-red with blood.

The Saurians used their hooked claws to scramble up the behemoth, working their way up the forelegs and flank, then climbing the neck. Ashley flinched at a sudden, gunshot crack. The monster's tail, short in comparison to the neck, was waving back and forth . . . and then it cracked like a bullwhip, generating a sound as loud as that of a cannon shot. The Saurians, however, were pressed in close against the dinosaur's sides, their razor claws biting into thick, scaled flesh, providing bloody footholds as they climbed, as they *swarmed* up that elephantine hide.

One of them, clinging halfway up the sinuous neck, opened its jaws wide, showing rows of teeth, then clamped down on the sauropod, ripping . . . tearing. ... .

There was an awful lot of blood. . . .

"MARK? WHAT'S wrong? Are you okay?"

"Nothing." He tried not to stare. "Sorry. . . ."

"You're allowed to look. . . ."

"I just . . . I'm not used to beautiful women throwing themselves at me like that."

"You do know, don't you, that your era, your culture, is obsessively inhibited about some very basic human behavior?"

"Such as . . . ?"

Elanna shrugged, which did delightful things to the anatomy of her upper torso. "Sex, for a start. And social nudity."

"And how is social nudity supposed to be an aspect of human behavior? Most of the people *I* know wear clothes!"

"Exactly. It's hardwired into the psyche of most humans in this era. You equate nudity with sex, and you think of sex as something private."

He finally allowed himself a long and appreciative look. After all, she didn't seem to mind. "Well, it's a pretty damn good start. . . ." He tilted his head to one side. "Do all of you run around like that in the future?"

"You saw Kalenviat Limbis. You saw Prime Center. We *do* wear clothing."

"Well, there *were* a few. . . ."

"The point, Mark, is that if clothing is not necessary for comfort in either a controlled or a pleasantly temperate environment, it becomes a means of self-expression, of decoration, not a matter of what you call 'modesty.' Human males all have very much the same anatomy, do they not? As do human females. Differences become means of expression and of comfort, which don't necessarily have anything to do with sex. Many in my time experiment with their bodily form, using genetic engineering to take self-expression far beyond mere textiles."

"Yeah, I saw a few of those, too." But *why* would someone want to change herself into a centaur? He shook his head at the memory.

Certainly, in Elanna's home time, people appeared to be quite free and easy with casual social nudity.

And for that matter, he and Geri had often visited a clothing-optional beach in California. And where was the harm in that?

Still . . .

"But, what the hell?" he demanded. "You take me to your quarters, sit me down on your bed, and all of your clothes dissolve. Are you telling me you're just getting comfy? Are you saying you're *not* trying to have sex with me?"

"Of *course* I am!"

Her matter-of-fact response startled him. "Sorry. I'm spoken for. . . ."

"You mean Geri Galanis?"

He nodded, embarrassed. "Well, yeah. Sort of. . . ."

The memory of Geri still ached.

Elanna looked genuinely puzzled. "You have an exclusive relationship with her?"

"Well . . ."

In point of fact, he and Geri had enjoyed an open relationship. Hunter's career as a Navy SEAL, however, had given him precious little time to play the field, as he'd once referred to it. When he'd had downtime or leave, he'd always spent it with Geri.

"I can see in your thoughts that you both had other partners," Elanna told him. She smiled. "It looks like you're halfway to the hundred and twentieth century already."

"You don't have exclusive relationships in the future?"

"It's . . . a very strange thought. No, not really. I suppose some choose that lifestyle. And a few prefer serial monogamy. But . . . why should the depth and sincerity and *passion* of a person's love be limited to just one person? Why should your ability to express that love physically and emotionally be limited to the boundaries of . . . of a certificate issued by the local government, or dictated by the rote words of a cleric? It's obscene! And it's not natural."

Despite himself, Hunter laughed.

"What's funny?" she asked him.

"Just thinking about how things have changed between my time and yours. Stuff we take for granted as moral you call obscene."

"Morals are, above all else, expressions of *culture*, Mark. Not of what a god has declared to be right, not of some universal and all-encompassing standard of right and wrong." She thought for a moment. "You know, on Earth, on some islands on the Pacific Ocean and not all that long ago, there existed some very moral people. Moral by *their* standards. They had no others close by with which to compare themselves. Among these people, these . . ." Reaching up, she cupped both breasts, presenting them. "*These* were for feeding offspring, nothing more. Attractive, perhaps, as a person's face might be thought attractive. They were *not* immoral, they were not . . . how do you say? Not *dirty*. They certainly were not something to be ashamed of. You understand?"

Hunter nodded. He was thinking of Geri on that California beach.

"The islands were warm, tropical, gentle. Neither men nor women wore much in the way of clothing. And the women routinely left their breasts bare."

"A Garden of Eden."

"Now, this same people had numerous taboos, rules of behavior given them, they thought, by the gods. One of those taboos was *kissing*. For them, to touch lips with one another was disgusting."

"They were okay with nudity, but not with kissing?"

"Exactly. And then one day the outsiders arrived."

Hunter closed his eyes. "Oh boy. I can see it coming. Missionaries?"

She nodded. "These foreigners had their own ideas about what was right, what was wrong, what was disgusting. For them, and according to their religious principles, it was shocking, it was *wrong* for a woman to expose her breasts. Those natives were berated for their immorality. They were forced to cover themselves up, to wear clothing, to abide by the religious laws of the newcomers, to feel *shame*. But why? They simply had different cultural values."

Hunter nodded. "I've heard things like that." Why did it make him feel so uncomfortable?

"I respect the way your culture has developed, Mark. I do not necessarily subscribe to all of its tenets. Casual nudity, casual sex . . . these are things to *celebrate*, not shame."

"So . . . you people think it's fine to have sex with anyone you meet?"

"For us, sex is simply a form of personal expression. It's joyful, it's freeing, it's fantastic recreation, it expands our emotional horizons . . . and it helps build *trust*. And, no, I wouldn't have sex with just anyone, any more than I would choose to live with just anyone. But when I wish to deepen a relationship with someone I like . . ."

Reaching out, she stroked the side of his face, and Hunter felt himself weakening.

And, after all, why resist? She was gorgeous, she was eager, and the sight and touch and smell of her had him fully and almost painfully aroused. He and Geri had not had any kind of exclusive relationship. With the demands of his career . . . how could they?

So where was the problem?

Of course, US Navy sailors had a certain . . . reputation when it came to sex. Sailors on liberty were expected to be sexual athletes. Hunter had never indulged in the stereotypes of Navy behavior, though. In this age of MeToo and mandatory sensitivity training, sexual recreation wasn't as simple as it once had been, and naval officers—at least in theory—tended to be more circumspect.

Elanna was gently unfastening the buttons on his utilities.

If a beautiful woman was throwing herself at you . . .

He helped her.

They touched. They embraced.

They kissed, long and deep and with fast-growing passion. Hunter honestly wasn't sure which of them had initiated it.

And when Hunter came up for air, he grinned and paraphrased *Casablanca*.

"Those Pacific islanders are going to be *shocked*! *Shocked*, I tell you!"

JULIA ASHLEY and James Bennett were meeting in the ship's main briefing room with members of the *Hillenkoetter*'s science team, as well as Captain Groton.

"You think that that behavior was some sort of *ritual*?" she asked.

"Almost certainly," Dr. McClure told them. "You know, on Paradies, Commander Hunter was telling us about the Saurians engaging in what he called a *Jagd*. Human prisoners were released, then hunted down by packs of Saurians who would run them down and tear them to pieces."

"I know," Ashley said, suppressing a shudder. "I saw, when I was RVing Paradies. It was horrible."

"The Saurians are evolved from pack-hunters," Karl Schroeder told them. Schroeder was a newly acquired member of the xenosophontology department, an expert on reptiles, on dinosaurs, and, by extension, on the Saurians. "Probably from something like Velociraptor or Deinonychus. When you saw them attacking a sauropod in the remote past, Julia . . . that might well explain their interest in running down humans for sport or ritual now."

"I've been doing some research, Julia," Bennett told her. "That huge sauropod you saw was probably an Alamosaurus."

"Alamosaurus?" Groton asked. "As in remember the—?"

"*Alamo* is a kind of cottonwood tree in New Mexico where the beast was first discovered," Schroeder told them. "It was found in a geological formation called the Ojo Alamo, which was named for a nearby trading post named for the tree, not the battle."

"So . . . a critter like Brontosaurus, I take it?"

"More like the Titanosaurs, down in South America," Bennett said, warming to the subject. "A real monster—thirty meters long and eighty tons."

"How the hell did you figure out what it was she saw?" Groton asked.

"The Internet is our friend," Bennett said with a wry grin.

Schroeder leaned back in his chair, stretching out his long legs. "Sauropods, they weren't usually armored. Toward the end of the Cretaceous, just before the asteroid put an end to the dinosaurs, lots of species were evolving armor. Seems the big killers like T. rex were pushing evolution along. Julia's sketches showed armored plates on what she saw, and that was Alamosaurus. They were lumbering around in the American Southwest at the very end of the Age of Dinosaurs . . . along with some nasty carnivores like the T. rex."

"And the Saurians," Dr. Clarence Vanover said thoughtfully. He was the ship's senior planetologist, as well as head of *Hillenkoetter*'s planetary science department. "Don't forget the Saurians."

"That's right," Dr. Simone Carter said. She was head of the ship's biological sciences division. "Their civilization was going strong then, I gather? Ms. Ashley's remote viewing session must have connected with that period."

"So what does that tell us about the Saurians?" Groton asked.

"I would think that it suggests they're singularly bloody-minded," Vanover said.

"We know that already," Groton said, "don't we?"

"If they're deeply attached to rituals," Carter told them, "we might expect them to be close-minded to some extent. And rigid."

"What do you mean?" Groton asked.

"With humans, ritual can be fulfilling, even healing. But taken too far it suggests a reliance on form over substance. It can even suggest a lack of original or creative thought."

"I'm not sure that follows," Groton said, looking thoughtful. "These guys are as intelligent as we are. At *least* as intelligent."

"This has nothing to do with intelligence," Carter told him. "Think of religious fundamentalists—and I don't care what the specific religion is. Christians, Muslims, whatever. 'God said it, I believe it, that settles it' expresses a willingness to let holy books or priests or age-old tradition do your thinking for you. Don't think because that can lead you into heresy. Don't change because this is how we've *always* done it."

"You're saying ritual is a way of avoiding thinking?"

"More or less. Ritual imposes order on our lives. It's comforting that way, and helps remind us of who we are and what our place in society is, okay? So far so good. But rely on it *too* much, and you end up losing life's complexity, and letting tradition dictate how and what you think."

"Then again," Ashley said, "maybe they're just really into tearing their prey into bloody bits."

"There would have to be a *reason* for that kind of behavior," Carter said. "Something in their evolutionary heritage that shaped their culture, their ethics, even the way they think."

"You know," McClure put in, "I'm reminded of the formalized mating rituals of some birds. Penguins, birds of paradise . . . They all have remarkably involved and intricate courtship dances. I wonder if they share some psychological traits with the Saurians."

"Birds of paradise aren't sapient," Bennett pointed out.

"No, she has a point," Carter said. "Birds evolved from dinosaurs in the first place. And birds as well as reptiles have some extremely elaborate . . . we can call them rituals, right? For courtship, mating, and for defending territory or mates, mostly. All instinctive, but we can imagine how those behaviors might be extended as a species evolves intelligence."

"So the *Jagd* ritual arose from the behaviors of more primitive critters?" Groton asked.

"Of course," Carter said. "At least the *tendency* is there in thinking creatures to recapitulate more primitive, more instinctive behaviors."

"I wonder," Ashley said, "what we humans do that started off as instincts?"

"Quite a lot, actually. We get pushed around, we get bullied or attacked, we respond with anger. Some of us fight back. Some people repress the anger and become submissive . . . which is just another way of avoiding threat."

"Fight or flight," Groton suggested.

"Exactly."

"Seems to me that's pretty basic for all life-forms."

"It's a big universe, Captain. There may be ways out there of responding to confrontation we haven't even dreamed of yet. And there are differences in degree and detail. We've already learned that the Saurians have a tendency to stay in the background, in the shadows, if you will."

"So . . . they like attacking huge things like that Alamo lizard I saw," Ashley suggested, "but they sneak up on it first?"

Carter nodded. "Partly. They also seem to like manipulating *us*. Trying to influence us covertly. That may be the biggest threat they present."

"And where would that trait come from?" Groton asked.

"Hard to say, Captain. We know they're evolved from pack-hunters. Maybe they were pack-hunters that were also ambush predators . . . like lions. Maybe they hunt in separate groups . . . one group serving to decoy or scare the prey, the others waiting to rush in at the end for the kill. In any case, keep in mind that it's all guesswork, and that intelligent beings *can* work against the evolutionary flow. They have choices that nonsapient species don't have."

"I'm relieved to hear it," Groton said with a wry grin. "I don't like the idea of giving orders as skipper of this tub, and causing all sorts of anxiety and anger when I do so."

"Tyrannosaurs," Schroeder said, a seeming non sequitur.

"I beg your pardon?" Carter said.

"What led the Saurians to hiding in the background? That's a no-brainer. They would have shared their landscape with some very large and very nasty predators. Tyrannosaurus rex, for one. Tarbosaurus, Dryptosaurus . . . all tyrannosaurids. There was quite a zoo of nightmare monsters running around at the end of the Cretaceous."

"Which means if our Saurian friends wanted to stay alive, they'd have to be sneaky."

"Exactly."

"That does explain their recent behavior, their tactics. They tried attacking with their saucers and they got their knuckles rapped. Instead of just attacking again in greater numbers, they tried a whole different approach . . . using their technology to drop combat teams inside our engineering spaces to cripple the ship. Almost worked, too. . . ."

"You know, the ritualized hunting might be a dominance thing, too," Carter suggested. "As a civilized species, they wouldn't need to hunt their own meals, any more than we do, but it becomes a way of saying 'Hey, look at me! I'm the tough kid on the block! You'd better watch out!'"

"Posturing," McClure added.

Carter nodded.

Groton sighed. "Well . . . everything we can learn about these critters is to the good. I just wish there were a way to tell them to fuck off and stay the hell off our planet. And make it stick."

"Remember, sir," Schroeder said. "Earth *is* their planet."

"Not," Groton said slowly, shaking his head, "anymore."

But he didn't sound convinced.

HUNTER AWOKE to the annoying chirp of his phone.

Of course, the device was in its holster in his utilities, which now were draped across the back of a chair on the other side of Elanna's quarters. Rolling out of bed gently so as not to wake Elanna, he got up and padded naked across the deck, fishing the phone from its hiding place. "Hunter."

"Sorry to bother you, sir," Billingsly told him. "We just got an alert."

That brought him fully awake. "Another attack?"

"No, sir. But the *Inman* has rendezvoused with us, and Admiral Winchester is shifting his flag. We've got an assembly on the flight deck, thirty minutes."

"Not full dress. . . ." There was no way the unit could get spit-and-polished in that short of a time.

"No, sir. Full armor, with weapons. I'm getting the unit squared away now."

"On my way."

Elanna was sitting up in her bed, her silver-blond hair spilling across bare shoulders in a glorious tangle. "Problem?"

"Sorry to wake you. The admiral's coming on board from *Inman*. Dog and pony show. I have to be down there to meet him."

"You are neither a dog nor a pony, Mark."

"No, but some things in the Navy never change." He looked at her for a moment. "I'm sorry, I hate to leave now. That was wonderful. But . . ."

She dimpled. "So . . . do you trust me now?"

"I don't think it's that easy, Elanna. I do feel . . . closer to you. And that's good." He thought a moment longer. "Right now, the question is . . . do *you* trust *me*?"

"Completely. But why?"

"I'm going to ask you to come down to the flight deck with me to meet the admiral."

"I would want to be there anyway. But why?"

"I may need you to vouch for me and my people. Even if you and your people disagree. . . ."

CHAPTER FOURTEEN

Reptiloids: Alien shape-shifting reptilians from the constellation Draco have lived on Earth for thousands of years, secretly intervening in human affairs and manipulating politicians, financial leaders, and policy makers. Numerous world figures, including both Presidents Bush and the Queen of England, are actually alien lizard-men who have shape-shifted into human form.

CONSPIRACY THEORY POPULARIZED BY AUTHOR
DAVID ICKE, *THE BIGGEST SECRET*, 1999

THE INTRUSION CAME as an icy shock, followed by a snakish slithering deep inside his skull. Albrecht tried to struggle, tried to scream . . . but the alien Lizard held him pinned—not by physical touch, but by the simple expedient of overriding his voluntary neural control.

At the first touch, he remembered. . . .

But the memories flooding through his brain weren't his. He felt as though he were drowning in that flood, strange, nightmare images of a place and time utterly alien and distant, memories not his but belonging to something else, something terribly other. He saw . . . towers, towers like enormous, flattened gold and bronze mushroom caps on slender stems rising from a thick forest, a city unlike anything he'd ever seen before.

Relax, *a cold voice said within his thoughts.* Relax, and this will be easier for you. I have no wish for you to injure yourself.

Albrecht forced himself to relax. There truly was nothing else he could do.

The real nightmare began a moment later, when Albrecht's arms moved of their own accord, examining his own hands. His head turned, again without him willing it to do so, and he looked at the screen of a television nearby displaying scenes of the riots in Berlin. He felt the . . . the thing looking through his eyes.

He was more certain than ever that this was what had happened to Kammler, a kind of living death possessed by an alien intelligence, unable to move or speak for himself, his body manipulated like a puppet dangling from its strings.

He was aware of several figures in the room with him— Eidechse.

The ice moved in his brain.

Das Sternenmänner.

The Starmen.

The invaders.

"ATTEN . . . *HUT!*"

At Master Chief Minkowski's bellowed command, the troops of the JSST snapped to attention with a sound like a gunshot that echoed through the cavernous flight deck bay. Only about half of the unit was present. The rest were divided between the engineering compartments, on guard against another Saurian incursion. In front of them, a shuttle, a TR-3W black triangle large enough to carry ten or fifteen people, had settled down on its tripod landing gear and extended an embarkation ramp. Standing off to one side of the formation, like the rest wearing his 7-SAS with the helmet visor up, Hunter watched as five men descended the ramp, Admiral Franklin Winchester in the lead. They were wearing the wood-land camo pattern utilities marking them as US Space Force, and Hunter suppressed a wry grimace. As more than one person had pointed out since the JSST had been subsumed into the newly created USSF: Didn't the designers of those uniforms know that space is *black*?

The shoulder tabs were a nice if somewhat larcenous touch, Hunter thought. They looked like the arrowhead logo from *Star Trek*.

Captain Groton and several members of his staff stood close by the ramp. Groton saluted, and the salute was returned.

"Captain Groton. Permission to come aboard." Even admirals had to go through that bit of formality, because the captain of the ship was the *captain*.

"Granted, Admiral. Welcome aboard."

"Thank you, Captain. Break my flag, if you will. I am transfer-ring it to the *Hillenkoetter*."

When the Navy and Marines had moved into space, a num-ber of ancient seafaring traditions of necessity had been changed. There would be no gun salute as the admiral shifted his flag to the *Hillenkoetter*, nor would a physical flag be flown from a mast. He would not read off his orders to the ship's company, since those orders had already been transmitted electronically to the ship's computer system.

In the creation of the 1-JSST, they'd had to make a number of adjustments to routine. Hunter would have been just as happy to dispense with the parade ground bullshit, but it was an extremely useful tool in the melding of personnel from a dozen different services and units into something approaching coherence.

And the brass hats seemed to like it.

Winchester and his staff approached, and Hunter rendered a crisp salute. "Sir! First Joint Space Strike Team, all present or accounted for, sir!"

Winchester returned the salute. "Thank you, Commander."

"*Comp*-ny, *puh*-rade . . . *rest*!" Minkowski thundered at Hunter's back. Technically, he was the senior NCO of the team's Alfa Platoon, but he served as the senior NCO for the whole unit when necessary.

With another gunshot crash, the men and women of the JSST spread their feet to shoulder width and clasped armored gloves behind their backs, or tried to. Parade rest was a drill field maneuver made difficult by the PLSS backpacks riding on their shoulders. The portable life support systems weren't as large or as cumbersome as those used by NASA's astronauts, but they still blocked them from holding their hands at their backs.

"Would you care to inspect the unit, sir?" Hunter asked.

Winchester nodded. "Very well."

"*Comp*-ny, atten-*hut*!"

Hunter walked a pace behind Winchester as the admiral moved down the three ranks of personnel. It was strictly pro forma, of course, ritual for the sake of ritual. Winchester couldn't check the team for haircuts or missing buttons . . . and many of them carried char marks and grease stains on their armor. There'd not been time to service their equipment since the fight on the engineering decks.

"Eighteen," Winchester said when he'd completed the final leg of the walk. "That's not your full complement."

"No, sir. We lost eight KIA kicking the Lizards off the *Hil-*

lenkoetter. The rest are on standby, just in case the enemy tries it again."

"Good. If you don't mind, I'd like to address the men."

"Of course, sir." As if his preferences made any difference to an admiral.

Winchester rejoined his staff in front of the formation. "At ease," he told Hunter's team.

The team members relaxed, but remained silent and attentive.

"Men . . . over these past months, the 1-JSST has done some spectacular work. I gather from Captain Groton that you are almost single-handedly responsible for saving this ship. Well done.

"Your original orders still stand. The enemy has taken over Ares Prime, our base on Mars, and I have been tasked under Majic command authority with that base's recovery. It is imperative that Mars not fall under Saurian control. To that end, LOC is designating this operation as Red Strike. . . ."

There was more, a lot more, but Hunter listened with only half an ear. Winchester rambled on about the JSST's importance in this operation and on how vital was the need for success.

In fact, Majic-12, or MJ-12 for short, was the ultimate voice in the prosecution of the highly secret and low-key war with the Saurians, something to which even presidents were not always privy. They superseded laws and borders, uniting with similar organizations in other nations and maintaining a secret alliance with the humanity of future eras. If they were worried about who controlled Mars, this op must be of deadly import.

Hunter wondered what the concern might be. Mars currently based only a few hundred humans, Talisians, and friendly Grays. The place was a frigid desert with no strategic importance of which Hunter was aware. A base from which the Saurians could attack Earth? Not really. Saurian technology was such that they didn't need bases for such attacks . . . and there were rumors of Saurian bases hidden on Earth's moon that were far closer. So far as he was aware, Mars was important for its several research facilities—hardly anything vital to the outcome of the war.

His attention snapped back to the admiral's speech when Winchester chose to address him directly. "Commander Hunter!" he said. "Is your unit prepared to execute Operation Red Strike?"

Hunter had been expecting this question or one like it, of course, but not in front of half of the JSST *and* the captain and senior staff of the USSS *Hillenkoetter.* But the man *had* asked. . . .

"Sir!" Hunter snapped. "We are ready to carry out your orders . . . with two provisos."

The silence was deafening. Hunter could imagine every man and woman in the ranks straining to hear what might come next, as Winchester's eyebrows jerked upward. He'd of course been expecting a short and sweet "aye, aye, sir" from a mere Navy commander.

"Excuse me . . . ?"

"Sir. With respect, we have two big problems to address in any attempt to retake the Martian base."

"And those are . . . ?"

"Sir, first . . . the JSST is ready and able to carry out this assault *if* we are properly equipped."

"And second?"

"Sir . . . the JSST will need some latitude in both planning and executing this assault. We are facing a determined enemy of unknown strength and superior technology, and our operational parameters insist we enter that base without compromising its air-tight security. That, sir, is impossible."

"Indeed? There are airlocks, you know. . . ."

"Yes, sir . . . and airlocks are extremely tight choke points with two sealed doors, one after the other, which an alerted enemy can quite easily defend. Unless you can provide us with magic Section Six teleportation devices, you're going to have to allow us to make our own door."

Winchester stared at Hunter for a long, cold moment. He had a reputation as a tough, no-nonsense officer, but he also listened to his subordinates. "There's something in what you say, Com-mander. This problem has already been raised back at LOC, and I plan to discuss options with Captain Groton. As for the other . . . what do you mean your unit is not properly equipped?"

"Sir. My unit has not been issued with the appropriate weap-ons and equipment to carry out its orders. The laser weaponry we were issued on Earth is crap, sir, and I gather that Captain Groton and *Hillenkoetter*'s supply officer have been ordered by Lunar Operations Command to withhold decent weapons, weap-ons which *are* now on board, and not issue them to us. Without those weapons, men and women are going to die on Mars when they might not have done so with appropriate logistical support, and that, sir, would be nothing short of criminal!"

Hunter remained at attention, breathing hard after his speech. He knew he was way out on a limb here, going over Groton's head and second-guessing LOC, but he saw no other way to deal with the problem.

If he didn't get the bastards to shake loose those weapons, he would have no choice but to refuse his orders . . . something he had never done in years of service as a Navy SEAL. If they ordered him to squander his people's lives in a frontal assault on a dammed airlock . . . same thing. He was responsible for both the lives of his people and the success of the mission, and that meant it was his responsibility to sound off if either were jeopardized.

Winchester stared at him for another long moment. "Commander," he said at last. "You are out of line. Our Talisian allies are concerned about us damaging the timelines of our future if we attempt to use those weapons without appropriate training. The orders out of LOC stand."

At this point, Hunter knew that he was skirting dangerously close to mutiny.

But he had to press forward.

"Sir. There is a Talisian here who might be able to convince you to rescind those orders." He didn't look around. He'd seen her moments before, standing near a bulkhead behind the formation, easily within earshot.

As she'd promised.

"Elanna!" he called out. "Front and center, if you please!"

"Yes, Commander."

"Admiral, I think you'll remember 425812 Elanna, one of our Talisian liaisons?"

"Of course." He sounded unsure of himself, but he gave her a respectful nod. "Hello, Elanna. . . ."

"Admiral."

"She and I have been butting heads almost since the moment I first met her, mostly over how our allies in the remote future can best help us. She believes that we twenty-first-century humans need to make our own way . . . insofar as that is possible. Right, Elanna?"

"Absolutely, Commander. If we give you everything you ask for, if we fight this war *for* you, you will not develop as a civilization, and that threatens our own existence."

"And at this point, I agree with her. I would much rather the future left us alone to grow and evolve on our own.

"*But* . . . the future has already intervened. Among other things, the Saurians and their human allies in the future, the Grays, gave extensive help and support to the Nazis. Not enough for them to win the war . . . but I think Elanna will agree with me when I say that their assistance may well have encouraged Hitler's megalomania, extended the war, and killed some millions of people, most of them civilians. The V-2 bombings alone—"

"Commander. I *do* know my history. . . ."

"Of course you do, Admiral."

"What's your point?"

At least he was listening. "My point, sir, is that Elanna's culture has been involved in our time as well, attempting to provide *balance*. Without them, the Grays and the Saurians would have wiped us off the map long ago, and with us the Talisian civilization. Is that a fair assessment, Elanna?"

"It is, Commander. Your use of the word *balance* is both succinct and accurate."

He could sense Elanna inside his thoughts. He was pretty sure she was reading him, reading what he was about to say, and encouraging him to go on.

"Commander," Winchester said, "it's not *just* the Talisians.

They're the ones who provided the new weapons, after all. But there are people both in the Pentagon and in Lunar Operations Command who feel our soldiers should not become too reliant on this technology."

"And that, Admiral, is bullshit. If we have it, we should use it."

Winchester gave an expression of mock surprise. "Oh, you mean like nukes?"

"Of course not."

Frowning, Hunter considered how best to approach this. The fact that Winchester hadn't simply slapped him down for having this discussion at all—in front of the assembled troops, no less— was encouraging. But Hunter knew he would have to tread cautiously.

"Admiral," he continued. "The Joint Space Strike Team is composed of men and women drawn from a number of elite US military organizations. Navy SEALs. Army Rangers and Special Forces. Special Operations Group. All of us are *very* good with weapons." He grinned. "You know, they say that *gun control* means hitting what you aim at. That, sir, is something at which we excel.

"We're also damned good at picking up a strange weapon in the field and putting it into operation immediately. Most of us are trained in the use of a wide variety of foreign weapons. And we're very, *very* good at what we do."

"Granted, Commander," Winchester said. "But if you're asking me to release those new weapons—"

"Sir. The new weapons have already been delivered." He was aware he'd just committed the unpardonable offense— interrupting an admiral—but he continued. "Somebody up there in the future has already decided we need them . . . need them to restore balance. And they sent them back here to be *used*, okay? Damn it, sir, if my people are being sent in to attack the Saurians on Mars . . . if Red Strike is so damned *important*, then we need those weapons if we're to even have a chance!"

Winchester stared at Hunter for a long, calculating moment. "Without proper training, son?" he said at last.

Hunter looked at Elanna. "Elanna? Do you trust me?"

Her large and expressive eyes widened, and he thought he might actually have caught her off-guard for a change. "Yes, Mark. I do."

Hunter glanced at Minkowski. He was thinking about the NCO's accidental discharge of an alien particle weapon into the wall of a lab back at S4.

"Do you trust me," he continued, "when I tell you that my people know what they're doing? That they'll follow my orders? That they won't . . . won't misuse their new toys?"

She hesitated, then nodded. "Yes, Commander. I do."

"And I trust *you* when you tell us that you have our best interests at heart, as well as yours."

"Thank you, Commander." She looked Winchester squarely in the eye. "Admiral, as formal liaison of the Talisian Confederation to your people, I authorize the release of those weapons. Effective immediately."

Winchester looked like he was about to give them both an argument, but then he smiled. "I can't ask for better than that. I'll want that in writing, though, Elanna. For when my superiors haul me over the coals for violating *my* orders."

"Gladly."

Hunter gave a deep, inward sigh. Hunter remembered reading

once that no less a personage than Abraham Lincoln had urged his own war department to purchase large numbers of newfangled repeating rifles during the American Civil War and been ignored. The generals, it seemed, were afraid that if the soldiers had such weapons, they would simply waste ammunition. . . .

Command myopia, he decided, was a problem for every military since the time of Sargon the Great.

"You may dismiss your troops, Commander," Winchester told him. "Have them muster in Armory Two and issue them new weapons. I will give the necessary orders. After that . . . stand ready for embarkation. I'll want your people deployed to the planet's surface within the next six to eight hours."

Hunter saluted. "Aye, aye, sir. Thank you, sir."

"Don't thank me, Commander. If I have any reason to regret this, it'll come out of your hide."

Hunter saluted again. "Aye, aye, sir!" Turning sharply, he told Minkowski, "Dismissed!"

And Minkowski turned to face the assembly. "*Comp*-ny, atten-*hut*! Dis-*missed*!"

Winchester and his staff walked out of the landing bay. As Hunter's group broke up, Groton approached him. "You were taking one hell of a chance there, Commander. I've known flag officers who've barbecued upstart commanders over a slow fire and had them for breakfast for less than what you just pulled."

"Sir?" Hunter asked, the word dripping innocence.

"Insubordination is a serious offense. Pulling that shit with me *and* your entire company looking on could have landed you in Colorado Supermax."

"The weapons are here," Hunter said. The confrontation with

Winchester had left him as exhausted as he'd been after the fight in engineering. "We should use them. If even one man gets killed because his four-shot toy laser runs out of juice . . . well, that's just criminal. I couldn't keep quiet about that. Sir."

"There's also the matter of going over my head. I told you I'd talked to the admiral . . . and that he said no."

"Yes, sir."

"Next time that happens I won't bother with Supermax. I'll just have you chucked out the nearest airlock. Understand me?"

"Perfectly. Sir."

"Carry on."

"Aye, aye, sir."

But Hunter knew that he would do it again if he had to.

War was bad enough without getting killed by your own top brass.

LIEUTENANT COMMANDER Hank Boland held his Stingray in tight formation with three other Hawks, adrift in endless, star-strewn night. The tiny, ruby beacon of Mars hung brilliant against the starry backdrop; he could just barely resolve it by eye as a disk, with one polar cap visible against the red as a gleaming white pinpoint.

"Hey, Skipper," Lieutenant Hobson, Delta Four, called over his headset. "How long are they going to keep us parked out here on the ass-end of nowhere?"

"Patience, Grasshopper," Boland replied. "All things come to those who wait."

But in truth, Boland was also feeling impatient. They'd been out here on CAP—Combat Aerospace Patrol—for hours already, and when they'd reached the end of their four-hour watch and requested permission to return to the barn, they'd been told to wait and hold. Something was brewing back there, but they hadn't been told what.

It seemed like the guys actually out on the cutting edge were never kept in the loop.

"All things?" Duvall asked. "Like maybe a whole squadron of dinodisks?"

"Dinodisks" and "saursaucers" were the aerospace wing's pet slang for Saurian fighters.

"Put a sock in it, Double-D," Boland said. "We do not need to hear it."

"Copy that, Skipper. Sock inserted, aye, aye."

The idea of fighting time-traveling intelligent dinosaurs, Duvall thought, was about as weird as it got. Perhaps the strangest part, though, was the realization that these critters had been interfering with human development, causing wars, even changing the course of evolution for centuries . . . and maybe since the beginning of the human species. There was every reason to suppose that the Reptilians were responsible for tales of devils, demons, and night-haunt monsters throughout human history.

So far as he was concerned, it was time to exorcise those demons, so that humanity could go to hell in its own chosen way.

"Starhawk Delta, Starhawk Delta," a voice called over the comm network, using the patrol's current callsign. "This is CIC. We need you boys to go and earn your keep."

"CIC, Delta, we copy," Boland replied. "Whatcha got?"

"Scouting run. They're setting up for a strike op now. Starhawk Delta will take point and lead them in."

"And how did it happen that we drew *that* lucky straw?" Duvall grumbled. "Our watch was up an hour ago!"

CIC heard the grumble. Perhaps assuming the voice had been Boland's, they replied, "Just lucky, Delta. Your four ships are in the best position to shape an approach vector for Mars. CIC, out."

Leaving Duvall to wonder if the people in CIC defined *lucky* the same way as he did.

"'BOUT TIME they gave these things to you," Master Chief Vic Torres said, grinning. "Doesn't do to have them in here collecting dust."

Hunter hefted one of the new hand weapons, a Sunbeam Type 2 Mod 4 laser pistol, a heavier, more cumbersome weapon than the Type 1 . . . but if its performance was any better he didn't mind that a bit. "What are the specs, Master Chief?"

"Forty megawatts, Commander. Settings for either pulse or beam, selector switch here. Improved battery in the grip . . . and you can plug in a second battery here, below the grip."

"Okay. How many shots?"

"With the additional pack, it should give you fifteen to twenty."

"Score!" Minkowski exclaimed at Hunter's side. "That's a hell of a lot better than four!"

"Yeah, at the cost of *two* batteries expended instead of one. We're going to be lugging a lot of battery packs with us, looks like."

"Can't get something for nothing, sir," Torres said. "Now take a look at this."

Hunter handed the Type 2 to Minkowski and accepted the

bulky rifle Torres was handing him. "Don't point that thing at a lab wall, Mink."

Minkowski stiffened. "Sir."

Torres was holding a new laser rifle. "Starbeam Mark 2," Torres told him with something approaching pride in his tone.

It was heavy . . . almost twice the weight of an M16A2 battle rifle. With a thirty-round magazine, the M16 came in at just under nine pounds; the laser rifle with its battery pack connected was sixteen.

But it would do. "It connects to our armor pliss?"

"Yup. Right here. Depending on the setting, it should hold you for a hundred shots. Thirty if it's on its own battery."

"That," Minkowski observed, "should do it for us!" He examined the uprated Starbeam closely. "Damn! I wish we'd had a few of these down in engineering!"

It was about time, Hunter thought. Maybe they had a chance now.

Lieutenant Billingsly examined a Sunbeam. "So why did Elanna's people finally come through?" he asked.

"Good question," Hunter said. He was painfully aware he still didn't understand Talisian policy, though he was beginning to suspect there were different, rival groups in whatever passed for Talisian government in the future. Liberals, perhaps, who favored arming their primitive ancestors against the Saurian threat, and conservatives fearful of a misstep that might wipe out their timeline, and them with it. Hunter thought the technology looked sleek and advanced . . . but probably was no more than a century or so ahead of what human arms manufacturers could produce now. He was still chewing on what Elanna had revealed—a trade network spanning time as well as space. Maybe these weapons had been acquired in the twenty-second century and brought back to the present. They *would* make a difference, though the weapons available in Elanna's home epoch must make these look like bows and arrows.

"The picture I get," Hunter said, "is of the Talisians in the position of Captain Kirk in *Star Trek*, bound by a policy of noninterference with primitive cultures."

"The Prime Directive," Billingsly said.

"Right . . . and the good guys are only able to make tiny and incremental changes where absolutely necessary for the plot of this week's episode."

"Fuck," Minkowski said. "Kirk violated that damned directive every week."

"And who decides when it's absolutely necessary?" Billingsly asked.

"That," Hunter said, "is something we're going to need to explore for ourselves." He handed the heavy laser rifle back to Torres. "Okay, Master Chief. I'll have the team line up, and your people can issue them these babies."

"Aye, aye, sir."

"And what's next, Commander?" Minkowski asked.

"Next . . . ?" Hunter grinned, willing to abandon the struggle to understand Talisian policies, at least for now. "Next we kick some sorry Saurian ass."

CHAPTER FIFTEEN

The JFK Assassination

John F. Kennedy, thirty-fifth President of the United States, was assassinated in 1963 by a conspiracy carried out by the CIA because Kennedy intended to shut the agency down....

or ...

JFK was assassinated by his vice president, Lyndon Baines Johnson, in a power grab and because Kennedy was about to dump Johnson as his running mate in the 1964 election....

or ...

JFK was assassinated in a conspiracy by the Russian KGB because they feared Kennedy....

or ...

JFK was assassinated in a conspiracy by the Mafia as a means of rendering his brother, Attorney General Robert F. Kennedy, powerless....

or ...

JFK was assassinated by the Cubans as retaliation for the Bay of Pigs as well as various CIA assassination plots against Castro....

or ...

JFK was assassinated in a coup by the US military and the military-industrial complex because he was about to sign an executive order ending American involvement in Vietnam....

or ...

JFK was assassinated by the CIA/MJ-12 because he was about to tell the public about UFOs....

And there are others. Take your pick.

CONSPIRACY THEORIES,
1963 AND ONWARD

VIKTOR ALBRECHT WAS *a prisoner inside his own body.*

He could hear and see and feel everything that was going on around him, but he was powerless to speak or move by his own volition. The cold voice somehow had entered his mind and taken over. Albrecht continued to breathe, his heart continued to pump . . . but he was trapped within a fleshy shell, unable to act on his own.

Like one of the imaginary demons of the Middle Ages, der Sternenmann *had possessed him utterly and completely.*

The intruder, he knew, was reading his thoughts, reading his memories, drawing from them his personal experiences during the glory days of the Third Reich. Albrecht carried very specific, very sharp and crisp memories of Hitler as he'd screamed his hatred and venom and searing emotion across the spellbound masses filling the Nuremburg stadium. Memories of the thunder of hundreds of thousands of voices yelling sieg heil *in unison . . .*

Albrecht had struggled to comprehend. Why him? Why bring a Nazi officer forward seventy-odd years to be . . . to be used in this fashion? He'd been walked out of the upstairs room and down into the darkened and smoke-choked rathskeller below, where he'd taken his place behind a podium and begun to speak. Perhaps a hundred people sat in the room listening—long-haired, unshaven, unkempt, undisciplined . . . but blank stares swiftly dissolved into rapt attention.

Surely the Starmen could have . . . recruited one of these unkempt students for the task. . . .

As he listened to himself speaking, however, he began to understand.

"Der Sternenmänner sind unsere Freunde," *he heard himself* *screaming into the smoky darkness,* "und zusammen mit ihnen werden wir über Deutschland, über Europa triumphieren, auf der ganzan Welt!"

He could feel his throat turning raw as he bellowed the promise of victory. He could feel the pain as his fists clenched so tightly the nails bit flesh.

And then, as he felt the cold entity drawing on his memories of Nuremburg, it struck him that the aliens were using his personal memories of der Führer *for their emotional content, for their ringing, mesmerizing thunder, for their ability to reach out and grab hold of the hearts and minds of the people listening.*

"Es wird kein Eurabia geben! Die muslimische Invasion hört hier auf!"

More than that . . . the Starmen were reaching out through him, using their minds to touch . . . to nudge . . . to change the listening human minds transfixed by his speech.

The aliens, Albrecht realized with an icy shock, were using him *to resurrect Adolf Hitler.*

"Deutschland! Deutschland! Deutschland über alles!"

"ALFA STRIKE One launch in three . . . two . . . one . . . *mark!*"

The first modified TR-3W lifted smoothly from the *Hillenkoetter*'s flight deck and drifted toward the newly repaired induction field that again held the huge ship's internal atmosphere safely inside. Behind, three more 3W Mod 2s lifted and followed, emerging from the glaring lights on the flight deck into the chill, black emptiness of space.

Each 3W shuttle carried an eight-wheeled Predator APC, an

armored transport that could carry up to sixteen JSST troopers. Currently, they were configured for twelve men apiece, with the extra space reserved for special weapons and equipment, including a Condor AG Scout Flier. The flight of four transports had been designated as Alfa Strike One; the rest of 1-JSST, designated Strike Two, would follow in one of the larger TR-3B heavy-haulers.

The TR-3Ws had been specially modified to carry the eighty-five-ton Predator vehicles fully loaded, slung to the shuttles' bellies with their upper hulls smoothly locked into the spacecrafts' cargo bays. Things were pretty cramped on board the Predators, with the passengers wearing full armor and PLSS units and carrying bulkier, more massive weapons—the long-awaited PEWs.

Although the Red Strike mission had originally called for just four TR transports ferrying about half of the JSST to the Martian surface, the attack on *Hillenkoetter* had convinced Hunter, Groton, and Winchester that a stronger response was necessary. *Hillenkoetter*'s shipboard Marine force would mount guard inside the ship's engineering decks. They knew what to look for and were on full alert. They should be able to fend off any further attacks.

Hunter hoped. If they couldn't, the JSST was going to be left hanging out on a very shaky limb. At least they'd had a measure of freedom in planning the actual assault.

If they had to kick in some doors to get inside, they would do so.

"Ten thousand kilometers," Lieutenant Jacobs, the TR's pilot, said in Hunter's headphones inside his sealed helmet. A small monitor inside the Predator's passenger compartment was currently displaying what the TR's pilot was seeing . . . a fast-growing orange-red sphere directly ahead—Mars.

"Just One, copy," Hunter replied.

It would have been a lot easier, Hunter reflected, to simply shift the *Hillenkoetter* across a few tens of thousands of kilometers of space before launching the transports. They'd made the decision to leave *Hillenkoetter* in place, giving the transports a longer approach. Winchester's reasoning seemed sound enough, Hunter thought. *Hillenkoetter* was not exactly a *stealthy* spacecraft, while the TR black triangles were. They had a much better chance of sneaking down to the Martian surface than they would if the enemy had been alerted by the *Big-H*'s approach.

And, of course, if the enemy did spot them coming in, hitting and destroying four small and stealthy shuttles would be a damned harder sight than simply blowing the *Hillenkoetter* out of the Martian sky.

Nevertheless, Hunter was feeling nakedly exposed as he sweated through every last mile of empty space between the spacecraft carrier and their objective. Several squadrons of fighters were deployed ahead . . . but would they be able to block for the Alfa Strike against superior Saurian tech?

That was still the big unknown.

"Five thousand kilometers, Commander."

"Copy." Mars had swelled rapidly to fill the television monitor, a pimply, acne-scarred wall of orange, ocher, and brown. The largest pimple—the ice-filled pockmark of Olympus Mons, the largest volcano in the solar system—lay almost at the center of the screen, while the ragged scars of the huge Valles Marineris stretched around the curve of the planet toward the southeast. They were coming in over the dayside; currently, the target was almost at the antipodes, 135 degrees to the east of Olympus Mons, at the Meridiani Planum where the Martian surface was shrouded in the frigid dark of night.

"Commander? Jacobs."

"Go ahead, Lieutenant."

"Message from Starhawk Delta, out front. They say we're all clear for atmospheric entry."

"Copy that. Pass along my thanks."

"Will do, Commander."

No Saurian spacecraft ahead. Were the Lizard forces stretched too thin to cover the approaches to the planet? Or were they lurking in wait somewhere out there, cloaked by their superior technology?

Decelerating sharply, the TR-3W arrowed almost vertically into the thin Martian atmosphere. At this altitude, the air outside was damned near to hard vacuum, but Hunter still felt the shock as they hurtled through the tenuous ionosphere.

In America's *other* space program, NASA scientists often referred to the entry into the Martian atmosphere as "seven minutes of terror." Each time they tried to land another robotic probe on the Martian surface, each time they used the Martian atmosphere to decelerate into orbit, the entire operation took place light minutes from Mission Control; the scientists could only wait in nail-biting anticipation as they waited for the radio signals to confirm success to make their way to Earth. Everything relied on the robot carrying out the right programmed instructions in the right sequence. By the time the scientists got the news of what was happening, the spacecraft had already succeeded . . . or been destroyed.

This, Hunter reflected, was like the seven minutes of terror. Strapped into the Predator, there was absolutely nothing he could do but wait it out.

On the monitor, the icy peak of Olympus Mons gave way to fairly smooth, descending terrain . . . and then they passed over the sheer cliffs and the broken, rugged tangle of canyons, chaotic terrain called the Noctis Labyrinthus—the Labyrinth of Night. Beyond gaped the vast and shadowed maw of the Valles Marineris, a canyon gouged out of the Martian surface five times longer and four times deeper than the Grand Canyon on Earth. The TR-3W continued to descend and to slow, its outer hull red hot now with friction as the spacecraft became a shooting star blazing through Mars's upper atmosphere. The broken ground below blurred with their speed as they dropped closer.

The Valles Marineris roughly followed the shuttle's course east and a bit south, opening up after a moment and giving way to the flat and boulder-strewn plain of the Margaritifer Terra. Craters and sand dunes dominated the landscape; in the distance, Hunter saw the towering, misty pillar of a Martian dust devil moving slowly along the surface, a tornado reaching five miles into a sky now tinted reddish pink.

Moments later, the light outside faded, the sky shifting from rusty pink to a deep, midnight blue to star-encrusted black—the depths of the Martian night.

Still no sign of the Lizards. It looked, Hunter thought, as though they might actually pull this thing off.

Then the Saurian spacecraft appeared, seemingly out of nowhere.

"CIC, DELTA Wing!" Boland called. "We have Arnolds inbound! Repeat, seven Arnolds!"

"Delta Three! Delta Three! Hobbie, break left!"

The four Stingrays of Starhawk Delta had been arrowing into the Martian night at an altitude of barely three hundred meters, flying fifty kilometers ahead of the incoming TR-3Ws. The enemy ships seemed to pop up over the horizon directly ahead, seven of the small Saurian craft called "Arnolds." Crescent-shaped and highly maneuverable, the Saurian ships were approaching the Stingrays head-on, and in an instant they'd passed through the human formation.

Lieutenant Frank Hobson, Delta Three, pitched his Stingray hard to port just as one of the flat silver crescents flashed past his starboard wing. The approach had been so sudden there'd been no time to lock on, much less to fire missiles.

Boland's first thought was that the attackers were trying to blow through the human fighter formation in order to get at the transports astern. As he pulled into a high-G turn, however, he saw the alien ships, after that first pass, were twisting around to come back at them from behind. Was it possible that Starhawk Delta was their target, that the Lizards hadn't detected the stealthy TR-3Ws yet?

He lined up a shot, heard the whine in his headset that confirmed a target lock, and pressed the firing button on his joystick. "Fox Three!" he called, using the standard brevity code for an AMRAAM launch.

His fighter gave a savage jolt, and a 335-pound AIM-120D dropped from its launch bay. The engine ignited, streaming a blue-white blaze of hot gas in the night.

The AIM-120 AMRAAM had originally been designed as a far-distance missile, a long-range killer that can travel over eighty miles, and is extended considerably by vacuum and zero G. This target, though, was still within easy visual range. The terminal phase radar switched on almost at once, arming the missile and guiding it in for the kill.

Flash . . .

"Target destroyed!" he exalted, squinting into the glare. He didn't hear the explosion, but there was enough air outside that he felt the compression wave, buffeting him with a tooth-rattling jolt. Bits of metal pinged off his canopy; that had been *way* too close.

He shifted to lasers.

The four human fighters closed once again with five Saurian craft; a second Arnold had been wrecked by Gatling fire from Duvall's Stingray. The odds were more even now, and the opposing forces tangled in what human pilots called a "furball," a reference to the twisting and intertwining contrails left by dogfighters in Earth's atmosphere. There were no contrails here, however, only targets and friendlies. The confusion and the danger, though, were as real as anything Boland had experienced as a Navy pilot flying F/A-18D Super Hornets over the Middle East.

"Delta Four . . . having trouble locking on!"

"Me, too. They're cloaking. . . ."

Fortunately, "cloaking" for them didn't mean invisibility at visual wavelengths, though there were plenty of stories about them being able to disappear completely. *That* would make dogfighting with them a real nightmare.

They would have to settle this inside visual range, with lasers and Gatling cannon.

"Watch it, Hobbie!" Duvall called. "Two bandits on your six!"

"I know . . . I know! Can't shake 'em!"

Two Saurian crescents were locked on to Hobson's tail. Boland angled his fighter sharply up, seeking the advantage of altitude to scrape those Lizards off his wingman's six. In aerial combat, altitude is speed and speed is energy, though the details differed with this near-magical gravitic technology. Rolling at the top of his climb, he angled back toward the surface, lining up on one of the enemy crescents and triggering the Stingray's twin pulse lasers. At a range of less than eight hundred meters he scored a clean hit . . . he was *sure* of it . . . but to no visible effect. The silver crescent, as it loomed large below him, appeared slightly blurred, the effect of its gravitic distortion field.

Human researchers had long known that the reason photographs of UFOs were almost invariably blurry and indistinct had to do with the gravitic and temporal distortion fields they projected around them. In fact, a crisp, clear, and detailed photo of such a craft was almost a guarantee of a hoax. Those fields also distorted incoming laser fire, which had to be held on a single part of the target for a significant fraction of a second to have a chance of damaging it.

Boland's fighter plunged between the two enemy fighters, decelerating sharply to avoid slamming into the night-shrouded desert floor below. As he fought for altitude once again, he saw the hostiles closing on Hobson.

"Watch it, Delta Three!" he warned over the combat channel. "Watch your six!"

"Break right, Hobbie!" Duvall added . . . and the Stingray began rolling to starboard, then disintegrated in a blinding flash of white light.

Still climbing, Boland switched to guns as he fell into line behind one of the two enemy craft. As he pressed the trigger, he could hear the shrill whine of the weapon conducted through his fuselage from the nose mount, the sound of 3,900 rounds leaving the weapon each minute. He felt the recoil as well as the stream of depleted uranium slugs kicked back against his Stingray's momentum.

The enemy's protective field disrupted incoming slugs as well as packets of photons . . . but unlike laser fire he didn't need to smash it all into a single small area. As his fighter bucked and shuddered, the Arnold came apart. The sharply pointed, sharply curved left wing shredded, and the rest of the spacecraft began tumbling in the thin, cold air. A moment later, another soundless explosion flared against the darkness up ahead.

Twisting to the left, he looked for the second Arnold but couldn't see it. What he did see was the very welcome sight of six more Stingrays arriving at the fight—the rest of Starhawk Squadron. It looked as though the Saurians had noted their approach, turned tail, and run. According to the plot residing in his computer, the planned LZ was just a few kilometers ahead.

"CIC, Starhawk Delta One," he called. "Looks like you're clear for approach and landing."

"Copy that, Delta One. But stick around, okay? We're going to be naked on the ground while we're dropping off our cargo."

"Will do, CIC. Delta out."

Boland began giving orders for the landing overwatch.

"WE'RE ON our approach, Commander," the TR's pilot warned. "Fifteen seconds!"

"Copy." Hunter relayed the information on to the rest of the men crowded into the belly-slung Predator. He'd seen flashes of light up ahead and assumed the fighter squadron was tangling with the bad guys, but there'd been no word as yet of how many there were, or whether they'd spotted the transports.

Fifteen seconds, though. That they could deal with.

And then the TR-3W jolted savagely to one side, slamming Hunter back against his seat. "What the hell?" Gunny Grabiak demanded . . . and then the transport lurched again.

Hunter knew better than to bother the ship's pilots, who likely had their hands full right now. On the monitor in front of him, something bright and metallic flashed past the 3W's nose.

They were under attack.

"SKIPPER! SOME of the bastards got through!"

Dave Duvall had just twisted his Stingray around in a sharp one-eighty to overfly the LZ when he saw the flashes of light a few kilometers off and guessed the worst: the four incoming TR-3Ws got beset by a dozen silver disks. He couldn't tell their type. He would need to get closer.

"Starhawk Leader, Hawk Three," he called. "I think the bad guys just jumped the Trews! Permission to break off here and lend support."

"Delta Leader, Three. Negative, repeat, negative. Leave it for the Sunhammers and the Firedrakes."

Duvall bit off a most unprofessional response. Boland was right, of course. Duvall's wing had been downed, and flying into another furball without a wingman was just begging for trouble. But to just circle the Ares Prime base while the transports came under attack was damned hard.

Where the hell had those Saurian ships come from, anyway?

They'd just appeared in front of the transports—coming up from the surface? Or were they using some sort of stealth cloaking?

Whatever they'd done, the firefight was rapidly moving closer. Pretty soon, Duvall wouldn't need permission to join the fight.

"Delta Flight, Delta Leader," Boland called to the entire group. "Stay tight! Let them come to us!"

The nine Stingrays of Starhawk Squadron continued to circle Ares Prime, though the base below was invisible in the Martian night. The tallest buildings and radio masts showed up on radar, but without a RIO in the back seat, Duvall was having to juggle piloting with his radar scan.

And then the TR-3Ws arrived, bringing with them a cloud of fighters, both human and Saurian. Duvall kicked his Stingray into a sharp climb, arced over, and tagged an attacker with a radar lock. As the tone sounded, he triggered an AGM-114L Hellfire missile, sending it streaking across the intervening distance to detonate with a blinding flash. He tagged another and realized the strong returns were fading. The Saurians were cloaking their ships again.

These targets were definitely not crescent-shaped Arnolds; each was thirty or forty feet across, a traditional, flattened disk shape with a dome on top. From up close, he was pretty sure these were Wall-class saucers, named for an American Army private who was attacked by a similar ship in the Korean War. He lined one up and triggered his Gatling cannon, sending a stream of depleted uranium into the dome, scattering fragments across the sky ahead and below.

"Damn!" Arnold called over the tactical channel. "How many of the buggers are there?"

"Just keep knocking them down," Boland replied. "You'll know when you reach the end!"

White light blossomed. "Mayday! Mayday! Hammer Three . . . I'm hit!"

"What the hell are they using?"

"Particle beams of some sort," Boland replied. "See that spike on your magnetometer?"

"Delta Six! Fox Three!"

"Firedrakes, Drake Leader! See if you can peel the bad guys away from the Tango Romeos!"

Tango Romeo—TR, meaning the TR-3Ws. Enemy saucers were closing on the four black triangles from all sides. Another brilliant white flare lit up the dark Martian night, and one of the 3W transports shuddered, its port wing dropping sharply and trailing smoke. The oxygen content of the local atmosphere was far too meager to support combustion, but white-hot metal and melting plastics left a visible contrail that roiled across the night.

"TR Bravo is hit! Bravo is hit!"

The enemy, Duvall thought with bitter realization, was far too advanced technologically for the human fighters to best in a stand-up dogfight. In past engagements, Stingrays had beaten Saurian saucers only when they possessed significant numerical superiority . . . or when they were being backed up by the fire-power of a capital ship like the *Hillenkoetter*. Right now, with the arrival of the new Stingray squadrons, the Earth fighters held a slight advantage in numbers . . . but that was more than offset by the Saurians' advanced technology. One of the Firedrakes exploded in a spectacular detonation that rained molten fragments of metal across the dark desert floor.

Duvall fell in behind an Arnold, who reappeared once the main enemy force had arrived. He pressed the trigger and sent a stream of Gatling rounds through the lightly armored craft, watching the Lizard ship disintegrate as it attempted to turn out of the line of fire.

But he couldn't keep using his Gatling on every target. With a fire rate of nearly four thousand rounds per minute, a Stingray's Gatling cannon could fire continuously for twenty seconds before it ran dry . . . twenty seconds *maybe*. Twisting hard to the right, he fell in behind a Wall-class fighter and triggered his lasers. He thought he saw a flash off the shiny dome, but he couldn't be sure, and the enemy machine kept flying long enough to fire its particle weapon into Delta 7's ship—piloted by a newbie named Kendrick. In a free-for-all furball like this one, it was almost impossible to keep a laser lined up on a fast-moving and highly maneuverable target long enough to bring it down. He tried to get a radar lock on another saucer . . . and failed. All of the Walls appeared blurred now thanks to the light-bending effect of their gravitics. He pulled in tight enough to deliver another burst from his Gatling, a very short, very precise burst that ripped through the silver dome and sent the craft into a wild tumble.

Saurian technology might be way ahead of human capabilities, Duvall thought, but their armor sucked. Their hulls were strong enough to hold atmosphere but they were paper-thin.

Tango Romeo Bravo was falling, trailing sparks of molten metal like stars.

ON BOARD TR-3W Red Strike Alfa, Hunter watched the unfolding firefight with a hard lump of nausea twisting in his gut, the entire operation now hanging in the balance. According to his charts, they were still some thirty kilometers short of Ares Prime.

Reaching a decision, he opened a comm channel to all of the TR-3Ws and the fighters. "All units, this is Hunter. Transports maneuver and ground immediately. Come down close to Bravo if you can. Fighters, get in close and give us cover. Ground teams . . . I want your RVs moving the instant you touch down. Get clear of your transports and get your weapons into the fight. Do you copy?"

Acknowledgments flashed back. His people sounded ready, and eager to go. On his monitor, another Stingray disintegrated in a spray of molten fragments. TR-3W Bravo hit the surface with a brilliant flare of light.

They had to get down; they were being massacred up here.

He felt the transport's deck tilt beneath him, and the craft dropped through the achingly thin air toward the desert surface. Their ops plan had called for touching down at the base itself, on the landing pad, if possible, just a short distance from the main, central structure. Thirty kilometers was a hell of a long way to move if the ground was contested, but the eight-wheeled Predator ARVX troop carriers were fast and they were armed with Bushmaster 30 mm chain guns in automatic turrets—weapons that could bring down a thin-skinned Lizard saucer if given half a chance.

The Predator's aft compartment overhead lighting switched to red. "Touching down, five seconds!" the transport's pilot called.

The time seemed a *lot* longer than that. . . .

CHAPTER SIXTEEN

Aum Shinrikyo: Founded in 1984 by a self-proclaimed messiah who called himself Shoko Asahara, the Aum Shinrikyo was a Japanese religious/political cult drawn from a mixture of Hindu, Tibetan Buddhist, and Christian beliefs. They taught that people with bad karma should be killed in order to save them from eternal hell, that a coming nuclear apocalypse between Japan, Russia, and the United States would destroy civilization, and that only cult members—the enlightened—would survive Armageddon to build the Kingdom of Shambhala. By the early 1990s, they believed Aum Shinrikyo itself was destined to begin the holocaust, though Asahara preached that sinister conspiracies by Jews, Freemasons, the Dutch, and the British royal family were attempting to thwart Aum's sacred mission.

Toward the end, the group attempted to create a number of chemical and biological weapons, most without success. They were able to stockpile successfully enough crude homemade sarin, VX, and other chemical agents, however, to carry out a number of assassinations and assassination attempts, including the Matsumoto sarin attack in 1994 which killed eight and injured over five hundred. On March 20, 1995, cult followers launched liquid sarin nerve gas attacks on five trains of the Tokyo subway system during rush hour. Fourteen people were killed in the attack, while over six thousand were injured, some critically.

The attack failed to trigger the onset of World War III. A number of Aum cultists were arrested in subsequent police raids, and thirteen, including Asahara, were sentenced to death. The group lost its protection as a religious organization, but was not outlawed. The group continues to exist today with numbers exceeding 2,100—with much of its current membership in Siberia—under the name Aleph. The group has renounced violence as a means of achieving its ends but continues to follow Asahara's spiritual teachings.

CONSPIRACY-BASED RELIGIOUS/POLITICAL CULT,
JAPAN, 1980S AND ON

CHARAACH STRUGGLED TO fully assimilate the human that had called itself Viktor Albrecht. The body, the suppressed mind, the human ego all were fighting back, resisting Charaach's attempts to fully integrate the human as a puppet life-form under the Vach's will.

Charaach had been controlling the Ghech that had been Maximillian Scheuer for decades now, ever since the former SS colonel had fled forward in time from the war and offered his services to the Return. Scheuer had been a good puppet, willing to comply with Vach control even when he was not actively possessed. Unfortunately, these humans had pathetically short lifespans, and Scheuer's body had been on the point of complete failure. Albrecht was still young and healthy, and a good choice for a new host.

The problem, of course, was that young and healthy humans tended to resist outside control, meaning that Charaach had a battle on her hands.

No matter. The Ghech body would conform and do what it was told, or it would be discarded.

After all, there were plenty more where this one had come from.

"BRACE FOR landing!"

The precipitous descent had promised a rough impact, but the TR-3W's pilot flared out at the last moment and the transport touched down on the desert floor gently enough . . . fortunately, since Hunter was already out of his seat and making his way forward to the control cab of the ARVX. The vehicle's driver and the gunner were crowded into a narrow space with high-def monitors mounted on bulkheads to give an all-round feed from cameras on the outer hull. The panorama helped keep the cab from feeling cripplingly claustrophobic, but it was still damned tight, especially for three men encased in seven-SAS armor.

"Get us clear of the ship, Gunny!" he ordered.

"Aye, aye, Commander," the pilot said, snapping off a row of switches on an overhead panel. Gunnery Sergeant Franklin Melrose was not directly a member of the JSST, but he was a part of the highly secret unit's logistical support infrastructure—a Marine detailed to the *Hillenkoetter* assigned as a Space Force vehicle driver. If he was upset by Hunter's telling him how to do his job he gave no sign. With a loud *thunk*, the magnetic grapples along the ARVX's hull released their grip, and the Predator dropped a few inches and landed on the surface with a jolt. "Rolling!"

The view overhead was completely blocked by the TR-3W's ventral hull, but black metal was replaced by star-clotted black sky as the ARVX trundled out from beneath the transport's belly. A tiny crescent glowed directly overhead—one of the two small Martian moons—while near the horizon he saw an extremely bright, golden-yellow beacon, almost certainly the planet Jupiter.

"We've got incoming targets, sir," the Predator's gunner told him. "Three dinodisks at one-seven-nine, range eight thousand . . ."

"Take 'em down."

"Arming weapon . . ."

The eight-wheeled, thirty-five-ton Predator ARVX was powered by fuel cells, mounting one of the new XM813 Bushmaster 30 mm cannons in its remote-controlled turret on its roof. That turret whined as it slewed into position, and Hunter saw the target on the gunner's monitor, picked up by a camera. The red cross-hair reticule slid onto the flat disk of a diving Saurian fighter, and then the Bushmaster chain gun opened up with a hammering *thud-thud-thud* that rang through the ARVX's cabin. The targeted saucer came apart, spilling glittering scraps of metal in its wake as it dropped from the sky. The turret slewed right, picking up a second target, knocked it down, then swung again to track a third. The weapon's radar tracking and stabilized mounting system let it hold pinpoint accuracy even when the Predator was jouncing and swerving at high speed over rough terrain. The troop transport could manage thirty-five miles per hour under one Earth gravity; in the lower Martian gravity it could manage twice that, though a high-speed turn with the lower ground pressure might well flip them. The driver seemed to know what he was doing, however, skillfully pulling well clear of the grounded TR-3W.

"Let's see if we can get to Bravo," he told the driver.

"I think they came down hard, sir."

"These things are *made* to come down hard. C'mon . . . pedal to the metal!"

"Aye, aye, sir!" And the Predator swung about in a wide circle and accelerated into the darkness.

CAPTAIN GROTON watched the main display in CIC, along with Admiral Winchester. "TR-3W Bravo just hit the surface," a rating seated at one of the consoles informed them.

Groton looked at the admiral over the plot board. "*Hillenkoetter*'s firepower could make the difference, sir."

Winchester considered this. "After the battering she's taken, Captain?"

"Repairs are good enough for both fire and maneuver, sir. And so far there's been no sign of a repeat attack."

"If *Hillenkoetter* runs into more than she can handle," Winchester said, "the JSST is going to be stranded down there."

"We have *Inman* in support. All of the enemy fighters appear to be concentrating on our people on Mars. Damn it, sir, we've got to get in close! We can't just leave them hanging in the breeze!"

Winchester considered this, then, finally, nodded. "Very well, Captain. I'll give the order for *Inman* to stick with us and provide close fire support. But be ready to yank us out of there if we come under a sustained attack."

"Of *course*, Admiral! 'Caution' is my middle name."

Privately, though, he was wondering if what counted would be his assessment of the threat to his ship . . . or the admiral's. There always was a delicate balance between what was acceptable risk versus unacceptable.

The ship's captain, after all, had the ultimate say in anything threatening his ship's safety . . . the *captain*, not the admiral.

Winchester might not see things quite that way, but Groton sure as hell was going to give it a go.

"THERE'S BRAVO, Commander . . . another hundred yards. Man, what a mess!"

"Punch it!" Hunter ordered. "Get us in closer! Gunner . . . keep those bastards off our backs."

"Aye, sir."

Hunter opened the tactical channel for the team. "Listen up, everybody. Check your pliss connections and get ready. We're going to exit the RV next to Bravo's transport. Thirty seconds."

"You sure about this, Commander?" Melrose asked. "It's freakin' hairy outside."

"Better running around outside than penned up in a tin-can target where one shot can take us all out. Once we're clear, maneuver away from TR-3W Bravo, okay? Draw their fire, and knock down as many as you can."

"Aye, aye, sir." Melrose didn't sound convinced . . . but he was a Marine gunnery sergeant and he knew how to shut up and follow orders.

Hunter made his way back into the passenger compartment as the Predator slewed to a halt beneath the overhand of one of the 3W's big triangular wings.

"Depressurizing!" Melrose called over the comm system, and Alfa Platoon stood and lined up in red-lit darkness, checking one another's suits and readying their weapons. A few moments later, the aft clamshell doors swung open and the ramp dropped, opening into the black, Martian night.

Hunter was at the rear of the queue, following the line of JSST troopers out, his laser rifle at the ready. For the first time, as he hit the ramp, he became aware of the significantly lower Martian gravity . . . a third of what he was used to on Earth. Even the massive Mk. 2 seemed light in his hands. He cleared the Predator's ramp with a bound.

"Spread out, people! Defensive perimeter. Herrera, Daly . . . set up a G-whiz. The rest of you keep an eye on the sky. . . ."

The Predator was already departing, moving clear of the downed TR's overhang. Hunter saw the Bushmaster turret topside swing sharply, tracking a fast-moving point of light in the sky. The weapon fired with no sound beyond the faintest of shudders in the thin air, and the repeated, three-times-per-second recoil of the barrel.

Without enhanced optics, he couldn't tell if they'd hit anything or not.

"Skipper!" HM1 Vince Marlow, Alfa's corpsman, waved Hunter farther along the downed transport's hull. "We've got survivors here!"

"On my way."

The TR-3W had come down on top of Bravo Platoon's Predator, partially crushing it and splitting its armored shell wide open along the right side. Armored JSST troopers were spilling through the gap, some assisted or carried by their comrades.

"Foster!" Hunter called over the company net. "Foster, report!"

"He's dead, Commander," Minkowski told him. "He was forward."

Damn. Army Ranger Joel Foster had been the platoon leader for Bravo Company. He almost hadn't made it on this op; he'd taken a round through his thigh on Daarish, out at Aldebaran, and had still been limping on a cane. Hunter had told him to stay on Luna.

But he'd insisted on deploying with his men, and Hunter had agreed. If it had been him, he would have wanted to deploy as well, and he understood Foster's need.

Hunter took a quick look at the Predator's cab, which had crumpled badly on impact. Driver, gunner, and Lieutenant Foster all had been crushed between the cab's bulkhead and the control panel when they'd hit.

"Minkowski!" Hunter bellowed.

"Yes, Skipper," Bravo's senior NCO replied.

"Platoon status."

"Sir! Not sure yet. At least five dead, including the skipper. Everyone else is dinged up . . . a couple pretty bad. I can tell you more when Doc finishes checking them all out."

"Okay, Mink. Bravo Platoon is yours. Keep me informed."

"Yes, sir."

It was a damned good thing the ARVXs were as tough as they were. Half of Bravo was still in commission . . . a small miracle given the violence of the crash.

"Mink. Check out the TR's cockpit. Take a couple of guys and see if anyone's alive up there."

"Aye, aye, sir."

The TR-3W had three crewmen—the pilot/commander, the copilot, and a cargo officer, all three Space Force personnel assigned to transport duty and not to be the combat company.

"Skipper!" Miguilito Herrera called. "We got company!"

Hunter hurried to the team's defensive perimeter some twenty yards out from under the loom of the crashed TR-3W. Sergeants Herrera and John Daly were setting up a G-whiz, one of the portable robotic sentries Torres had told him about. Designated as a ground-interdiction weapon system or GIWS—the source of the "G-whiz" nickname—the weapon was derived from the highly successful CIWS robot guns used on naval vessels as a last-ditch defense against incoming antiship missiles, suicide boats, or aircraft. It mounted an M61A1 Vulcan rotary gun which could crank out six thousand rounds a minute, guided by a K_u band fire-control radar and powerful AI software. The system was considerably lighter and smaller than its CIWS predecessors, designed to be set up in moments by a couple of people. Hunter had decidedly mixed feelings about the system but was grateful they had it with them now. Each TR-3W carried three units to assist in maintaining a defensive perimeter. Hunter only wanted one for the moment, as temporary fire support against incoming Saurian targets.

"Whatcha got, Sergeant?" Hunter asked Herrera.

"There, sir," the big man said, pointing to a cluster of six bright lights hovering above the Martian horizon. "They showed up just a minute ago."

"Range?"

"Seven thousand meters."

Hunter's eyes narrowed as he tried to assess movement. "Okay. Are they in approach?"

"Tell you in a sec, Commander," Daly said. He completed the plug-in of a data cable and switched on the unit. A flat-screen monitor mounted on one side of the sentrybot lit up . . . and the weapon itself suddenly came to life, elevating and traversing in one swift, fluid movement.

"They're coming at us, sir," Daly confirmed. "Slow—about ten meters a second. They might be playing it cautious, not knowing what to expect."

"Tell your robot friend to hold fire until they're closer."

Daly typed something into the sentrybot's display with clumsily gloved fingers. "Yes, sir. How close?"

"Whites of their eyes, John. Call it five hundred meters."

"I don't think the Lizards have whites in their eyes. Five hundred meters, yes, sir."

Hunter was taking a risk, of course, letting the enemy ships get that close, but the Predator and the rest of the platoon was watching them now as well, and if they made a threatening move they'd be taken down in short order.

But the Vulcan had an effective range out to fifteen hundred meters—and Hunter didn't want to scare the bad guys out of killing range if he could help it. Those saucers were damned fast, and the sentrybot would get only one crack at them before all hell broke loose.

If the bad guys didn't know what was waiting for them . . .

"Incoming has increased speed to four hundred meters per second."

"Stay with them."

It was eerie, Hunter thought, watching the sentrybot's cluster of six rotary barrels making minute tracking adjustments left and right, up and down, as it followed the targets. They were spreading out somewhat, now. Almost certainly they'd picked up the K_u band radar from the sentry . . . but they might not know what it was connected to.

"They're fading out, sir," Herrera reported. "We still have positive target lock."

The saucers were warping space around them as they approached . . . but so long as Hunter and the others could see them in visible light, the sentrybot's sensitive radar could see them as well. The signal might be somewhat scattered or distorted, but enough would reflect back to the unit's receivers to maintain the targeting lock.

"Here they come!" Daly called, as the six enemy craft grew

suddenly brilliant in the sky. An instant later, the G-whiz opened up, the buzz-saw shriek of its Gatling gun distorted by the vanishingly thin atmosphere into a mosquito's whine. Spent brass fountained across the area in the light Martian gravity. The weapon, programmed to conserve ammo, fired in quick, successive bursts. One of the incoming saucers seemed to twist and shatter, breaking into dozens of gleaming pieces. A second target began rolling over and over, falling out of control . . . and then the three men were bathed in an actinic light, a glare like the beam from a searchlight bringing with it a wave of hot, tingling sensation.

Hunter glanced down at his arm. He'd read reports of Malok weapons that burned, and which seemed to illuminate the target in X-rays, rendering bones nakedly visible.

But . . . no bones, no horrific glimpse of his own skeleton. This might be the same weapon he'd read about, but the JSST's 7-SAS armor was shielding them.

A third Malok ship exploded in glittering fragments as the stream of Gatling fire touched it . . .

. . . and then the three remaining saucers vanished, hurtling out of range and out of sight in a blurred instant.

"You guys okay?" Hunter asked.

"Felt like I was in a microwave oven for a second there," Daly said, "but, yeah. I'm okay."

They would still need to get checked out in *Hillenkoetter*'s sick bay when this was over. So long as the man hadn't been killed outright, Talis medical technology could reverse most of the damage caused by high radiation.

Still . . . that had been damned close.

Other Malok ships circled in the distance . . . unwilling, Hunter thought—unwilling Hunter *hoped*—to get within range.

It looked like they were tangling with the fighters.

DUVALL TWISTED hard to the right, falling in behind one of the Malok saucers. Definitely Wall-class, he thought . . . fast, maneuverable, and deadly. But if he could get close enough . . .

The saucer was on the tail of one of the Firedrakes, and Duvall watched as the Stingray lit up in X-rays, glowing white-hot. Damn! *No!*

He fired a burst from his Gatling gun and watched the enemy ship go into an uncontrolled tumble, but it was too late to save the Drake. "Mayday! Mayday! Firedrake Two! I'm hit!" the pilot called, and then the Stingray slammed into the desert floor.

Duvall released another burst of depleted uranium slugs . . . then bit off a curse as a red light flashed on his console. "Hawk One, Hawk Three, black on ammo," he called. "Black on ammo" was the code phrase indicating he was empty, or damned close. He still had missiles on board—a Hellfire and three AMRAAMs— but he was having trouble locking on to targets, which appeared blurred to the naked eye.

A second Stingray exploded in glittering fragments.

"Pull back, Skyhawks," Boland called. "Everybody pull back!"

But disengaging from a technologically superior adversary was a lot tougher than that simple order suggested. Another Stingray went down, fried by a Malok particle beam. Damn, how many good guys had been killed already? There seemed to be a lot fewer friendlies in the sky now, after just seconds of combat.

"This is Sunhammer Eight! Hammer Eight! Get this guy off my tail!"

Duvall saw the attack unfolding less than half a kilometer ahead, a Stingray in a sharp dive, furiously twisting left and right, trying to shake a saucer hot on his six. He was in the perfect position for an intercept; almost without thinking, Duvall accelerated, turned, and dropped in behind the enemy ship. "Break high, Sunhammer Eight," he called. "I'm on his six. . . ."

He was in the perfect position. The only problem was that he was out of ammo, his remaining missiles useless, his lasers useless . . .

He didn't hesitate. He gunned it.

The saucer *almost* managed to slip out of the path of Duvall's Stingray before they collided. The left edge of the F/S-49 Stingray's sleek, diamond-shaped hull clipped the Malok craft, splitting it wide open. Duvall felt the jolt of the impact; he also felt a peculiar twisting inside his body as he brushed through the saucer's space-bending fields. It wasn't painful, exactly, but it shook him, dropping him for an instant into a bottomless black abyss.

As the enemy ship broke apart, Duvall had just a glimpse of the pilot.

No! It's not possible!

But Duvall had other things to worry about. The Stingray's left flank crumpled, knocking out his port-side gravitic lifters and stabilizers and sending him into an uncontrollable tumble.

Punch out!

That was his immediate reaction, one honed by intense training . . . but it was useless here. Even at one-third of a gravity, he would need a truly immense parachute to slow him enough in this painfully thin atmosphere that he wouldn't be killed when he hit the ground. For that reason, he didn't even have a parachute.

And he was going down. . . .

A SAURIAN beam weapon struck the sharply canted flank of the downed TR-3W, erupting in a dazzling flash of lightning and a cascade of glowing droplets of molten metal raining across the armored troops sheltering beneath the transport's overhang.

"Shit!" former Air Force Master Sergeant Charles Briggs snapped. "I thought it didn't rain on Mars!"

Army Staff Sergeant Lynn Pauly gave a bitter laugh. "Stay out of *that* rain, flyboy," she said. "It'll ruin your whole day!" The JSST's 7-SAS armor would protect them from being burned, but molten metal could fry delicate electronics and melt external antennae and equipment mountings. Enough of it might burn through the tough but flexible material at elbows and knees and hands, causing explosive decompression as well as severe burns.

Quickly, Hunter checked the temperature outside his armor, a reading displayed by a tiny glowing number on his helmet visor. A chilly minus 115 degrees Fahrenheit . . . a typical nighttime low on this frigid desert world. At those temperatures, the tiny drops of liquid metal would freeze solid in seconds; he could hear a clatter on his helmet, like BBs sprinkled across sheet metal. Unless someone got clobbered by a droplet the size of a basketball, they should be okay.

The dinodisks were gathering again above the horizon, readying another assault.

"Cut the chatter!" Hunter yelled over the team's tactical net. "When they get close to five hundred yards, light 'em up!"

Why didn't the bastards break off? Hunter wondered. They'd taken heavy losses so far, and a forty-foot saucer couldn't be cheap . . . though he had no idea of how Saurian economics might work. Maybe they didn't care about individual lives the way humans did.

There were too many unknowns in the equation.

Hunter raised his Mark 2 to his shoulder, using the sight-camera to aim at one of the glowing disks. He held his breath . . . held it . . . held it . . . then pressed the firing button, sending a bolt of laser light into the target . . .

. . . with no effect. The enemy saucer was blurred by the warped space around it, and the Starbeam's energy was dissipated by the effect. He saw a flash from the distortion field, but no indication that he'd damaged the thing at all. Nearby, Herrera and Daly crouched beside their sentrybot. The weapon tracked, slewed right, and then fired. The stream of depleted uranium sliced through the oncoming saucer's distortion field, and ripped the craft into a spray of glittering pieces.

The ground erupted twenty meters away, shaking the overhanging cliff of the TR-3W, and tossing several JSST troopers aside. An enormous dust cloud billowed across the dark landscape, obscuring the lights set on either side of the helmets. Martian dust was extremely fine, and in the planet's light gravity field it boiled up like silt on the ocean floor.

"Daly! Herrera!" he yelled, pointing. "That one! To the left!"

"Got it, boss!"

Other sentrybots were joining in, now, as the other two RVs on the ground moved clear and disembarked their troops. The sky was filled with lights. Bolts of high-energy particle beams slammed into the ground around him, erupting in more geysers of dust and blocking visibility even more.

The attackers seemed utterly unconcerned about their losses, and Hunter wondered about that. He knew the Saurians ruled large numbers of the Grays . . . not all of them, but enough that Grays made up the vast majority of Malok forces. He also knew that most of the saucers were piloted by Grays. Grays had been in the two saucers that had famously crashed at Roswell seventy-five years ago and had been seen in countless Saurian-directed abduction cases. What were they to the Saurians? What kind of hold did the Lizards have over them?

If humanity could crack that puzzle, could make use of it, the Lizards would be put into a serious disadvantage.

And, suddenly, the lights were gone. What the hell?

The dust overhead was slowly settling, and Hunter looked up to see the stars of Orion being blotted out, one by one, as something . . . something huge, drifted slowly across the sky. . . .

CHAPTER SEVENTEEN

Ginsberg Hoax: Supreme Court Justice Ruth Bader Ginsberg did not die on September 18, 2020, but in fact had either died a year and a half earlier or been placed in a medical coma. Numerous public appearances were orchestrated by fake-news manipulators using a body double. This conspiracy was apparently carried out by liberals in order to make certain President Donald Trump did not appoint a conservative justice to SCOTUS immediately before the election. QAnon and other sources also claimed that a Trump appointment before the November elections would result in civil war.

Despite this, Ginsberg was replaced on October 26, 2020, by the confirmation of conservative Amy Coney Barrett to SCOTUS.

POPULAR CONSERVATIVE CONSPIRACY THEORY,
2020 AND AFTER

ALBRECHT TOOK THE measure of the invader. It appeared to have left him and his mind alone . . . but he knew with chilling certainty that it would be back. Its control over him appeared to relax when it slept, but it always returned. Always . . .

But when the thing slept, it didn't appear to be aware of his thoughts. Luckily, he had full control over his body at those times. The Eidechse *had walked him into a tiny room, a cell, really, somewhere in the rathskeller's basement, before abandoning him. He was locked in, in the dark, no way out.*

He held up his hands, flexing them, unable to see them in the darkness, but savoring the feel of their movement.

Yes . . . they belonged to him now.

How could he take advantage of that?

There must *be a way out. . . .*

"COMMANDER!" RM1 Colby called out. "Check fire! Check fire! We have friendlies inbound!"

His first thought was that the Stingray fighters were moving in close to drive off the saucers, but that couldn't be right. There were too many of the Malok craft, and their gravitic field distortion made laser fire and radar locks anywhere from difficult to impossible. The surviving fighters had pulled back.

"What friendlies? Where?"

"Right overhead, Skipper!"

Hunter stared up once more toward the zenith, and just then realized what he was seeing. A long dark flattened cigar-shaped ship . . . The *Hillenkoetter* drifted low overhead, slowly occulting the stars.

No wonder the Malok saucers had fled.

Hunter opened a ground-to-ship channel. "*Hillenkoetter, Hillenkoetter,* this is Red Strike. Do you copy?"

"Red Strike, *Hillenkoetter.* Go ahead."

It was Groton's voice. "Sir," Hunter said. "We have wounded down here. We also are going to need cover for the run in to Ares Prime. Can you assist?"

"Copy, Red Strike. That's why we're here. We're preparing shuttles to come medevac your wounded. As for Ares Prime . . . what are your intentions?"

And Hunter told him.

DUVALL STRUGGLED to right his tumbling Stingray. All of his portside gravitics were out, and as he fell through the thin atmosphere, his speed was great enough to create lift on the starboard side, lift that threw him into a counterclockwise roll.

With no way to punch out, all he could do was ride the craft down. By juggling the controls for his remaining gravitic lifters, he slowed the roll, bringing the nose up to use the Stingray's broad, flat underside to slow his velocity in the thin air. At the last possible moment, he cut in every lifter that still worked, killing more speed as his tail dragged through sand and fighting to keep the Stingray from flipping over on its back.

A savage jolt rattled his teeth as the Stingray hit a sand dune and skipped . . . skimmed . . . then hit again, dragging a long furrow through the desert floor before the final slam of an impact.

Duvall blinked. His head was spinning and his ears ringing. He could hear the shrill squeal of air escaping into near-vacuum, and managed to give thanks to the universe that his pressure suit was sealed, his helmet locked shut. A quick check of his control panel showed the expected: all power was out, communications were out, life support was out. His F/S-49 Stingray, arguably the most advanced aerospace craft in humanity's current arsenal, had been reduced to an inert and twisted pile of junk.

He was pretty sure he'd been unconscious for a time. How long? With his wristwatch inside the sleeve of his pressure suit and his control panel dead, he had no way of knowing how long he'd been out.

His helmet display showed the ambient air pressure—about six one-thousandths of the pressure at sea level back on Earth. Why the hell hadn't they put a time function into the display?

Obviously because the designers had figured he would have a working control panel with a digital time readout.

Out. He had to get out. His pressure suit was connected to the Stingray's air reserves. Fumbling, working by feel, he disconnected from the Stingray's life support system and reconnected to an emergency four-hour bottle stashed beneath his seat.

The canopy release failed to operate. Squeezing his knees up to his chest in the tight confines of his cockpit, Duvall managed to get his boots up to head level and kick, *hard*, wincing at the sudden, sharp pain in his side that felt like a bad bruise from his harness. Ignoring the pain, he continued kicking again and again, until at last the partially sprung canopy popped up and broke away, taking with it the remaining air inside the cockpit in a near-silent gush. Unclipping his portable air supply from under his seat, he pulled himself out, scrambling clear of the wreck and sliding down the heat-scorched hull to the broken, rocky ground.

Alive . . . yes, and achingly alone.

It was still night, so at least his unintended nap hadn't lasted too long. A tiny, misshapen half-moon disk hung among the stars halfway down from the zenith. The information didn't help him; he didn't know which directions were which. Ares Prime should be somewhere to the east, something like thirty kilometers distant.

"Red Strike, Red Strike, this is Starhawk Delta Four. Do you copy?"

He heard no reply.

"Red Strike, Red Strike, Delta Four. Come back, please."

Nothing.

Well, the TR-3W transports had been pretty low to the ground, so they would be below the horizon from him. The other fighters, though . . .

He shifted to the Starhawk's general comm frequency. "Starhawk Delta, Starhawk Delta, this is Double-D. Do you copy?"

According to an amber light on his helmet display, his suit radio was working. Unfortunately, no one seemed to be listening.

Most likely, they were out of range. His suit radio was good for short-range communications, five or ten kilometers, maybe more . . . but it was intended for use with a partner close by. He couldn't reach any of the Martian comsats overhead, and he had to be in line of sight to reach anyone else on the surface. How far was the Martian horizon? He wasn't sure, but it wasn't very far.

So the question was . . . should he walk or stay put? Eighteen miles was a hell of a hike, especially at night, in a desert, and with, at best, only a few hours of life in his bulky air tank. Even under the light Martian gravity, it would be a stretch to hotfoot it that far, that fast.

Much worse . . . Mars had no magnetic field to speak of, so his suit's compass wasn't working. Which way was east?

Possibly he'd be better off sticking with his downed Stingray. In flight training and survival school back home, they'd always hammered at the theme that it was best to stay with your spacecraft if you were downed. The wreckage of a fighter was a lot easier to spot from overhead than a solitary human figure alone in all of that barren emptiness. The wreck should be broadcasting a distress signal, but he wasn't picking anything up on his suit radio, and so as far as he could tell all of the Stingray's electronics were dead.

Still, if someone had caught his mayday earlier, they *might* at least deploy a fighter to come check him out.

The fighter squadrons had been pretty busy when he'd collided with that dinodisk. A lot of Stingrays had been destroyed in that furball, and he was one of many out here. He just happened to be alive. . . .

He sagged. Hell, maybe he'd be better off walking. At least he would be *doing* something, even if he never made it to Ares Prime.

Duvall looked up again at the Martian moon, which had visibly dropped toward the horizon just during the past few minutes. He remembered having heard that the inner Martian moon went around the planet pretty fast, fast enough that you could actually see its movement in the sky, moment by moment. Okay . . . if it was setting, it would be in the west, which would be in *that* direction. He knew he was standing on the equator, so west would be directly beneath the quickly and vertically descending moon. Turning in place, he looked in the opposite direction, noting the stars above the horizon. One stood out brighter than the rest. *That*, near enough, would be east.

Back on Earth, he'd done long-distance runs regularly, including a couple of marathons, and he was in decent shape, regularly clocking a mile in ten minutes. He should be able to get to Ares Prime in three hours easily and with an hour to spare . . . *if* he could keep up that pace for that long, and if he didn't get lost along the way.

On the plus side, he was certain of his overland navigation skills. Three hours of jogging, using the stars to hold to a straight course, should at least bring him within range of the Red Strike transports as they attacked Ares Prime, close enough that he could make contact over his suit's radio. He'd just keep going until he heard the JSST chatter, then yell for help.

He secured the air tank over the shoulder of his pressure suit.

Four hours of life . . . eighteen miles . . .

Yeah, he should be able to pull that off, with no problem.

He began walking, then broke into an easy, ground-eating jog.

"CALL IT two minutes, Commander," Captain Groton said over the radio. "Almost there."

"Rog."

Once again, Hunter was squeezed into the troop bay of an ARVX Predator slung beneath the belly of a TR-3W black-triangle transport. All three surviving 3Ws were skimming east above the night-cloaked desert while, somewhere overhead, the star carrier *Hillenkoetter* paced the transports, providing overwatch.

In fact, only 3W Alfa was carrying a strike platoon inside an RV. The other two were flying escort, providing a waiting and thoroughly alerted enemy with three targets instead of just one. It was a cold application of tactics, but Hunter knew they needed to squeeze every advantage they could out of the tacsit, even the slimmest. Bravo, Charlie, and Delta Platoons were bringing up the rear in their RVs, high-tailing it overland across the Martian desert. While Predators could clock forty kilometers per hour off-road—faster, probably—under Martian conditions, they were traversing unknown terrain, rugged in some places, blocked by sand dunes in others. Still, they should reach Ares Prime within thirty minutes, providing the attack with an excellent tactical reserve. Hunter had put the team's XO, Billingsly, in charge, with orders to get all three platoons to Ares Prime as quickly as possible.

And that, Hunter thought, was one of a very few bright spots in a mission that had all but gone to hell. Red Strike's op-plan still called for an attempt to get into Ares Prime without shooting the place up . . . but the fact that they'd been accosted by a fleet of Saurian spacecraft had pretty well deep-sixed that idea. Hunter's plan, as he'd relayed earlier to Groton, called for a two-pronged attack on the base.

And Alfa Platoon was the sharp point of the spear.

"There's the doughnut," the TR's pilot reported over the comm system. "Thirty seconds."

Hunter could see it on his monitor. The sun was just beginning to light up the eastern horizon, and the sky was bright enough now that he could make out the shape of the huge, central torus of the base. Red strobes blinked atop several radio masts, and a handful of the small *Zdal*-class scout saucers were scattered across the landing pad. The larger craft were nowhere to be seen. Had they fled? Or were they simply regrouping somewhere for another assault?

"Those scouts could cause us trouble, Captain," Hunter said. "If you would be so kind . . . ?"

"Already on it."

The *Hillenkoetter* possessed powerful high-energy lasers, particle beam weapons, and a spinal railgun that could accelerate small lumps of metal to serious velocities. It was the laser banks to which Groton addressed his next command. "Batteries one and three! Target those grounded saucers! *Fire!*"

Light glared through the television monitor on the Predator's bulkhead as, one by one, the ships on the tarmac flared into white-hot incandescence. With no shields, no special distortion fields, they were reduced to charred and unrecognizable fragments in seconds.

"Ten seconds, Commander!" the TR-3W pilot said through their headset. "Hold on!"

The black triangle flared into a nose-high touchdown just a few dozen yards from the curving shell of the doughnut. An instant later, the magnetic grapples released the Predator, and the eight-wheeled vehicle lurched forward, clearing the transport and racing into the open. This was the deadliest moment of their assault. If the Saurians had had time to mount weapons on or near the aboveground portion of the command center, the platoon would be driving full-tilt into a crossfire. Hunter was counting on the probability that the enemy hadn't had time to harden the unarmed base's defenses.

But nothing was ever certain in combat.

The lone RV slewed to a halt, and the rear ramp dropped. Twelve JSST troopers spilled out and rapidly dispersed, forming a loose defensive perimeter, their new weapons out and at the ready.

"*Hillenkoetter*, Red Strike," Hunter called. "We're on the beach. Request you deploy the door-kicker. . . ."

In close-quarters combat, a "door-kicker" was the guy on point who blew open a locked door, giving admittance to the rest of the team. He might be someone like Minkowski with his shotgun . . . or the demo guy who employed thermite or C4 who would literally break the door down.

"Commander Hunter," a new voice said. "This is Winchester."

"Yes, Admiral."

"I remind you to keep damage to the facility to an absolute minimum."

"Roger that, sir."

Hunter wasn't going to argue any further. He'd already presented his arguments, and he knew that Groton had later and privately argued himself blue in the face to convince Winchester that breaking things to get into Ares Prime was going to be necessary.

He just hoped the brass wasn't going to yank the rug out from under at the last moment . . . or try to micromanage 1-JSST to death.

He could picture Winchester hovering over Groton as *Hillenkoetter*'s skipper tried to manage the assault from the sky.

"Taylor!" Hunter called. "Time to shoot off some fireworks." He pointed. "Right there."

The side of the doughnut closest to the tarmac was set off by what looked like a large garage door. That would be the main ground-level storeroom, Hunter knew. He'd studied schematics of Ares Prime's layout to plan the attack. He'd indicated the garage door . . . and EN1 Thomas Taylor was crouched beside it, opening a canvas shoulder bag.

Taylor had been told off as Alfa's boomer—the demolitions man. In this case, however, he wasn't blowing anything up. He pulled out a large squeeze tube of Neelymite.

Neelymite had been invented by Kelsay Neely as part of her master of science thesis before going on to work as an aerospace engineer at NASA. The name was a portmanteau created from Neely's name and thermite—the rust, aluminum, and magnesium cocktail that burned at over 5,100 degrees Fahrenheit and which had been used by military forces worldwide for well over a century. Neely's contribution to the formula was to make a 3D-printable *paste* with the consistency of peanut butter. Taylor used the squeeze tube to lay out a long string of the stuff onto the garage door, defining an oval five feet high and perhaps three wide. An extra dollop of paste went onto the top of the arch. After carefully putting the tube away, Taylor took a magnesium binary igniter, pushed it into the thermite blob, and crushed the glass capsule on the free end.

"Everybody stay back and stay down!" Hunter ordered.

Hunter watched from a safe distance, thinking thermite was wonderful stuff. Based on iron oxide—rust—it carried its own oxygen supply, and so could be used underwater, in space, or here in the vanishingly thin atmosphere of Mars. It needed the heat produced by burning magnesium to kindle it; ordinary blasting caps or det cord simply weren't hot enough to set it off. Once ignited, though, there was no way to put it out, and it would cheerfully melt through engine blocks, the breech of an artillery piece, or, in this case, a solid steel pressure door.

"Fire in the hole!" Taylor yelled, then gathered up his bag, turned, and bolted for cover in the light Martian gravity. It took several seconds for the binary chemicals in the igniter to combine, grow hot, and ignite the magnesium, which in turn set off the thermite paste with an eye-searing white heat that left a temporary oval shadow across Hunter's vision. It burned . . . burned . . . and then it *did* explode, the cut-out section of door hurtling out into the desert on the end of a piledriver of escaping atmosphere. The brief wind created a fireball as oxygen escaping from the building fanned vaporizing iron and aluminum. The jet raised a whirling storm of dust in front of the doorway. Much of the dust was iron oxide and that caught fire, too, briefly.

Then the last of the air inside the room on the other side of the garage door dwindled away to almost nothing. The edges of the newly cut entryway glowed red hot in the predawn darkness.

"Let's go, people!"

The twelve JSST troopers rose from their positions and rushed to the hole. Behind them, the ARVX opened up with its Bushmaster, sending a stream of depleted uranium slugs tearing through the opening and into the room beyond. Dust raised by the depressurization continued to hang over the tarmac, and provided them with a welcome measure of cover as they ran.

During the initial planning, Hunter and Groton had considered using *Hillenkoetter*'s primary weapon, a railgun running the length of her keel, a magnetic accelerator that could hurl relatively small slugs of metal at speeds of tens of thousands of meters per second. They'd eventually settled on thermite paste, however, which was more . . . surgical.

The hole looked to Hunter as if a slug had punched cleanly through, like a bullet through sheet metal. Precision meant that at least the entire command center hadn't been reduced to junk like those scout ships outside.

As the team neared the opening, the Predator's Bushmaster ceased fire. By now, the hurricane of escaping air had faded to nothing. Sergeant Aliya Moss was the first one through.

"Tight fit, Skipper!" she called from inside. "And watch the edges! They're hot!"

Hunter had expected as much. Seven-SAS armor should protect them all from the molten-hot edges of the metal shell, at least from an accidental brush. Herrera was next through, stooping nearly double to fit, followed by Daly and Colby. Hunter followed.

The room beyond, which was right next to the landing tarmac, turned out to be a large airlock. "Taylor!" Hunter called. He pointed at one of the sealed doorways. "Blow it!"

"Aye, aye, Skipper."

Again, Taylor applied the detonator. The team retreated back outside, out of harm's way. The magnesium detonator lit up the darkened room as the thermite took fire, and once again a neatly cut-out section of pressure door rocketed into the center of the storeroom, bringing with it a roaring blast of air.

That roar lasted for a much longer time before it dwindled away into still silence. Beyond that was the base cargo receiving area, a large storeroom with rows of metal shelves and stacks of aluminum crates and a large number of steel cylinders of compressed gas all thoroughly trashed by *Hillenkoetter*'s shot. The room was pitch-black, the contents revealed in dancing confusions of light and shadow as the platoon moved into it, partially illuminating it with their helmet lights. Movement caught Hunter's eye and he turned. An oxygen cylinder, its valve cracked by the blast of escaping air, spun wildly and silently on the floor.

Several doors were spaced along the storeroom's inner walls. Gunnery Sergeant Joan Nicholson hurried over to one and tried the handle. "Sealed," she announced.

Hunter had expected this. "Just like back on the *Big-H*," he said. "When the pressure started dropping, every door in the place slammed shut and sealed tight."

The base on Mars, he knew, had been constructed with the knowledge that meteor strikes on the planet's surface were common. The heavily cratered landscape gave silent testimony to the threat; the thin Martian air couldn't vaporize the majority of incoming rocks as was the case on Earth. Habitats on the planet either needed to have numerous and separate pressurized compartments, or they needed to be built underground. Ares Prime had both aboveground structures and subsurface living quarters protected from ultraviolet radiation and meteor impacts.

"Briggs," Hunter said. "That door. Taylor, give him a hand."

Master Sergeant Charles Briggs had been an Air Force combat control specialist, a forward observer until his transfer to the US Space Force. His training was heavy in combat communications, but had included a heavy dose of electronics in general. The two men found an access panel next to a keypad to the right of the sealed pressure door and began working at it. The pressure door's technology was akin to that of a garage door opener on Earth; Briggs had used a small, handheld computer to cycle through the ten thousand possible combinations of four digits in a few seconds.

"Red Strike, CIC," sounded in his helmet speakers. It was Admiral Winchester rather than Groton, not entirely to Hunter's surprise. "Talk to me. What's going on in there?"

"We're through the airlock, sir," Hunter replied, "and inside the main cargo area. Working on the inner door now. If we can open the thing without blowing a hole in it, we will."

"Good. Keep me informed."

"Aye, aye, sir."

Winchester's concern for the local architecture certainly was understandable, Hunter thought . . . but if his boomer and his electronics specialist weren't through that door in three minutes flat, he'd have Taylor use the Neelymite.

The plans he'd studied told him beyond this door was a long hallway that ran in a circle through Ares Prime's ground-level floor. If they could evacuate that, they would have access to the interior of the building, and Saurians on this level would be trapped inside their individual rooms. If they could get through this door the platoon actually would have a significant advantage. The Lizards would be trapped, even if they had pressure suits of their own, while Red Strike could move where it wanted.

The problem was in deciding where that might be. According to the floor plans, there was a command-control center one level up, and an engineering deck one level down. Both would have plenty of armed Saurians inside. Attacking the upper deck would have the advantage of decapitating the enemy's command staff.

But Hunter wasn't yet sure that that would be the best option.

"CIC, Red Strike," he called. "Put me through to RV-Eye."

"RV" in this instance didn't refer to the Predators, but to remote viewing. Julia Ashley would be in her quarters on board the *Hillenkoetter*, using her uncanny psychic skills to peer inside Ares Prime, a literal RV-Eye in the sky. She'd done it before, and ought to have a fair idea of where things were by now.

At least, he hoped.

"This . . . this is Julia," she said. "I'm here."

"Hey, Julia. This is Mark Hunter, inside the base, ground level. I need to know where the Lizard teleport equipment is."

"I've been watching it, Mark. There are a lot of Saurians there. Maybe twenty . . . twenty-five. And I think it's underground."

"In the basement. You're sure?"

"That's what I've been getting. There are big generators in there, some sort of a power plant. Lots of electrical cables, some of them as big around as my arm. I think they set up their stuff where they could draw on the base power plant directly."

"That would make sense. Are we over it now?"

There was a long hesitation. "No. It's a big, circular room

carved out of bedrock, and it's directly below the doughnut's central column."

"Okay. Stand by. I'll call you back."

"Commander!" Briggs called. "We're ready to pop this puppy!"

He was holding a hand controller, like a television remote. The access panel was off, and Hunter could see a tangle of wires inside. The remote was directly attached to the wires by several alligator clips.

"You found the code?"

"I think so, sir. Got a green light when we hit the right numbers."

"Right. Now hear this, everybody! Get back and hang on! We're about to open another door!" He braced himself, holding his Mark 2 Starbeam at the ready. The team took shelter against the storeroom walls, well back from the door.

Holding his breath, Briggs pressed a button on his controller.

The door began to open as the now familiar pile driver of air exploded into the storeroom.

CHAPTER EIGHTEEN

Vaccination: The use of vaccines against various diseases has been linked to autism in children. . . .

or . . .

The use of vaccines is actually part of a systematic and nefarious plot against Muslims/Blacks/poor people/excess population/political undesirables. . . .

or . . .

The use of vaccines is actually a means of injecting nano-technic surveillance or mind-control devices into the general population. . . .

or . . .

The use of vaccines is actually a means of sterilizing undesirable populations. . . .

or . . .

The use of vaccines—from the Latin *vaccinae*, meaning "from cows"—introduces bestial humors into humans and can give them cowlike features. . . .

or

The use of vaccines is an offense against God. . . .

Take your pick.

ANTI-VAX CONSPIRACY THEORIES,
1794 AND ON

"SSST! HALLO! WHO is there?"

Albrecht leaned against the solid, wooden door, speaking in a fierce whisper. If the Eidechse *that possessed him really was asleep, he didn't want to awaken it.*

Could he awaken it? Technically, it still had a body of its own, though somehow it was able to override his own brain's higher functions and substitute for them its own. It wasn't as if the Eidechse *was actually inside his skull.*

He didn't think that was the case.

He hoped *it wasn't. . . .*

He could hear someone moving just outside the door. He was taking a fearful chance trying to get their attention, but somehow, he had to get out of this tiny, locked room.

He heard the scrape of a bolt being drawn. . . .

The door opened, and Albrecht squinted into the light outside. His rescuer was a young woman, the blonde he'd seen dancing onstage earlier . . . though she now was wearing a white robe.

"Herr Oberst!" she cried aloud. "What are you doing in there?"

"Never mind! I've got to—"

And the Eidechse *awoke.*

THE JSST assault team stayed crouched against the walls as the chamber beyond the next door emptied itself of air. Hunter found himself fascinated by what looked like white vapor emerging from the open door with a shrill roar, then realized he was seeing water vapor in the air entering the minus-100-degree ambient temperature and condensing into a visible cloud of tiny ice crystals—just like watching your breath on a cold day.

After a moment, a body came through . . . one of the small Grays. Hunter wondered if the being had been one of the human allies at the base, or if it had worked for the Lizards. Either way, it was dead . . . or would be in another minute or two.

The thundering roar raised in pitch and dwindled, until it had faded away into inaudibility.

"Red Strike Alfa, this is Billingsly. Do you copy?"

"God, yes, copy! This is Hunter. Go."

"We're just coming up on Ares Prime. Where do you want us?"

Hunter felt a warm rush of relief. The other three platoons had arrived. While he'd taken advantage of the tactical opportunities he'd encountered so far, attacking an unknown hostile force with twelve men was *not* sound military tactics.

"The garage door at the tarmac. You'll see the mess we made. C'mon in!"

"On our way."

"Let's go," Hunter said . . . but before the team could move into position a black figure came through the door. Seven feet tall and covered with gleaming, metallic skin, the figure appeared to be one of the big Reptilians, wearing close-fitting combat armor and a long, curving helmet. The creature was armed with a device that might have been some sort of laser weapon, sleeker and less bulky than the JSST's new Mark 2s. Unlike the Gray, it was fully in control of itself as it stepped into the storeroom and bashed Briggs aside with the weapon's stock. Hunter raised his own laser weapon and triggered a burst of high-energy coherent light; four other JSST troops fired at the same instant, and the armored Lizard twisted, pinwheeled, and collapsed on the floor, blood and freezing vapor jetting from black-rimmed vents in the suit.

"Someone grab that weapon," Hunter called. "Let's see if we can make it work."

Master Sergeant Coulter, Alfa's senior NCO, stooped and retrieved the weapon. "Got it, boss!"

JSST personnel, as Hunter once had remarked, were *very* good with weapons, even those of foreign manufacture. Hell, you couldn't get much more foreign than that thing, but he trusted Coulter to be able to figure it out.

Beyond the opened door was a long, gently curving passageway, a corridor that Hunter knew from the floor plans ran all the way around the interior of the doughnut. Several more unarmored Grays lay dead on the floor, suffocated by the sudden decompression.

Hunter led the team toward the right.

"RV-Eye, this is Red Strike. Which way to the basement?"

"There's a stairway ahead of you, Mark," Ashley's voice told him. "But there are Saurians waiting at the bottom."

"In armor? Space suits?"

"Some of them, yes."

"Does this hallway we're in pass over the basement?" He was trying to recall subtle details from the floor plans he'd studied, but was having trouble remembering how the ground level fit over the large power plant room one level down.

"Do you see a stairway? You should be close."

"Affirmative." A pressure-sealed doorway ahead was marked "Stairs." A small, square window looked into the stairwell beyond.

"About ten feet to the left of that door. That's right above the center of the lower level."

"Got it."

Hunter ordered Taylor to squeeze out an oval of Neelymite, a *big* oval some twelve feet long and four feet wide.

Coulter was leaning against the door to the stairwell, clutching the alien laser. "Hey, Skipper?"

"What?"

"I can see a pressure gauge on the other side of the door. It's dropping."

Shit. Those stairwells served as airlocks between floors. Dropping pressure meant—

"You see any Lizards?"

"Uh . . . yessir! They're coming up the stairs now! Heavy armor and weapons!"

"Stay clear of that window. Herrera! Nicholson! Dumont! Cover that door! You, too, Coulter! If they come through, pin them in the bottleneck!"

"Aye, aye, sir!"

Four sets of laser weaponry were aimed at the sealed door. The rest of the team stood well back from Taylor's oval on the floor.

The door swung open as the pressure on the other side dwindled to zero, and a half dozen armored Lizards surged for the opening. The waiting JSST troopers opened fire, cutting into the mass of enemy figures as they jammed up against one another in the narrow opening. One of them managed to get off a shot, catching Sergeant John Dumont in his helmet and dropping him instantly to the floor. Coulter fired the massive alien weapon from the hip and vaporized the shooter's chest plate, then swept the beam across the other Lizards crowding in behind.

A moment later, Taylor called "Fire in the hole!" and triggered the magnesium detonator. The thermite oval flared to a silent, deadly brilliance as droplets of molten metal scattered across the passageway. A forty-eight-square-foot section of the deck shot straight up, propelled by the blast of escaping air, struck the ceiling, and shattered as freezing vapor exploded from the hole beneath. The human troops edged up to the steaming hole, firing into its depths, the haze of freezing vapor making the beams from their lasers starkly and radiantly visible.

Hunter peered over the rim of the hole and saw movement below, blurred by swirling vapor. The drop was roughly twelve feet; in Martian gravity the impact would translate to about four feet on Earth. "Just-One!" he yelled. "With me!"

He stepped off into empty space. "*Hoo-yah!*" He screamed the Navy SEAL battle cry as he fell, dropping through the mist. He got off several wild shots before he hit concrete, flexing his knees to absorb the impact, then immediately rushed forward to get out from under as armored 1-JSST troops followed. More battle cries of other military services rang over the tactical channel, a mangled cacophony: "*Ooh-rah!*" Marines. "*Boo-yah!*" Airborne. "*Hoo-ah!*" Army and Space Force. Half a dozen armored troops dropped down through the ceiling, landing on the hard deck, moving out. Hunter killed a tall Reptilian with three quick shots to its plastron, then took cover behind the shoulder of a massive turbine. A laser bolt struck the mechanism, splattering molten metal. He returned fire.

A door marked "Stairs" several yards away swung open, and three more armored shapes burst into the generator room—more Saurians. Herrera, Nicholson, and Coulter had cleared the stairwell and reached the lower level in a somewhat more conventional fashion. Their emergence from the stairwell caught a small group of crouching Saurians from behind, and in a few more moments the fighting was over.

"RV-Eye!" Hunter snapped. "Red Strike! Check the generator room for me! Any more of the bastards hiding?"

"I see eight . . . no . . . ten behind that partition to your left," Ashley's voice replied. "They . . . I think they're teleporting out!"

Hunter led his team around the wall in time to see the last three Saurians leaping through a kind of door or window . . . a parallelogram framework held upright between metal poles, with a blue glow flickering in the middle. The thing was ten feet tall and wider at the base than the top. Several of the Malok Grays remained, unmoving, unarmed, staring at the humans with huge, black eyes.

Hunter felt a sudden, cold shock; the bad guys were teleporting back to the *Big-H*!

Then he realized that the space he was seeing beyond that framework was like nothing he'd ever seen, not on board the *Hillenkoetter* . . . and nowhere else in his life.

CAPTAIN GROTON had asked Ashley to report to him in the CIC, and she and James Bennett had made their way through the ship past Marines and damage control parties. So far, the Saurians hadn't tried a repeat of their attack on the ship's engineering spaces, but the ship was now on high alert against the possibility of another teleportation assault.

Groton was leaning against a plotting table with the ship's XO, Commander Haines, and with Captain Macmillan, *Hillenkoetter*'s CAG.

"You asked to see us, Captain?" Bennett asked.

"I asked to see Miss Ashley," Groton replied. He looked at her. "So . . . how are you with missing persons, ma'am?"

"As in finding them?" She shook her head. "I don't know. I've never tried."

"Who's missing?" Bennett asked.

"One of our fighter pilots," Macmillan told him. "Lieutenant David Duvall, the Starhawks." He scowled. "We lost seventeen fighters from four squadrons in that last dustup. Three pilots were recovered by SAR flights. They found Duvall's ship, crashed out in the desert, but he was gone."

"Gone?" Ashley asked. "Was he picked up by the Saurians?"

"We don't think so. The kid knocked a Lizard ship out of the sky. Destroyed it. We didn't track any other of their saucers in that area."

"He must be trying to reach Ares Prime on foot," Haines said.

"Footprints?" Bennett asked.

"His fighter came down on rocky ground," Macmillan said. "No prints."

"Thing is, he was eighteen miles from Ares Prime," Haines added. "That was over three hours ago. We've had SAR flights and fighters crisscrossing the entire area between his crash site and Ares Prime, looking for him. With no success."

"And he has, at best, four hours of air with him. *Had*, I should say. He'll be running dry pretty soon, now."

"Maybe he wandered off in the wrong direction," Bennett suggested.

"I don't think so," Macmillan said. "With his training, he wouldn't have set out on foot unless he knew which way to go. Now, it is possible he got off course. It's a big desert down there, and compasses don't work. That's why we wanted to see if Miss Ashley could help narrow the search a bit."

"I really don't know if I can help," she told them. "I would need some sort of RV coordinates. But maybe I could use . . . a photograph of the guy?"

Groton nodded to Macmillan. "Give her Duvall's file, CAG."

"Right."

"Why is this one pilot so important?" Bennett asked.

Groton turned on him, angry. "You, sir, can just shut the fuck up. I will *not*, under any circumstances, leave one of my people behind. We bring back Duvall, or we bring back his body."

Ashley watched Bennett as he began to reply, then thought better of it. She'd never seen the ship's captain this angry, and it looked like that anger had just stopped her handler cold.

"I . . . might be able to do something," she said. "Since my . . . my mental encounters with various aliens, I've been . . . I don't know. More sensitive to thoughts? To minds? Let me go back to my quarters and I'll try."

"Do so, Miss Ashley," Groton said. "Call me here if you pick up *anything*."

"Yes, sir."

She left the CIC wondering how she would make good on that promise.

LIEUTENANT DUVALL finally stopped his endless march, looking at the sky with a despairing horror tempered by exhaustion. How was this even possible? The sun was rising . . . but *behind* him. Rising from what he'd *thought* was the western horizon.

He'd not been aware of it until his own shadow had appeared, standing out stark and black on the ground in front of him. Dawn had come suddenly with little atmosphere to scatter the light. Overhead, the stars were swiftly fading out . . . stars that might have given him the clues he'd needed if he'd been paying attention. Damn it, he'd had a class in celestial navigation after joining the Space Force training program, sure . . . but most of that had been focused on using his fighter's computer to find given stars in order to get from point A to point B. He'd never been especially good at picking out constellations in the sky . . . and that task was made far more difficult when the Martian night sky was as clear and as star-clotted as it was in open space.

It wasn't fair! He'd seen that moon moving down the sky! He'd been *certain* he was headed east!

Somehow, he still didn't understand why he'd been moving *west*, not east. Or . . . had he wandered in a circle? He knew that could happen to people, of course, but he'd been careful to line up distant landmarks or stars and use those to maintain a straight bearing.

How much time had passed? Four hours? He was having trouble breathing. No . . . probably less than four hours had passed. He'd been breathing heavily ever since flat rock had given way to soft sand, using his air at a faster rate. He'd stopped his ground-eating jog when that happened, but soon each step was a struggle. However long it had been, Duvall estimated he was around thirty-six miles from Ares Prime, give or take.

He could turn around, but he would never make it.

Duvall was at the fringes of a dune sea, now, standing atop a sand dune with an endless expanse of smooth-sided ridges of sand stretching away to the horizon. His strength was spent. His side, bruised in the crash, shrieked at him. Each breath was a searingly painful attempt to drag oxygen from the dying trickle of compressed air.

He took another step forward, more from force of habit than in any attempt to reach a destination . . . but his legs crumpled under him and he fell and rolled and slid and tumbled all the way down the face of the dune, coming to rest flat on his back at the foot of the wind-shaped hill.

Duvall stared up into a deep, violet sky.

He couldn't get up.

He didn't have much longer. . . .

THE CIC intercom chirped, and Groton opened the channel. "Captain Groton?"

"Yes, Miss Ashley."

"I think I touched him. Duvall, I mean."

"Excellent!" Macmillan put in. "Where is he?"

"That's the problem, sir. There are no reference points. No coordinates. I . . . I saw him lying in the sand, but I have no way of determining where he is, what direction, or how far. I think he's west of the crash site, but I don't know. It's *all* sand and rock and frozen desert out there, thousands of square miles of it!" She sounded like she was losing it.

"Okay, Julia," Groton said. "Calm down. I've had the search and rescue craft scouting to the west just because he obviously isn't in the east. Maybe they'll get lucky."

"Captain? There was one funny thing."

"What's that?"

"I . . . I touched his mind. Just a little. Enough to get a feeling of intense confusion . . . like he couldn't figure something out."

"What?"

"Well . . . I know this sounds weird, but he seemed upset that the moon had been wrong. He'd been using the moon to figure out where east was, and it had *lied* to him, somehow!"

"Miss Ashley," Macmillan said, leaning closer to the intercom's pickup. "Mr. Duvall likely is suffering from hypoxia . . . he's running out of air. That can degrade his thought processes, even make him hallucinate."

"No!" Groton said sharply. "That's not it! That's not it at all!"

"Sir?"

"What do you know about the inner Martian moon, CAG?"

Macmillan shrugged. "Phobos? It's tiny—a few kilometers across. And it's pretty close to the planet's surface."

"Exactly. About thirty-seven hundred miles, in fact. So close it orbits the planet faster than Mars rotates! Meaning—"

Macmillan's eyes opened wide. "Meaning it rises in the *west*, not in the east like any sane natural satellite!"

"So what if our hotshot pilot got out of his fighter, looked up, and saw Phobos setting? It's so close to the planet you can see it move with your naked eye. If he didn't know about the moon's quirks, he might have thought it was setting in the west."

"When it was setting in the east. My God!"

"Thank you, Julia!" Groton said, rushed. "You've been most helpful!"

"Mr. Toland!"

"Sir!" the rating seated at the CIC's communications center shot back.

"Make to all SAR vessels! Concentrate the search *exactly* west of the crash site, out to eighteen or twenty kilometers. He may be unconscious by now. Use his suit's transponder to tag him and get a fix."

"Aye, aye, sir!"

"Damn it, I should have thought of that, Andrew," Groton told Macmillan. "We were assuming Duvall must have wandered off in any direction, blindly. But he knew *exactly* what he was doing. He just forgot that Phobos goes backward in the Martian sky!"

Macmillan shook his head. "I must have known that once," he said.

Groton shrugged. "Understandable. Hell, we've been training for missions out among the stars, not right here in Earth's backyard. We can't keep track of *everything*." He looked up at the main CIC screen, which showed the rust and ocher expanse of the desert hanging below them. "I just hope the SAR guys reach the poor bastard in time."

HUNTER STARED into the eerie blue glow . . . and through it. He could see movement, but he was having trouble understanding what he was looking at. He could make out the shapes of Grays moving within a very large and empty space, as well as a few larger figures that looked like Saurians, blurred and distorted by the glow.

He didn't want to touch that glow until he understood it.

"Careful, Commander," Billingsly said at his side. "If they can see you . . ."

Wordlessly, Hunter held up a pen between thumb and forefinger he'd found on a desk across the compartment a few moments before. Carefully, he extended his gauntleted hand and pressed the end of the pen into the translucent light.

The opening was blocked, a solid yet invisible wall. He tapped the pen against it several times. There was no sound, but the feeling was that of a stiff rubber sheet, slightly yielding.

Billingsly was startled by the demonstration. "What the fuck . . . ?"

"A force field," Hunter told him, "something like *Hillenkoetter*'s magnetokinetic induction screen. At least it acts like it."

"What do you mean?"

"I don't see anyone wearing pressure suits over there, do you?"

"Yeah . . . you're right."

"Looks like they're at normal atmospheric pressure on that side, while we're at close to vacuum. The good news is if we can't get at them, then they can't get at us. I *think* . . ."

"So . . . where is that?"

"Best guess? Earth."

"How can you tell?"

"I've been watching them. Watching how they move . . ."

The room on the other side was as distorted as if it were being viewed through a sheet of wavy and imperfect glass, but some details could be seen. Hunter could see a number of other teleportation frames set up in a large circle, as though the one he was peering through was one of perhaps a dozen all facing inward in a circle. The moving figures were engaged in various activities at a central kiosk or control desk. He could make out screens and glowing panels that seemed to float in midair, and instrumentation that had a hazy, translucent look to it. It appeared that one very large Reptilian was overseeing perhaps ten or twelve Grays; Malok Grays.

As they watched, a Reptilian stepped from one of the frames.

He appeared to stagger as he stepped onto the floor; for an awkward moment it seemed he would fall.

"See that? See how he moves? On the Moon or here on Mars, lower gravity means you walk with a kind of sliding, gliding step. More efficient. That guy just stepped from low gravity into high gravity. I'd need to see someone drop something to be sure, but I think they're under one standard G."

"So . . . a hidden base on Earth? Maybe underground?"

"I think," Hunter said slowly, "that it's underwater. And I think someone on board the *Big-H* has seen it before."

"Who?"

"Julia Ashley."

"The psychic girl?"

"The remote viewer. I read one of her reports."

That report had included a detailed description of both the exterior and interior of an undersea base in the Pacific Ocean. Her sketches and descriptions had been of a site six miles off the Malibu Coast, at Point Duma, not far from Los Angeles. The sea cliffs there dropped into inky blackness two thousand feet down, but a single mesa or seamount rose from those depths to within four hundred feet of the surface, a geological anomaly given the improbable name of Sycamore Knoll. The plateau—one could actually see the thing clearly on Google Earth—was strangely artificial in its appearance, a huge egg shape a little over two miles across, its top smooth, as though neatly razored off. Seven large domes rested atop the mesa in an interconnected circle, an alien undersea base in a region that was a hotspot for both UFO and USO activity.

And inside . . .

Julia hadn't seen much of the base's interior . . . but she had seen enough to get Hunter's undivided attention. She'd had at the time a photograph of Geri Galanis, and somehow that visual cue had taken her to an enormous room inside the underwater base filled with transparent upright cylinders.

Most of those sealed cylinders held humans, submerged in green liquid and seemingly asleep. Hunter and Billingsly both had seen exactly the same thing before—at Zeta Reticuli and again at Aldebaran. Human abductees, submerged in a perfluorocarbon compound, naked, sealed in, and stored away in a kind of twilight sleep for some unimaginable purpose at which Hunter could only guess.

His guesses tended all to be nightmares.

"Ever since President Eisenhower signed a secret deal with extraterrestrials," Hunter told his XO, "they've been abducting our people. Thousands of them. Tens of thousands. We don't know why. Apparently, Eisenhower agreed that they could abduct a few of our citizens now and again; after all, how could he stop them? And in return they gave us technologies straight out of *Buck Rogers*."

"I've heard the stories."

"Thing is, the Grays and their Reptilian bosses have been abducting our citizens ever since. *Way* too many for occasional random medical examinations. And now we know that the Lizards are from Earth—survivors from the Age of Dinosaurs. Why would they want to run medical experiments on us? We're a different species, but same biology."

"I've been wondering about that," Billingsly admitted.

"At Aldebaran, we think the Lizards were preparing an army.

There aren't that many of them, and it's not like they could launch an invasion of Earth themselves, right?"

"But with an army of reprogrammed abductees . . ."

"Exactly."

"So what are we gonna do about it, boss?"

Thoughtfully, Hunter ran the glove of his pressure suit along the outside edge of the frame. There were power cables there, thick ones snaking across the deck to a jury-rigged console nearby. Several Grays, killed by the explosive decompression, lay beside the controls.

"I need to talk to Groton," Hunter said after a moment. "And Elanna. But I think we might have a weapon now that would give us a fighting chance. . . ."

"KYLE! KYLE, over here!"

HM1 Raymond Latimer crouched in the sand, brushing sand away from the pressure-suited figure half buried at the base of a towering dune. Marine Sergeant Kyle Mallory slid down the face of the dune in a spray of sand, reaching Latimer's side. "How is he, Doc?"

"Alive," Latimer said. "I think. . . ."

The rescue team had arrived moments before in one of the SAR black triangles, following the weak and short-ranged transmission of the pilot's emergency beacon. Latimer checked the gauge on the man's O_2 tank: in the red at dead empty. The name tag on his pressure suit read "D. Duvall." Latimer couldn't take a pulse through the suit's fabric, but he thought he saw Duvall's eyelids flutter.

Mallory was carrying a spare O_2 tank, and was busily disconnecting the empty bottle and replacing it with the full one. He cracked the valve . . . and Duvall's chest rose convulsively.

Alive.

"Let's get the ship over here," Latimer told the Marine. "We need to get him back to sick bay, stat."

Latimer watched a towering dust devil snake its way through the dunes in the distance. Duvall had been partially covered; had one of those devils buried him completely, the SAR team would have never found him.

The guy was damned lucky to be alive.

Whether or not he retained any brain function remained to be seen.

CHAPTER NINETEEN

Alternative 3: For decades, the global elite has known that a global catastrophe is imminent—through overpopulation, nuclear war, pollution, ozone depletion, polar shift, global warming, an ice age—and sought a solution. Two alternatives were to blow holes in Earth's atmosphere to release pollution or build vast subterranean cities; both were considered and dismissed.

A third alternative was then implemented.

In the 1970s, authorities noted an unusual increase in the number of disappearances of top scientists, including many who'd been part of the canceled Apollo program. This so-called brain drain was only a fraction of the mass disappearances of ordinary people, beginning in the 1960s. Popular conspiracy theories suggested that these were abductions by alien Grays, but in fact the abductors were human, part of the secret Alternative 3 program. The vanished, mind-controlled citizens had been taken to the Moon where they were forced to construct secret bases. These bases would become sanctuaries for the world's elite when the inevitable planetary catastrophe destroyed all civilization on Earth. The stories of abductions by Gray aliens were simply a cover story for the real cause of those disappearances.

AS SUGGESTED IN THE BOOK *ALTERNATIVE 3*,
LESLIE WATKINS, 1978

ALBRECHT SHRIEKED, THROWING himself about wildly, trying desperately to avoid the waves of sheer agony exploding from his tortured brain. In his mind, he ran down endless black corridors, a monstrous thing composed of ravening pain close on his heels, lashing him, burning him, dismembering him piece from bloodied piece. He tripped, pitching forward, falling, falling, landing at last in a vision of hell drawn from his Lutheran childhood . . . and still he shrieked as flames engulfed him, searing . . . blackening . . . an agony that went on and on and on for an eternity of pain. . . .

And then he stood at the door of the small room, staring into the face of the blond girl who'd opened it. She clutched her robe together at her chest. "Are you well, Herr Oberst?"

Cautiously, he drew breath. The pain truly and blessedly was gone, though he was so weak he could scarcely stand. He put a hand out to steady himself on the doorjamb.

The Eidechse's *voice thundered inside his brain. "No! No! Ghech! Obey!"*

The being sounded like it was disciplining a particularly stubborn and disobedient dog.

Again, the Eidechse *insinuated itself into his brain, crowding and bullying Albrecht's mind back into a tiny pocket and locking it away, as Albrecht's ego continued to shudder after its brief taste of living hell.*

AT HUNTER'S request, a small crowd of *Hillenkoetter*'s senior officers and scientific personnel had gathered in Briefing One, the large CIC briefing room. Groton and Haines both were there, as well as Captain Macmillan and *Hillenkoetter*'s CHENG, Commander Ramsey. Admiral Winchester was seated next to Groton, and Hunter knew those two would be the ones to convince. A number of senior civilian scientists were present as well—Doctors Carter, McClure, Norton, and Bennett, and, of course, Julia Ashley.

He'd brought along his senior people as well—Billingsly, Minkowski, Layton, and Coulter. Hunter fully expected intense pushback from the ship's command staff. He would need some stiff support at his back, and those four were just the men to provide it.

And . . . there was Elanna. He tried not to look at her, but he could feel the Talisian's large eyes watching him. Possibly, she would be the toughest of those present to convince.

Could he trust her? Damn those evolved pheromones. Mentally, he tried pushing the distraction aside.

It didn't work. *Maybe if I think about icebergs. . . .*

"Welcome back on board, Commander," Groton said. "That was excellent work down there."

"Thank you, Captain. We're not done yet. The upper levels of the base, including the control center, are still under Saurian control."

"Casualties?"

"Five dead, sir," Billingsly said. "Eight wounded."

"Not bad at all," Winchester said.

Hunter glowered but kept his thoughts on the matter to himself. So far as he was concerned, five dead was five too many.

Casualties in a war were inevitable, but he didn't have to like it.

"We got lucky, sir," Billingsly said.

"We never would have had a chance," Hunter pointed out, "if Miss Ashley hadn't been on the team. We knew exactly where to hit them."

"You told me when you asked for this debrief," Groton said, "that you had some ideas. Something about building on our success here and taking the fight to the enemy."

"Yes, sir. We have an absolutely perfect opportunity here to take out the Malibu USO base."

"Malibu?" Winchester said, his brow wrinkling. "On Earth, Malibu?"

"That's the one, Admiral." He began explaining what he'd seen in the basement level of Ares Prime . . . the teleport frame looking into another place, his observations of the local gravity. "Miss Ashley might be able to verify for us whether or not we're actually looking at the target she scouted for us before . . . an alien base four hundred feet down off the coast of California. A base with a large number of people being held prisoner."

Groton made a face. "Commander . . . we've been over this before. . . ."

"We have, sir. And the . . . the moral imperative has not changed. For decades, now, the Saurians have been kidnapping our citizens in large numbers and holding them captive. They're holding them indefinitely in a kind of suspended animation, and we don't know why!"

"And tell me, Commander," Groton said, "would you be this fired up if your girlfriend wasn't one of those captives?"

Hunter blinked. He honestly wasn't sure where his feelings about that might be right now. "The Lizards have no fucking right to abduct our people, sir. I don't care what Eisenhower's treaty said. . . ."

"Just what is it you propose, Commander?" Admiral Winchester asked. "Teleporting into that base from Ares Prime? You would have no idea at all how many Saurians you would run into there. Or where anything is, or how to get at it, or even whether or not you'd be able to come back. . . ."

"That's why I'd like to enlist Miss Ashley's services."

"The fact remains, Commander," Winchester told him, "that

your assault force would be seriously outnumbered, outgunned, and out-teched. Hell, even if you managed to fight through to where they're keeping the, uh, the abductees, getting them out would be a medical and a logistical nightmare. If you couldn't transport back here for whatever reason, you and the prisoners would be trapped at the bottom of the ocean, with no means of calling in support."

"And why the hell wouldn't we be able to transport back, Admiral?" Minkowski asked. "We step through the door. We do our thing. We step back."

"You step back *if* no one in the Lizard control room decides to cut power to your transporter."

"I have to agree with the admiral," Dr. Joshua Norton said. "We don't understand the Saurians' teleportation technology. We'd be like a toddler who's never seen a flame before. We could get burned."

Hunter looked at Norton for a long moment before answering. The former RAND tech expert had gotten a boarding party into serious trouble during *Hillenkoetter*'s recent investigation of an extrasolar planetoid, and Hunter didn't trust the man's judgment. His disagreement actually sounded like he was being supercautious, now. No more shoot-if-they-look-hostile mindset . . . which, all things considered, would be a very *good* thing.

"We *do* have a means of crippling the enemy's defenses before we even set foot in that base," Hunter told them. "And we would *not* be going in blind. Not with Julia here on our team."

"Just what is it you have in mind, Commander?" Groton asked. He sounded intrigued.

Hunter straightened, took a deep breath, and began explaining.

He was interrupted almost at once by shouted protests, and he knew this was going to be an exceptionally hard sell.

"FOR WHATEVER it's worth, Commander," Ashley told Hunter, "I do agree with you. We've got to do *something.*"

They were seated on *Hillenkoetter*'s mess deck having a late dinner. Long windows along one bulkhead looked out and down onto the rust-colored surface of Mars. Only a handful of other personnel, just coming off watch, were in the place, and their table gave them a quiet and out-of-the-way place to sit and talk.

Hunter gave her a long stare. "*Why* do we have to do something, Julia? What did you see?"

She gave a shrug, trying to appear nonchalant. "I . . . I *did* see the girl in that photograph you showed me, Mark. Or her body, at any rate . . . sealed into one of those awful glass tubes. I can't imagine being confined like that, submerged in liquid, unable to move. . . ."

Hunter nodded understanding. "How long have you been claustrophobic?"

She exhaled softly. He *understood.* "Since I was a little girl. I accidentally got locked inside a dark closet in the basement. It was hours before my father heard me and let me out." She suppressed a shudder. "Actually . . . I kind of think the experience helped me with RV. When I'm remote viewing, it's like I'm no longer confined inside my body. It's . . . it's incredibly freeing. It's like a trauma victim being able to dissociate . . . leaving her body to escape. . . ."

"I understand that feeling now," Hunter told her. "Elanna took me on a kind of mental tour of the far future. It was like I was just a disembodied viewpoint, sailing through walls, going anywhere at all with just a thought. . . ."

"That's it exactly!" Julia exclaimed. "No walls, no boundaries, no limits. But sometimes you . . . you see things you really wish you hadn't. Things that get stuck in your mind, and you can't ever get them out."

"And when you saw Geri . . . it was like that?"

She nodded. "How can they even breathe like that, submerged in that green liquid?"

Hunter toyed with his half-eaten supper. This conversation as well as pure exhaustion had killed his appetite. "There's a chemical compound called perfluorocarbon that holds a great deal of oxygen," he told her. "We've been experimenting with the stuff for decades, actually, for extremely deep dives. You have to inhale it, or rather drown in it, but then it keeps your blood oxygenated . . . I don't know. Indefinitely, I suppose. They must have equipment to feed free oxygen into the tank as it's used up."

"Can we change the subject, please? It's kind of squicking me out."

"I'm sorry."

"It's okay. I just . . . well . . . it *hurts* thinking of all those people bottled up like that. I wish we could help them."

"Unfortunately," Hunter said, "Captain Groton and Admiral Winchester don't agree." He pushed his half-full plate from in front of him. "In fairness . . . Winchester is constrained by his superiors . . . the Defense Department, the President . . . and above him, I guess, by MJ-12. And the Talisians wouldn't like my idea either . . . not if it leads us and them into all-out war with the Saurians."

"But I thought you were in command of the JSST?" Ashley said. "Not Captain Groton."

"I suppose so," Hunter said. "We're kind of working in parallel here, though he does outrank me. But he's the one responsible for the ship, just as CAG Macmillan is in charge of the aerospace wing. Winchester is in command of the whole task force, and that does include me and my people. The JSST doesn't belong to me. I can't just hare off on my own. . . ."

"And the lives of those people at Malibu don't count?"

Hunter made a sour face. "Are the people at Malibu worth the risk of all-out war with the Lizards? Suppose we take out their base. Will they start taking out our cities? Worse . . . will they break their informal agreement with the Talis and maybe do something nasty to our timeline? Change our history so we're no longer a threat? I gather that could happen."

"I've never really understood this stuff about a time war," Ashley admitted.

"I'm not sure I do either. In a way, the past is already set, right? If we go back in time and change something, we spawn a whole new parallel universe with new situations dictated by that change. Our old universe is still there, but we're stuck in the new one. At least . . . that's my understanding of it."

"But aren't we changing the Talisian future every time we do something here in the present? *Our* present is *their* past . . . and it must be just as set for them."

"Absolutely right. And that's where my understanding kind of leaves the building. But I get the impression that the Lizards have been making small, incremental changes all along . . . and their long-term plan *is* to rewrite our future. The Talis are working to stop any changes that rewrite *their* present, somewhen up in our future."

"None of which explains why the Saurians should be allowed to get away with mass kidnappings."

"The problem is that we don't know how far we can push them. Push too hard, and they decide we're too much trouble and just step on us. And they could, too. Probably without raising a sweat."

"I didn't know reptiles can sweat."

Hunter smiled. "You know what I mean."

Ashley was thoughtful for a long moment. "I'm wondering, Mark . . ."

"What?"

"Dr. Bennett and I have been working for a while on a different problem, one that involves time travel and changing the future."

"What problem is that?"

She drew a deep breath. "Shag Harbour."

"That crashed alien spaceship?"

"The . . . the people on board are called the Zshaj. That's what the Talis call them, anyway. They're . . . they're stuck in my mind. I can't get away from them. They want me to help."

Hunter looked alarmed. "What . . . they're in your head?"

She shook her head. "Not like that. Not like they're controlling me or anything. But the *memory* won't go away. Sometimes, like in my dreams, it seems like they're still talking to me, even though I'm not trancing out."

"And what are they saying?"

"'Help us.'"

"So what do you want to do about it?"

"I've been talking to Dr. Bennett. I think I have him convinced to act. See . . . the Zshaj are trapped inside their time ship submerged at the bottom of Shag Harbour in Nova Scotia. That means they're separated from the rest of the time-space continuum, right? If they all die down there . . . or if we rescue them, it doesn't matter to the rest of the timeline."

"Well . . . it might," Hunter said. "If, say, they were here to invade the Earth and they got shot down, that might pose a bit of a problem for us if we showed up and rescued them."

"They are *not* here to hurt us, Mark," Ashley said, stubborn. "We rescue them, they go home, and we never see them again."

"You're sure of that?"

"Trust me. I *know.* . . ."

Hunter shook his head. "Either way, Julia . . . even if it doesn't affect us, whether they go home or die on Earth, that's going to affect the future of *their* world. Do they have families?"

"Of course they do." She glared at him for a moment. "Just like you have Geri Galanis. If you manage to rescue her, won't you be changing *her* future?"

Hunter winced. "Ouch. Touché."

"Dr. Bennett has been talking to your Captain Groton, trying to convince him. If he does, I think the idea will be to use the *Hillenkoetter* to go back to 1967."

"And do what?"

"I don't know. Make direct contact? Maybe call in other Zshaj ships to help? Or maybe we can help them repair their vessel. I think I could get a lot more information if I was there in their time."

"Groton and Winchester are going to need a lot of convincing. Elanna, too."

She hesitated, building up the nerve to ask. "If you'll help me, Mark, then I'll help you."

"You'll help me save my people, if I help you save your aliens?"

"Something like that."

Slowly, Hunter nodded. "I'm not sure I can offer any real help," he said. "But I'll sure as hell try. I do think I might have an idea. . . ."

IN THE end, the Saurians on the upper decks of Ares Prime's doughnut surrendered. They had little choice in the matter, since the humans now controlled the base's life support system and power, and they held the ultimate hole card in their willingness to depressurize the remaining sealed compartments and kill the surviving Malok.

Groton had been concerned about taking on board an unknown number of Saurian prisoners; those things were known to be able to control human minds at close range, and their technologies extended to nanotech and other powerful magics that might well be impossible to detect or counter. The Saurians themselves had offered Groton a deal: permit them to escape, and Ares Prime would be left to the humans.

"What I don't understand is how we keep them from sending an army through that transport gate in the basement. They could just walk right in and take over the doughnut again the minute we're gone," Groton told Hunter in his office aft of the CIC.

"Well . . . Admiral Winchester is bringing in some of the Marines with the squadron to take charge of the base," Hunter reassured him. "We can alert them on what to watch for . . . set up a 24/7 guard in the base engineering section, that sort of thing. The fact that there is very little air in the doughnut's basement means the enemy would need an airlock on the other end if they wished to jump through."

Groton nodded. "That should be adequate. At least until we restore pressure throughout the Ares Prime facility."

"By which time, we'll have the teleport apparatus dismantled," Hunter said. "I imagine our xenotech people will want to examine that stuff thoroughly and see how it's put together." Hunter hesitated a moment, then added, "If I may, Captain, I have a new proposal I'd like to discuss."

"*Not* a plan to attack the Malibu undersea base."

"No, sir. Dr. Bennett and Miss Ashley have already been talking to you about this one. Shag Harbour . . ."

"Ah. Our Talisian allies have already made it clear that intervening in that . . . incident would be a bad idea."

"Did they outright forbid it, sir?"

"Not in so many words. . . ."

"I suggest we bring Elanna in here and discuss it with her. It's my contention that if Earth is still a sovereign world . . . if humans are still acknowledged to be masters of their own world and their own destiny . . . then it's really up to us to decide what we will do, what guidance we shall accept, what we will tolerate."

"That, Commander," Groton said carefully, "is an extremely dangerous stance for Humankind . . . wouldn't you agree?"

"Perhaps. But I submit that interceding on behalf of these stranded aliens in our past will not be changing history in any way. According to our records, the object that crashed in Shag Harbour in 1967 was joined by another craft underwater."

"Excuse me. How do we know this?"

"Both the Canadians and our own Navy had ships in the area soon after the event," Hunter explained. "They watched what happened with sonar. According to those records, the two unknown craft remained together for a time, then moved off together before they were lost. All military records, including those sonar scans, were immediately classified, of course."

"Of course." Groton considered this. "So tell me, Commander . . . why would we want to get involved in the first place?"

"Sir, *if* humans are a sovereign species, in charge of our own affairs, then we have a right to decide for ourselves if and when we're going to contact other species, if and when we're going to establish diplomatic relations with them."

"We already have treaties with some of them . . . with the Saurians and with some of the Malok Grays."

"Of which the Malok have been . . . let's say . . . taking outrageous advantage. If we establish peaceful relations with other species who happen to be visiting our planet, humanity will be in a *much* better position to assert its rights as an independent species, one able to chart its own course." Hunter spread his hands, imploring. "Sir, we *can't* let the Talis do our thinking for us. We can't let them make decisions for us. And we *damn* sure can't let the Lizards run our planet!"

"The Talis *are* human, and in a better position to make decisions than we are." Groton smiled, which Hunter took for a good sign. At least Groton hadn't thrown him out on his ear.

"Sir, what they're afraid of is that we're going to screw up their timeline, their history, okay? This operation we're proposing will prove that we can keep events isolated in space *and* in time and preserve their timeline as well as our own."

Groton leaned back in his chair and considered Hunter's words carefully. "Actually, Commander . . . I'm inclined to agree with you."

"You are?" Hunter sounded startled, and Groton chuckled.

"You make some good arguments. For a long time I've been concerned that the Talis are using the US Space Force as a kind of mercenary unit, doing their dirty work. Remember Aldebaran?"

"How can I forget?" *Hillenkoetter*'s task force had been deployed to investigate a kind of Saurian concentration camp on a planet called Daarish. The Talis, unwilling to get their hands dirty, had nudged the human force into taking the place down . . . without getting involved themselves.

"What you propose would go a long way toward establishing ourselves as an independent galactic civilization in our own right. *But . . .*"

"But?"

"You have to admit that the Talis have a better perspective on things than we do," Groton said. "They know how it all works. They know what they're doing when it comes to time travel. They know how everything is supposed to turn out in the end, while we don't know what the fuck we're doing."

"Which is why Shag Harbour is a good place for us to start taking our first steps on our own. As long as we're not caught by those Navy ships, we'll simply leave them with a mystery which is already documented in history. And we'll make some new friends."

Groton sighed. "You make it all sound so easy, Mark."

"Isn't it?"

"First and foremost . . . you know as well as I do that the military does *not* set policy. The civilians are in charge.

"Second, the stakes in this game you're proposing are astronomically high. If we screw this up, it's not just our independence we're gambling. It's existential, understand? The Lizards get pissed enough . . . *and humanity, past, present, and future gets wiped off the map*!"

"Sir, that's why I'm suggesting we look at intervening at Shag Harbour. We should be able to stay completely out of sight."

"The operative word in that sentence, Commander, is *should.* " Groton thought about it for a moment more. "Tell you what, Commander. I'll discuss the idea with Elanna, and see if she'll pass it up with her recommendation to LOC . . . maybe to MJ-12. We've *got* to have their blessing on this before we move."

"I understand, Captain." He wondered if Elanna would go along with the idea . . . and if she would be able to convince the higher-ups at Luna and on Earth. The problem was that the Space Force would still be working under Talisian control. Hunter wanted to see the human defenses being overseen by twenty-first-century humans, not people from the far-off future.

But then . . . it *was* all a matter of perspective, wasn't it? Shag Harbour could become existential for the Talis as well as for the present-day world; if the humans of the twenty-first century were wiped out, the Talis, too, would become extinct.

Groton touched a switch on the intercom unit on his desk. "Mr. Toland? Get me Elanna."

"Aye, sir."

"Shall I leave, sir?"

"No. Stay." He grinned. "If the answer is no, maybe you'll take it better from her than me."

425812 ELANNA leaned over the still figure in the bunk in sick bay. She rarely intervened directly in cases like this; twenty-first-century human medicine was generally sufficient to treat the wounded brought back to *Hillenkoetter*.

This one, however, was special, and required her immediate and personal attention.

"Hold on to me, Lieutenant," she whispered in the man's mind. "Don't leave me."

She heard only a broken, grasping sob as his answer. Duvall's brain had been starved of oxygen for too long. She wasn't certain she could bring back the mind.

But she did have one clear image, a memory burned into Duvall's awareness during that last desperate battle above the Martian surface. Shock had etched the memory in perfect clarity . . . though she doubted that Duvall was now consciously aware of it.

Deliberately, Duvall had hurled his Stingray into a Malok fighter. He'd watched the alien saucer break into pieces as he blasted through its gravitic field.

He'd watched as the Malok pilot had been kicked free of his ship, mouth open, eyes open, screaming as he fell through the bare wisp of atmosphere.

The image she watched in Duvall's mind rocked her. Unexpectedly, the enemy pilot was not Saurian, was not Malok Gray.

He was *human*, a human of the current epoch.

Like some Grays, abducted humans had been enlisted to the Malok cause.

CHAPTER TWENTY

Project Pegasus: Since the 1960s, teleportation chambers operated by DARPA and the CIA have allowed instantaneous travel between Earth and Mars, where covert bases were established for the purpose of acclimatizing Earthlings to Martian conditions, and for accustoming the humanoid Martian inhabitants to the terrestrial presence. NASA, meantime, has kept the actual surface conditions on Mars secret from the general public. While thinner than on Earth, the Martian atmosphere is as thick as that in the Peruvian Altiplano, and breathable without special gear.

As well, time travel has allowed the CIA to enlist teenagers for training programs, after which they are assigned duties at the Martian bases. They serve for twenty years, then have their memories erased all the way back to the moment they were first contacted. Simultaneously, their bodies are physically regressed, and they are sent back in time twenty years to resume their lives at the exact spacetime coordinates where they first were abducted. This project was exposed only because the memory erasures didn't always hold, and some people were able to recover the lost memories of a twenty-year tour of duty on Mars.

One of the whistleblowers who wrote about Project Pegasus reported that in the early 1980s he met a nineteen-year-old named Barry Soetoro twice on Mars—aka Barack Obama, the future President of the United States. Reportedly Soetero's mother, CIA officer Ann Dunham, was there as well.

Both the Pentagon and the White House have denied that President Obama ever teleported to Mars.

But then, of *course* they would deny it.

ALLEGATIONS OF WHISTLEBLOWERS
ANDREW BASIAGO AND WILLIAM STILLINGS, 2012

"WERE IT UP to me," the reptile's voice whispered in his skull, "I would eliminate you now. You are not as tractable as most of your fellows."

They were standing in the middle of an empty field east of Berlin, under a star-filled night sky. Albrecht could not answer the Eidechse. He could not do anything but listen to the creature, and feel the rising sick horror within his soul.

"On Daarish, we had a game we enjoyed," the creature told him. It was no longer inside his head—not exactly—though its voice was. Physically, the Eidechse stood next to him, holding him mute and motionless by sheer force of mind.

"In German, the game was called Jagd. 'The hunt.' You, I believe, would make excellent prey, struggling and fighting to the last.

"Unfortunately, that is not the quality I need in a puppet. You were a superb choice: an actual officer from the war, with knowledge and experience difficult to find now, seventy years later. My fellows have decided that you are simply too valuable to . . . waste on mere sport." Albrecht sensed the Saurian at his side watching him, one clawed, three-fingered hand tightly gripping his upper arm. There was no way to escape it . . . no way to engage his own, deeply suppressed will.

In the sky above the southern horizon, a bright light appeared . . . and grew brighter. At first, Albrecht thought that he might be seeing the landing lights of a small aircraft, but moment by moment, as the object became more luminous, he began to realize that he was watching one of the Eidechse ships.

"We are taking you to . . . a place, one of our bases on this *planet. There we shall find ways to make you more tractable, more amenable to our will."*

Silently, the flat, dome-topped saucer hovered above the field, hesitating, then grounded. Albrecht felt the Eidechse *grip his arm tighter, felt its mind move within his skull. Step by stumbling step, the Saurian forced him toward the ship.*

The flight was brief, a matter of just moments as the craft flashed across the night-shrouded landscape into daylight, then maneuvered toward the surface of the ocean. He felt no shock at all as the saucer penetrated the waves.

But he felt quickening terror as they dropped into abyssal darkness.

HILLENKOETTER REMAINED in place, hovering a few hundred kilometers above the surface of Mars. Below, the Marine shore party had taken over Ares Prime. The last of the Lizards—and a number of their Gray allies—had boarded ships and departed, abandoning the base. The Marines had investigated all of the outlying structures, discovering a number of humans trapped there by the attack and rescuing them. The last of the 1-JSST had been brought up to the ship, including several survivors of the aerospace dogfight who'd crashed in the desert.

Captain Groton had gathered in Briefing One with Admiral Winchester, Elanna, and members of the ship's senior staff. Winchester, as expected, was dead-set against any "extratemporal adventurism," as he put it.

But to Groton's surprise, Elanna was not.

"Commander Hunter's suggestion has merit," she told them.

"Perhaps it *is* time for twenty-first-century humanity to take charge of its own affairs."

"That's . . . unexpected," Groton said. He exchanged a glance with Macmillan; the CAG looked as surprised as he felt. So did "Ops," Commander Kelly. "I thought you were afraid primitives like us would screw up your timeline."

"New information has reached me," she said. "Information that significantly changes the situation."

"What information?" Commander Philip Wheaton asked. The ship's senior intelligence officer looked across at Kelly, then returned his full attention to Elanna.

The Talisian was silent for a long moment, as though considering exactly what she could say. Groton knew she was often precariously balanced between giving modern humans too much information, and too little.

"Two points of data," she said at last. "First . . . Julia's discovery of an attack by Saurian craft on a Zshaj exploration vessel."

She made an obscure gesture with her left hand, and a large monitor on the forward bulkhead came to life. On the screen, an immense, ebon-black rectangular spacecraft drifted toward Earth, which loomed in the background—swirls of white cloud overlaying ocean blue. The image was of crystal clarity and extraordinarily high definition. As the ship dwindled against the planet, four more ships appeared in close pursuit, classic Saurian flying disks.

They were firing weapons, the effects visible as bright flashes against and around the larger vessel.

"Where the hell did you get *this*?" Wheaton asked, eyes wide. "CGI?"

"Not computer graphics, no," Elanna said. "When we saw Ms. Ashley's report, we sent a covert drone to 1967 and scanned local space for artificial gravitic fields. We found this . . . encounter and recorded it."

Closely pursued, the rectangular slab entered Earth's atmosphere. Bits and pieces were breaking away from the falling craft, blazing like fireworks in the fiery stream of hot plasma.

"We've been able to verify," Elanna went on, "that the larger craft is a Zshaj explorer. My people checked their records in the hundred and first century and learned that the ship *did* return safely. However, we found no details of the event. We don't know exactly what happened."

"Which means we're clear to insert ourselves into the historical record," Groton said.

"*Carefully*, Captain," Winchester said, "*carefully.*"

"What was the second data point you mentioned?" Groton asked her.

"One of your Stingray pilots, a Lieutenant Duvall, rammed one of the Malok saucers, then crashed in the desert."

"I saw the report," Macmillan said. "An incredibly heroic act."

"Indeed," Elanna said, nodding. "He survived, somewhat miraculously, and has been brought back to this ship. I . . . investigated his mind. I wanted to determine if there would be permanent damage due to oxygen depletion."

"Is there?" Macmillan wanted to know.

"Uncertain. There *is* damage, but I don't know if even Talisian medical technology can repair it. However, I found one extraordinarily clear image in his mind. As the Malok saucer disintegrated around him, Duvall caught a glimpse of the pilot. I saw that memory clearly. The pilot was human."

Winchester looked puzzled. "A Gray . . . ?"

"No, Admiral. A human of *this* epoch."

"We knew they were training human pilots on Daarish," Groton said.

"For a planned invasion of Earth, yes. This suggests that they may be using human abductees from *this* time period for the same purpose."

"It might have been their Nazi abductees from Daarish," Winchester said. He didn't sound entirely convinced.

"It might have been," Elanna agreed. "But your people did quite a good job at shutting down the Malok operation on Daarish and freeing the humans held there. It's more likely they're getting new, ah, *recruits* from the twenty-first century . . . as well as some held over from the twentieth."

"They've been kidnapping our people for a long time," Wheaton observed.

"And bringing some forward from Nazi Germany. We haven't been certain why . . . but at least some are being trained as soldiers. Probably mind-controlled soldiers," Elanna added.

On the screen, the Zshaj rectangle had leveled off above the cloud deck, four bright orange orbs still in pursuit. It made a sudden turn, as though trying to elude its attackers, and descended. As it broke through the clouds, a large landmass was just visible below and ahead, picked out by isolated clusters of lights.

"How does any of this change things, Elanna?" Groton asked her. "Why should we get involved now?"

"You'll have to admit, Captain, that *now* is an extremely flexible and relative term. If twenty-first-century Humankind takes the lead here, defending that explorer ship over fifty years ago from Saurian aggression, you will have taken a tremendous step toward securing your civilization's independence, your self-sufficiency, and your sovereignty within the galactic milieu."

The rectangle descended, the black water below rushing up to receive it.

"And just what is it we're supposed to do?"

"As you suggested, Captain, you can insert the *Hillenkoetter* into the historical record."

Winchester scowled at Elanna. "I must say, ma'am, that I don't like this idea. By rights we should await orders from . . . higher up."

Elanna's head tilted to one side. "By that you mean Lunar Operations Command? Or from MJ-12 itself? Admiral . . . I can't say very much about this, but I should tell you that my command authority has long suspected that your MJ-12 has been penetrated by enemy operatives."

"A *mole*?" Wheaton cried. "Inside Majic-12?"

"I believe that's the term used by your current intelligence agencies, yes. Request orders from your superiors, and you'll be sending us into a trap."

"But . . . but we can't just *ignore* them. . . ."

"Admiral, that is *exactly* what we shall do." She hesitated. "I am invoking Warden's Command."

Winchester, Groton noted, went white. He didn't know what it was that Elanna had just invoked . . . but Winchester clearly did, and he clearly didn't like it.

"Then I assume, ma'am, that you take full responsibility for this action."

"I do, Admiral." She smiled sweetly. "I always have."

"In writing."

"Don't worry, Admiral. Your career is quite safe. . . ."

Winchester's face reddened, and for a moment Groton thought the man was going to explode with rage . . . but he caught himself, forced the anger down, and held his response to a low growl. "That, madam, was not my concern here."

"I know, Franklin," Elanna said. The informality was like a slap across the face. "Like the Talis, you fear for our mutual future."

"My *career* indeed," Winchester huffed.

And the meeting was at an end.

"SOUNDS LIKE an exciting meeting," Hunter said. "I'm glad I wasn't there."

"You didn't miss a great deal," Elanna told him. "They've agreed to a temporal raid to rescue the trapped Zshaj ship."

They were in Hunter's cabin, sitting on his bunk. Once again, Hunter was deeply aware of her closeness, and of her intense sexuality. Those eyes captured his and held his gaze, and Hunter wondered if he would ever be able to understand the mind behind them.

"I'm not sure I see the point," Hunter said. "If you've seen the records and we know the Zshaj ship gets back to its own world safely, like you say, why do we need to do anything about it?"

"You—*we*—have a part to play in this."

Hunter's eyebrows crept up his forehead. "Is there something about all of this you're not telling us? Does the universe come to an end if we *don't* rescue them?"

"Mark . . . there are *many* things we can't tell you, and you know that quite well."

Hunter grinned. "Maybe I do. I just wish I didn't have to walk this tightrope blindfolded."

She looked puzzled. "'Tightrope'?"

"Sure. I have to carry out my duties, perform certain tasks, obey lawful orders. Usually, my superiors tell me what I have to do, okay? But now you tell me we have to act on our own, outside of the chain of command. We have to act for ourselves . . . but you won't tell me if a given action is right or wrong. If I'm wrong, if I step the wrong way, I fall off the rope and the whole human race goes with me. That's kind of a large weight to carry on my shoulders."

"I, *we*, rather, are still here to guide you, Mark."

"I'm glad to hear it. I still can't see where I'm stepping, and it's a long way down."

She smiled at him. "Trust. Remember?"

"How can I forget?"

"Perhaps we need a refresher. . . ."

Once again, she touched the gem at her throat, and her nano-tech garment vanished.

Hunter was tempted. *God*, he was tempted. Elanna was hauntingly beautiful, achingly desirable, passionately eager. But . . .

"No," he said, shaking his head. "Thank you . . . but no."

Her face fell. "But why?"

"*Trust*," he said slowly, "does involve other things than sex, don't you think? Besides, I need to get together with my platoon leaders and work out what we're going to do . . . what was the place in Nova Scotia?"

"Shag Harbour."

"That's the place. Funny name."

"*Shag* is what I want to do with you. . . ."

He gave her a quizzical look. "I thought that was a British euphemism."

She shrugged. "I've been stationed there, too."

"Well, I like shagging, too. But I'm afraid it will have to be later." He stood. "How long do we have to prepare?"

"As long as you like. With time travel you can go any *when* you want, any *time* you want."

"Unless the bad guys move first."

"The target year is 1967, Mark. The Malok have done nothing in all that time . . . save attack the Zshaj explorer in the first place."

"And as soon as the Malok figure out what we're doing—perhaps pick it up telepathically from one of our people—they'll be first in line to crash the party."

"There . . . is that. . . ." Elanna looked off to her side, probably wondering what she could share.

"Hey . . . tell me." Hunter reached out to her.

"If I can."

"That jump gate down in Prime's basement . . . it can really reach Earth?"

"Yes."

"Can it reach Earth *in 1967*?"

"Not really."

"What do you mean 'really'?"

"Earth is moving. So is Earth's sun."

"And . . . ?"

"The sun is moving at about two hundred kilometers per second. That works out to almost seven hundred million kilometers in one year."

"You're saying that Earth has moved a fair piece since 1967."

"Something like forty-two billion kilometers—about two hundred and seventy-seven astronomical units. The accuracy necessary to hit such a fast-moving target a few meters across at that kind of range requires computing power and fine control that you—or we, for that matter—simply do not possess."

"Sorry I asked. So . . . how about loading the gate into *Hillenkoetter*? Can we make it operational using *Big-H*'s power plant?"

Elanna looked thoughtful. "Possibly . . ."

"Please find out. It will be simpler if we can use that gate to drop in on our new friends."

"You should give some thought to what those new friends will think of humans materializing out of thin ammonia."

"Is that what they breathe?"

"A gas mix similar to Titan's. Mostly nitrogen, with about five percent methane and ammonia. Ambient temperature is minus one-eighty Celsius."

"We'll need our mittens."

"To say the least."

"Tell us what we need to do to move that jump gate, okay? We need the information yesterday."

"I assume you're speaking metaphorically." She chuckled. "The temporal paradox resulting from—"

"Just do it, Elanna. Please. Fast as you can."

And he left her sitting there nude in his quarters.

FOR GROTON, this was the first time he'd attempted to specifically take the *Hillenkoetter* through time as distinct from space. Travel between stars required time travel as a part of the process;

to reach a star ten light-years away, you simultaneously moved forward in space and backward in time, reducing the trip's apparent duration from ten years to a matter of days or weeks. The head of the ship's astrophysics lab, Dr. Lawrence Brody, had tried explaining it, but without much success.

And the trick was less than precise.

"What do you mean we missed our target date?" he demanded. "By how much?"

Groton was in the CIC with Hunter, Elanna, and Dr. Brody, along with Commander Donald Kelly and members of the ops staff. Winchester was conspicuous by his absence. The squadron's admiral, disgruntled by Elanna's trespass of his authority, had shifted his flag back to the *Inman*. They had not, Groton thought, heard the last of it.

The forward screen showed Earth half a million kilometers ahead, with the much larger moon drifting off to the left as *Hillenkoetter* maneuvered past it.

"It's confirmed, Captain," Elanna said. She was pressing something like the bud of a Bluetooth into her left ear, listening. "According to the Talis watch station, the date on this half of the planet is October 6, 1967. The Shag Harbour incident occurred two days ago, on the fourth."

"Shit," Groton said, with deep annoyance. "We used the precise metrics you provided. . . ."

"I told you," Brody said, "that there would be some wiggle room in the calculations. Between relativistic effects, the movement of planetary bodies, and the nature of time travel itself, pinpoint accuracy is simply not possible."

Groton glanced at the moon as it slid past the ship to port. Almost two years to go before Neil Armstrong's "one small step." According to Elanna, a Talis watch station had been set up in the crater Aristarchus centuries ago to keep an eye on the Earth of this epoch. The station, he'd been given to understand, was largely automated, with little in the way of resources the expedition could use.

Which meant it would be up to the *Hillenkoetter* to resolve this mess.

"Any sign of the bad guys?"

"No, Captain. They appear to have left the area shortly after the Zshaj ship crashed."

"Good."

"There's something else, though. . . ." Elanna felt the need to interrupt the conversation.

"Yes?"

She listened for a moment more. "The watch station has been monitoring communications in the target area. Especially military communications. The target has moved."

"It flew?" Hunter asked.

"No. I believe you call such sightings 'USOs'?"

Kelly nodded. "Unidentified submerged objects, yes."

"The target was tracked by Canadian and US vessels moving at high speed underwater. It was picked up by undersea listening devices at a place called Government Point, about twenty-five miles northeast of Shag Harbour."

"But it's still there?" Groton asked.

"Yes, Captain." She hesitated. "There are a number of military surface vessels in the area, apparently monitoring it."

"That could make things . . . difficult," Hunter said. "We can't have any interaction with the locals."

"Agreed," Groton said. "But maybe we won't have to." He looked at Elanna. "Are you sure you want to do this?"

"Of course. How else are you going to find out what they need to repair their craft?"

"Assuming we have what they need. Okay." He picked up a handheld microphone. "Maneuvering . . . put us in a hover over Government Point. One hundred kilometers, and maintain position."

"Aye, aye, sir," Brody said.

"Engineering. We'll need to be invisible for a while."

"Aye, Captain," Commander Ramsey replied. "No guarantees, sir."

"I understand, CHENG." The gravitic distortion field that propelled *Hillenkoetter* through space and time could also scatter or absorb incoming radar waves—the ultimate in stealth technology. A ship as large as the *Big-H* wouldn't become optically invisible . . . but it *would* be blurred and distorted, as generations of would-be UFO photographers had discovered.

The important thing was to keep something the size of a Navy supercarrier invisible to radar.

The planet before them rapidly swelled on the screen as the sun dropped below the curved horizon and they descended into the planetary night. Groton could see the dark mass of Nova Scotia, edged by orange lights. West, in a ragged strip, lay more lights—the Maine coast—separated from Nova Scotia by the black void of the Gulf of Maine.

Groton looked at Hunter. "We're in position, Commander."

"Yes, sir," the 1-JSST CO replied. "I'll go get suited up." He looked at Elanna. "Coming?"

She nodded and followed.

HUNTER WONDERED if Elanna was angry or hurt by his rejection of her advances earlier. She'd seemed uncharacteristically reserved in the CIC, her voice a bit cold. Strange thought— a twelve-hundred-year-old woman from the far future acting *hurt* . . . but perhaps that simply confirmed the fact that she was still *human*.

When he was confronted by her casual use of near-magical technologies, Hunter sometimes had trouble remembering that.

The VBSS team had already gathered on the flight deck. They stood just below the open maw of a TR-3W. Just forty feet across, it could carry ten or fifteen troops, not counting the three-man fight crew.

Today, however, it would be carrying just seven.

VBSS stood for "visit, board, search, and seizure," a term describing maritime boarding tactics used by military and law-enforcement personnel. Normally, it applied to SEAL or Marine units sent to capture or search a foreign vessel—one suspected of drug-running or piracy, for example.

This time it would apply to the boarding of an alien spacecraft at the bottom of the Atlantic Ocean.

"Team's ready, Commander," Billingsly said, saluting. The exec was not suited up, but he'd been checking the others— Minkowski, Nicholson, Daly, and Briggs, anonymous in their bulky 7-SAS gear. Due to the cramped conditions on the target vessel, they would be carrying their Sunbeam sidearms, but nothing heavier. The VBSS party would also include Hunter and Elanna, as well as the ship's CHENG, Commander Ramsey. Julia Ashley stood nearby with Bennett. The idea was that she could supply mapping data from the *Big-H*, and also serve as the *Hillenkoetter*'s relay for telepathic communications.

"We're a mixed bunch today," Hunter said, looking at the other suited personnel. That had been deliberate—Hunter and Minkowski from the Navy, Nicholson from the Marines and Delta Force, Daly from the Army, and Briggs from the Air Force. The idea from day one had been to take personnel from various elite military units and forge them into a distinctly US Space Force assault team, but that goal had not yet quite been realized. They did function as a unit, and functioned well . . . but these people would always remain loyal to their original services. For Hunter, it was once a SEAL, *always* a SEAL, no matter what the change in designation or personnel record.

Well . . . he'd done his best.

And *they'd* done their best. And now they faced a new challenge.

"Okay, people," Hunter told them. "No fancy speeches. The op-plan is to go on board an alien spacecraft and make contact with the beings on board. We've had no communications with them, and we don't know for sure how they'll react. Miss Ashley has said they've requested our help. Whether they'll recognize armored humans dropping onto their quarterdeck as help remains to be seen. We will be going in armed just in case, and because we don't know what to expect. However, you will *not* fire unless you receive specific orders to do so. I don't want anyone putting a hole in the bulkhead. Understand?"

The response was immediate, loud, and enthusiastic. *"Hoo-yah!" "Hoo-ah!" "Ooh-rah!" "Sir, yes, sir!"*

"Questions?"

Briggs raised a hand. "Can't our mind readers here just *talk* to the aliens? Do we really need to go aboard their ship?"

"Elanna?" Hunter said. "Care to answer that?"

"We can't really communicate with any precision across a distance," she told them. "Feelings . . . impressions . . . yes. But information on what they need for repairs? Not so much."

"Other questions? No? Right. Let's saddle up!"

They filed up the TR-3W's ramp and took their seats along the narrow cargo compartment. The aft section was filled with the ungainly shape of one of the two Saurian jump gates, dismantled and brought up from Ares Prime on board this same 3W. The thing had been directly wired to the transport's power plant with massive cables snaking across the deck and was under the control of the flight crew engineer.

He'd been told that the unit would only function when the black triangle had powered-down its other systems. That would leave the transport vulnerable for precious seconds as the VBSS team made its insertion.

But there was nothing for it.

Hunter strapped in next to Elanna. "You okay?" he asked her.

"I'm fine," she said. He couldn't see her expression behind the reflections off her visor, but her voice sounded cold. "'Hoo-yah.'"

And then the TR-3W's drive engaged and the ship drifted out past *Hillenkoetter*'s now-operational induction screens.

Moments later they dropped toward an alien vessel marooned in an alien time.

CHAPTER TWENTY-ONE

The Flat Earth: The Earth is not a sphere but is instead either a flat disk or an infinite plane, as suggested in the Bible which refers to "the four corners of the Earth." NASA has faked the evidence otherwise, and GPS devices are rigged to convince aircraft pilots that they are flying around a globe. Photographs of the Earth from the Moon were either Photoshopped to show a spherical Earth, or they show Earth's circular but two-dimensional shape from directly above. The reason the government has been concealing the true nature of the Earth from the people is to discredit biblical truth.

CONSPIRACY THEORY BASED ON BIBLICAL PASSAGES,
MID-NINETEENTH CENTURY AND AFTER

ACCORDING TO HIS captor, the undersea base was called Rachallich, though Albrecht didn't know what that word meant. It was a place of wonders, of glass rooms and towering ceilings, of white plastic and endless hangars holding the smooth, brooding shapes of Eidechse saucers.

He'd expected to be dragged from the ship that had brought them, but one of his captors simply pointed at him, and gravity—at least for him—vanished. One of the smaller, huge-eyed servitor beings moved him through the air with a touch to guide his flight.

At the end of a long and convoluted path, they brought him to an immense room with gleaming rows of tall, upright, transparent cylinders. Each was filled with a viscous green liquid . . . and most held a nude and seemingly unconscious human.

*They floated him toward the nearest empty tube. His clothing . . .
what the hell had happened to his clothing? He struggled—
uselessly.*

At some point in the proceedings, one of the Eidechse *touched
his forehead, and he lost consciousness.*

THE TR-3W plunged into the ocean nearly ten miles from the current
location of the alien ship. Her inertial control shielded the crew
and passengers from the shock of impact; the drive field allowed
them to slip from one medium to another with barely a splash to
mark the passage, and accelerated the ship to a higher underwater
velocity than any submarine could manage, silently, without cavi-
tation. The same technology allowed such ships to move through
air at hypersonic speeds without the window-shattering crack of
a sonic boom. In minutes, the pilot had guided the craft into the
target area, the cockpit monitors showing nothing but inky blackness in all directions.

Hunter stood behind the pilot and copilot, bent forward in the
cramped cockpit to watch the visual displays. "How the hell do
you guys see where you're going?"

The copilot, Lieutenant Chavez, laughed and indicated a small
display on the console. "Got it covered right here," she told him.
"This sweet little computer pulls together data from every sensor
we have: sound, optical, laser, IR, water pressure, even gravitic
effects off our drive field. It pools them and makes sense of them
right here on this screen."

Hunter stared at the screen, noting what was clearly the ocean
floor picked out in thousands of points of green light, and the

ocean's surface in blue. There was detail enough to show large rocks on the bottom and the keels of a dozen large ships overhead.

"Huh. Is that our technology? Or . . ."

"Ha! We don't have anything like this, Commander. Not yet. Not this sensitive, and not in this kind of detail. And in 1967, all the other guy can do is listen in through SOSUS, or ping us with active sonar."

Hunter knew that SOSUS—the Sound Surveillance System— had been a vast network of passive sonar detectors deployed during the twentieth century to pinpoint Russian submarines.

"The records of this incident mention passive sonar at Government Point."

"That's it—the northern end of one of the arrays, Nova Scotia all the way to Barbados. Don't know if the guys listening here are Canadian or American, though."

Hunter almost told her that Canadians *were* American, but thought better of it. "Is that important?"

"Sure is, sir. Even back in this time period, US sonar operators are the *best*."

"Oh? Do I detect just a hint of nationalistic pride, Lieutenant?"

"Maybe a bit of *professional* pride, sir. I was a ping jockey on the USS *Seawolf* before I transferred to the Space Force. Counting change."

Hunter chuckled. He'd heard the stories. The joke was that if a sailor on the target ship accidentally dropped a pocketful of change on the deck, the US sonar operator listening nearby could tell that the coinage totaled forty-eight cents, one quarter, two dimes, and three pennies, and which of the coins had turned up "heads."

"Looks like we might have company," the pilot said. He pointed. "What do you think, Chav?"

Chavez pressed a button several times, each push showing a different angle, then pulled up an ID from the computer. "Yup. Submarine . . . but not one of ours."

Hunter had been expecting it. Some of the unofficial stories floating around in the wake of Shag Harbour suggested that a Russian sub had joined the party off Government Point and been tagged by passive sonar. Those stories, it seemed, were true.

"Let's stay out of his way," Hunter said.

"Not to worry, Commander," the pilot told him. "We'll leave him eating our wake."

Sure enough, the black triangle began smoothly pulling away from the cigar-shaped image of a submarine. In another moment, though, Chavez said, "Contact! There's our target!"

Hunter saw it, lying at an angle on the bottom just ahead. It looked like a flat brick picked out in orange pinpoints of light. "How big *is* that thing?"

"One hundred twelve meters, Commander," Chavez told him. "Range three hundred and fifty meters."

More than the length of a football field—*huge*. "Get us as close as you can," he ordered, "then bottom out. I'll get my team ready. Thanks for the lift."

"Good luck, Commander," the pilot said. "Bring us back a souvenir."

Assuming they could *come* back . . . but he didn't say that out loud.

In the passenger compartment aft, Ramsey was studying a breadboard controller board connected by a tangle of wires with the jump gate. "So, CHENG, you know what buttons to push?" Hunter asked, grinning.

"Hope so," Ramsey replied. "I guess we'll find out when you step through."

Hillenkoetter's engineering crew hadn't had much time to study the alien equipment at Ares Prime. The VBSS party was taking an ungodly chance, here.

"The gate mechanism is fairly straightforward," Elanna told him. "This rig has worked with the tests we were able to perform."

Somehow, the Talis agent managed to look sexy even inside her 7-SAS armor . . . something about the way she moved. He pushed the renegade thought aside. "Julia?" he asked, turning. "Have you made contact?"

"N-not very well, Commander," she replied. "It's . . . not exactly the best working conditions."

Hunter had been afraid of that. Generally when the remote viewer did her thing, it was on a couch or her bed in a darkened room and with no noise. The interior of the TR-3W was claustrophobically cramped, and she was further restricted by her heavy suit.

"Anything at all?"

"Just a . . . just a feeling, sir. Emotions . . . fear, worry, maybe anger. I haven't been able to talk with them at all."

"Okay. We'll hope they're not angry at us." He looked at Ramsey. "We ready to go?"

"As we'll ever be."

"Then open 'er up."

Ramsey worked something on the board, and the gate came to life. Ramsey looked through the opening into the night sky well above the surface of the ocean.

"How the hell do we steer?"

"With this." The chief engineer had wired what looked like a game controller to the circuit board. Using a thumb on each of the two control sticks, he began moving them with delicate adjustments until the view was looking down on the black waters off Nova Scotia. Several Navy ships were visible in the darkness below, marked by their running lights. The viewpoint zoomed down toward the water between two of the vessels, plunged beneath the surface without a ripple, and moved through underwater darkness.

Tension mounted on the transport's passenger deck as minutes crawled past. Ramsey was operating in the dark, with suggestions from both Ashley and Elanna. Even with their psychic guidance, it was nearly an hour before the gateway's opening suddenly flashed to a dim red illumination, to smoothly rounded surfaces, and to several huge dark sluglike things with tiny legs and wrinkled hides.

"Bingo!" Ramsey said. He adjusted the controller. "We're locked on."

Hunter reached out and touched the invisible barrier between that side and this. "Can we go through?"

"Just push your way through. The field will slide over you but maintain pressure. Or it *should*."

He extended his gloved hand, feeling the give of the invisible membrane, watching as the surface seemed to flow up the surface of the armored shell covering his forearm. Elanna had told him the atmosphere on the other side was ammonia-nitrogen at minus one-eighty. Nasty stuff.

"It better," he said. He straightened up, drawing his uprated Sunbeam pistol. "Okay. I'll go through first. Watch me for a signal. Elanna, you try to stay with my thoughts, okay?"

"Sir," Minkowski said. "I still don't think—"

"Don't give me an argument, Mink. All of you just stand by."

The truth was he refused to order one of his people to perform a task he would not. Gripping the pistol, he bent forward and stepped through, pressing ahead against heavy resistance.

And then he stumbled through, nearly losing his balance. The deck was tipped by a good twenty degrees, and the change in the gravity field caught him by surprise. The gravity was also a lot less than Earth-normal, similar to what he'd felt on Mars.

Three rod-shaped Zshaj shuffled about on their myriad, stubby legs, turning to face him with glittering constellations of eyes. *Don't be afraid*, Hunter thought, throwing everything he could into the attempt to communicate. *I'm here to help.*

There was no obvious reaction from the aliens, and Hunter heard nothing in his mind.

Telepathy between mutually alien species is always . . . tricky, Elanna's voice said in his mind. It sounded muffled and distant, almost unintelligible. *Different ways of thinking. Like being on a completely different frequency.*

"Then what am I supposed to do?" Hunter shot back. "How do I make them understand?"

Hold on, we're coming through, Elanna replied, and a moment later she stepped across the threshold, materializing out of the quadrangle of light behind him. A moment later, a second armored figure appeared; the name tag on her suit read "Ashley."

For several moments, Ashley, Hunter, and Elanna stood in front of the looming masses of the three aliens. Maybe, Hunter thought, the match in numbers itself was a message: *We're here to help, not to fight.*

"Okay," Ashley said over the comm after a moment. "I think we're okay. . . ."

And the three Zshaj lowered their bodies to the deck, completely hiding their legs.

HAVE YOU to hunt us come?

The words hammering into Julia Ashley's skull were crystalline clear and distinct, the mental volume high enough to make her wince. She was used to picking up psychic imagery in wisps and almost-not-there trickles, not in the torrent she was experiencing now. When she'd brushed these minds with her own once before, it had been across unimaginable gulfs of space and time. She'd been able to pick up the gist of what they were saying, but not clearly, and not with anything even approaching this clarity. These beings, she realized, these *Zshaj*, were true telepaths, communicating between one another and with alien species through the agency of thought alone.

The word order she heard was a little strange, the sentences choppy and brief. Were they asking if the humans were hunting *for* them? Or had arrived to hunt them, as prey?

One of them—she sensed the name *Kedawa*, though that might have been a title—opened what might have been a mouth beneath what could have been its head and extended a sinuous purple tentacle ending in three filaments. A tongue? But a tongue evolved as an arm and hand. It was clutching a silvery device of some sort. A weapon?

"We're here as friends," she told them carefully, trying to impress the idea in their minds. "We want to help you."

Damage to valitiz zolijop, Kedawa told her. It gestured with the device held by its tongue. *Attacked by Ve'hrech'na. Far-thought useless. Sensory loss. Drive crippled.*

Ve'hrech'na, Ashley knew, meant "We Surviving Few" and was a name used by the Saurians to refer to themselves.

"You know the Surviving Few?" she asked them.

Enemy! another said, its mind dripping acid. She sensed its name: Dorova. *Know them, yes, hate them, fear them ancient sickness.*

And Ashley saw a vivid image in her mind, a scene of Saurian disks dropping from a deep violet sky, a bleak and frozen wasteland below with clusters of bright red domes and rounded towers rising from the ice. . . .

Of a dazzling flash of actinic light that vaporized ice and structures alike, leaving a vast crater opening down into a boiling sea.

Our world . . .

Impressions flooded into Ashley's mind. The Zshaj had evolved on—or, rather, *within*—a world much like Titan in Earth's Solar System. The frigid moon of an ice giant, a world with a planetary ocean a thousand kilometers deep capped by ice frozen as hard as granite.

She wondered how had such an environment fostered *technological* life? How does an intelligent species even develop *fire* when it is locked away within an ice-capped ocean?

It seemed impossible.

The third being—referred to as Aladao—blinked its eyes at her in a rapid-fire and unintelligible pattern. *Learned we that the Ve'hrech'na evolved here, on this world*, it told her. *Come we here to learn of them. This time, too much we learned. . . .*

We had a hand in this, Elanna said within Ashley's mind. *The Talis and many other branches of humanity have fostered technic civilization on tens of thousands of worlds across the Galaxy. Species locked away in ice-bound moons. We helped them discover the cosmos.*

"Then . . . then you know these . . . these people."

Of course. They are our children. Which means they are yours *as well. . . .*

"But intelligence and civilization on a world like this . . ."

Trust me, Julia. Worlds with ice-capped planetary oceans far, far *outnumber worlds like Earth, perched uncertainly within narrow bands of habitability. The sun alone hosts many such— Europa, Ganymede, Callisto, Titan, Enceladus, Triton, Pluto . . . so many worlds ripe with the promise of life! And there is only one Earth.*

"But they're all so small and cold! How can anything live there?"

Europa, orbiting Jupiter, is about the size of Earth's moon. Beneath its icy exterior, it has an ocean one hundred kilometers deep. Julia, that is enough water to form an ocean two to three times more massive than all of the water on Earth. Such worlds outnumber rocky planets like Earth by hundreds of thousands to one. The Galaxy truly is brimming over with life.

"You mean all of those moons in the Solar System, they have life already? All those moons . . . and, my God, and *Pluto*?"

Let's just say that your people have some surprises in store as they continue to explore the worlds in their own backyard. In the meantime, our . . . children here need help.

Ashley grimaced at the thought. These "children" clearly were far more ancient than Humankind. Even with Talis help it had taken an incredible span of time to achieve star travel.

But, then, the Talis had time travel. The Galaxy embraced a teeming civilization occupying unimaginable vistas of space *and* time.

"How can we help them?" Ashley asked. "I can't understand a lot of what they're saying."

And hell, she thought to herself. *Why can't you help them, anyway?*

We cannot oppose the Malok directly, Elanna's voice said. Evidently, she'd heard Ashley's thought as though she'd spoken it aloud. *You know that. A time war would destroy civilization across the entire Galaxy.*

"But we can. Is that it?"

If you wish to take your place within the galactic milieu as an independent technic species . . . yes.

"It sounds," Hunter's voice cut in, "as though they need a good engineer. I suggest we get Commander Ramsey in here. Maybe you two can translate what it is they need." Evidently, Hunter had been party to the entire conversation, both spoken and telepathic.

Exactly right, Elanna said. *If you can help them repair their ship, they may be able to reach safety.*

Ashley nodded. "They say they have damage to their *valiz zoli*-something . . . whatever the hell *that* is."

"Then we'd best get started," Hunter told them. "CHENG! We need you over here. . . ."

"I'D LIKE to know how they were able to get that thing up and running," Ashley said.

Hunter grinned. "It just proves that the Talis are into this up to their sexy necks."

The two of them stood on one of *Hillenkoetter*'s observation decks. Through the large, deck-to-overhead transparency they could see Earth, with most of the visible hemisphere now shrouded in night. Scattered clusters of golden pinpoint lights marked the big cities—Boston, New York, Washington, and the coastline in between. To Hunter's eye, the nighttime lights of the US coast were not nearly so bright or as thickly strewn in 1967 as they were in his own time.

A monitor some forty feet square hung to one side. At the moment, it showed only the slowly rolling swells of a black ocean. A broken line of lights in the distance marked the horizon; several nearer lights might have been ships. Canadian and US warships had been patrolling the area with relentless determination the entire time.

It had taken three days, but the repairs to the alien ship, jury-rigged and fragile, were completed at last. Hunter had acted as liaison, using the teleportation frame taken from Ares Prime to shuttle back and forth between the TR-3W, the *Hillenkoetter*, and the Zshaj vessel, helping to organize the damage control party and getting the needed parts. *Hillenkoetter*'s chief engineer had supervised the fabrication of those parts in the *Big-H*'s machine shop and directed their installation in the alien vessel's power plant. Elanna had served as translator with the alien visitors, while Ashley had used her remote-viewing skills to peer deep into alien mechanisms, describing what she saw and providing measurements and detailed descriptions.

And now, the TR-3W had returned to the *Hillenkoetter* still hovering overhead, moving first through the water to get clear of the circling warships.

One warship was of particular concern. Neither Canadian nor US, it had been picked up by *Hillenkoetter*'s sensors edging in toward the perimeter of the surface naval operations—a Soviet Russian submarine.

According to the historical records, the Russian sub had approached, listened, then left . . . but *Hillenkoetter* was watching it carefully just in case.

"So what *are* the Talis up to?" Ashley asked after a long silence. "You're saying they made the parts we used to repair that ship?"

"Not quite," Hunter replied. "But they were involved."

"How?"

"Well, they'd use different measurements, different tolerances, different voltages, *everything* would be different. We wouldn't stand a chance in hell of carrying out repairs. But we got lucky."

"Commander Ramsey did say that the Zshaj power plant and gravitic drive were a lot like ours. Same principles, anyway."

"Right. I thought at first that we were seeing a kind of parallel evolution in engineering. We both use ZPE to power our ships, and we both tap that energy in pretty much the same way."

"'ZPE'?"

"Zero-point energy. The lifting of unimaginable quantities of power from quantum fluctuations within the vacuum."

She made a face. "If you say so. Quantum stuff gives me a headache."

"Ha. Me, too. But the only way we know of to harvest that energy is what the Talis use. The Zshaj *valitiz zolijop* was similar enough to the *Hillenkoetter*'s vacuum power tap that Tom was able to cobble together a working fix." Hunter shook his head. "The guy is scary."

"Elanna told me that if the Zshaj can just reach orbit, they'll be able to contact their mother ship."

"That's the idea. I gather they have some sort of telepathic amplifier . . . what they call a 'far-thought,' according to Elanna, but it doesn't work underwater, or even in-atmosphere."

"You said 'at first,' a little bit ago," she said. "You don't believe it now?"

"Believe what?"

"Parallel evolution."

"Oh. Right. No. I've decided that that's simply way too simple of an explanation. The Zshaj had help. *Lots* of it."

"The Talis."

"Exactly."

"You know, Elanna told me the other day that the Zshaj had evolved within an ice-capped ocean on a gas-giant moon in another star system. Apparently the Talis helped the Zshaj evolve eons ago."

"Stands to reason, doesn't it? The Talis gave *us* the principles of power taps and gravitic drives, right? They went so far as to help us build the *Hillenkoetter* and all of the other Solar Warden ships, and then show us how to use them. Obviously, judging by that explorer vessel down there, they gave those technologies to the Zshaj as well, giving them what they needed to break through their ice ceiling and push out into the Galaxy."

"So Zshaj technology and ours really *are* the same."

"Exactly. Hell, the Zshaj would have needed outside help just to figure out how to smelt metal, right? No fire—not underwater, and not in a nitrogen-ammonia atmosphere like Titan's."

"They might have used volcanic vents," Ashley suggested.

"Maybe. They might have started with that. But . . . my God! The Zshaj wouldn't even have known there was a whole universe outside! Their whole world would have been that icy deep-ocean darkness where they evolved! The Talis *must* have shown them."

Hunter wondered if the Talis might have tinkered with the Zshaj genome, but he didn't mention it to Ashley. How else can one explain a species leaving the dark and comfortably claustrophobic security of its abyssal cradle and evolving to live on their world's frozen surface?

Well . . . they *might* have done that on their own. Earth's animal life had made a similar change a few hundred million years ago, moving from the oceans to land and evolving along the way. Perhaps the Zshaj had simply done the same.

"Elanna told me that the Talis think of the Zshaj as their 'children,'" Ashley said. "Maybe their help was more than just helping them discover fire and build starships. Maybe they helped them *evolve*."

"I've been thinking the same thing." Hunter was thoughtful for a moment. "The Zshaj today don't look much like aquatic creatures, do they? All those legs."

"I'm beginning to think that the Talis have been running around the Galaxy for a long time, uplifting primitive species. What do you think they're doing . . . making lots of allies for themselves?"

"Could be. That could explain why the Saurians attacked that explorer ship. They might have the electronic equivalent of no trespassing signs put out . . . and real quick trigger fingers if anybody ignores them."

"Like us?"

"Mm. Maybe. But I don't think the Saurians see us as trespassers. They see us as *property*."

Ashley made a face. "Ugh."

"Kind of puts this galactic war in focus, doesn't it? The Saurians fighting for their . . . property. The Talis fighting for our independence from the Saurians, because eventually *we* turn into *them*. Their parents. . . ."

Hunter was silent for a moment, pursuing a sudden, new course of thought.

"What is it, Mark?"

"You know . . . if the Talis are in effect *our* children, the offspring of modern-day humanity . . . damn."

"What?"

"Does that make us the Zshaj's *grandparents*?"

Ashley laughed . . . then pointed at the monitor. "Look! I think they're moving!"

"Finally!"

On the screen, a dim light could just be made out beneath the rolling black waves, with a ripple as if from something very large and massive moving beneath the surface. The camera pulled back, showing now two nearby vessels—cutters of the Canadian Coast Guard. The light, barely visible but circled by a white targeting cursor, slipped between the cutters and accelerated, heading south. The *Hillenkoetter*'s long-range cameras followed.

"I hope those repairs hold," Ashley told him.

"I think they will." Hunter grinned. "I mean . . . we know how this turns out, right?"

"Sure. Unless we're sitting here changing history."

"I think I'd rather believe that we're just part of the picture, making happen what's *supposed* to happen."

Miles south of Government Point and the coast of Nova Scotia, well out into the North Atlantic, the Zshaj vessel broke the surface with very little in the way of splash or spray.

The Zshaj explorer, a huge, flattened, black brick with a band of light around its periphery, cut smoothly through the air and out into space.

"All hands, all hands," Groton's voice called over the intercom. "The alien explorer is away."

"What now?" Ashley wondered. "Back to Mars?"

"Back to Mars," Hunter said. "Definitely. We still have some unfinished business to take care of."

"I thought the Malok had left."

"They did. I'm talking about the unfinished business on *Earth*."

CHAPTER TWENTY-TWO

I Am Legend: In the 2007 movie *I Am Legend* starring Will Smith, a vaccine against cancer goes horribly wrong when most vaccine recipients die and the survivors turn into zombies. The anti-vax movement has taken this movie and turned it into a meme. "Remember," the meme warns, "in *I Am Legend*, the sickness didn't make the zombies. The vaccination did."

ANTI-VAXXER PROPAGANDA,
2020 AND AFTER

Note: The screenwriter for the movie was forced to issue a clarification to the effect that the movie was *fiction*, not a documentary.

HUMANS, CHARAACH DECIDED, *were unbelievably stupid creatures, far below the Vach on the scale of intelligence. Sometimes it seemed that they would believe* anything *you told them.*

She had again entered the mind of the human called Albrecht, staring into its thoughts through the transparent acrylic of one of the holding tubes. It was still fully conscious. It had struggled fitfully as it drowned . . . then showed the expected shock when the liquid surrounding it rushed into its lungs with the creature's final, gasping inhalation . . . but it didn't die. Instead, the last of the air within its lungs belched out into the green liquid in a huge bubble, and then the human continued to breathe.

Perfluorocarbon, the liquid it was now breathing, provided more than enough oxygen to keep it alive and conscious as Charaach began its lessons.

The Ghech fought her at every turn, its helplessly ineffectual mental struggles reminding Charaach of a flying insect from the swamps of her lost home, lightly and harmlessly fluttering against her face.

You will learn discipline, Ghech, *she told the human, speaking within its mind. Around her were the vast and shadowed recesses of the specimen storage lab, dark and with a high-vaulted ceiling, filled with row upon ordered row of holding cylinders. Charaach strengthened her connection with the human, feeding it images of the quiescent forms within each.*

We selected you, human, because you came out of the holocaust that was Greater Germany. You witnessed those events. They are part of you. We believe you capable of instilling discipline, loyalty, and patriotic fervor within your fellows in this modern era. But to instill those qualities, you must possess them yourself. Do you understand me?

The creature might have answered in her mind, but all that came across the mental link was a kind of mewling despair. Perhaps, Charaach thought, it had been pushed too hard. A pity, if so. If its mind was ruined, the human would be discarded.

Of course, there were many more where this one had come from. There were hundreds of specimens right here, all around her.

We will train you. The training will not be pleasant, but you will emerge stronger, more tractable, more able to carry out the instructions of your masters. Or . . . you will be disposed of.

She felt the human's violent, wordless shudder and knew she had gotten through.

It was difficult, but these creatures could *be taught.*

"THE ANSWER, Commander," Winchester told him, "is still *no*."

"With respect, Admiral," Hunter replied, "we *must* take charge of our own destiny. We cannot allow others to direct our path . . . not if we wish to survive as a species."

They were gathered in Admiral Winchester's spacious office suite on board the *Hillenkoetter*, aft of the CIC. Winchester and several members of his staff were on one side of his massive desk, and a number of personnel Hunter had brought in for this meeting were on the other, seated in a semicircle of folding chairs. Elanna was there, and Julia Ashley, as well as the young fighter pilot, Duvall, who'd been released from sick bay only hours before. Sitting behind Winchester were Captain Groton and several of his senior officers, including Commander Kelly, head of the ship's intelligence department, and Ramsey, the ship's CHENG.

Winchester gave Hunter a sharp look. "You are making the claim that this decision is . . . existential?"

"I am. If we don't make a stand here and now . . . well, we face planetary suicide."

"Because you claim the Saurians are using our own people against us."

"Yes, sir. Mr. Duvall here saw a *human* fall out of that enemy saucer he knocked down. Right, Lieutenant?"

"That's right, sir. I got a good look. The guy damned near bounced off my Stingray's cockpit!"

"We know the Malok recruited German Nazis from the Second World War," Winchester said. "And they had that Nazi colony at Aldebaran. There were suggestions that they were being turned into an army to use against us . . . but that threat *has* been blocked."

"Has it, sir?" Hunter asked. "We have proof that the Saurians have been, ah, *collecting* humans, abducting them over the course of fifty or sixty years, and keeping them on ice at an undersea base off the coast of California. And that's just the one base we know about. There are almost certainly others. Our Talis liaison here tells me that they're using telepathic manipulation to program some of their prisoners to spread Saurian misinformation all over the world."

Winchester actually smiled. "So-called fake news?"

"*Yes*, fake news. Admiral, can't you see how our entire civilization has been under assault for . . . for *years*, now? QAnon, InfoWars, Disinfomedia, and a hundred others . . . *all* of them cranking out fake news stories as fast as they can, spreading lies, gossip, and wild conspiracy theories manufactured to deliberately undermine people's faith in the government."

"Some would say," Groton put in, "that a healthy skepticism about the government is a *good* thing." He chuckled. "Don't quote me."

"Ever since Watergate," Hunter replied, "yeah, I agree. But our enemies are using lies to push their agendas. Even other governments—Russia planting false stories to sway US voters. North Korea, Iran, Hamas, the Taliban, *all* of them cranking out lies and propaganda to win friends and influence people."

"Commander," Winchester said, "are you actually claiming the *Saurians* are behind all this? That's crazy."

"Commander Hunter is right, Admiral," Elanna told him. "There is a technique, a kind of psychological warfare at which the Malok are very, very good. We call it 'memegineering'—the creation and implantation of ideas that take on a life of their own, designed for the purpose of persuasion."

Winchester looked puzzled. "'Meme' . . . ?"

"Admiral, a meme is like a *gene* in biology," Commander Kelly told him, "but it's a unit of information, not a sequence of nucleotides. Like genes, they self-replicate, mutate, and change according to the laws of natural selection."

"I've heard the term used in social media," Winchester said, "but didn't know where it came from. I thought a meme had something to do with cats."

"Essentially, the Saurians can infect someone with a set of ideas they've created," Elanna said. "That person will infect others, and they'll infect still more until an entire culture has been changed . . . corrupted."

"Okay. But it sounds like you're just talking about propaganda. Nothing new in that."

"Admiral, what you think of as 'propaganda' is as far removed from Saurian memegineering as a stone knife is from a Starbeam laser. The Saurians have refined their tools and techniques over the course of many millennia. They use them with the precision of a surgeon. Believe me, Admiral, when I say that memegineering—getting into the brains of a target audience and changing them at will—is as much a weapon of mass destruction as a thermonuclear warhead."

"So the Lizards are using super-propaganda on us?"

"They've been doing so for thousands of years, Admiral. The

Saurians, remember, are relatively few in number. They don't have the numerical strength to take on the entire human population of the planet in a stand-up fight. But if they can corrupt a sizable fraction of that population, get cultures and nations and religions and political factions and even individual people at each other's throats, they've won. Control of Earth will fall right into their scaly laps."

"Yes . . . but *all* propaganda?" Wheaton asked, shaking his head.

"Not *all* propaganda comes from the Saurians, certainly. Not all fake news, or disruptive memes, or conspiracy theories are Malok plants. But we have known for some time that some of the stories being fed into the Western media, especially *social* media, are deliberately planted to cause chaos, confusion, fear, and a loss of trust in government. This is being carried out by enemy agents . . . the Malok. And we now have evidence that the Saurians are using their human abductees to spread those stories, to foment unrest and destabilize governments, and even to engage us directly militarily. If you don't confront them with strength, you will be overwhelmed."

"I thought the Talis were more . . . more conservative than that," Winchester said. "No all-out confrontations with the Lizards. No all-out war. No *time* war. . . ."

"Remember, Admiral," Elanna said. "We Talis are as human as you. And that means we can be wrong."

"And that," Winchester said, settling back in his desk chair, "may be the scariest thing I've heard this morning."

"The Talis have been wrong, yes, sir," Hunter said. He gave Elanna a sidelong glance. "They helped the Nazis in the years before World War II because their understanding of that part of Earth's history was . . . incomplete."

"We were attempting to counter the efforts of the Malok, who were actively attempting to help the Germans win the war. But we were unaware of some of the details." She tilted her head, her large and expressive eyes on the admiral. "Tell me, Admiral . . . do you believe in *evil*?"

Winchester looked uncomfortable. "Well . . . what's evil for one culture might be considered good for someone else. . . ."

"Including the torture and extermination of millions in concentration camps?"

"Well . . . obviously no."

"Sir, the Talis have a fairly simple take on the idea of evil. *Evil is that which intentionally distorts or destroys the human spirit.* By that definition the Nazis epitomize the very concept of evil. So do the Soviet communists, the Maoists of the Great Leap Forward, the church inquisitors of the Medieval era, and the sponsors of slavery all over the world ever since the Neolithic Revolution. And the state-sponsored genocides in China, Turkey, Cambodia, Rwanda, the Americas—"

"Please, Elanna," Winchester interrupted. "We get the idea."

"The Malok represent a distinct and extremely dangerous *evil*, Admiral Winchester. They must be stopped."

"I think it's also important," Hunter added, "for us, for Solar Warden, to take charge, here, to be more than pawns in the struggle between Talis and Malok."

"I understand your feelings, Commander. But Solar Warden exists under the aegis of the National Command Authority. We do not make policy. And that means we can't rush off to punish evildoers without direct orders from—"

"The President?" Hunter asked, completing the sentence. "But my understanding is that the President, today's President, doesn't even know about Solar Warden . . . right? Eisenhower, maybe Kennedy, maybe Nixon . . . they knew. But at some point, the office of the President was . . . snip!" His fingers imitated a scissors motion. "Cut right out of the loop. So was the Defense Department . . . and National Intelligence, though I'm sure there are individuals within those offices who know what's going on. Today, Solar Warden is run by . . . who? Majestic-12?"

"MJ-12 directs all classified activities *above* Crypto 17," Winchester admitted. There were twenty-eight levels of the Top Secret Crypto system of security classification. The President of the United States was supposed to be at level seventeen.

"*And*," Captain Groton said, staring at Elanna, "we have reason to suspect that the enemy has already penetrated MJ-12."

"Warden's Command, Admiral," Elanna said softly. "Remember? We must do this."

"What," Groton asked, "is this 'Warden's Command'?"

"Warden's Command," Winchester said, "refers to the fact that the Talis are, ultimately, in charge of Solar Warden. They—and the Grays working with them—gave the technology to us in the first place, starting back in Eisenhower's day. They showed us all of what we know. Part of the agreement with them stipulated that they maintain control overall. They promised to keep hands off . . . most of the time. But when there's a serious breach in security, or a threat we can't handle . . ." He let the sentence trail off.

"They take charge," Groton said, nodding. "Understood."

"The idea all along," Elanna told them, "was that twenty-first-century humans should be eased into galactic culture *gently*. It would have been complete idiocy to give you star travel and high-tech weaponry and just toss you into shark-infested waters on your own, without support."

"Especially if you want us to survive," Hunter put in, "so that someday *we* can become *you*."

"Precisely." Her eyes closed, and she smiled. "It's something of a tightrope balancing act."

"Okay, Elanna, so you've invoked Warden's Command," Winchester said. "For a *second* time, now. What is it you want us to do?"

"We want you to carry out a measured response against the Malok. They have a number of secret bases on Earth—that's common knowledge. The one we're interested in, however, is Sycamore Knoll . . . the Malibu USO base." She nodded at Ashley. "Your remote viewer, here, has accurately seen inside that base. We know they have several hundred human abductees, there. We believe the Saurians are using their captives as a resource—a pool of vectors for memetic infection, and of personnel for military duties . . . like the pilot Mr. Duvall saw."

"How many Malok are inside that base?" Kelly wanted to know.

"Unknown."

"How many human prisoners?" Hunter asked.

"Also unknown."

"Then I don't see how we can effectively carry out your instructions," Winchester said. "The JSST consists of a hundred men and women, more or less. What if there are a thousand of your Malok down there? What if there are a thousand captives? How do we get them out? How do we even *reach* them . . . ?"

"We do have a useful tool in that regard, Admiral," Hunter pointed out. "The Dimensional Gateway."

"Which won't help one bit if we *are* up against a thousand enemy troops."

"Actually," Hunter said, smiling, "I have some ideas on that. . . ."

"Which are . . . ?"

"First off, sir, we need to get the gateway we captured back into Ares Prime. . . ."

JULIA ASHLEY lay back in her bunk, eyes closed, mind open to . . . that place. She was having considerable trouble focusing. It was like the Zshaj were still inside her head. She could see them when she closed her eyes, watching her. Those long, purple tongues . . .

She shuddered.

Both Bennett and Hunter were in her room with her, Bennett with a recorder, Hunter asking gentle, guiding questions. Something about his voice helped steady Ashley, helped her concentrate on the task at hand.

And, somehow, the Zshaj were a part of the process.

"I think they're still here," she said.

"Who, Julia?" Bennett asked. "Who's still here?"

"The Zshaj. They're in my head. I think . . . I think they want to help us."

"Paying us back, maybe," Hunter said. Ashley felt his smile in the semidarkness.

"Something like that. I think they're . . . they're *interested* in us. In who we are."

"Try to focus on your assignment, Julia," Bennett told her. "The Malibu base . . ."

This was a huge leap from normal remote-viewing protocol, but lately Ashley had become used to the idea. The trick had been convincing Bennett that the process was legitimate. Instead of being given a string of coordinates, she was now able to pick up on a given location she'd already visited.

The hard part was letting her mind drift into the target without preconceived notions of what she would find. That sort of thing swiftly led to her seeing what she wanted to see . . . or what she believed she *should* see . . . and not what was actually there.

Reality, Ashley was learning, was a slippery, twisty beast that could change if you simply looked at it.

She found the memory of the Malibu base, four hundred feet beneath the surface of the Pacific Ocean. Sycamore Knoll . . . funny name. She couldn't decide if it meant that oceanologists didn't have much imagination when it came to naming marine features . . . or if it meant that they had too much.

Seven domes laid out in a now familiar arrangement, six small bubbles around a large central structure. They gleamed like silver, and she noticed that there wasn't enough light at this depth to see anything.

So just what was she seeing? *How* was she seeing?

That sort of second-guessing would jolt her out of the session *real* quick. She let her mind slip down into the central dome, seeking out a place she'd been before. "I'm in the forest," she told the others.

"Sherwood Forest," Hunter's voice said.

"I don't see Robin Hood," she replied. "Why Sherwood?"

"I was on a boomer once, during a SEAL op. A submarine with sixteen launch tubes for Poseidon nuclear missiles. The tubes are lined up side by side in two long columns of eight each inside a single huge compartment. *Big* suckers. The sailors on board called the place Sherwood Forest."

She saw the kinship at once. Her mind had stubbornly insisted on calling the place a "forest," though there were no trees in sight. Instead, she again saw the row upon row of translucent, upright cylinders, each filled with green liquid, each holding a nude human. Most appeared to be sleeping; in a few, the occupant was clearly, nightmarishly awake and struggling . . . until they slipped back into some kind of an alien, twilight sleep.

Ashley was rapidly sketching on the notebook beside her. She also described what she was seeing out loud for the benefit of Bennett's voice recorder.

"I'm not sure how many tubes there are," she said. "But hundreds, certainly. A few are empty. Most are . . . occupied."

She felt Hunter stir uncomfortably beside her. She knew that Hunter had his girlfriend inside one of these things, and he was driven to try to find her.

Ashley had actually seen Geri Galanis during a past exploratory visit to this place of horrors. She considered going there immediately, but knew she had to focus on the larger mission first. They wanted her to determine just how many people were being held captive here.

"The cylinders are all sealed," she told them. "I can't be sure, but it looks like you could just lift them off their pedestals and cart them away. I see wiring and mechanisms on the caps on top. My guess is life support."

"Power supply?" Hunter asked.

"I think it's built in, Mark," she told him. "I can *feel* power flowing through them. It's not coming from outside."

"Thank God for that," Hunter said softly. "That gives us a chance, at least. . . ."

"*Please* refrain from the running commentary, Commander," Bennett said. "Julia mustn't analyze what she sees, understand? She just reports."

"I . . . I see someone," Ashley said. "A human!"

"There are hundreds of humans there, Julia," Bennett told her.

"No! This is a man . . . he's inside one of the containers. But he's awake! There's a Saurian outside the tube, looking at him. . . ."

"Can you describe him?"

"Not really. I'm just getting . . . I don't know. Feelings, really. He's . . . he's not wearing any clothes . . . but I'm getting a sort of a sense of some kind of uniform overlaying what I'm seeing."

"Mental projection," Bennett said. "If he's under a considerable stress, his mind might be putting out impressions of what he's used to. If he was military, say, and found comfort or purpose or identity in his uniform. . . ."

"What kind of uniform, Julia?" Hunter asked.

"Black . . . lots of straps and brass . . . There's a German Iron Cross at his throat . . . that cross-shaped medal? Oh . . . and a swastika armband, left arm."

"A Nazi soldier, then. Can you get anything besides the uniform?"

"Blue eyes . . . sharp features. And, he's in pain."

"He's injured?"

"No . . . not that kind of pain. I . . . I'm getting a kind of weird double-image. He looks like a human, but there's something else inside his head!"

"Tell us what you see, Julia."

More than once in the past, Julia Ashley's roving mind had encountered other alien minds, ones with powerful telepathic potential, that were *aware* of her, able to *see* her, even though she was not present in the flesh. Now, she looked into the icy blue eyes of the prisoner, and she could see, superimposed on the image, another face staring back at her—golden eyes with slit pupils, like a snake's . . . scaly brown skin with just a hint of iridescence . . . a snout with large nostrils above a mouth filled with curved teeth. . . .

In the past, when confronted by one of these aware and knowing gazes, Ashley had fled. This time, though, she stood her ground. She was reasonably certain the thing couldn't reach her, though her every instinct was to flee.

"It's the Saurian," she told Hunter and Bennett. "The man is . . . is *possessed* by the Saurian outside the tank. God, it sees me. It knows I'm here. . . ."

Abruptly, the reptile face vanished, leaving the human behind. Like a string-cut puppet, the human crumpled into unconsciousness within the tank. The uniform faded away with the man's awareness.

"A Nazi," Hunter said softly.

"Apparently. Why a Nazi *here*, though, off the coast of California?"

"They've cropped up in modern times before," Hunter said. "Hans Kammler and 'the Bell.'"

"I don't know what that means."

"Ancient history. A Lizard spacecraft came down outside a little town in Pennsylvania . . . 1965, I think it was, at a place called Kecksburg. The alien pilot got away, but the Army found a Nazi inside the ship, an SS general named Hans Kammler. We're pretty sure the ship was a Saurian time machine from twenty years earlier."

"Are you saying this guy Julia sees is Kammler?"

"Maybe. But my guess is it's just another time-traveling Nazi."

"Do you still see the man, Julia?" Bennett asked.

"Yes. I think he's unconscious."

"Can you pick up anything else about him?"

"I'm . . . trying. I think . . . I think I got a word from his mind. '*Albrecht.*'"

"'Albrecht'?" Bennett asked. "Is that part of the overlay you're seeing?"

"I think so. Like the uniform . . . part of his identity . . . who he is."

"So . . . is this Albrecht working with the Saurians?" Bennett asked. He almost smiled. "*That's* convenient. Nazis and aliens in one neat package."

"Sounds more like Herr Albrecht is being *ridden* by the Saurians," Hunter said. "I wonder, though . . ."

"Wonder what?" Ashley asked.

"How many old stories of demon possession were *real*."

Bennett shrugged. "We'll have to ask him."

"If we get the chance. Julia? Do you see anyone else in that room? Besides the prisoners, I mean. Other Saurians."

"No. It's empty now. I . . . I kind of get the sense that there are a lot more Saurians and Malok Grays nearby, though. Maybe in the surrounding domes."

"Can you find some sort of control room? A central office, or something like that?"

"Let me look. . . ."

Ashley continued to drift through the Malibu base. The place was huge. There were several hangars filled with various types of Saurian spacecraft, from the sleek, crescent-shaped little Arnolds up to transports that might carry a hundred passengers. There were storerooms aplenty, filled with crated, tanked, or packaged supplies . . . sleeping quarters, several occupied by the current off-watch mess decks—she tried not to look at the bloody, raw meat. . . .

Worst, though, was the room she thought of as the laboratory, sleek and clean and gleaming white. Five Grays and one Reptilian were gathered around a large, rectangular table beneath a suspended cluster of probes or sensors of some sort.

And on the table was a screaming man. He was nude, and though he was struggling wildly, he appeared to be held in place by invisible restraints. A circlet embraced his head, and Ashley had the sense that he was being fed images of some sort through that device . . . *horrible* images . . . that he was somehow being *trained*. . . .

The large Saurian touched the man on his forehead, and the prisoner at once lapsed into unconsciousness.

And then they saw her. As one, each Gray and the Reptilian who Ashley instinctively thought of as the leader turned its head and stared straight at her disembodied viewpoint.

"They see me!" she cried. She could feel the force of a powerful mind behind that gaze. Was it the Saurian? Or was she feeling the combined gestalt of the tall Reptilian with its five Gray helpers?

The power behind that gaze was like a hammer blow . . . and *this* time, she fled.

"OUR RECONNAISSANCE of the objective has been completed," Hunter told the men and women seated around the table. In front of him was a stack of crude sketches and handwritten notes. Julia Ashley sat beside him, looking drawn and tired.

They'd gathered in Briefing One aft of the ship's CIC . . . Hunter's senior people in the Just One were gathered around the table, along with Captain Groton, Captain Macmillan, and Elanna.

Admiral Winchester was conspicuous by his absence.

"The TR-3W we used at Shag Harbour has returned to our flight deck," he continued. "The ship's CHENG and his black gang are hooking up the Dimensional Gateway there. Commander Ramsey tells me they should be ready to rock in another two hours. The other gateway, the one in the Mars Prime basement, is powered up and ready to go."

Hunter tapped the notes and drawings on the table before him. "Julia, here, has given us quite a lot to work with." He picked up several large sheets of white cardstock and passed them around.

"These are the floor plans we've been able to put together based on Julia's observations. You'll notice that only a handful of compartments have been positively identified. This place is huge . . . and Julia wasn't able to check all of it out. But we have the important places nailed down—control center, hangars, sleeping quarters, the lab, and the Forest."

"So . . . we'll pop into the Forest," Minkowski said, studying one of the maps. "What do we do then? Those tubes are three or four hundred pounds each with the liquid in them . . . and the weight of a full-grown person on top of that. What are we gonna do . . . rent a forklift?"

"That," Hunter said, "has already been taken care of." He looked at Macmillan. "Right, CAG?"

"If you break 'em, Commander, you've bought 'em."

"I'll keep that in mind, sir." He took the map from Minkowski and turned it so everyone could see. "Now we need to look at F and M. . . ."

CHAPTER TWENTY-THREE

Would we, if we could, educate and sophisticate pigs, geese, cattle? Would it be wise to establish diplomatic relations with the hen that now functions, satisfied with mere sense of achievement by way of compensation? I think we're property.

CHARLES FORT,
THE BOOK OF THE DAMNED, 1919

ALBRECHT WAS FREE... *after a fashion.*

The Eidechse *had left him for reasons unknown . . . but Albrecht in his current state could barely register the fact. He was underwater . . . he was* breathing *water . . . and he didn't know how that was possible. The effort generated intense pain in his chest each time he inhaled.*

Albrecht felt physically sick . . . betrayed . . . violated. Over the past days he had become more and more convinced that the Eidechse *were simply using the Reich for their own secret purposes, their own agenda . . . but the fact that they'd stuffed him into this tank with the promise of* training *him . . .*

The consuming anger he felt over his betrayal, strangely, was fading. In its place was an overwhelming lassitude . . . a need for sleep. Was it something in the liquid? Or something transmitted mind to mind?

He didn't know.

Physically, he could only give in . . . relax . . . accept . . .

But he would continue to fight these . . . these demons for as long as he drew breath.

No matter what he was breathing at the time.

HUNTER, ENCASED in his 7-SAS, crouched in the Ares Prime basement, peering through the aperture of the captured Dimensional Gateway. "It looks fuzzy, CHENG," he said.

"It does," Ramsey replied. The chief engineer, like all of the other people currently working in that basement area, also wore a pressure suit. The air down here was still as thin as out on the surface of Mars. "But what do you expect?" Ramsey continued. "We're zeroing in on a few cubic meters at a range of over a hundred and sixty million kilometers. Of *course* the damned thing is fuzzy!"

"Yeah . . . but when we step through, what kind of condition will we be in on the other side? If light's being distorted through this thing, what's going to happen to biology?"

"That's not the way to think of it," Ramsey said. "Right now, Mars is a hundred and sixty million kilometers or so from Earth, yeah. But through this thing?" He fondly patted the frame of the transporter. "It's more like five meters. We're not going *through* space. We're stepping *past* it."

"At least it looks like you managed to compensate for the velocity difference."

"That took a while," Ramsey replied. "I should have said we're zeroing in on a few cubic meters that are moving a few thousand kilometers per hour in *one* direction, while we're going just as fast in another. The base computers do seem to be keeping the two frameworks steady now relative to each other. Thank God."

As Hunter stared across . . . no, as he stared *past* all of those empty kilometers, he could still see a bit of drift to the right, and up wasn't quite the same *there* as it was *here*. The team should be able to handle it, though.

He could just make out the tall, ordered rows of acrylic tubes on the other side, their contents little more than vaguely humanoid shadows.

Hang on, Geri, he thought. *We're coming to get you. We're coming to get* all *of you. . . .*

"Mark?"

It was Julia Ashley, fetchingly clad in a blue pressure suit identifying her as a civilian, with a NASA tag on the chest. She handed him an iPad.

"Hi, Julia!" he said. "Do you have it?"

"It's all here." She touched a button, and the screen of the handheld device winked on. It showed images pulled from the large, cardstock drawings taken from her notes. "All of the levels are on here." She pointed. "I also did what I could to identify the actuator mechanisms, like you asked."

Hunter studied the current page, noting small, red icons at obvious doors and entryways. "Excellent. We just might be able to pull this off."

"Are you going to want me coming along?"

Hunter considered this. It was tempting. Julia had a remarkable talent for getting into blind corners and the interiors of mechanisms with her mind and being able to describe what she saw. That talent, so far as Hunter could tell, was getting stronger and stronger every time she interacted with telepathic beings.

"No, Julia. We need you on this side. Elanna will be going

through because she can talk with the Lizards. I'll want you to stay linked to her, okay? If we need you to 'look' at something, she can bring you in and show you what it is."

"I guess that makes sense." She seemed to sag a little. "I'm just as glad, actually. The Lizards can see me, and when they do it scares the crap out of me. I feel . . . I don't know . . . paralyzed. Or hypnotized, like I can't move."

Hunter smiled. "People used to think that snakes hypnotized their prey just by looking at it. Maybe the Saurians do something like that."

"And maybe I'm just scared stiff. You . . . you be careful over there. Please?"

"Absolutely. Oops . . . watch out. . . ."

A large ordnance hauler off the *Hillenkoetter* had just emerged from the broad ramp that connected the basement with the ground level above. It was pulling a large flatbed trailer behind, and several regular forklifts were following in its wake.

Ashley stepped aside and watched them pass. Briggs stood a few yards away, waving his hands to direct the loaders and haulers into a compact parking area. "Those were on the shuttle that brought me down," Ashley said. "For the tubes?"

"That's right. We're going to need to get those people loaded up and back here just as quickly as we can."

"Don't drop any of them."

Hunter pointed to a line of men and women entering with the equipment, each with colored vests draped over their pressure suits to identify their place in the flight deck ballet. "We have a small army of deck personnel coming along to drive," Hunter said. "They know what they're doing."

"Okay. I'd better go get settled in. Dr. Bennett is waiting for me."

"Control room, yeah. Good luck!"

"You too, Mark. I'll be . . . watching."

He watched her leave, squeezing past the influx of personnel and equipment. He wondered about her loyalty to Bennett. The guy didn't appear to do anything but carp and try to protect her from the rest of the world.

Or . . . maybe that was precisely what she wanted.

"Attention on deck!" someone called over the radio channel.

"Admiral on the deck," echoed another.

"As you were," Winchester's voice said.

Surprised, Hunter turned and came to attention. What the hell was Winchester doing down *here*?

"Admiral," he said. "Sir."

"Commander," Winchester said. "Hope you don't mind the intrusion. I came down on the 3B with the flight deck gang."

Hunter wondered if Winchester was here to pull the plug on the operation at the last moment. Or did he just plan on launching a last-second lecture about not screwing up the timeline?

"Not a problem, sir. What can we do for you?"

"Just stopping by to see you off, son."

"You didn't have to shuttle down here for that, sir." Hunter grinned through his helmet visor. "There's this wonderful new invention, you know. It's called 'radio.'"

He looked off to Hunter's left. "Hmm. Some things are safer spoken in person."

Hunter followed Winchester's brief glance. Elanna was about ten yards away at the jury-rigged control panel that ran the Dimensional Gateway. He wondered if the admiral was aware of how easily she might be able to read their minds.

But all he said was "Yes, sir."

"Commander, I am on record as opposing this plan . . . as you well know. I'm under oath to uphold the Constitution of the United States . . . and that means I take orders from my commander in chief, the President. Even if the President is not in the loop over what's happening, he still has the final authority."

"Does he have authority over MJ-12?" Hunter asked. "I've always wondered. . . ."

"Technically . . . yes. MJ-12 is not in the *official* chain of command . . . but when they give the orders, the DoD, the Space Force, and Solar Warden all jump." He looked again across at Elanna. "Lately I've come to see your arguments in an entirely new light."

"My arguments?"

"About how humans need to take charge of their own future."

"Even when that future is defined by our . . . children?"

"Especially then. We can't have the kids always telling us what to do."

"It seems to me, Admiral, that we could benefit quite a bit from having the kids tell us what to do. How to unscramble what we've done to the environment, for instance. How to avoid getting slammed by a space rock. There are quite a few existential threats that we can't do much about right now. Maybe *they* can."

"I agree. But the first existential threat on the agenda is the Saurians, and . . . you're right. We have to deal with that threat ourselves, if only to prove that we can."

If this was supposed to be a don't-screw-things-up lecture, Hunter thought, it was taking an unusual course.

"So," Winchester added, "officially, I'm out of the picture. If I was *in* the picture, I would need to insist that we clear this thing with MJ-12 first. With Elanna invoking Warden's Command, I can sit back, put my feet up, and wish you and your people the very best of luck."

The genuineness of Winchester's benediction caught Hunter completely by surprise.

"Thank you, Admiral. That is very much appreciated."

Winchester's eyes twinkled through his visor. "Just don't screw up Elanna's precious timeline, okay? She would be thoroughly pissed if you did."

Hunter tossed Winchester a jaunty salute. "We'll certainly do our best, sir."

And Winchester returned the salute with grave formality. "I know you will, Mark."

Hours more passed, but the JSST at last was ready to roll. Hunter had gone down the lines of SAS-suited men and women, checking weapons and dropping encouraging comments. Their mood seemed almost buoyant. They understood the importance of finally taking the war to the enemy on Earth, even if that meant widening the undeclared war.

And above them, on board the *Hillenkoetter*, the rest of the 1-JSST, under the command of Lieutenant Billingsly, were gathered with over a hundred of the ship's flight deck personnel, each wearing a colored vest over their pressure suit—the red ordnance "mag rats" who ran the ship's magazines, the yellow deck handlers and aircraft directors, the blue plane handlers, and the green maintenance personnel. Most had transferred to Solar Warden right off the decks of various US aircraft carriers. All had long experience moving heavy and delicate loads about the flight deck. Their code name was Rescue.

But down here in Ares Prime, the JSST assault force tagged "Spearpoint" would lead the attack.

Ramsey would be staying with the electronics and computer personnel manning the Ares Prime gateway, but a number of machinist's mates and electronic specialists under the command of Lieutenant Commander Winslow were on the *Hillenkoetter*'s fight deck with Rescue, ready to jump across the 150 million kilometers currently separating Mars from the Earth.

Hunter saw Elanna with them, and she was linked mind-to-mind with Julia, on board the *Big-H*.

Everyone in their place . . . everyone ready.

Time for Humankind to take a stand.

"Right, people," Hunter said over the unit's tactical frequency. "It's showtime. Remember to check your fire. There are a hell of a lot of civilians in the AO. Everybody ready? Be sure to brace yourselves for the blow." He looked at the twenty JSST troops closest to him, at the front of the pack. "Spearpoint!" he called. "Stand by to move out!"

They chorused back at him with a blend of *ooh-rah*s and *hoo-yah*s. He really had to find a single, unique battle cry specific to Solar Warden. The Army's *hoo-ah* was also supposed to be the battle call of the new Space Force, but Hunter still wanted something more, something with meaning.

"Gateway! On my mark, drop the M-kiss! In three . . . two . . . one . . . *go*!"

Wind at hurricane force blasted through the wide-open gateway framework.

The interface between one gateway and the next, the rubbery-feeling force field called a magnetokinetic induction screen—or MKIS—switched off, and the atmosphere within the Malibu base began blasting into the near-vacuum in the basement of Ares Prime. The event, Hunter thought a little wildly, was a nice piece of payback for what the Saurians had done to the screen across the large entrance to *Hillenkoetter*'s flight deck. The armored troops within the Mars base crouched and held on as the wind buffeted them, rushing past and up and through the labyrinth of evacuated compartments within Ares Prime.

The sudden drop inside the Malibu base had the same effect as the earlier pressure loss on board the *Hillenkoetter*: sensors throughout the structure detected the drop and activated the emergency doors, which slammed shut with reverberating booms.

"Mark!" Ashley's voice called in his head. "The doors are closed!"

"Right! Mr. Ramsey! Raise the M-kiss! Spearpoint . . . *go*!"

The silent hurricane of outrushing air snapped off, and the twenty men of the lead strike team surged forward through the Dimensional Gateway. The magnetokinetic induction screen, now holding back the air within the Malibu base, closed around the armor of each JSST trooper as they pushed through, a sensation like moving through a viscous wall of molasses.

Hunter stepped across the threshold, stumbling a bit as gravity three times greater than what he'd felt on Mars dragged at him, and the room seemed to shift to a different up-down orientation. Ahead, Herrera and Minkowski both had dropped to a kneeling crouch, weapons at the ready. Behind him, Joan Nicholson seemed to materialize out of thin air, her Starbeam Mk. 2 at her shoulder, seeking targets. At the right angle, the gateway's framework was just visible hanging in the air, with just a hint of motion-filled darkness beyond.

"Spread out!" Hunter barked. "Perimeter defense around the LZ!"

The LZ was a twelve-meter stretch of empty deck between the ordered ranks of Sherwood Forest and a broad ramp leading up to a sealed double door. The incoming troops created a broad circle, facing out against any potential threat. Laser fire snapped to Hunter's right, where EN1 Taylor and Sergeant Alvarez engaged a lanky, armored Saurian near the sealed pressure door at the top of the ramp. The Lizard turned, trying to get off a shot at the humans from the weapon strapped to its torso, but the uprated PEWs cut the being down in a volley of blue-white flares of light.

Was that the only Lizard guarding Sherwood Forest? Hunter signaled his men to keep spreading out, searching for any more enemy guards.

"Looks like we're clear, Skipper," Minkowski told him. "No more bad guys."

"Stay alert. Commander Ramsey?"

"Receiving you loud and clear, Commander." Radio, fortunately, could transmit through the gateway, offering Hunter an ingenious means of bypassing Einstein. He could talk to Ramsey, in Ares Prime . . . and Ramsey could communicate with the *Hillenkoetter* above the Martian surface.

"Let Billingsly know," Hunter told him. "The LZ is secure. Start bringing Rescue through."

"Roger that, Spearpoint."

Hunter turned his attention to the rows of vertical storage tanks. "Elanna?" he called. "Ask if Julia can guide me to the guy she saw earlier, the Nazi. Is he still conscious?"

"She can't tell, Mark," Elanna said after a moment. "She thinks he's to your left . . . all the way down that row in front of you, four from the end."

"Gotcha. Mink . . . Nicholson . . . Bostwick . . . with me."

If the captive Nazi was still awake, they might be able to question him. Hunter knew from previous rescues that it took time to awaken the unconscious prisoners, that they were muddled and often incoherent until they'd had a chance to recuperate. Not always.

A few had awakened screaming.

In any case, he didn't want to smash his way through the Forest at random trying to find someone who might or might not have some useful information about this place.

"There he is," Ashley said over Hunter's helmet radio. "On your left."

Hunter saw the man . . . and realized that Albrecht now saw him, too. The blue eyes were wide open, bulging in terror, as he struggled within the tight confines of the liquid-filled cylinder. Hunter knew that these cylinders were equipped with some sophisticated alien electronics that could render the prisoner unconscious. Evidently, Albrecht had been left awake . . . that, or he'd been awakened by the Reptilian Ashley had seen from Mars. The man hammered his fists against the transparency, the blows slowed by the liquid to ineffectual shoves.

"Winslow!" he called. "Get a rescue team over here. Second row back, far end."

"On our way, Commander."

"Bring Marlow with you." They would need the corpsman to start reviving these prisoners.

In moments, Winslow arrived, leading Vince Marlow and a half dozen technicians and one of *Hillenkoetter*'s ordnance carts.

"Get him out of there," Hunter told Winslow. "We'll want to talk to him. And we'll probably need a German translator."

"Aye, aye, sir. Chief Krueger is with us back at the LZ." And Winslow began snapping off orders.

Christian Krueger was an ENC, an Engineman Chief assigned to *Hillenkoetter*'s black gang—the old-time slang for men working in a ship's engine room, in the days when a coal-fired boiler was what propelled the vessel. He'd helped translate for rescued German prisoners at Aldebaran.

As they waited, Hunter prowled among the vertical tubes, searching. Julia had found Geri for him once before, using a photograph to pinpoint her position. She was in here *somewhere*. . . .

"Julia?" he called. "Do you remember where Geri Galanis is? You found her when you first found this base."

"I'm . . . not sure, Mark. She's in toward the middle of the Forest, I think. I didn't get a lock on her exact position when I was here before."

This way, then. . . .

Damn it, he knew he shouldn't be looking for his girlfriend *now*, not when—

"Skipper! We have incoming!"

Hunter turned at Briggs's warning and pounded back to the perimeter. Four Saurians had just materialized inside the defensive perimeter, close beside the cluster of ordnance carts and flight deck crew. As Hunter approached the group another appeared out of emptiness . . . and another . . .

Saurians elsewhere in the undersea base had pinpointed the human incursion and were sending troops in to deal with it. The JSST troopers had already opened fire at the newcomers, but they were handicapped by the fact that the enemy was appearing *in-side* their defensive circle, alongside the flight deck people, which meant that they would hit their own comrades in the crossfire if they weren't damned careful with their aim.

The Saurians wore gold-colored armor, etched with intricately shaped loops and whorls, with helmets molded into cartoonish, fiercely reptilian visages. Each carried a chest-mounted weapon that left their arms free, a device like a flat box strapped onto the front of their torso. Curved blades, like savage claws, extended from their gauntlets. Hunter had never seen Malok troops like this and wondered if they represented some sort of elite soldier—a Saurian special ops force.

A dazzling flash seared Hunter's retinas, and a JSST soldier nearby went down, his helmet and the upper part of his torso vaporized. The Saurian was hit by immediate return fire, the light and heat from four Sunbeam lasers flaring off his armor until he collapsed.

But two more Lizards stepped through out of emptiness and into the center of the LZ. A blue-vested crewman went down . . . then a red-vest mag rat crouching behind a cart. Lizard warriors were pouring through into the center of the human defenses with a shrill clatter of steel, killing with indiscriminate abandon.

With sudden, aching dread, Hunter saw Elanna, standing out in the open, seemingly frozen. The Lizards hadn't shot at her yet . . .

or hadn't noticed her, but that would change in an instant. Or . . . was it possible there was a very deliberate truce between Talis and Malok, that they *knew* her as Talis and wouldn't kill her if she didn't threaten them?

No time to think about that now. *"Elanna! Get down!"* Hunter yelled. "Tell the *Big-H* we need help in the LZ!"

His words seemed to startle her, but she dropped behind an ordnance cart. "Done, Mark."

But what the JSST could not afford was a stand-up fight with superior forces. If they got bogged down here, the Lizards would swiftly scrub them right off the deck.

An armored Saurian leaped onto the flatbed of an ordnance trailer, looming directly above Elanna. Hunter fired his Sunbeam Type 2 pistol and hit the Lizard squarely in the visor of its intricately shaped helmet. Arms flailing, the Saurian pitched back off the cart and into the surging mass of its fellows behind.

More Saurian warriors poured through the second gateway, along with a number of unarmored Grays. What the hell were *they* doing here?

"Concentrate your fire!" Hunter yelled over the tactical channel. It had worked when the Malok were boarding the *Hillenkoetter*.

JSST troops began firing into the vaguely defined patch of air through which the enemy was forcing its way. Eight or ten uprated-PEW beams at a time punched through gold armor, and in seconds the dimensional doorway was filled with a tangle of bodies, some dead, some still struggling. Within moments more the transporter gateway was engulfed in sun-bright energy, and the entire LZ as far as the nearest reaches of Sherwood Forest was wreathed in greasy smoke.

Hunter reached Elanna, who was still crouching behind an ordnance transporter. Technically, radio signals could be sent through an open transporter gate, but the angle had to be just right for decent reception—that, or the receiver had to be right inside the gateway's mouth. It was faster and more certain to bypass the electronics and use the Talisian's telepathic abilities instead.

"Tell Ares Prime to execute Plan Bravo!" he told her. "Now!"

"Done, Mark." She paused. "Commander Ramsey requests that you make sure your end of the gateway is clear."

Good point. Hunter wasn't sure what would happen if someone was half on one side of the gate and half on the other . . . and the gate closed. The result, he imagined, was probably quite messy.

"We're clear!" he called. "Hit it!"

A moment later, the dimensional portal between Mars and the Malibu base closed.

Combat does not afford the luxury of making battle plans on the fly. Whenever possible, various alternate plans were worked out ahead of time, given code names, and used to coordinate tactics with a minimum of discussion and wasted time. "Bravo" was the second of six tactical responses Hunter, Groton, Ramsey, and Elanna had worked out to counter possible Malok threats.

It was also the most dangerous response on the list. By closing the gateway between Mars and here, the JSST troops and support personnel already inside the undersea base were completely cut off—no retreat, no reinforcements, and no communications until Ramsey and his team decided to reestablish contact.

If they could reestablish contact.

Meanwhile, golden Lizard warriors continued to pour into

Sherwood Forest, stepping across the stacked and savaged bodies lying in front of their own Dimensional Gateway. The JSST Spearpoint continued to edge closer to the gate, firing through the Lizards' opening as quickly as they could cycle their weapons.

And thank the high-tech gods of modern warfare, Hunter thought, squeezing off shot after shot with his Sunbeam Type 2. Spearpoint would not have stood a snowflake's chance in hell if they'd not been packing these uprated PEWs. Between battery life and the long power recycle time between shots, their old gear had never been up to extended firefights, putting them at a distinct disadvantage in rodeos like this one.

He could still wish for more punch in the hand lasers. That damned Saurian gold armor drank coherent light like soda through a straw. He was finding that by aiming for spots blackened by the fire from heavier lasers, though, he could make his shots stick. A seven-foot Lizard with charred armor over his torso went down when Hunter drilled him with two precise shots.

And then the Saurian troops were withdrawing, stepping back through their open gateway as the JSST closed in around them. Lizard warriors were undeniably fierce in combat, but they seemed to possess powerful survival instincts. Hunter thought about what he'd heard in various briefings—how there were relatively few Saurians left in the wake of the impact event that had annihilated the dinosaurs. Apparently, they didn't care for stand-up slugfests any more than Hunter did.

He realized that was the key to defeating these things. Hit them, hit them hard, *keep* hitting them, and make them bleed. Sooner or later, they would decide they'd had enough and back off. Hunter remembered an expression—to step on someone's foot until *they* apologized. He couldn't remember where he'd read that . . . but that might well be the way Humankind would get the Saurians to acknowledge that Earth had new masters now.

And that humans were no longer *things* to be abducted, to be kept in bottles, or to be the subjects of alien experimentation. He looked off into the rows of tanks with their shadowy captives. No more of *that*. Humans would be their own masters now.

"Can you talk to Julia now?" he asked Elanna. He wondered what was happening back on Mars. He'd heard somewhere that telepathic communications actually bypassed the space between two subjects, cheating Einstein.

"No, Mark," the Talis said. "It's much too far."

So much for that. They would simply have to sit tight until Plan Bravo had its hoped-for effect.

"Spearpoint! Spearpoint!" a woman's voice called. "This is Nicholson! Lizards coming through!"

"Layton!" Hunter snapped, looking for troops close by. "With me! Bring your squad!"

Ten of them clattered across the open deck, racing for the far end of the tube forest where Minkowski, Nicholson, and the rescue personnel with them were still gathered about the cylinder holding the German captive. Four gold-armored Saurians had just stepped out of a new Dimensional Gateway and were closing on the small group.

"Take 'em down!" Hunter yelled, and he opened fire with his pistol, even though none of these suits of armor was vulnerable as yet. For a mad five seconds, energy beams snapped back and forth between three warring groups. These Lizards had heavier, hand-carried weapons rather than the small boxes strapped to their chests, and a dazzling flash of actinic light caught Briggs just a few feet to Hunter's right, wiping away his helmet and upper torso in a spray of vaporized blood and tissue.

Laser fire from the two human groups pinned the Saurians in a vicious crossfire, killing one. Another Lizard snapped off a bolt of energy at Minkowski's group and missed, smashing the top of the translucent cylinder holding the German prisoner.

Green perfluorocarbon sprayed across the area, some of it flashing instantly to steam. The cylinder, cut from the mechanisms holding it upright, toppled, spilling Albrecht onto the deck in plastic shards and liquid.

"Corpsman!" Minkowski yelled.

Vince Marlow, the team's corpsman, was at the man's side immediately, as energy beams continued to flash and snap. Alvarez, Moss, and Layton crouched side by side, burning down the remaining Lizards who appeared to be trying to retreat, now, through their open gate.

The gate snapped off, cutting a wounded Saurian neatly in two.

Mark! Elanna's voice called in his head. *We have a gate connection again with Mars!*

And moments later, Lieutenant Billingsly arrived, along with several troops from the JSST's reserve.

The fierce and deadly firefight for Sherwood Forest was over.

At least for the moment. . . .

CHAPTER TWENTY-FOUR

Any sufficiently advanced technology is indistinguishable
from magic.

ARTHUR C. CLARKE,
PROFILES OF THE FUTURE,
1973 REVISED EDITION

*VIKTOR ALBRECHT FORCED himself to hands and knees, coughing
and gagging on the green fluid as he expelled it from his lungs.
He gasped in air—real air—and nearly collapsed again with the
pain. He was cold and wet and in agony with the effort of trying
to breathe air once more.*

*"Sei einfach," a voice said close by, amplified over a pressure
suit speaker. "Wir sind Freunde."*

Be easy. We are friends.

*Albrecht wasn't certain if he could believe that. The armored
person leaning over him was human, at least in a general way,
and not* Eidechse, *but Albrecht's mind now was shrieking with
paranoia and in need to get away,* anywhere *away from this
nightmare chamber.*

*Someone helped him stand and draped a towel over his shoul-
ders.*

*When he'd begun this voyage in time, he remembered, he'd
not trusted the Reptiles. They'd promised technology, weapons,
a victorious outcome to a war grown increasingly hopeless . . .*

and never delivered. The anger he'd felt then was nothing at all compared to the desolation and betrayal he felt now.

"Hier entlang," *the voice said, an arm guiding him. This way.*

Unable to resist, unable to think, Viktor Albrecht stumbled off with the pressure-suited men.

THEY'RE GOING *to cut you off again,* Julia's voice said in Elanna's mind. *Captain Groton sent through Billingsly with reinforcements to help you hold out. We . . . we think the Hunter Maneuver is working. They've found where the Lizards have their dimensional transporters set up inside the Malibu base, and they're going to blast it.*

Thank you, Julia, Elanna though back. *We'll be here waiting.*

The mental link was broken.

The Hunter Maneuver. An appropriate name, Elanna thought. Hunter had come up with the idea and argued vehemently for its use. It turned the Malok gateway system into a weapon of mass destruction, at least on a small scale.

She still wasn't certain what she thought about that.

As long as the MKIS was engaged, the temperature and atmospheric pressure on one side remained separate from those of the other. Turn the MKIS off, however . . .

Hunter had used the trick—a kind of test run—to trigger the pressure sensors inside the Malibu base and seal off the various compartments from one another, allowing the team to secure the Malok's holding chamber. When the Saurians began pouring their elite *G'paku* warriors through their own portal, however, Plan Bravo was solidified, opening a portal within the Malok control center and leaving it open to the vacuum of the Martian atmosphere.

Elanna still wasn't quite used to the change in the planet between her home time and this. The Mars she knew, the world of
Prime Center in the 101st century, was green and pleasant and held
an atmosphere as breathable as Earth's. The Mars of Ares Prime
here in the twenty-first century was a very different world indeed.

The portal likely hadn't been open long enough to completely
evacuate the Malibu control room, but the Earthside pressure would
have dropped enough at least to incapacitate the Malok inside.

With enough time, the pressure inside the Malibu base would
drop to one sixth-thousandth of the surface pressure on Earth; the
question was whether the evacuated high-tech dome would even
be able to withstand the external pressure. Elanna looked up at
the vaulted ceiling overhead. How long would it hold?

For now, at least, the air pressure inside the holding chamber
was steady at roughly twelve psi. The Solar Warden team working
on the portal device back on Mars had just shifted its opening to
a different chamber within the Malibu base, sucking the air from
the place where the Malok had their own dimensional projection
equipment. Once the portal opened, conditions inside the chamber were like those at the heart of a city-wrecking storm.

CHARAACH CROUCHED behind a console, clinging to the edge as
the hurricane shrilled and howled around her. Only once had she
ever experienced anything quite like this . . . in another epoch tens
of millions of years ago, when Apocalypse had fallen from the
skies to exterminate the golden civilization of the Vach.

At least this time fire was not falling from a storm-savaged sky.
In moments, however, it might not be fire . . . but billions of tons
of seawater.

Somehow, the humans had opened a portal between Rachal-lich and . . . someplace else with an extremely low atmospheric pressure, probably Mars, possibly Earth's moon. The wind inside the small compartment was a shrieking, vicious thing. Several Grays, without suits, were already unconscious; two *G'paku* soldiers, armored and with life support, could still breathe, but could barely stand against the storm.

Charaach, without a pressure suit, could not breathe, could hear nothing but the thunder of disappearing air, and knew that she had only moments to live.

She had remarkably few options. Through that open portal on the far side of the room lay only death, the vacuum on the surface of another world. The Vach projector next to her still was targeted on the holding chamber, with breathable air but held now by the human invaders. It would take several minutes to reset the projector to some other target—another chamber within the Rachallich base, or possibly another Vach base somewhere on or within the Earth.

Minutes she knew she did not have, even if she could have made the projector function within this nightmare of destruction and death.

Charaach saw only one way out. She hit the broad, flat button on the console that reenergized the Vach projector, watched the framework fill with the image of its target, and with the last of her breath and strength, managed to drag herself upright.

Somehow, then, she pushed past the protective field membrane and stepped through to the other side.

THEY'D HALF guided, half dragged Viktor Albrecht down a long line of nearly transparent cylinders. Their goal seemed to be an open expanse at the far end of the chamber where space-suited men encircled a knot of carts or strange-looking tractors. Groups of those men were moving off in different directions with smart precision; for a crazed moment, Albrecht wondered if they were, in fact, SS.

Then he caught a ghostly image leering at him out of the corner of his eye.

He knew that face. . . .

The shock of recognition had left him broken, crumpled, unable to move or speak.

Der Teufel! How could this possibly be . . . ?

The last time he'd seen Heinrich Müller had been in early 1945, in Berlin. Chief of the Gestapo—head of the secret police and one of the senior architects of the solution to the Jewish problem—he'd been one of the most powerful men within the Third Reich.

He didn't look powerful now, nude, shrunken, wrinkled, trapped in a glass bottle with eyes squeezed shut and mouth hanging open in a silent scream.

And in the very next tube was *SS Obergruppenführer* Hans Kammler, the man in charge of the Reich's secret *Wunderwaffen* that was supposed to finally win the war. Albrecht had seen Kammler only a day or two before writhing on the floor in the grip of apparent insanity, shrieking, pathetic.

He was even more pathetic now, a twisted, naked specimen imprisoned within a giant test tube.

The overwhelming sense of betrayal rose again in Albrecht's chest and throat, a blinding fury that threatened to consume him. The Starmen had promised Germany *victory*, weapons, power over the entire planet . . . but their agenda, obviously, was to reduce humans—even the most powerful men of the Third Reich—to *property*, to things to be used and cast aside, to vermin to be exterminated when they became inconvenient.

My God . . . my God . . . how could we be so blind!

Ahead, near the defensive perimeter of the soldiers, a Lizard popped into existence, stepping out of emptiness.

And Albrecht's mind exploded in searing, red-black hatred. . . .

"STOP RIGHT there!" Hunter ordered, his Sunbeam gripped in two gloved hands, aimed at the creature's blood-smeared face. "Don't move!"

He wasn't even sure the thing understood English . . . but it did stop, wavering on unsteady digitigrade legs. Its golden eyes seemed glassy, unfocused, and its clawed hands came slowly up to chest height, showing they were empty. The creature stood over seven feet tall; even bloodied and injured, it projected a terrifying presence.

Elanna stepped out beside Hunter, and the Saurian's eyes widened in recognition. *Talis! You've broken the Covenant!* Hunter heard the words clearly in his mind.

The humans of this age signed no Covenant, Elanna's voice replied. *They choose to make their own future. I suggest that you honor this.*

This planet, the Saurian replied, *is ours!*

Hunter gestured with his pistol. "Funny way you have of surrendering, Lizard," he said aloud. "Or did you come here to start an argument?"

The Saurian's head swiveled, fixing Hunter with those unnerving eyes.

We . . . yield, human. Allow us to leave and Rachallich base is yours.

Like on Mars, Hunter thought. Call a truce and flee . . . and the problem is still there.

"We don't particularly want your base, Lizard," Hunter said. "We want the people you've imprisoned down here . . . alive, unharmed, and *free*. Understand?"

The Saurian looked back to Elanna. *These Ghech are incapable of understanding. At least your people are civilized.* The words were as clear in Hunter's head as if the Lizard had spoken them out loud.

Not as civilized as you might think, Elanna's mental voice replied. *The Ve'hrech'na must relinquish their claim on this world. There are many, many other worlds across this Galaxy, and timelines without number. Find another place and time.*

The Lizard showed its teeth, curved and glistening. *The Ve'hrech'na Council will never agree. This world is sacred to us. You have unleashed a skyfall doom that may annihilate the Galaxy.*

Then to escape the doom, you must convince your Council.

The Lizard closed one fist, then opened it. Hunter had the impression that the gesture was the same as a human's negative shake of the head. *You . . . do not understand. You should have enforced the Covenant,* made *the humans accept, bent them to will and to reason! They must be* taught*!*

In that moment, Hunter heard an unearthly shrilling, a scream garbled by fear or rage or insanity or all three. A man raced across the deck out of the shadows of Sherwood Forest, stark naked, bare feet slapping on the deck, eyes bulging, arms outstretched, face contorted in a ghastly caricature of what might once have been human.

Julia's Nazi . . .

Hunter pivoted, tracking with his pistol, but the former captive was too fast, the surprise too sudden and complete. Viktor Albrecht seemed to go airborne eight feet away from the Lizard, sailed through the intervening distance and crashed into it, knocking it down. Hunter had seen the lightning reflexes of Saurians before . . . but this one was so injured or weakened it couldn't turn or block the attack.

Albrecht landed on top. The Lizard's mouth gaped wide as it tried to bite; instead, the German slammed his fist and arm past those glistening teeth, thrusting his arm down the Saurian's throat all the way to the shoulder. The Saurian gagged, struggled, and hissed while thrashing beneath Albrecht, unable to escape. Clawed hands closed over Albrecht's naked back, digging in, tearing, shredding, exposing his spine and ribs.

And still Albrecht continued to hang on, his arm buried down the Lizard's throat as he shrieked something unintelligible over and over again.

At last the jaws snapped shut and Albrecht rolled off, blood gushing from the severed stump at his shoulder. The Lizard continued to thrash and struggle beside him, unable to breathe.

Hunter dropped the pistol and threw himself down at the creature's side. Its face, its jaws were covered with blood, its bloodied hands now clawing at its own throat.

Not the brightest thing I've ever done, he thought . . . and he shoved his arm into the Lizard's gaping mouth, trying to grab the severed arm.

Mark! No! Elanna screamed in his head.

He continued groping, trying to get a secure handhold on bone or tissue. It was slippery . . . his *glove* was slippery . . . and now the Saurian was clamping down on his armor in an involuntary reflex.

"Damn it!" he yelled into the Lizard's face. "Relax! I'm trying to fucking help you!"

Through his glove, he could feel the bitten-off end of Albrecht's arm. He managed to clamp down on it and pull . . . and with agonizing slowness, it started to give way.

Then the Saurian convulsed, vomiting blood and arm and a foul raw-meat mass that likely was the Lizard's most recent meal.

Hunter lay on the deck, his suit drenched in blood and other, less pleasant matter. Doc Marlow was kneeling next to him. "Skipper! You okay?"

"Even with the armor," Hunter managed to say, "I think I need a shower." He struggled to sit up. "Is he going to be okay?"

"The naked guy? He's dead."

"No, idiot. The Lizard!"

"We'll check him out, but I think he's going to live. Why the hell did you save him?"

Hunter looked down into the Saurian's bloody face. The gold, vertically-slitted eyes stared back at him. "Because this scaly bastard is going to make peace with us if I have to fucking kill him!"

ELANNA REACHED for the Saurian's mind. *You heard? You understand? Mark Hunter . . . he saved your life. He wants to make peace. But on his terms, not yours.*

I . . . heard. The Council still will never approve.

What's important right now is peace between us and the Saurians still inside this base, Elanna thought, pouring every ounce of her will and determination into the words. *Can you order the rest of the Surviving Few within this base to cease fire? To board your ships and leave?*

The Saurian hesitated, seeming to think about it.

Yes. The base commander is Bright Fang. He is of the Kagag faction, which favors negotiations with the Ghech. He will agree. The eyes closed. *If he still lives, of course. I will try to reach him. . . .*

HUNTER WAS worried. The base had begun making unpleasant noises.

An hour after the Saurians had surrendered, the evacuation of their captives was well underway. A steady stream of ordnance vehicles continued threading back and forth between the Forest and the portal leading back to *Hillenkoetter*'s flight deck. A small army of space wing crewmen and technicians worked among the upright cylinders, dismantling them and carefully removing their occupants. They'd counted a total of 217 people in the cavernous room; extracting them from their tubes, waking them up and getting them to breathe room air. Once the captives caught their breath, the team dried them off and dressed them in clothing brought over from Ares Prime.

It was going to take hours more to clear the chamber . . . and Hunter was beginning to wonder if they would have enough time.

With nearly all of the air sucked from the compartment holding the Saurian dimensional transporter gear, parts of the main undersea dome had become seriously weakened. Hunter could hear the series of low, painful groans from somewhere overhead as the dome's structure struggled to hold back the relentless weight of water.

Almost two hundred pounds of water was pressing down on each and every square inch of the main dome's surface. Even the high-tech materials and construction techniques employed by the Lizards would not hold it back for long.

Hunter had discussed the situation with Ramsey; could they use the transporter on Mars to bring air back into the evacuated chamber? The answer, it turned out, was no. The surface pressure of the Martian atmosphere was still one six-thousandth that of Earth. You couldn't pressurize a vacuum from another vacuum, after all.

Could they use the transporter on the *Big-H* instead? Possibly, but that would be extremely ill-advised. *Hillenkoetter* was a spacecraft, after all . . . an enormous one, but still a self-contained vessel with a limited air supply. Trying to repressurize part of the Malibu base would threaten the space carrier's integrity. It would also put a halt to the evacuation, since the rescued prisoners couldn't be shuttled through to Mars. There weren't enough space suits for them all.

Could Hunter take a team to that chamber and blow a hole in the sealed door, letting air back in from the rest of the station? Perhaps, but at the risk of weakening the bulkheads enough to bring about an immediate total collapse of the entire structure.

Better to keep working at the evacuation, as quickly and as efficiently as possible. *Maybe* the dome would hold for long enough. . . .

And if it collapsed, he thought, the disaster would be his fault.

His original plan had called for sealing off Sherwood Forest, holding off the Saurian counterattacks while the flight deck crews removed the abductees back to the *Big-H*. Plan Bravo had been put in place in case the Saurians had their own Dimensional Gateway, and he'd gambled that the super-technology of the Lizards would keep the ocean out.

Another groan echoed through the chamber, followed by a sudden series of sharp cracks and pops.

How much longer . . . ?

And then he found Geri.

Her cylindrical prison was ten down from where the team currently was working. Hunter's immediate thought was to bring the deck personnel over and free her right away . . . but he fought the urge. The rescue work was following a carefully articulated plan; to interrupt that plan and start working out of order would guarantee chaos . . . and possibly delay the entire evacuation.

Hunter stood next to the cylinder, watching the young woman apparently asleep within her fluid-filled cell, knowing that his people were releasing others ahead of her . . . knowing that some of those others might well be Nazis ripped from their home time, like Albrecht.

But most were ordinary people—mothers and wives, fathers and husbands, even children abducted over the years and held for whatever dark evil the Lizards had had in mind for them. There was no way he could pick and choose which ones would be freed, which ones might die when the ocean crashed in . . . and the realization was sheer torture.

The rescue crew was now working on the next tube closer in line. *Come on . . . come on . . .*

She was beautiful, pallid wrinkled skin and all. He was scarcely aware of her lack of clothing; his attention was fixed on her face.

He was glad to have finally found her, but still he was perplexed to find that the years of her absence somehow had left him . . . empty. He knew he'd grown, changed.

Had she?

And what had the Lizards done to her in all that time? That fighter pilot on the *Hillenkoetter* had confirmed that some abducted humans were being used to pilot enemy ships, but Geri wasn't the fighter-jock type. But he remembered that conference back on board the *Hillenkoetter*, where he and Elanna had tried to convince Winchester and his staff that Humankind needed to assume responsibility for themselves. Elanna had talked about Saurian memegineering . . . about how they used abductees to spread fake news, propaganda, lies designed to poison society, spread chaos, and disrupt governments.

Was that what they'd done to Geri? With what lies had they infected her?

Hell, did she even still love him? That, perhaps, was the biggest question of all right now. That . . . and . . . well . . . did *he* still love *her*?

"Excuse us, Commander," a young man with a brown vest over his 7-SAS armor said. "This one's next." He grinned. "Quite a babe, huh?"

"Just do your job, mister," Hunter growled. "Belay the fucking commentary."

"Aye, aye, sir."

He helped them detach her tube from the mechanisms overhead that kept her supplied with nutrients, drugs, and fresh breathing fluid. They'd encountered these devices more than once before and knew the perfluorocarbon would keep her oxygenated for some hours—long enough to get her back to the *Hillenkoetter*. A forklift hoisted the cylinder off the deck and gently laid it on an ordnance cart flatbed with several others. A red-vested mag rat strapped her down, and the cart trundled off toward the LZ.

From overhead came the echoing groan of the failing dome.

"I'M IN the room with the Lizard transporter," Ashley said. "The roof . . . the roof is . . . is crumpling inward. I think it's going to fail. . . ."

"Don't interpret," Bennett's voice said at her side. "Simply observe."

"But we should *warn* them!"

"Speed of light delay, Julia, remember? What you're seeing happened eight minutes ago."

"Bullshit!" Ashley snapped back. "I know what I'm sensing! You *know* I do! This is happening *now*!"

Ashley was being bombarded by sensation and by intense emotion. She could feel the icy chill in that dark room, see the ceiling beginning to crumple and bulge inward, hear the rumbling groan and whine of metal pushed beyond its structural limits. She was *there*, now, this instant.

There was still acrimonious debate within RV circles about whether or not telepathy and psychic awareness moved at the speed of light . . . or faster. Ashley believed the phenomenon propagated *past* space, an instantaneous direct connection between here and there, as though what happened in one brain instantly registered in another, without having to traverse the space between.

Bennett was old-school. He didn't share the convictions of her experience.

Thunder boomed around her, followed by squeals and staccato pops. She felt a throbbing and claustrophobic terror, a need to flee . . . even though she knew her body was safe on the sofa back on board the *Hillenkoetter* over ninety million miles distant.

With an ear-piercing shriek, a beam appeared in the darkness just ahead of her, spearing from the ceiling to the floor like a solid shaft of gleaming metal. Ashley had seen something like this before . . . on board the Oumuamuan asteroid-ship, when a scientist named Kellerman had tried using a laser to pierce a wall in order to take a sample—a wall with water under unimaginable pressure just behind it. The shriek deepened to a bone-rattling roar.

What looked to her like a solid shaft of metal was a stream of water under a pressure of very close to two hundred pounds per square inch.

Ashley realized that the water pressure here was far, far less than what she'd sensed within the confines of the rock shard called Oumuamua, the "messenger from afar who arrives first." Her memories of that encounter, however, colored what she was viewing here, adding urgency to an already desperately urgent situation.

She was feeling the same dark terror she'd felt there, within an alien starship.

"Dr. Bennett!" Ashley cried. "The dome is failing! *Now!* Right *now*! *Please* tell them!"

HUNTER HAD escorted the tractor carrying Geri to the portal and helped pass her through to the medical personnel waiting on the other side, on *Hillenkoetter*'s flight deck. He wanted, he yearned to step through with her, but that would be an unthinkable dereliction of duty.

"*C'mon*, people!" Hunter bellowed over his suit speaker, turning to survey the scene. "*C'mon*! Pick up the pace!"

The tortured squeal of bending metal somewhere overhead added an urgent exclamation point to Hunter's order. The carts continued coming, one following another, with men and women from *Hillenkoetter*'s crew waiting to haul the heavy cylinders across the threshold from Earth to Mars. At first they'd been decanting the captives here, in the base . . . but they were rushing now to escape the inevitable collapse, hauling them to *Hillenkoetter*'s flight deck before releasing them.

There'd been some discussion about the possibility of moving *Hillenkoetter* from Mars to Earth. Doing so would have simplified communications and allowed him to talk directly with Julia. Groton had been unwilling to abandon the sizable shore party at Ares Prime, however. The base had only recently been abandoned by the Malok, and Winchester and Groton both were concerned about the enemy returning if the *Big-H* wasn't there standing guard.

Instead, Groton had dispatched a couple of squadrons of Stingrays to Earth to keep an eye on things from overhead. What they could possibly do to help Spearpoint and Rescue, four hundred feet underwater, was something Hunter simply couldn't imagine.

Not my circus, not my monkeys, Hunter thought, with only a mild scowl. Having the *Hillenkoetter* a couple of hundred miles overhead wouldn't have afforded that much of an advantage. Winchester and Groton together were doing what they thought best for the ship and for the mission.

Still, it would have been nice to have had the moral support of a Solar Warden carrier right outside.

The deck shuddered beneath Hunter's feet, and thunder boomed through the compartment. He'd lived in Southern California for a number of years, and his first thought was . . . *earthquake*!

Then the double doors at the top of the ramp bulged inward, admitting a stream of water.

AN EON or two ago—all the way back in 2014—David "Double-D" Duvall had been a Navy aviator flying F/A-18 Super Hornets off the USS *Nimitz* when he and his RIO had played tag with an alien spacecraft above the ocean off the coast near San Diego. The encounter had actually been declassified a few years later—at just about the same time that Duvall had transferred to the newly minted Space Force under the aegis of Solar Warden.

Now he was back in very nearly the same airspace, this time flying an F/S-49 Stingray, and he once again was watching something weird.

"What the hell is that thing?" Lieutenant Iverson, his rear-seater, called over the intercom. "Looks like a fucking flying brick!"

"I'm not sure, Ivy. You got a lock?"

"Now and then. I tag it with radar, and then it fades out."

"I'll try getting closer."

They were just a few miles south of the dark bluffs off Malibu, California. Somewhere below was an alien undersea base being assaulted by a JSST strike force. Duvall's squadron had been ordered to return to Earth, and Duvall had pulled strings to come along. The doc back aboard ship had recommended he take light duty for a while, recovery time from his ordeal in the Martian desert.

For Duvall, though, there was a pressing need to get back in the saddle of the horse that had thrown him. He'd gone to Captain Macmillan and asked, no, *demanded* that he be able to join the flight.

And Macmillan, somewhat against his better judgment, had agreed.

Below, the object—an obsidian-black brick with a bar of brilliant light running around its edges—was hovering low above the surface of the water. That surface was roiling and bubbling fiercely, now, and Duvall wondered if the thing was using some sort of a weapon on the undersea base.

He dropped the Stingray in a sharp drop until he was just above the thing, half expecting it to lash out with high-tech weaponry . . . and grateful that it appeared to be ignoring them.

And then it descended into the water below, descended in a bubbling mass of sea-foam and spray . . . and vanished.

"What'll we *do*, Double-D?"

"Damfino, Ivy," Duvall replied. He shook his head. *Hillenkoetter* was over eight minutes away by radio, and the strike force below was insulated by four hundred feet of ocean, with all radio communications blocked. There was nothing they *could* do. "They didn't cover this very well in preflight, did they?"

Odd. The bubbling and frothing below had stopped.

IN THE Malibu base, a final earthquake jolted through the structure . . . and then everything became still. Water continued gushing through the partially breached doorway, but there was no longer any pressure behind it . . . no force raging to crush the dome. The team, frozen with that last shock, very slowly relaxed, stood upright, and began talking among themselves.

Hunter watched the inflowing water for a moment, judging the threat, then signaled the others. "Keep going! We're okay!"

Mark! Elanna's voice said. *It's the Zshaj!*

"Where? Where are they?"

Their ship! It's outside, right above us! I don't know how . . . but they've stabilized the dome.

Hunter blinked with surprise. He'd not expected to hear from those many-legged telepaths again. How the hell had they known to return to Earth *now*, over fifty years after Shag Harbour, just in time to prevent the Malibu base's collapse?

They must be using the gravitic field around their ship, he thought. Using it to block off the ocean . . . or reduce the weight of the water on the dome . . . or . . . hell. What was it they always said about "any sufficiently advanced technology . . ."?

Ten minutes later, the last of the nightmare cylinders was disconnected, hauled across the deck of Sherwood Forest, and manhandled through to the other side.

Hunter took a last look around. "Elanna?"

I'm here, Mark.

"We're clear, here. Tell our . . . ah . . . new friends: *thank you.*"

Will do.

And Hunter was the last one through the portal.

Now, it was time to go back on board the *Big-H* and see Geri.

EPILOGUE

"IS SHE GOING to be okay?" Hunter asked.

"Should be, sir," Marlow told him, withdrawing the hypodermic needle from her shoulder. "Just be warned, okay? Some of them come around with symptoms of severe emotional trauma."

They were kneeling on the flight deck of the USSS *Hillenkoetter*, next to the unconscious body of Geri Galanis. Around them were the over two hundred other rescued human captives, lying on makeshift stretchers or blankets or on the cold metal deck. Doctors, med techs, and corpsmen moved among them, administering drugs to counteract the Saurian soporifics, reassuring them, getting them water and clothing. Perhaps half of the evacuees were awake, now. Occasionally someone else would come to with a piercing scream.

"Like what?"

Marlow gave a shrug. "Ever wake up from a nightmare screaming?"

"I've been worried about brainwashing."

"It's possible. I gather the Lizards have been using captured humans to spread some pretty weird stories. 'Man never landed on the Moon.' That kind of crap."

"Undermining people's faith in the government, in the system. Stirring them up with things like riots in Europe, tearing down statues, assassinations, anything to weaken and divide us."

"It's been working, too, hasn't it?"

"So how do we deal with it?"

"I don't know, sir. Therapy, maybe. Trauma counseling. A *lot* of tender loving care. . . ."

Geri's eyes fluttered open, then widened as she saw Hunter's face. She drew a deep breath, looking like she was about to scream.

"Easy, miss . . . *easy!*" Marlow said, holding her shoulder. "It's okay! We're US Space Force. We're here to take you home. . . ."

"Space . . . Force . . . ?" She shook her head, keeping her eyes locked on Hunter's. "Mark Hunter . . . I do *not* like the company you keep!"

A DAY later, Hunter sat on *Hillenkoetter*'s observation deck, feeling as broken, as *rejected* as it was possible to feel. Marlow and the ship's doctor both had told him that neurochemical changes in Geri's brain might, *might* have changed her perceptions, changed the way she thought of people she'd known. It happened sometimes in stroke victims.

Her brain chemistry might go back to what it was.

Might . . .

"I heard what happened down there, Mark," Elanna said. She'd stepped up behind him without his being aware. "I'm so sorry."

He stood, and she took a seat next to him. "I'm honestly not surprised," he told her. "It's been a long time. People . . . change."

"You think you've changed?"

"Oh, I know I have. And poor Geri has been stuck in a fish tank for . . . how long? Months and months. That's enough to traumatize anybody."

"I . . . looked into her mind, Mark. It's going to take a while, but I think she'll be okay. Humans are *very* resilient."

"She said she doesn't like the company I keep."

"Can you blame her? Every time she woke up, she'd find herself staring at a Gray or a Saurian. It was the Men in Black who kidnapped her in the first place—probably hybrids like your friend in Las Vegas."

"'Jack.'"

"She's wrestling right now with what you do for a living. I think she was okay with Mark the Navy SEAL. She's having trouble with Mark the Defender of Humankind."

"I figured that out, Elanna. Trouble is . . . I've found a home here. I don't see myself giving up the Space Force for . . . anyone."

"I . . . I know how you feel."

"Well . . . sure. You just read my mind, and—"

"It's not that."

Hunter suddenly realized that she sounded as lost and as rejected as did he. "Something . . . about your people?" he guessed. "Up in the future?"

She hesitated, then nodded. "I am now on . . . you might call it administrative leave, Mark. They're . . . unhappy with me."

"Is there going to be a time war?"

She shook her head. "Probably not. Bright Fang and Truthful Lies both think the Saurians couldn't win such a conflict. *Especially* since the Zshaj seem to have joined with us a few years from now."

Hunter thought about this. Time travel demanded a new grammar. What was more, thinking about aliens required a completely new and expanded worldview. The Grays, the Talis, and modern humans all were human, but as mutually alien to one another as the passing millennia could make them. The Saurians were more alien still . . . but undeniably were part of Earth's evolutionary heritage.

But then there were the *really* alien species. Hunter had heard a term tossed around by the ship's xenobiologists: *xenoalithis*, the "truly foreign." The Xaxki, out at Zeta Reticuli; the "Dreamers" in their virtual worlds; the K'kurix, the Dreamers' Guardians; the Oumuamuans in their cold, dark ocean contained within an interstellar sliver of rock. These were beings so different that they had almost nothing in common with humans, no common ground at all. The Zshaj . . . well, at least humans had been able to communicate with them. And, evidently, they shared the human desire to pay back debts.

By comparison, humans, Talis, Grays, and even Saurians were close brothers. It was an interesting thought.

"Maybe we'll find other allies," Hunter said. "We'll need them."

"Yes. . . ."

"But I guess I kind of forced the issue in rescuing the Zshaj," Hunter said. "We changed the future . . . is that it?"

"A little. Our records now show a very early, very strong alliance with the Zshaj that we . . . weren't aware of before. Not enough of a change to wipe out the Talis . . . but it *is* a change."

"Well, the Zshaj *did* save our asses down there. . . ."

"And I'm glad they did. Actually, my command authority is concerned about a combination of things. They're worried about giving your people your heads without consulting them. There's a real possibility that *your* command authority, MJ-12, has been compromised. Even more . . . well, my work with the Nazis, back in the war. I *did* help them, Mark."

"I know."

"You understand, don't you? The Malok were *everywhere*, interfering, changing things, appropriating Nazi goals, threatening to rewrite history! I and some of my colleagues tried to nudge things the other way." She shook her head. "We were only partly successful."

"If there's one thing I've learned about time, Elanna, it's that the stuff is terribly messy. We're changing time every moment, with every decision we make. *That's* what it means to be responsible for our own future . . . to be willing to act and to live with the result."

"It seems my future is back here in the twenty-first century," she told him.

He wondered . . . was there an invitation behind her words, in her voice . . . ?

"I'm sorry, Elanna. And it was my fault. . . ."

She smiled at him. "It was no one's fault. It was . . . a shifting in the currents of time."

"Maybe things will change." He grinned. "Assuming we don't screw up the future."

"*Always* assuming that, Mark." She sighed. "We're entering a terribly dangerous temporal node—a point in the time stream where our decisions, and the decisions made by our enemies, can have enormous consequences. The Malok may be driving Russia's actions in Ukraine. They may be pushing the Chinese to invade Taiwan . . . or the North Koreans against the entire world. A misstep anywhere could lead to World War III, and a Malok takeover."

"What's our course of action? What do we do?"

"Stay the course. Keep blocking the Malok where we can." She reached out, almost tentatively, and touched his arm. "Keep doing what you do so well. . . ."

The feeling of an invitation was more powerful than ever. Was it chemistry? Or his own wishful thinking?

He might ask her . . . but later. He needed time, a bit of distance, a lot of thought.

He emphatically did not want her evolved pheromone chemistry or his sexual response to cloud his mind.

In the meantime . . .

Hunter glanced at his watch. "Ah. I have to get down to the flight deck."

"Why? What's down there?"

"The Just One. We're being reviewed by Admiral Winchester. Medals and commendations, probably . . . if we don't get chewed out for destroying both Ares Prime and Malibu base. Want to come?"

Minutes later, Hunter and Elanna walked onto the flight deck, where the men and women of the 1st Joint Space Strike Team had already fallen into ranks, having shed their battle-scarred armor and donning instead dress US Space Force uniforms—complete with that ridiculous woodland camouflage pattern.

He would have to see about changing that. Maybe midnight black instead. *That* was the way to go.

Billingsly saw Hunter walking in and snapped off a sharp "*Comp*'ny . . . atten . . . *hut*!"

With a crash of booted feet on metal deck, they came to attention.

"Just One!" Billingsly bellowed. "Battle cry!"

And the JSST's new war cry echoed across the flight deck.

"Hyu-*man*!"

Hunter grinned. Not "hoo-*ah*." Not "hoo-*yah*" or even "*ooh-rah*." He'd thought of the variant just hours ago, suggested it to Billingsly, and his XO had run with it. *Human*.

It was a small thing, silly, even . . . but it distinguished the Space Force and Solar Warden from the rest, marked them out as the guardians of Earth and of Humankind. Let the enemy know just who it was they faced. Let them know that humans were a force to be reckoned with, and respected. Let them know that humans would never again allow *anyone* to kidnap humans, imprison them, breed them, use them.

Let them know that humans had at last grabbed hold of their own future.

Humans, past, present, and future.

ABOUT THE AUTHOR

IAN DOUGLAS is one of the many pseudonyms for writer William H. Keith, *New York Times* bestselling author of the popular military science fiction series The Heritage Trilogy, The Legacy Trilogy, The Inheritance Trilogy, The Star Corpsman, and The Star Carrier series. A former naval corpsman, he lives in Pennsylvania.